Orinoco

ORINOCO

JAMES A. CIULLO

+ Betty

FIVE STAR

An imprint of Thomson Gale, a part of The Thomson Corporation

To Ron + Marcia
Jim Ciullo
Oct 4, 2013

THOMSON
GALE

Detroit • New York • San Francisco • New Haven, Conn. • Waterville, Maine • London

THOMSON
GALE

Set in 11 pt. Plantin.

LIBRARY OF CONGRESS CATALOGING-IN-PUBLICATION DATA

Ciullo, James A.
Orinoco / James A. Ciullo. — 1st ed.
p. cm.
ISBN-13: 978-1-59414-553-7 (hardcover : alk. paper)
ISBN-10: 1-59414-553-9 (hardcover : alk. paper)
1. Political candidates—Fiction. 2. United States. Congress. Senate—Elections—Fiction. 3. Political campaigns—Fiction. 4. Political fiction. I. Title.
PS3603.I94O75 2007
813'.6—dc22 2007008154

First Edition. First Printing: June 2007.

Published in 2007 in conjunction with Tekno Books and Ed Gorman.

Printed in the United States of America on permanent paper
10 9 8 7 6 5 4 3 2 1

To

All those who have served in the Peace Corps

Book I

Chapter 1

Burlington, Vermont
April 1998

He felt the pit in the bottom of his stomach. Can't turn back now, he reasoned. Why'd I let 'em talk me into this? Shit, just when I was enjoying the peace in my life.

"About ready, Joe?" Judy Bennett asked, barely making eye contact as she whisked by. It was her first opportunity to manage a big-time campaign. No more gopher jobs. No more small-town crap. Finally, she had a big fish, a figure known nationally, a man who might become a U.S. Senator.

Ready, my ass. The self-doubt still buzzed around in his mind. He peered out into the TV studio. They were all there—the press from all over New England, maybe even from upstate New York. He listened to the crescendo of their anticipating voices. Like seagulls trailing an ocean liner, they awaited the official announcement. The lances were at the ready. The jousting would soon begin.

Better suck it up, Joe. Get the juices flowing. Reach back for the confidence, man. Or, they'll have you for lunch. What a prospect. Well-known college professor with new-age policy ideas not ready for prime time. Gotta rise to the challenge, baby. Can't wimp out now.

He heard the familiar voice. A George "something or other." Williams, maybe. Or was it Williamson? Anyway, he was the host of Green Mountain Forum, the local version of Sunday political talk. George "something or other's" final phrase, ". . . the soon-to-be U.S. Senate candidate from Vermont, Joseph LaCarta," was the cue.

The applause fueled his determination as he stepped to the podium. The lifelike mural of the rolling green mountains spanned the back wall. The TV lighting would give the impression that he was standing in front of an oversized window with an unobstructed view of the Northeast Kingdom. He smiled. He waved. That's what all candidates do before speaking, right?

The reporters were at the ready, pads and pens, cameras, three or four laptops. And there was one guy in the back, tall, stately, early fifties, far enough removed that no one paid much notice as he punched a number into a cell phone. He did not represent any of the newspapers or radio stations. His press pass was obtained from other sources.

"Thank you, thank you," Joe began. "Thanks for coming here. I feel flattered. Well, I suppose it's time to end the speculation. A lot of folks urged me to do this, and you know what they say—be careful what you wish for." He chuckled.

"So without further ado, I'm making it official. I will run for Vermont's open U.S. Senate seat. I will maintain my status as an Independent. And if I am so fortunate as to be the choice of the good people of this state, I will pursue those policy goals and reforms that I've been promoting when I get to Washington.

"Since you all have heard me a million times before, and you know what I stand for, I think the TV viewers would prefer a dialogue rather than a speech. So have at it. I'm open for questions."

The attractive fortyish woman in the front row immediately caught his eye. Not bad, he thought. Why haven't I met her before? He was delighted that she had her hand up. "Yes, the lady in the front." He pointed. Yes, the lady with the lean figure and the wavy hair, who he thought was holding back an admiring smile.

"Professor LaCarta, Victoria Rivier, Rutland Free Press," she began. "Running as an Independent, won't that be a considerable disadvantage? Do you really think you can win? And if so, how much influence would you really have when you get to Washington . . . that is, without Party affiliation?"

Sexy voice. Graceful manner. She was appealing. Not the voluptuous trophy babe that some midlifers chased. Her allure was about something more intricate. More complex, like a fine wine.

"First of all, please, you needn't address me as 'professor.' 'Mr. LaCarta' is fine." He almost asked her to call him "Joe." He was pleased to associate the face with the name. He had read her news stories. And her weekly Sunday column had grabbed his attention on a few occasions. Attractive to go with the perceptive, he now noted.

"Ms. Rivier." He paused, catching himself before saying something like "nice to meet you." ". . . No, it will not be a disadvantage. Granted, I won't be as well funded as my opponents. But since I stand for reforms in campaign financing, I would not avail myself of the special-interest money anyway. And as we all know, the voters in this state are themselves quite independent. They will vote on the issues.

"As for being powerless in Washington, it's time for a unifier to get down there and end the partisan bickering and the stagnation. There are responsible people on both sides of the aisle ready to break ranks and to bring back good old common sense. I think I can help play such a role, maybe even be the catalyst."

To say that some of the established interests were threatened by such a prospect would have been an understatement. And this explained why his two opponents were so well funded. The Democrats and Republicans were playing their usual numbers game. The open Senate seat was another playoff game on the way to the Super Bowl.

"Mr. LaCarta, Mike Fitzpatrick, *Boston Tribune*. You call for a total revamping of our so-called War on Drugs. Aren't your ideas reckless? Won't it just lead to more drug use?"

He knew this question was coming. It was these views of his on the drug war that had gotten him on all the talk shows—CNN, Fox News—he couldn't remember them all. Sometimes he felt like everything else he stood for was little more than window dressing. This Fitzpatrick and the *Boston Tribune* were particularly critical. Joe was aware that they wanted him stopped in his tracks. Their editorials were meant to dissuade his candidacy. Fortunately, the other New England papers were keeping an open mind.

"Mike, as you know, I want to control it. My premise is to shift our focus. Instead of drug dealers getting rich, instead of kids falling for the lure of the quick buck, I want it regulated and taxed. And then we can use the revenues for rehabilitation and for education and job training. The only ones who go to prison will be those selling outside the regulations, and those committing crimes under the influence. For them justice will be swift and severe.

"I know you're skeptical. But look what we have now. Prisons are full—some violent people are even getting paroled because bed space is scarce. Law enforcement devotes a disproportionate amount of time to it. There's a shortage of treatment programs. Neighboring countries are dominated by drug cartels and officials on the take." He shook his head. "We Americans are a resourceful people. We can design a system that works."

As usual, Joe LaCarta provoked a thoughtful dialogue. The flow of ideas energized the press corps. Pens streaked across the writing pads. The keyboards on the laptops clicked rapidly to the tapping fingers. Flashbulbs occasionally lit up the podium.

Only one person left before it was over. When he finished with his several cell phone calls, the tall man with the phony press pass proceeded through the back exit of the studio. He was already well aware of what Joe LaCarta stood for.

Northern Baja California, Mexico
April (later the same day)

"Eh, Pancho, take me with you. I want to work in San Diego."

"No, not him, Pancho, take me. I'm stronger, and not as lazy."

It was a familiar refrain. Every time he approached his car to leave, the kids would gather around. He wondered if they'd really come along if one of these times he swung open all the doors and told them to pile in. Sadly enough, their time would come. In a few years, perhaps. It was inevitable. They'd have to make their own way. Many would head for the border. They couldn't remain at the orphanage forever.

Not that Padre Villa would kick them out. It was just that there were only so many mouths that could be fed, and so many cots that could fit in the makeshift dormitory.

As was the custom on Francisco "Pancho" Morales' once-a-month weekend forays to volunteer at the orphanage, the energetic young priest walked him to his encircled black Volkswagen Jetta when it was time to leave.

"Back off, *muchachos*, let Pancho get going. Haven't you kept him busy enough. The poor man is tired, can't you see?"

"The poor *old* man," Pancho corrected Father Villa.

"I'll be as old as you in about a year if I keep up this pace," Villa commented. He was barely thirty. But his dedication and his youthful idealism had captivated Pancho. That, along with the surname.

Father Villa had convinced Pancho that he was indeed descended from the legendary Pancho Villa, perhaps an offspring of one of the many family branches that sprouted during the Mexican Revolution. The famed Mexican revolutionary, or bandit, depending on one's point of view, had always been a source of fascination for Francisco "Pancho" Morales. And he relished being a member of the brotherhood of "Franciscos" nicknamed "Pancho."

"Well, Padre, I guess I'll see you next month. Hopefully, that foundation in Ensenada will like our proposal. This place may be a few pesos richer by then."

"*Si Dios quiere.* God willing. If not," the priest shrugged his shoulders, "we'll be here anyway."

"And so will I," Pancho promised.

They gave each other a parting *abrazo.* Pancho waved to the kids. "*Hasta la proxima vez.* And study your little asses off. Sorry, Father," he caught himself and then smiled sheepishly at the priest who was young enough to be his son.

The car pulled away from the dilapidated stucco building, leaving a cloud of dust in the unpaved driveway. In the rearview mirror, Pancho could see them waving good-bye right up until he turned onto the main road.

I'm beat to the ass, he thought to himself as he fidgeted for a mariachi tape. He needed some lively music to help him stay awake. Shit, he looked at his watch. Should've left hours ago.

He liked to drive in daylight. He never tired of the scenic stretch above the rocky coastline between Ensenada and Tijuana. Now, the sun was setting out over the Pacific. In a few minutes, the only scenery would be that illuminated by his headlights.

These weekends away were becoming a sacrifice. He'd met a new woman back in San Diego. And he missed her on these monthly excursions. She was a great cook, as evidenced by his expanding waistline. And lazing around in her bedroom, it was still exciting. But he didn't want to abandon Father Villa. They were so close to getting the funding the orphanage needed. And besides, he liked having a project that was less cushy; one that offered a connectedness to his younger days, when he mingled at grassroots levels.

Sure, rubbing shoulders with the shakers and bakers of San Diego was gratifying. It was a long time in coming. Working at a level where he could make a difference on a wider scale certainly represented a coming of age. He was part of the proverbial establishment after a career of activism, years of fighting the good fight. Now even the most conservative elements in the community invited "Frank" Morales to their cocktail parties.

The peppy Volkswagen streaked northward up the roadway following the beams of its headlights. Pancho raised the volume on the tape deck as he continued to combat drowsiness. Maybe he should sing along with the lyrics—it might jumpstart the adrenalin. God, please don't let the line of cars at the border be too long, he prayed, just before joining in with the mariachis.

It was beginning to work. He experienced a renaissance of alertness, aware enough in fact to notice the flashing blue light approaching from the rear. "What the . . . ?" he said aloud. It caught him by surprise. He looked at the speedometer. He was beyond the limit, but who wasn't? He usually drove much faster.

Strange, he thought. Why no siren? Yet there was no question in his mind that he should pull over. He veered as far over to the right as he could. He looked over his shoulder through the back window. Transit police. Shit. How much will this cost me? he wondered. He squeezed the wallet out of his back pocket, preparing to pay the fine. Or the bribe, whichever category it fell into. Maybe he could explain his volunteer role at the orphanage; maybe get off for being a do-gooder.

Suddenly, another car, a grayish sedan, pulled off the road and snaked in front of his Jetta. It was starting to get confusing. And it got more so when the police car pulled out and streaked off, up the roadway, only to be replaced by another plain car inching up Pancho's rear bumper. Quickly, the car ahead backed towards his front bumper to block any attempt at escape.

He was not being stopped by police! He was about to be robbed! The transit cop had to be in on it. What kind of kickback was he going to get from the modest amount of cash Pancho was carrying?

"Get out, *pendejo*," the Spanish-speaking voice came from the open window on the passenger side. The accent didn't sound Mexican. Two men from the front car came scurrying out of the darkness towards the driver-side door.

Getting out was the last thing Pancho wanted to do. "Here," he shouted, holding his wallet out the driver-side window with his left hand. "Take it. It's all I have." All of a sudden, he was almost ashamed for acting so naive. Why would they go through this trouble for only a few bucks? Why would they need to draw the cop into it? This had to be about something other than his cash.

He saw the revolver now being held through the passenger-side window. It looked like something out of the Wild West. Then the same voice, more emphatically, "I said get out of the car, asshole. And I mean now."

What choice did he have? But now *he* was pissed. It had been a while, but Pancho Morales was starting to lose his famous temper. Angrily, he pushed open the driver-side door. Its force hit the smaller of the two men standing to the car's left.

"*Hijo de puta!* Son of a bitch!" came the angered response.

"You're the assholes. Go fuck yourselves," Pancho challenged, clumsily unfastening the seat belt and emerging out onto his feet. "Who do you think you're messing with?"

Pancho was ready to take them on, whoever they were. But the man from the passenger side had calmly shuffled around from the rear of Pancho's vehicle to reassert his control of the situation. Pancho felt the cold steel of the revolver against the side of his neck. And the iron grip he felt on his crotch squelched any inclination to take the battle to the next level.

With no other choice, he calmed. "Okay, okay goddammit. What d'you want? Talk to me." Please, God, he prayed to himself. Let there be a way out of this.

The two figures in front of him came into focus. There was the map of thuggery on each of their faces, the larger one in particular. Had he seen the man before? He was built like a bull, although an aging one. He had those unmistakable features that were hard to forget. A stone face with a steely stare. A thick head of graying straight hair. Very Indian. The Andes, maybe.

It was Pancho's last conscious thought. The aging bull's right uppercut crashed into Pancho's frightened gaze. His eyelids shut. His knees buckled. A glob of blood ran through the nostrils of his broken nose.

"Híjole, Colombiano!" exclaimed the smaller thug as he bent over Pancho's limp body. "You still have iron in those fists."

The aging bull flashed a stare at his admirer, a stare that seemed to say, And don't ever forget it, friend.

The orders came from the *pistolero,* the man placing the revolver back inside his shirt and into his belt. "Come on, let's get him back into the car." The aging bull was quick to grab Pancho from under the armpits. He didn't need much help. In a matter of seconds, Pancho, out cold, was back behind the wheel of the Volkswagen.

"Okay move the front car out of the way," barked the pistolero. The aging bull jumped to the command. "Come on," the pistolero said to the smaller thug. "Help me push this car over the cliff." He gestured towards the opposite side of the roadway.

"Over the cliff? With him in it! I thought we were just gonna work him over. I thought we were just sending a message."

"Well, there's been a change. The stakes have been raised.

The 'message' needs to be more emphatic."

"But . . . but murder wasn't supposed to be part of the deal. My boss, he didn't say anything about killing the bastard. I . . ."

"Well, my boss did. And he'll square it with your boss. Now shut the fuck up and let's get going. Or 'El Colombiano' here will toss you over the cliff, too." The menacing bull was fast approaching to contribute his brawn to the task at hand. The little thug's dissenting opinion evaporated into the night air.

They chose a spot high above the crashing waves on the opposite side, a spot from which the car could easily be rolled over the cliff. They started the engine, shifted it into neutral, and waited for the right moment. With no cars approaching from either direction, they pushed it to the edge, then over. As it tumbled, the steel scraping against the rocky cliff sent sparks out over the ocean spray below. The culminating crash signaled the end of Pancho Morales' fifty-odd years on Planet Earth.

"It's beautiful," the pistolero concluded. "El Espanto will be pleased. He can call it an accident if he wants. Or, he can call it murder. Whichever serves his purpose best." He let out a sinister laugh as he led his two cohorts back to the parked cars. They acquiesced. The little thug didn't know what the pistolero was even talking about. The aging bull simply grunted.

Chapter 2

The TV was still on. He had slept pretty well considering its light and sound had remained present. He noticed it was already 9:30 a.m. It was nice not having to get up and get over to UVM to teach classes. Yes, the sabbatical was going to be nice. Well, it would be if he didn't have a political campaign on his calendar. But the intensity was for later, he hoped. No harm in approaching it more gradually at the outset.

His fifty-year-old body was always a little stiff in the morning. It was all the more so after a day of celebration. But yesterday's all-day congratulatory therapy had been necessary. It was important that he savor his last day on the friendly side of the battle lines. From here on, he'd begin to experience unfriendly fire across the bow of his ship as it forayed into uncharted political waters.

He lumbered into the kitchen and fired up the coffeemaker. As the water gurgled down through the filter, he headed for the front door to grab the Monday morning edition of each of the Burlington papers he read each day. Sure enough he was on the front page of both. Above the fold, even. It must be true, then. He really was doing this. It was as if the media were the ones who made it official, and not he.

Strolling by his in-home office, he booted up the computer. He hadn't checked his E-mail since Saturday some time. The list of names scrolled down the screen. More than the usual cyber traffic. Probably all his friends wishing him well, offering support, etc. Too many to read before the caffeine fix, he figured. But when he saw Pete Donovan's name, he clicked on it right away.

Crazy Pedro, he smiled to himself. Haven't heard from him in a while.

José,

What's this I hear about you becoming a senator? Guess, I shouldn't be surprised. You were always the schmoozer, always the diplomat. Maybe when you win, I can finally get you down here to stay a while and show you the hotspots. Let me know if I can help from my end. Have a few contacts here in D.C.—

Saludos, Pedro.

Contact with his old Peace Corps cronies always floated the nostalgia balloon. Especially so when it came from his inner circle. Joe, Pete, and Francisco "Pancho" Morales had been like the three musketeers. All for one, one for all. But it was amazing, almost disturbing, how the years had diminished their contact. Little by little. Year by year. At first they all got together once or twice a year after they left Venezuela. Now it was down to E-mail. Hell, Pancho didn't even have that yet. It probably wasn't folksy enough for him.

Joe poured his coffee and headed for the all-season sun porch overlooking Lake Champlain. A pleasant spring day was taking shape. The birds were returning from wherever they went. There were some traces of humanity along the bike trail that paralleled the lake's eastern shore, just north of the city. He noted an occasional in-line skater, several bikers, one or two seniors coming out of hibernation for a morning stroll.

The coffee and the newspaper in the privacy of his own home. Nobody else around. Peaceful. All that's missing is a good woman, he sometimes thought. His only marriage had failed.

He and Sherry were still friends, but they'd never had a family. This missed opportunity was always a source of "what if" for Joe. The Senate race was sure to keep his mind off things so mundane, at least for a while.

The newspaper coverage of his announcement was straightforward. Editorial comment would gather momentum as the contest unfolded. For that, his sword had better be kept sharpened and at the ready. Tomorrow's worry, he rationalized as he savored the moment. He looked out over the lake. He came to depend on these moments of solitude—to do his thinking, to formulate his cutting-edge ideas. Soon it would be warm enough to take in the evening sunsets with a good cigar.

Despite the coffee and the close-to-home topic of the first front-page article he'd just completed, Joe was ready to doze off again when the phone rang.

He stretched his relaxed body as he gathered to his feet. He thought about letting the machine take it, and almost plunked himself back down into the easy chair. Better not. Maybe it's Judy Bennett, his campaign manager, with news of some important booking or other.

He grabbed the receiver from his cordless and instinctively started back towards the recliner facing out over the lake.

"Hello," he began, expecting to be greeted by Judy Bennett's focused demeanor.

But the female voice was of a much sweeter quality. "Joe La-Carta? José?"

"Yes. Who is this?"

"José, it's Marialena Morales, Pancho's daughter. Remember?"

"Of course, of course I remember. How could I forget? How're you doing?" He had met her two and a half years before when she had come east to enroll at the University of Massachusetts. Her father and she took a little side trip to Vermont to pay Joe a visit.

But the pause at the other end of the line hinted that her answer wouldn't be the superficial "fine, thank you." The sob and the short stutter spun him quickly into a state of apprehensiveness. His lower back tensed as if he could sense the impending bad news.

"H-he's dead, José. Papa's dead."

"What? What d'you mean, Marialena? He . . . Oh, my God!"

"A car accident. In Baja. You know, Mexico, where he was helping out at an orphanage."

"Yeah. I remember. He mentioned it last time . . . last time we spoke." Joe couldn't really remember when that was. "How'd it happen, Marialena?"

"Not really sure, José. He was alone. The car went over the cliff on the coastal road. He fell asleep at the wheel, maybe. Don't know."

Pancho dead! The reality began to sink in. What about Pancho's family, his ex-wife and Marialena, how were they holding up?

"How are you doing with it, Marialena? You were close." Joe recalled seeing them together. He had been envious. He'd wished he had a daughter as bright and as impressive as Marialena. And Joe remembered how she seemed to idolize Pancho. She had chosen an eastern university to experience a different part of the country from her native Southern California.

"I'm okay for now. I keep hoping it's just a bad dream. But I know better. I'll keep it together for another day. Gotta make the flight tomorrow."

The flight? Of course. Back to San Diego. "You're flying tomorrow?"

"Two twenty-five p.m. From Hartford."

"From Hartford? . . . From Hartford. Listen, why don't I try to get on the same flight? I can drive down and pick you up."

"I could really use the company."

Chapter 3

The senate race seemed to diminish in importance as Joe sped along I-89 towards its junction with I-91 South into Massachusetts. The prospect of never seeing Pancho again kept churning over in his mind.

It wasn't so much that his friend's life was cut short. After all, Pancho had made it to his early fifties. Probably, it was the idea that Pancho was finally at the top of his game, that he no longer labored on the activist fringes. Old Pancho, the Pancho Villa aficionado, finally had settled into a comfortable life. He had told Joe that the orphanage thing was mostly a reminder of what he had stood for, a protective coat against becoming complacent.

Joe seemed to be recalling every escapade that he, Pancho, and Pete had ever taken on back in their Peace Corps days, especially the big one, the one he had almost managed to put out of sight and out of mind. As if it had been something that they'd heard about, instead of having perpetrated. We must've been out of our ever-loving, mother-freaking minds, he thought, shaking his head as he peered down the endless highway. God, I hope Pancho never mentioned it to Marialena, he pondered. No. Not even Pancho was that crazy. A secret best kept from everyone. Even family.

Pancho had always been the most macho of the group. Sure Pete had been the party guy, and Joe the social networker. But Pancho, he was the one who'd get in the face of anyone who rubbed him wrong, usually those he considered to be out of touch with whatever "good cause" he was pushing.

Pancho had grown up in East Los Angeles, the son of Mexican immigrants. He had had to be tough. Consequently, he was that much more worldly than Pete and Joe. He was speaking fluent Spanish from day one when they arrived in Venezuela. But it wasn't long before they all had become fixtures in their assigned community. They had accomplished a lot. More than most, perhaps. I should hope so, Joe contemplated, after the rather unorthodox measures that they had taken.

In just under three hours, Joe found himself knocking at the door of the duplex in Northampton, Massachusetts. He had had no trouble following Marialena's directions.

A thickly built woman with short hair answered and invited him to step in. She called upstairs for Marialena, and offered Joe a seat in the living room. Joe noticed a third young woman, a roommate, as Marialena would later explain, the partner of the woman who had answered Joe's knock.

The roommates seemed to be aware that Joe was some sort of politician from Vermont and made some small talk along the lines of wishing him well.

Within minutes, Joe heard the graceful steps descending the stairway. He stood to greet his friend's daughter as she entered the room. Two and a half years had worked added magic to the pretty young girl he'd met only once before. Now she had grown to the brink of womanhood, an exotic beauty with flowing black hair and a radiant smile, despite the circumstances, on her smooth olive-skinned face. The almond-shaped eyes had weathered sadness, yet they reflected an inviting warmth.

Stunned by her beauty, Joe almost stopped in his tracks. But recalling the gravity of the situation, he continued forward. When they reached one another, they embraced in a heartfelt and consoling hug. Neither let go until the tears passed.

Chapter 4

It wasn't just his imagination. People both in the terminal and on board the plane had flashed a few stares. Maybe it was just Marialena's distinctive beauty. But maybe it was also the fact the twenty-one-year-old was in the presence of a man well over twice her age.

Not that Joe was an unattractive guy. He still had a full head of hair, although graying rapidly. He stayed in shape. His stomach was still toned. His penchant for red wine and pasta had not exacted much of a toll on his physique. Nonetheless, Bradley Airport in Connecticut was only two states away from Vermont. And he certainly could do without being recognized. No bimbo factor here. It wasn't just a question of protecting his public self. He sincerely wanted Marialena spared from such rumors as well.

They managed seat assignments in the same row. He had to settle for the window while she gracefully slid into the middle seat.

"I hope this goes by quickly," Joe began. "Flying is not my favorite activity. Imagine you'd like to get it over with, too?"

"Normally I don't mind it. But I'm anxious to see Mom."

"She never remarried?" Joe remembered her from Pancho's newlywed days.

"Nah. But she's happy. Happier, even. Papa had a new girlfriend, though. You'll meet her. Name's Angela Arroyo. She owns a small fitness center." Marialena let out a quick laugh.

"Didn't do Papa much good. I think it was her cooking that held the attraction. He started to pork a bit." She gestured toward her midsection. "He should've had you around for a role model. You're in good shape for . . ."

"For an old geezer," he laughed. "Go ahead you can say it."

"Fifty's not old anymore. Look at you. You're making the career move of your life."

"That's not youthfulness," he pointed out. "That's a reflection of craziness. Don't ask me what the hell ever possessed me . . ."

"Okay, whatever possessed you?" she quickly interrupted with some harmless sarcasm. "That, I'm really curious about. God, I'm in the presence of a celebrity. Soon the whole country will know you."

"Who said I'm gonna win?"

"I'd vote for you."

"That's reassuring. Does that mean I'd get the young people's vote. Or just the votes of those who know me personally?"

"I know more about you than you think."

"And you'd still vote for me?"

"Don't be so self-effacing," she chided. "I know from what you stood for twenty-five years ago, that you couldn't possibly have gone wrong. Papa told me all about your Peace Corps days."

"He did, eh? And you were interested? Nobody else ever seemed to be, once we returned. But, he was your father. So I guess . . ."

"Yes. And I'm sort of following in his footsteps. I'm majoring in human services. I want to get involved. Don't know if I'd join the Peace Corps. There's plenty to do here. I've stayed around Western Massachusetts to work summers in community mental health."

"Really? And you never came to Vermont again to visit?"

"I know. I should have. But you know how it is. I kept waiting for Papa to come, so we could go to Burlington together. Then he met Angela, and . . . and he stayed in San Diego and got a little settled."

"It's to be expected," Joe concluded, thinking he might do the same if he'd gotten involved in a new relationship. "Did you go home much?"

"Holidays. We spoke by phone at least once a week. You know how he was, he was always involved in all kinds of community stuff, the cause du jour."

The use of the past tense "was" resonated in Joe's mind. If it was hard for him to think of Pancho as a "was," he could imagine how difficult it must have been for Marialena. The plane reached its cruising altitude when he shut his eyes to relax and think.

Minutes later, the flight attendant came by to offer drinks. Marialena asked for mineral water. Joe still had hopes for a nap so he chose some decaf.

As they lowered their trays, the relaxed conversation resumed. Joe was pleasantly surprised by how easy it was to have a free-flowing, nonacademic exchange with someone so much younger. Never having had children, he was not accustomed to one-on-one cross-generational situations.

"So, how are you gonna change the country?" she began. "When you get elected."

"What makes you think I have any such grand plan?" he joked.

"Oh, I checked you out. I've heard that you've been on a few talk shows. CNN. Fox News. Something about drugs."

"Drugs. That's what everybody seems to remember most. Wish they'd talk a little more about campaign finance reform, tolerance of one another, energy independence, health care, stuff like that. But, drugs . . . drugs are a pretty big deal. It affects everybody. It's pretty visible."

"So what are you, for legalization?"

"To some extent. Decriminalization, at least. We need to reform our policies, mostly. I really believe if we redirected our efforts and resources, use would not go up, at least not significantly. And I'd expect crime to go down. Drug traffic, as we now know it, would be taken out of the hands of the criminals. And law enforcement could concentrate more on other crimes. We would put violent people away for longer stretches."

"Makes some sense. Now, we put users and traffickers away and fill the prisons, right?"

"Right. And others take their place on the streets. The users commit crimes to support their habits. And society pays the bills, the taxes, the insurance premiums. I say let them all pay their own way. We'll use our tax dollars to offer them something better maybe, and to prosecute other crimes."

She nodded. "It sounds like it has some logic." Then she shook her head. Joe could tell she was a thinker, mature beyond her years. "Somehow, though, I can see it'll be a tough sell."

"Oh, you got that right."

"It must've been a lot simpler when you were younger."

Joe thought about that comment. Maybe her political sense was better than her historical sense. He recalled his college days, the Vietnam War, civil rights, the assassinations of the Kennedys and of Martin Luther King.

She elaborated, "I don't mean the times. I meant, for you. And Papa. Your Peace Corps days, for example."

"Yeah that," he concurred. "There, just about anything we did was something that was needed. We started from scratch, nowhere to go but up. And the people . . . hell, they appreciated anything we could do. And they demanded little, if anything.

Pretty straightforward." Up until the end anyway, he reflected to himself.

"Papa told me all about it."

"All? As in everything?" Joe was nervous about such a prospect.

"Well, I assume he did a few things that a father wouldn't tell a daughter."

Joe chuckled. "Yeah, that you can assume."

"I meant about your work. Your projects," she continued.

"He told you all about those? And what sticks out most in your mind?" It was time to cut to the chase.

"He was particularly proud of how you guys got that Foundation in the Cayman Islands to fund your program into perpetuity."

"Perpetuity," the word piqued his curiosity. He hadn't used it much since his Peace Corps days when he and Pancho and Pete had become preoccupied with the survival of what they had helped create. So many good Peace Corps successes failed to survive the departure of the volunteers. They had been determined to not let that happen, so much so that they were willing to succumb to a strange temptation.

"He told you all about that?" Joe probed. "Including how we got the money?"

"Well, no. I just assumed you approached the Foundation with some kind of proposal. Right?"

"Yeah, something like that. If I remember correctly." Whew, he surmised. She didn't know about it.

Chapter 5

Joe arrived at the funeral home around mid-afternoon. Unusually, he had slept late that morning. Maybe it was the jet lag. Maybe it was the uncharacteristic depression he was combating over Pancho's death and that growing shadow of mortality even U.S. Senators couldn't deny.

Nonetheless, he felt rested. He had stayed in a downtown hotel after arriving the previous night. Marialena's mother had met them at Lindburg Airport and offered to put him up. But Joe wasn't family, and he refused to impose, even in the slightest.

It was a closed casket affair. Damn, he wouldn't even get to lay eyes on his old friend ever again. He wondered if Pancho's family had had the opportunity, or the horror, to view his face, and perhaps his mutilated body, one last time.

He knelt at the casket for the traditional several minutes before rising to pass through the greeting line. Pancho's mother was slumped over in a sofa overcome with grief. Joe had never met her. He knew Pancho had lost his father during his college years. Marialena intercepted Joe's approach and introduced him to her grieving grandmother. Joe held the octogenarian's hand and expressed his condolences. She gave credence to what he'd long since realized—a mother's pain when she is predeceased by a son.

Joe greeted Marialena's mother and kissed her on the cheek.

Then Marialena introduced Joe to Angela Arroyo, the grieving girlfriend.

"I've heard a lot about you, I'm so glad to meet you," she said softly, as she stepped away from the greeting line.

"Likewise," Joe said.

"And you may be hearing even more about him," Marialena interjected. "José, I mean Joe—Papa used to call him by his Peace Corps name—is going to be a U.S. Senator."

Joe waved his arms as if to say it was a big "if," and that it was no big deal anyway.

But Angela was impressed. "Really? Well I wish you all the luck . . ."

"It seems strange talking about luck," Joe consoled. "I wish I could've given you whatever luck is due to come my way. This must be awful for you."

"Of course. But what choice do I have? I'll get through it. We all will." Joe had just met Angela. But for some reason he could see she had been a good fit for Pancho. She was self-assured and exuded a certain grit in her eyes and in her facial expression. She was reasonably attractive, mid-forties, perhaps. It was evident that she was a client of her health club as well as the owner.

"It's a real waste," Angela continued. "Life was really good for us. For him." She shook her head as she spoke. "The funeral directors couldn't even make him presentable."

"Papa was thrown from the car," Marialena explained. "The rocks at the bottom of the cliff . . ." She didn't need to elaborate.

"Funny, though," she added after a brief pause and a passing sob. "The driver's seat didn't get separated from the car itself. We saw pictures. And Papa was fanatical about wearing his seat belt. He impressed that upon me ever since I was a little girl. I can't believe he would've been driving without being strapped in."

Angela shrugged her shoulders as if to say, What difference would it have made? "It wouldn't have saved him, Marialena. Who knows? If he fell asleep at the wheel, he must've been exhausted. If he was that tired, maybe he just forgot. He was getting a bit absentminded, you know."

"I know it wouldn't've made a difference. It was just strange, that's all. Maybe I wouldn't be so curious if it'd happened on this side of the border."

"Suspicious?" Joe asked, noting Marialena's expression. "You don't think there was any foul play, do you? I thought it sounded pretty straightforward."

"Oh, don't mind me," she shrugged. "Maybe my imagination's getting the best of me. You know how you read about all the corruption and stuff around Tijuana."

"Don't get hung up on that, Marialena," Angela advised. "Even if it were a remote possibility, we'd never get any answers."

She was right, of course, Joe concluded. If there were anything resembling a cover-up, then that cover-up would also be covered up. It was counter-therapeutic to even consider. "I doubt there was any foul play," Joe added, trying to put Marialena's curiosity at ease. "Why should there be? He didn't have any enemies, did he?"

Marialena shrugged her shoulders. How would she know?

"None," Angela answered. "Everybody liked Pancho. He was endearing, even when he lost that temper of his on occasion."

Joe smiled. He remembered how intense Pancho could get.

Marialena also flashed a smile. "Yeah, I can't remember anyone ever staying mad at him. He didn't have any enemies from his younger days, did he?" she asked Joe, almost kiddingly.

"None that I can remember," answered Joe, thinking how

that might've been different had their little secret been discovered.

As Joe sat and watched the people flowing through, he discovered first-hand that Pancho did indeed have many friends. It didn't require much speculation to surmise that virtually every segment of the community was represented. Joe could see that there were a few of the shakers and bakers as well as those who looked to be more down on their luck. Then there were those who were obviously part of his inner circle, as Joe once had been—those close friends and confidants that Pancho saw regularly.

Contemplating close friends and confidants, Joe's attention was abruptly directed to the lumbering stroll of the balding man who had just appeared at the end of the line. Pedro! Damn, he made it.

Joe had tried calling Pete Donovan before leaving Vermont. Then he called again from Marialena's apartment in Massachusetts. But he had gotten neither an answer nor an answering machine. He had figured that he would connect in person, and therefore had chosen not to inform Pete by e-mail. He was beginning to feel guilty about that decision, thinking that if Pete did not find out in time, it would be Joe's fault.

But Pete was here. Somebody had to have called him. Marialena, perhaps? No, she would have mentioned it. Besides, Joe didn't think they'd ever met. But at least now his own feeling of guilt was turned back.

Joe anxiously waited where he sat while Pete worked his way through the greeting line. Joe watched as Pete introduced himself, somewhat uneasily, to Pancho's family and to Angela Arroyo. Funny, he thought, Pete usually was quite comfortable in such situations. Why should this be any different? Maybe he was a bit fried after the trip. Knowing the old Pedro, Joe figured that he had had a few cocktails on his cross-country flight.

When Pete noticed Joe staring in his direction, he seemed anxious to phase out of his conversation with Angela and Marialena. When he pulled away, he walked ponderously towards Joe, without the mischievous grin that he normally sported at such reunions. Is he all right? Joe wondered.

Barely forcing a smile, Pete shook Joe's hand when he stood. There was no seat available next to Joe, so they spontaneously walked together to an outside foyer.

"Pedro, I was afraid you wouldn't hear about it in time. Shit, thank God you found out. Glad you made it."

The worried look remained on Pete's face. Was it Pancho's death that had derailed his otherwise upbeat personality? Maybe it hadn't sunk in yet. All he knew was that Pete kidded about almost everything, even when he was down.

Pete fidgeted. Then shaking his head, he finally acknowledged Joe's opening remark. "José, we gotta go somewhere and talk."

Joe gave him a puzzled look. Why not here? he wondered.

"You won't believe it, José. You're not gonna believe what I have to tell you."

Book II

Chapter 6

Puerto Ordaz, Venezuela
October 1972

"What's taking Pedro so long with the *cerveza?*" complained Pancho. "Another *Cuba Libre* and I'll have a helluva *ratón* tomorrow." Raton meant hangover in the Venezuelan vernacular. Pancho knew from experience that mixing rum cokes and beer was a recipe for Tuesday morning nausea.

"You know him. Probably his usual—checking out who's at the beer hall," explained Joe. "He knew we were down to our last beer, so he won't keep us waiting too long. He better not, the crazy drunk. Besides, he's a Giants fan, and he won't want to miss the game."

"It's almost kick-off now. Turn it up," Pancho pointed to the radio as he swirled the ice in his empty glass.

Listening to Monday Night Football on Armed Forces Radio had become a ritual for Pancho, Pete, and Joe. And since they stocked the refrigerator for the event, it was customary for some of their gringo friends working in the area to drop in.

For the moment they were alone in the modest apartment. The three Peace Corps volunteers lived together, each having his own room off a short hallway. The common living room area was sparsely decorated, and was furnished with the barest essentials. They had assembled chairs sufficient enough for sitting around over beers or *Cuba Libres.* An old wooden table was plunked down in the corner dining area for those few occasions when any of them did not eat out in one of the cheap eateries in town.

The apartment was part of a complex that was financed with public and private capital to house new workers flocking into the fast-growing city. The urban development was being fueled by the rich iron and mineral deposits in the surrounding area.

The complex was conveniently located near the downtown, about a fifteen-minute walk in the sweltering heat. More often than not, they used the Peace Corps jeep assigned to their program to get around.

"Here he comes now," said Joe. "I can hear the jeep pulling up." The apartments had open-air vents in lieu of glass windows. Even from their third-floor perch, outside sounds were as audible as those in the next room.

They recognized Pete's heavy footsteps as he stormed the stairway with the case of Polar beer braced on his shoulder. Entering through the open door, Pete cheerily lowered the cargo to pull out three of the ice-cold green bottles. "Enjoy," he exhorted before continuing towards the fridge and hoisting the rest of the box into its position of honor on the top shelf.

"Game start yet?" he asked as he returned to within earshot of the English-speaking voice fighting through the static. "Go Giants! They're gonna kick some ass tonight." He held up his bottle, and then took a hefty swig.

"Redskins just received the kick. First down around the twenty-five. You just made it. Where the hell you been?" scolded Pancho.

"I stopped for a quick one at the *Cervecería.* Ran into crazy Carlos. He was sitting with a fresh batch of *señoritas* he'd just met. You know. Slinging his usual line of crap."

"Any nice lookers?" Joe beat Pancho to the inevitable next question.

"Actually yes, better than his usual entourage."

"Carlos isn't that choosy. Long as they don't need to shave their faces," Joe said, taking a gulp. "And as long as they shave their legs."

"I don't know about that last requirement. Carlos mentioned getting together this Sunday. Maybe go to the river. Have a picnic. Naturally, he invited his new lady friends. We should get a group together." Pete guzzled the remainder of the beer in his bottle and got up to grab another.

"Hey, great idea. It's Anita's birthday this weekend. We'll make it into a special celebration," Joe suggested. "Anita" was Anne Jeffries, a nurse who worked as a Peace Corps volunteer in the city. She lived nearby and hung out with the guys on weekends.

The more they drank and conversed, the more they missed the broadcast of the play-by-play. As was the custom, they were more interested in the score and whether or not the point spread was being covered. For the second straight year, they were running a weekly football card in the American community. This enterprise raised a few extra *bolivares* for their community projects.

The weekly ritual fulfilled a community need for those expatriate Americans on assignment with some of the area companies. They missed their pro football. The opportunity to bet re-piqued their interest. And they knew even if they lost, the profits went to a good cause.

Joe had become a proficient handicapper. He established the point spreads by himself early in the week so they could distribute and retrieve the cards by the weekend's games. When the English-speaking paper published the official point spreads on Fridays, Joe discovered he was generally within a half point of the official lines. Maybe Las Vegas was in his future.

"We're better off this week if the 'Skins cover? That's what you said, right, José?" Pancho asked.

"By two hundred *bolivares* or so."

"Good job again with the point spreads. Maybe you can get a job with the New England mob when you leave here. What else are you Italians good for?" Pancho chided.

"Beats being a two-bit bandit like your great Pancho Villa," Joe kidded back. "And watch your mouth, I have a cousin who's working his way up in the New England mob."

"Yeah, a real genius, I'll bet."

"Sure, like Professor Pancho Villa. Couldn't even count up to the number of wives he had."

"The man was a stud, what can I say?"

"I don't care about the money this week," Pete butted in. "I prefer that my Giants win outright." His partisanship superseded his altruism, at least for this particular game. Pete was raised in New York City.

"You guys still talking about raising money?" boomed the happy-go-lucky voice from the hallway. The guys were momentarily startled. They hadn't heard the approaching footsteps. The beer must've dulled their senses. All at once they looked up at the tall figure of Big Don Buchanan striding through the open doorway with his signature mischievous smile.

"Tío Don! Where you been hiding?" Joe asked.

"Let me get the man a *cerveza.*" Pete popped up. He needed to grab another for himself anyway. To Pete, a beer bottle that was empty was a waste of good hand space.

They liked calling the tall balding man "Tío," meaning "uncle." Big Don was older than his young friends by a full generation. A Marine Corps veteran of World War II, the fiftyish expatriate never settled into the postwar, "Father Knows Best" lifestyle. For him, life was a series of business deals and other sundry adventures. What his young friends possessed in idealism, El Tío matched in worldliness.

El Tío was an upbeat and fun-loving sort who enjoyed mixing

with the younger crowd, and not just for the young señoritas they attracted. It was as if he needed to prolong his youthfulness. He was the kind that needed to feel he was viewing the world prospectively.

Presently, El Tío, or Tío Don, was making a lot of money in the trucking business. With all the development going on in the area, it had become a can't-miss venture. Nonetheless, he always had his antennae up for new enterprises, schemes that would pay big dividends in the future.

Because he was in the shipping business, he often drove the trucks or accompanied his drivers. Sometimes he was gone from Puerto Ordaz for long stretches. His young friends, whom he often referred to as his *sobrinos*, meaning nephews, usually missed his charismatic presence when they didn't see him for a while. Their Venezuelan friends also enjoyed having El Tío around. Even though his Spanish was packaged in a heavily wrapped gringo accent, his storytelling skills more than compensated.

"I was in Caracas," El Tío answered, as Pete handed him a cold bottle of Polar Beer. "Had to deal with some bureaucratic shit. Seems the government and I disagree on how much I owe in taxes. They may shut me down till I see it their way, the bastards. Wish they could take a joke," he laughed. "How's the game going?"

"Pretty close right now. José and I want the Redskins to cover the spread. It means a few extra *bolivares* for our projects," explained Pancho.

"You guys are always nickel-and-diming," Tío Don chided.

"Yeah, well, our project needs all it can get, especially with us leaving soon," Pancho retorted.

"Be nice to have a permanent money source," Joe repeated the familiar refrain. "When we leave, all our work will probably just flush down the Orinoco."

"Ain't that the truth," Pete chimed in between chugs on his latest bottle. "Got any big ideas, Tío? You're the businessman around here."

Big Don bellowed out a laugh. "As a matter of fact I do." Then, his face turned dead serious. He paused until all three pairs of eyes were riveted on his. "I just found out that there's over six million dollars worth of Nazi loot in a warehouse near here. And all we gotta do is go and steal it!"

Chapter 7

The Orinoco was Venezuela's major river. Its wide brown waters flowed past Puerto Ordaz on their easterly journey through Venezuela's northeastern Delta Amacuro before draining into the Atlantic. The Caroni River rambled northward from the Guyana Highlands in the south to join the Orinoco between Puerto Ordaz and its sister city to the east, San Felix. The confluence of the two large rivers was generally referred to simply as *la confluencia.*

Whereas the Orinoco was a lifeblood of commerce, the rugged fast-flowing Caroni was not navigable. It had many fewer river "beaches" than did the more tame Orinoco. The Orinoco afforded any number of popular weekend gathering spots, and was the river of choice for the locals who wanted to get wet.

The Sunday picnic idea proposed by Carlos to Pete the previous Monday evening gathered momentum. Spurred on by Anita's *cumpleaños,* or birthday, word-of-mouth preparations were made, and a willing group was pulled together.

Reminiscent of Ben Cartwright and his three sons in the TV western *Bonanza,* El Tío and his "three nephews" rambled forward proudly in his pickup truck, assembling the needed supplies along the route—cold beer, snacks, cola to mix with the Cacique rum.

Anita Jeffries, the birthday girl, drove the jeep and brought her two roommates, Carmen and Marta, young Venezuelan teachers at the local high school. Like so many young professionals in the area, the two *profesoras* hailed from other parts of the country, Carmen from Caracas, Marta, nicknamed "La Maracucha," from Maracaibo.

The two vehicles arrived almost simultaneously. The ladies chose a cabana near the shoreline and carried in some dishes that required a little more preparation. The men unloaded the pickup and popped open their first round of beers without breaking stride.

"Where's ours?" Anita chided.

"Oh, sorry," Joe answered sheepishly. "What do you prefer, beer or rum?" He held up the Cacique bottle. The sunlight glistened off its golden contents.

"*Cuba Libre* for me," Anita stated in Spanish. Carmen and Marta followed suit. Marta flashed Joe an especially friendly smile. They had had a brief fling the year before, but it dissipated when Joe's experiment with monogamy left too little wind under his wings. They remained friends and liked to flirt with one another.

Like Pancho, Joe was anxiously awaiting Carlos' arrival. Pete's scouting report on this new group of señoritas had piqued some curiosity. Joe looked up each time he heard a car engine cresting forward along the dirt road that carved through the wild green shrubbery.

"Where the hell's Carlos?" Pancho seemed to be directing the interrogation at Pete.

"Don't worry, he'll be here. It was his idea. Remember? When would he ever miss a party? You know Carlos."

"Yeah, we know Carlos," Joe deadpanned. "That's why we know he's always late. Pedro's right. He'll be here."

"Who cares about Carlos?" Pancho added sarcastically. "It's the señoritas I care about. As long as he brings them, he can leave after that if he wants."

"Nice talk, Pancho. If he leaves, who's gonna play the guitar?

You? Pedro?"

"Well it sure as shit won't be you with your repertoire of two songs. What's that one Carlos taught you?"

" 'Mexico Lindo.' It's his theme song. And I'm getting good. Didn't you notice Marta swooning at the last fiesta?"

"Yeah, she was swooning all right," Pancho laughed. "She was saying to herself, 'I'm glad I dumped this asshole.' "

"Dumped *me?* Hell I'm the one who called it off, not her." Joe caught Marta smiling in his direction as he said this. But since they were bantering in English, she didn't understand that she was a part of the subject matter.

"There he is now," Pete pointed as Carlos' old white Ford sedan came into view. A bronze colored elbow was noted in the passenger window, and long black hair was noticeable through each of the rear windows.

"Let's go check them out. I mean, let's go see if they need any help carrying," Joe chuckled.

Carlos and his three young guests piled out of the two-door sedan and greeted the three approaching young men carrying the green Polar bottles. They all exchanged smiles as they shook hands and said their *mucho gustos,* "pleasure to meet you's." Courteously, Pancho, Pete, and Joe each lent their one free hand to carry a few items from the car to the cabana. Carlos carried his guitar.

"Not bad," Pancho whispered to Joe in English.

"I like the tall, thin one." Joe staked first claim.

"Well then you're lucky, 'cause I like the one with the coconuts in her T-shirt," Pancho mumbled. "The skinny one's all yours."

"What about Pedro and Carlos?"

Pancho shrugged his shoulders. "Carlos'll take whoever's left over."

"That's true. And by the time Pedro's drunk enough to

bother, it'll be late in the fourth quarter."

Tío Don had already forged ahead into the water. They could see his six-foot four-inch frame smiling above the water line with a paper cup in his right hand.

"Are you guys going in?" Anne "Anita" Jeffries asked. She was decked out in a new bathing suit and her ample bustline caught Joe's eye as it often had. Too bad she's a little too old, he thought to himself. She was in her late twenties, pushing thirty perhaps. Even though it was her birthday, she wouldn't divulge her age. Hell, can't ruin a good friendship, he concluded for the ninetieth time, as if Anita wasn't wise to his act, as well as to that of Pancho.

Within minutes everyone was in the water. Even Pete took some time away from the cooler. The guys started tossing a waterproof version of an American football around. It was an effective attention-getter. The señoritas were intrigued by its nuances. And the guys didn't mind offering up-close tutorials in the art of throwing and catching the odd-shaped projectile.

By late afternoon it was time for the birthday cake. Carmen and Marta took it out of the cooler as everyone gathered around inside the open-air cabana. Everyone was still going strong with the drinks. The fresh air and the exercise facilitated alcohol absorption. Or, at least so they all figured.

"So, how many candles, Anita?" Pancho kidded, as he awaited the dirty look.

"Put twenty on there, and shut the fuck up," she responded in English. The use of the vulgarity was very uncharacteristic. Anita served notice that it was the end of the subject.

"Wait till you're all my age," El Tío laughed, also in English. "Hell, I had a twenty-five-year-old last week, and twenty-five goes into fifty twice. But when fifty tried to go into twenty-five twice, hell, I almost had a stroke."

"Hilarious, Tío," Anita scolded.

"Which whorehouse was that in?" Pete whispered near El Tío's ear.

"I'll take you there later if you wanna go," he joked.

Carlos tuned up the guitar and they sang "Happy Birthday" in Spanish. Anita cut the cake and passed it around while Pete grabbed some beers and Carmen and Marta mixed a few more rum cokes. Pancho and Joe maneuvered themselves into one-on-one conversations with the two new señoritas they'd staked out. The third young girl that Carlos brought along seemed to be enraptured in his music and song.

That time of the late afternoon when jungle daylight rather abruptly flipped over to full darkness was fast approaching. In the tropics, it didn't seem to happen gradually. Nightfall drove out the intense afternoon heat, replacing it with lukewarm river breezes that served to refresh both mind and body.

Her name was Nora. But she told Joe that everyone referred to her as La Flaca, or the "thin lady." La Flaca had just accepted Joe's invitation to join him at the Cervecería Bavaria, the local beer hall, for sometime later that week. He got that out of the way—he was assured of seeing her again.

The two had separated from the group for a short moonlight stroll near the river. "We'd better not wander beyond the glow of the lights," La Flaca cautioned. "You never know. There may be caimans or anacondas. Can't see 'em in the dark."

That was a possibility. But Joe had other things on his mind. Nonetheless, he had little choice but to heed his new friend's excuse to remain within view of her friends. But he was in no hurry to rejoin the group. With the guitar music resonating through the palms and waltzing with the breeze and the flow of the river, the right mood was developing.

Spontaneously, Joe and La Flaca began to dance to the beat of Carlos' guitar. The choreography was a bit out of synch.

Nonetheless, they established a dialogue without conversation.

When the music stopped, they strolled back towards the cabana. "How long have you known Carlos?" she asked Joe. "He's quite the charmer."

Joe wasn't sure whether or not to feel threatened. Was he, Joe, her second choice? Nah. Can't be. True, Carlos was a charmer with the ladies, and he had the gift of guitar and song. But hell, he had a wide girth, and was considerably out of shape for a guy who wasn't even thirty.

"Over a year," Joe answered, getting past the self-doubting pause. "Funny, I don't even remember how we met him. He just seemed to appear. Says he works for the Agricultural Ministry. Works with the farmers in the surrounding area. Not sure what he does, exactly. None of us have ever gone with him."

"He's Mexican, no?"

"*Sí.* He claims he's from a politically connected family in Mexico City. His last name's Santiago. Claims he's here out of the goodness of his heart. Why? What'd he tell you?"

"The same. But he wanted to talk more about my friends and me."

Of course, one of Carlos' little secrets, Joe recalled. When you meet women, talk about them, make them feel they're the center of attention.

"Carlos is quite a character," Joe acknowledged. "I've gotten to be good friends with him. Sure, he's a lot of fun. But he's also got some great perspectives on things."

"Like?"

"Oh . . . Like Latin American Politics. Economic development. Education of the masses."

"You mean he has a serious side?"

As they neared the cabana, Joe noted that Carlos and Pancho were locking horns in a serious conversation. It wasn't the first time that a few drinks had spurred on the two of them.

Joe chuckled to La Flaca. Pointing to Carlos and Pancho, he said, "Listen and take note."

Carlos tried not to get too serious. As usual, it was Pancho who was getting hot under the collar. Carlos just liked to instigate, and then go away laughing about it.

"Pancho Villa and his two-bit revolution was the worst thing that ever happened to Mexico," Carlos was saying. "The country's been ruled by bandits ever since. It's who you know, who you can bribe."

"And what was it before?" Pancho responded. "Just a bunch of bandits who happened to be wellborn. They cared only about themselves. At least Pancho Villa gave the poor some dignity. *Viva Villa!*" he bellowed, talking through the alcohol.

"Sí, Viva Villa," Carlos repeated sarcastically. "That revolution was a joke."

Joe could see that the drinking was driving Pancho from his party self to his intense self. The señorita with the "coconuts in her T-shirt" was now talking with Anita. Maybe she felt upstaged by alcohol and politics. Meeting a man who romanticized about Pancho Villa instead of young women may not be what she'd had in mind.

"Hey, Carlos, what's the matter, you tired already? We wanna hear more music. Come on." It was Joe's way of restoring decorum. "Play, or I'll have to take over."

There was a chorus of voices exhorting Carlos therefore to play. Pancho, Pete, El Tío, Anita, Carmen, and Marta did not hold Joe's guitar skills in the same esteem that Joe himself did.

The music resumed. Pancho got up and wedged himself into the conversation between Anita and the señorita he'd temporarily forgotten about.

Joe wondered why Pete hadn't moved in after Pancho had gotten sidetracked. He's probably shit-faced, Joe figured, as he headed towards the cooler. At the same instant, Pete got up from his conversation with El Tío and joined Joe in grabbing another cold one. He seemed to be walking pretty straight, Joe noted.

"José, how you doing with that skinny chick?" Pete asked.

"Skinny? You guys are nuts. If they're not top heavy, you assholes don't give 'em a second look. These thin ones have staying power. They'll look good even when they're thirty-five and old."

"Who gives a shit about how they look when they're thirty-five and old. What a' you gonna marry 'er? Wake up, man. We'll be out of here soon."

Joe took it in good humor. "You sound like El Tío. Invest little and get a lot. He's like that with women and with business."

"He's smart that way," Pete said, seriously enough to sound like a disciple. "Say, José, you should hear him out on his plan."

"Plan? What plan is that? Is he opening up another whorehouse?"

"No. You know what plan. Remember the other night? The Nazi loot? It's there, José. Paintings and sculptures stolen from museums and private homes during the war."

"Sure. And we're gonna steal it from the Nazis? What're you nuts? What do we look like, a bunch of commandos? Do you think the Nazis are just gonna stand by and watch?"

"That's the beauty of it. It's just sitting there. It's not being watched, because nobody's supposed to know it's even there."

"According to El Tío. The world's most reliable source. Don't you know he'd take a risk just for the thrill of it?"

"José, he ain't been to jail yet."

"Well, maybe that's his next adventure. Get caught, so we gotta break out of El Dorado prison. You remember driving by there, don't you? In the middle of the most God-forsaken jungle known to man. The one that Papillon, in his memoirs, said was the worst one of all he'd experienced."

"Papillon? You mean that bullshitter whose book was the all-time bestseller here in Venezuela? José, hear him out. This ain't bullshit. He's got a plan. He's even staked the place out."

"Pedro, you've had too much *cerveza.* El Tío's a hot shit, but let's just stick to the partying and the occasional run to the whorehouses with him."

"No, José, I'm not drunk. Think about it. Six million bucks. Think what we could do with our share. Wait till El Tío tells Pancho the plan."

That prospect sent a ray of uneasiness up Joe's spine. Pancho was just macho enough to take it on. Just hope he's not crazy enough to be swayed by El Tío, Joe thought. And by Pete, if it really is testosterone, and not alcohol, spurring his thoughts.

Chapter 8

"I knew it, goddammit. Pancho, the rum and the *cerveza* has finally fried your brain. Those assholes've really got you thinking about it, don't they?"

"Just hear El Tío out, José. Then make up your own mind. He's got it worked out, I tell ya. He'll be here any minute."

Joe took a seat across from Pancho at the wooden table in the corner of the living area. "It's Pedro, too, ain't it? El Tío's convinced him. And now he's cheerleading the idea. When did you have your session with them?" Joe had feared that the winds of folly would sweep through and disrupt the calm waters of their final months of service.

"They didn't pressure. Wasn't them so much," Pancho admitted. Joe couldn't help but notice the gritty expression on Pancho's face.

"Come on, Pancho. You got more brains than that. Pete's always half in the bag. And El Tío always brings out the worst in him. But hell, I figured you to be capable of distinguishing between worthiness and craziness."

"It's not that crazy, José. It rang true the minute I heard it. Think about it. The shit's just sitting there. El Tío lucked out getting the inside information."

"So? You were serious from the get-go? From the first time you heard it?" Joe was disappointed to think that maybe it was Pancho who was breathing life into the far-fetched idea. Joe slouched back in the chair and took in a deep breath. He stared off at the open door to the hallway. "Pancho, do you really think it's just sitting there unguarded? Give me a break."

"So maybe there's a watchman. Yeah, there's a watchman. So what? El Tío figured on that much. We just work around that. Shit, it's not like we're storming the Bastille."

Joe shook his head in continued amazement. "I can't believe this is happening. What the hell's gotten into you guys? Don't you want to get home and get on with your lives?"

"Hell yes. As much as you do. But won't you enjoy it more knowing we set up our program financially? Forever? To live on after we're gone?"

At least that was a relief, Joe thought. They weren't thinking of going after the money for themselves. It was not unusual for Peace Corps initiatives to have a short shelf life after the departure of the assigned volunteers. This prospect had been like a stone in their shoes. Like having unfinished business.

"To live on after we're gone," Joe repeated Pancho's words. "And your plan includes us not getting caught, I take it?"

"Hey, what makes you think I wanna go to prison any more than you do? I know about El Dorado prison down there in the asshole of the Earth. José, listen to me. If the plan isn't foolproof, we don't do it. End of story. That's it."

"Gee, Pancho, that's a relief. You guys just give it your stamp of foolproof-ness, and I'll feel as safe as an altar boy at Sunday Mass. Give me a break."

"Planning is everything, hombre."

"Pancho . . . Pancho Villa. *Viva Villa!* Take from the 'haves' and give to the 'have-nots.' That's what this is all about? A chance for you to follow the dream of The Great Revolutionary? That it, Pancho?"

"No dreaming here, José. How did the fucking Nazis get it? By robbing their victims. Well, their victims are probably all dead. And if not, they have no chance of ever seeing the stuff again. So why not take the profits and put them to good use? So some good people, victims in their own right, can benefit? What, would you feel better letting the Nazis keep it?"

"If I could wave a magic wand . . . of course, I'd snatch it from the bastards. Of course I'd fund our programs into perpetuity. But, it's not like it's risk free. I don't care how good the plan is. There are always contingencies. Especially here. How much of what we've accomplished has gone according to plan?"

" 'Perpetuity'? That's a good word. Nice ring to it," Pancho kidded. "So we'll have a contingency. You just said it—we're experienced with contingencies. We'll handle whatever contingency."

"We?"

"José, it has to be all of us. Or it's out of the question."

This didn't relieve Joe's uneasiness. Now he felt the pressure of having veto power. He felt a tension in the back of his neck, as if he had steel weights on each shoulder.

"Pancho, we're out of our league. We're just a bunch of pussy-assed do-gooders. We're not made for this shit."

"Don't sell us short. I did some pretty ballsy things in my youth, back in L.A. Pete grew up in the Bronx. You pulled some risky shit to pay for college. Come on.

"Besides, a lot of guys our age have put their asses on the line in Vietnam. We probably won't have to. And that's good for us 'cause the policy sucks. But here we've got a cause we *do* believe in. So maybe we've got an obligation to risk our butts this time, for a greater good."

"Maybe you've lived a little closer to the edge than I have, Pancho. I never did anything I thought might end me up in some rat-hole of a jail." Joe paused and thought for a moment. "On the other hand, I have to admit . . . what could be more gratifying than knowing those poor kids and their families would have these services forever, compliments of the Nazi underground?"

"The concept is beautiful."

"But it's still *pura locura.*" He used the Spanish term for "pure craziness." "That kind of loot can't be just sitting there with our names on it."

They heard El Tío's pickup truck coming to a halt outside the building. His and Pete's cheerful voices bantered back and forth as they ascended the stairway towards the apartment.

"Hell, no escape. I'm gonna be late meeting Carlos and the ladies," Joe lamented. "They're waiting for me at the Cervecería Bavaria." The Bavaria was a small beer hall, or *cervecería,* with a German motif that the group frequented.

"Relax," counseled Pancho. "You're only gonna be here a few more months. Not enough time to get anywhere with that chick. Especially when you tell her you're leaving. Trust me."

"I think I'd rather make a fool of myself with her than be some thug's girlfriend at El Dorado prison."

El Tío's and Pete's footsteps slowed to a halt in the entryway. "There they are. My two crack commandos," El Tío chided, as they stepped in.

Joe shuddered.

"A round of *cervezas?*" Pete proposed. He proceeded towards the fridge without waiting for responses.

"Yeah, let's make it quick. I've got to get over to the Bavaria," Joe repeated his priority. "Okay, Tío, you're on. Let's hear it. Especially the foolproof part. I don't want to piss my pants before my date."

El Tío let out a mischievous laugh. "Sit back 'n enjoy your beer, son. It's an opportunity we can't refuse. The señorita at the beer hall will wait. She'll probably be late anyway. If not, she's got Carlos and the other broad to keep her company. No loss for conversation there."

It took one bullshitter to know another, Joe thought.

El Tío began by giving a little background. On his recent trip to Caracas to meet with his banker, he was privy to some loose talk about a shipment of valuable paintings and art objects from Zurich, Switzerland. The materials had been crated and shipped through the port of Marseilles, France, to Venezuela. The cargo was offloaded at the nearby port on the Orinoco River to await transshipment down the eastern coast of South America to its destination in Argentina. And the crates were sitting in an open-air warehouse that El Tío's trucks had hauled cargo into and out of quite regularly over the past few years. It was a warehouse that, according to El Tío, "didn't exactly have the security of Fort Knox."

Allegedly, the bank in Caracas was partly owned by the bank in Switzerland that sent the shipment. The Venezuelan bank was responsible for guaranteeing the reloading of the cargo onto an Argentina-bound freighter sometime before Christmas. When El Tío inquired kiddingly, as was his custom even in serious business meetings, if it was going to some kind of underground group of ex-Nazis, the bankers recklessly revealed that he had actually made a lucky guess. Evidently, the bankers in Caracas were feeling some discomfort over the origin of the pieces, and were only handling the transshipment because they had no choice.

According to El Tío's descriptive account, the bankers' looks, gestures, and cryptic verbalizations unmistakably conveyed the fact that the portraits, sculptures, and other artifacts had been looted during the War from victims of the Holocaust and from museums in conquered territory.

Carelessly, the Caracas bankers had also revealed the value of the cache. They must've felt that El Tío was a man who could be trusted. They claimed its worth to be around six million dollars. El Tío's business sense led him to figure that the bank must've held an insurance policy commensurate with the value of the cargo.

Being in the trucking business, El Tío had occasion to go in and out of warehouses in the area, and he was especially familiar with the one in question, the one at the river port. When he'd returned from Caracas, he'd made it a point to wander through its large storage area until he noticed a cluster of large crates with markings "Zurich-Mars" in large black letters. These had to be the ones. The "-Mars" part must have meant Marseilles, the port of embarkation.

The crates were only a short distance from where El Tío had rented space to store some mining equipment he had purchased as an investment. Over and over, he reconstructed the spatial layout of the vast warehouse in his scheming mind. Were the essential elements in place? Would conditions ever be more favorable to pull off a surprise heist? To succeed in a get-rich-quick adventure?

Now, almost every night, El Tío was finding an excuse to drive into the area to case it out. The warehouse was a large open-air shed with an extensive roof of corrugated metal. A barbed-wire fence defined the outside perimeter. Just to its inside there was a roadway, just wide enough for large trucks to circle and load.

During the nighttime hours, there was only one watchman stationed at the warehouse entrance. He was armed with a rifle, and he carried a two-way radio. This had to indicate that he could access back-up assistance very quickly from port security officers. El Tío was making it a point to get to know the watchman on a friendly basis. He claimed he'd even gotten the man to accept a shot of rum from him on his last drive through.

El Tío described the crates as large and cumbersome. He'd counted twenty-four of them, one truckload on his largest flatbed.

Then he detailed how they'd pull off the heist. It would be a semi-inside job. He made it sound convincingly easy. He outlined steps that sounded feasible and convenient. But what about foolproof? Joe kept going back to this most stringent criterion.

One thing was certain, however. The circumstances seemed designed by fate to be dangled tantalizingly before their idealistic young eyes, so they would be tempted, so they would feel obligated to perform one enduring act on behalf of those to whom they had developed an unwavering commitment.

"You make it sound like picking bananas," Joe conceded to the choir poised for his response. "Just one big question for you Einsteins. Just how do we get the six million bucks? I haven't seen any want ads to buy Old World masterpieces boxed in huge crates. Or maybe this demand will all of a sudden emerge. Maybe once they all realize the Nazi underground is biting at our asses. I can just see it. We'll probably end up paying someone to take it. Won't that be a kick in the balls?"

El Tío stretched back in his chair and washed down the remaining brew in his green bottle. "Be patient there, young fella. I'm still working on that part of the plan. It'll come into focus. There's always a logical answer."

For Joe the only logical answer at this point was to hope that the idea would just blow out on the same river breezes it rode in on.

Chapter 9

"Gringo, where've you been," Carlos Santiago greeted Joe as he approached the booth. "These Americans have no concept of time." Carlos got the two señoritas sitting with him to giggle. Nora, "La Flaca" looked up at Joe to see if the irony had sunk in, for it was the Americans who traditionally stereotyped the Latinos for their liberal interpretation of punctuality.

"Sorry," Joe apologized. "But I was unavoidably detained. Very unavoidably."

"No hay problema." Nora spoke up. Nobody much minded. Social meeting times in Venezuela really were only approximations.

Carlos and the two señoritas were already laughing it up, making small talk. Joe's arrival didn't disrupt the melody. He quickly picked up the beat and became part of the ensemble.

The Cervecería Bavaria, or Bavarian Beer House, was a new business in town. Those who had steady jobs in the area gathered here regularly. Its popularity as a nightspot was instantaneous. The steady influx of patrons included business people, government agency people, politicians, and the like. And on any given night, there was an international flavor to the clientele. The developed countries of the world were well represented in Puerto Ordaz, as many specialty skills were needed to propel the city's young industrial and business economy forward.

It seemed at least one of the Peace Corps volunteers checked in at the Bavaria almost every night. The contacts they could make here proved invaluable for their projects. And since they had no phone at their apartment—domestic phones were still quite a luxury, messages from the Peace Corps office in Caracas were received at the Cervecería Bavaria.

The drinking section purported to replicate a traditional German beer hall, but on a much smaller scale, of course. There were, perhaps, twenty tables and booths. A semicircular bar with about fifteen bar stools extended out from the far inner wall and back kitchen.

By day, the air-conditioning and cold draughts provided a jolt of refreshment from the oppressive heat. In the evenings, there was usually someone at the piano. And on weekend evenings, the pianist might be accompanied by a vocalist.

There was also an adjoining German restaurant by the same name through a double doorway and hallway on one side. Whereas the beer hall was generally filled to capacity with a mixed crowd, the more quaint restaurant was patronized primarily by those from the area's German community. The restaurant sported a typically rustic Bavarian decor, and it enjoyed a solid reputation for the quality of its German dishes.

Young Venezuelan women loved to be invited to the Cervecería Bavaria. It was a respectable place even if it was a bar. They were not likely to be exposed to, or subjugated to, some of the baser elements of machismo. It was relatively easy, even for the gringo volunteers, to interest young señoritas in being their guests for drinks. Not a bad situation, this. They mixed social life with the opportunity to make important contacts. And it was the closest thing they had to an office phone.

For Joe, the little gathering with Nora, and Carlos and his "date," was not atypical. It was standard fare in his social schedule. Storytelling, laughs, planning of future gatherings or *fiestas* while sipping cold drinks, it was better than slouching in front of a TV after work each night, like might have been the case if he were back home in the U.S.

After another hour or so, the young ladies announced they were approaching curfew. Carlos offered to drive them home. Joe rode along. The ladies were each let off at their nearby homes in a newly developed working-class neighborhood. The friendships were in the infancy stage, too new for Carlos or Joe to jockey into position for more romantic pursuits, especially on a weekday night.

"She's in love with me," Carlos boasted to Joe in Spanish after they were alone in the car.

"Sure. And as soon as you lie and tell her you love her, she'll start sleeping with you. Then you'll tell her you're gonna marry her to keep it going. She'll think you'll take her home to meet the family in Mexico."

Carlos burst into laughter. "Gringo, you're on to my tactics! How are you doing with La Flaca?"

"She's very nice. But since I'm morally superior to you," Joe kidded, "I already told her I'd be going back to the United States in a few weeks. Alone."

"Pendejo!" "Fool!" It was one of Carlos' favorite words. He turned from the wheel quickly to shake his head mockingly at Joe. In Carlos' view, a few weeks were more than enough time to pursue a new *conquista,* a new conquest. Joe, on the other hand, seemed content to simply run out the clock.

"Yo tengo hambre," Joe changed the subject, declaring he'd like to get something to eat.

Carlos concurred. They headed to an all-night eatery for a late-hour pig-out, a youthful bad habit that only the twenty-somethings could get away with.

The open-air restaurant was a busy place at this time of night. It attracted drinkers and revelers whose only nutrition to this point may've been alcohol and bar snacks called *pasapalos.* The aroma of the chicken on the rotisseries floated on the calm breezes and extended an invitation to anyone within range. The lure was almost irresistible, even to anyone who may've already dined. Carlos and Joe were entrapped. They each ordered a half chicken. And some strong Venezuelan coffee to counteract lingering effects from the beers.

Joe had become good friends with Carlos. They had more in common than just partying and talking about women. Carlos was very well versed in politics. The association provided Joe with the opportunity to develop some valuable insights of his own, especially as they pertained to Latin America. Joe got a kick out of how Carlos teased Pancho over his romanticized interpretations of the exploits of his idol, Pancho Villa.

Carlos and Pancho regularly entertained the group with their arguments about the Mexican Revolution. Pancho's grandfather allegedly rode with Villa and he, Pancho, was named after the legendary leader. Carlos, on the contrary, claimed his grandfather and his great uncles rode with a competing army because Pancho Villa couldn't be trusted. The differing perspectives always intrigued Joe. Joe's grandfather didn't ride with anybody.

Joe felt challenged by Carlos' grasp of the bigger picture. The Mexican seemed to have a knack for putting everything in its proper framework, especially whenever anyone drew a simplistic conclusion based on a narrow perspective.

"Tell me," Carlos began. "What was that nonsense El Tío was discussing with Pedro at the picnic Sunday?"

Joe flashed a quizzical look in Carlos' direction. Don't tell me, he thought to himself.

"Something about robbing Nazis?" Carlos continued matter-of-factly.

Joe now wondered how wide the secret circle had become. El Tío talked too freely. Such matters were best discussed when alcohol was not in the mix. Joe always suspected that Carlos did indeed have a respectable understanding of English, despite the disclaimers. If he learned about the heist from overhearing El Tío Don speak with Pete, then Joe was all the more convinced that Carlos could pick up on English conversation.

"They mentioned it to you?" Joe acted surprised. Nevertheless, it occurred to him that before getting serious about such a scheme, he would want Carlos' opinion, if not his active involvement. If Carlos were to participate, it would serve as a confidence booster. Joe reckoned Carlos to be a clever, calculating individual, one who was not prone to careless indiscretions, at least where it concerned matters of such gravity.

"Sort of," Carlos responded cryptically.

The plates of roasted chicken arrived, along with the deep dark coffees. Was now as good a time as any to seek Carlos' advice, to find out his level of interest? Or his degree of disapproval?

Joe mulled it around as they each attacked the golden mound of meat with their forks and greasy hands. Each time they came up for air they took a sip of the warm coffee, the complementary add-on to the late-night dining experience. By the time they got down to tweaking the last vestiges of meat from the chicken bones, Joe had made a decision. Why wait? Having already been conceived, the heist idea was already beyond the embryonic stage.

"Okay, amigo, let me tell you about it. In confidence, of course."

"Of course," Carlos responded. "I'm only disloyal in matters of love."

Joe proceeded to outline the plan. He did not editorialize. He wanted to give an honest account so that Carlos, in turn, would give his honest appraisal.

"Idiotas!" Carlos didn't mince words. "When something that big looks that easy, it usually isn't. Count on that. Where're you

going to unload it, even if you are able to steal it?"

"Then I guess you're not joining up," Joe said sarcastically. He felt somewhat relieved. If Carlos were in favor, it would plunge Joe deeper into the vortex of group pressure. Now, in contrast, he could line up behind Carlos and hold out, linking his own reticence to the latter's sage advice.

"I've got to talk with those *pendejos.* Make them come to their senses. They're out of touch with reality," Carlos was shaking his head. "What a crew. An old adventurer who never grew up. A drunk. And a reinvented Pancho Villa. Why are you the only one showing any sense?"

"Because I don't think we can get away with it. And . . . and they have no idea about how to turn the stuff into cash afterwards."

"Those are reasons enough," Carlos agreed. "Not to mention that the heist itself would probably get fucked up. I don't care what El Tío might've done in the big World War Two. You'd still be amateurs."

"So, tell them that when you talk to them. And good luck," Joe warned. "Pancho's ready to follow in the footsteps of his namesake. And Pedro . . . you know him. He'd follow El Tío down to the source waters of the Orinoco."

Chapter 10

The following Saturday was a workday. Saturdays were valuable. Schools were vacant and classrooms could be borrowed or rented to do trainings for community volunteers. The young trainees themselves were more available. On weekdays they were generally occupied as students, apprentices, or the like.

And it was easier to get doctors to do free exams in the barrios on Saturdays. Most closed their offices. And there was a distinct scarcity of tee time on the one area golf course.

Pancho and Pete were running a training course in Puerto Ordaz. Joe took off to a barrio in San Felix on the other side of the Caroni River.

Joe had arranged for the free physical exams. These were offered by physicians on a rotating basis in barrios throughout the city. Joe did the logistical coordination with two of the young community volunteers. They also did follow-up after the exams, tasks such as hustling donations of eyeglasses for kids who otherwise couldn't see well enough to continue in school.

Families were already lined up for the exams when Joe pulled up on a borrowed motorcycle. The community volunteers, one male and one female, were already on site interacting with the families, especially the kids. Everyone waited just outside the small elementary school.

The inhabitants of the barrio were, for the most part, recent arrivals from rural towns and villages. They dreamed of a better life in the city. They came because of the industrial growth and the demand for workers. If they were lucky, they could acquire the necessary skills and get the good jobs. If not, they counted on spillover opportunities being available even for the unskilled. But there were, however, major adjustments to be made, transitions from the simpler lives they had known. City life presented new challenges. And many new pitfalls.

Soon the two doctors arrived, accompanied by a nurse assistant. Joe spoke with them briefly to find out how they wished to proceed. Within minutes, the process was set in motion. The line pushed forward as the first patients were invited in.

Every so often, the nurse called Joe into the examination room. The medical team advised him as to necessary follow-up measures on behalf of any of the patients. Joe and the two volunteers would divide up the responsibilities over the following week.

In one instance, the doctors diagnosed a serious leg infection with a boy of about ten, a precocious youngster named Orlando Vallarta. The name stuck with Joe not only for the double "O's," but because the kid boldly declared that when he became president of Venezuela, there would be free medical care for all. The doctors felt he needed hospitalization. To Joe this translated into convincing one of the hospitals to provide a free bed for a few days or so. The hospital administrators were at the point of hiding whenever they saw Joe coming. It seemed he was forever trying to talk them into "this one more time." What was one more time for a future president of Venezuela?

By early afternoon, the line was dwindling. Good thing, Joe observed, as he lounged on the shady side of a surrounding wall. Once the doctors broke for lunch, there was little hope of their return on the same day. He too was looking forward to a few cold ones, maybe getting a head start on the Saturday night festivities.

"*Hola, Señor Americano,* what brings you here today?" Joe

turned to observe the two young men approaching from across the street.

Who the . . . ? He searched his memory. It took a few seconds. But it hit him. More déjà vu, than memory. He hadn't come across them in a while. They were community organizers from the Venezuelan Communist party, *Partido Comunista de Venezuela.*

The Spanish acronym was PCV. This was ironic, as it was also the acronym for Peace Corps Volunteer. And they had been in competition on several past occasions around the city. Well, "competition" was how the Communists viewed it. Joe and his colleagues weren't about to begrudge any accomplishments on behalf of the people of the various barrios, no matter who got the credit.

He couldn't recall either of their names. No matter. Since they'd referred to him as "Señor Americano," it was evident they didn't remember his, either. Funny, he thought, as the picture of recall came into sharper focus. It didn't stop these guys from spreading rumors last year that Joe, Pancho, and Pete were CIA.

What a joke that was. "Why would there be CIA in Puerto Ordaz?" Joe remembered laughing to Carlos.

"Because of all the mineral wealth, because it is a prime Orinoco port," the Mexican reminded him at the time, making Joe feel a bit naive.

"Long time no see," Joe finally responded. The two young men before him were well-educated post-university types, perhaps a few years older than Joe.

"Routine physical exams," Joe continued. "Two doctors from Puerto Ordaz, volunteering their Saturday. Pretty nice of them, no?" Joe really didn't expect them to be appreciative. A one-day sacrifice paled in comparison to what Doctor Che Guevara, M.D. had given up.

"Perhaps we should talk about this," one of the men suggested. "We've been working this barrio for a while now. Maybe we should take on this responsibility in the future. You know, we're trying to get a community clinic built. It'd serve some of the surrounding barrios as well."

We'd be all for that, Joe thought. But they were really a very minor political party. They didn't carry much, if any, clout with the heavy hitters who were always in power. So Joe was aware that their aspirations exceeded their promise. And besides, he could not help being suspicious about their real priorities. Did they really want to help the people? Or did they just want a few visible successes to show off so they could gain recruits and strengthen their geopolitical position in the grander scheme?

"Always interested in putting something permanent in place," Joe acknowledged, still preserving decorum. "I'll speak with my Board of Directors. We'll discuss not duplicating efforts. We prefer to work where we're most needed."

Pleasing these guys was not a high priority for Joe, nor was it for his colleagues. Promising to bring it up before his local Board of community leaders was a polite and effective way of putting them off. The Board was not about to take the Communists very seriously, anyway. Joe realized this. His political sensibilities had evolved at least that much. Scary, he thought. Maybe there was politics in his genetic make-up.

"*Gracias.* We would appreciate that. Maybe we could come to one of their meetings," the other young Communist finally spoke up with this rather pushy suggestion.

"I'll mention that. Someone will get back to you. Take care. See you later," Joe ended the discussion with a collegial smile.

The two men politely walked off.

Joe deliberately turned and walked towards the doorway to the school where the examinations were finishing up. Interesting little twist, he thought. Maybe they'll have all the barrios to themselves if our project fades away after we're gone. The concept troubled him.

Maybe we should tell them about the Nazi loot. Leave it for them to steal. Maybe they'd put their *cojones* on the line. Yeah, right. If they got their hands on six million dollars, what would they do with it? Channel it to community projects? Maybe. Maybe, if there was anything left after it was applied to political purposes. Maybe even Fidel would be in for a cut.

Chapter 11

"How'd the training go today?" Joe asked Pancho and Pete as he slid into the booth. He was happy to see they'd gotten to Cervezería Bavaria ahead of him. He didn't feel like being the one waiting.

"Fantástico," responded Pete. "Everybody who'd said they'd be there showed up."

"Impressed the hell out of me," Pancho added. "And a real good group. Some of the best and brightest around. Hope they stick it out."

"And the doctors' exams?" Pete asked Joe.

"Like clockwork for a change. Gotta get one kid into the hospital as soon as possible. Bad infection ascending up his leg. Good thing they caught it in time. The kid had some real spunk, claimed he was going to be president of Venezuela some day and give free medical care to everyone. Other than that, lots of routine stuff. You know, eyeglasses, some dental work. Oh, remember those Communist organizers in San Felix?"

"Yeah, those assholes who wanted everyone to think we were CIA," Pete answered.

"Well, they were there today, doing whatever it is they do. They're still singing the same tune—that we need to divide the action. Strange. They act like anything we accomplish is like a shiv up there asses."

"Forget about 'em," advised Pancho. "They're small potatoes. We've got more important things."

"That's right. Almost forgot. Pancho Villa was the only 'right kind' of revolutionary," Joe kidded Pancho.

"Speaking of more important things, José . . . you discussed the heist with Carlos, didn't you?" Pete inquired, obviously knowing the answer.

"First of all, he got wind of it last Sunday at the river. The son of a bitch understands more English than any of us realizes. And second of all, quite frankly, his opinion counts for something. If I risk my ass, and I'm not saying I am, I'd like to have him along."

"Well, you can forget about that ever happening," Pancho said. "He's dead against it. Tried to talk us out of even considering it. Said it was lunacy, and that we were asshole amateurs who'd fuck it up for sure."

"Pretty complimentary of him." Joe felt that Carlos could've done without the insults. They could only serve to egg on a guy like Pancho. And he himself didn't appreciate being told he was inept even if he was. Carlos may not have realized it, but he may've employed bad psychology in his dissuasion attempt.

"He did tell me he was going to make you guys see the light."

"Well, we also respect Carlos' opinion," Pancho pointed out. "But you know which way Pedro and I are leaning."

"José, if we can come up with something, a plan to get rid of the stuff afterwards . . . I think the heist itself will be a piece of cake," reasoned Pete, just before downing the rest of his draught.

"This is not what I want to hear on a Saturday night, guys. Let's change the subject," Joe begged, disguising the fact that he himself was getting tempted, that he himself was fighting back a surge of adrenalin. He pulled up short of admitting to himself that a viable plan to liquidate the goods might now be enough to sway him as well.

Joe had now concluded that the concept was indeed beautiful. To leave Venezuela knowing that their accomplishments would live on was temptation enough. But the realization that the resources would be redirected from the Nazi underground, perhaps from some sinister purpose, added yet another dimension. In such a scenario, perhaps the rightful owners might not have been victimized in vain. Perhaps, in its own way, the injustice could be counteracted. The question kept haunting him. Was the confluence of these factors preordained by fate? And if so, should it be viewed as a mandate?

And unbeknownst to the others, Joe was beginning to view the venture as a test of his mettle—as a challenge to his willingness to take a risk for something he stood for. Hell, was Pancho's romanticizing about the likes of Pancho Villa beginning to get a grip? Was romanticism itself penetrating his shield of logic?

Sure, Carlos' lack of interest in participating disappointed Joe. Sure, if Carlos had at least outlined some pros to go with the cons, it would've boosted his optimism. But Carlos' opinion was now accepted as a given. He was on record. And he was not going to join up. Okay, so at least there'd be one less share to divide up, one more share going to the program, three fourths instead of three fifths.

They ordered another round of Polar draughts. As Joe had suggested, the subject was changed—they began discussing their plans for the evening. Joe suggested that Pancho and Pete meet him later at a disco. The señoritas they were with at the river fiesta would be there, and they had promised to bring along some additional friends. Carlos was also slated to make an appearance.

"Count me in," Pete agreed, while Pancho nodded. "As long as there's beer."

Just then the main door swung open ushering in a subtle gush of warm air. Followed, perhaps, by some not-so-subtle hot air, Joe observed sarcastically. The charismatic presence of El Tío, fresh from a day of wheeling and dealing around town, was about to grace the premises. The tall, lanky essence of gringo-hood was in his typically jovial mood. Per usual, he knew about half the people in the place. He circled through, making upbeat small talk before shuffling over and plunking himself down in the booth with his three "nephews."

"El Tío, what's the good word?" Pete was the first to greet his mentor.

"The good word? I'll tell you what the good word is, 'Colombia.' Colombia, as in the country just to the west of Venezuela. That's where we're gonna unload the crates after we steal them," he said in a low voice and with the signature grin.

"That's a load off my mind."

"Take heart my young friends. The puzzle has been solved. Colombia is the only country we can go to by land, right?"

This was true. Even though they were much closer to British Guiana, there were no roads between the two countries. Diplomatic relations did not even exist. And a road through southeastern Venezuela down to the Amazon region of Brazil was only in the dream stages. But there were several roads in and out of Colombia. And contraband did pass in both directions.

"We'll drive it across the border and sell it," El Tío announced, proud that he'd finally solved the dilemma, at least in his own mind.

"And to whom? The first guy we see with six million bucks hanging out of his pocket?" Pancho was beginning to sound like Joe with this bit of sarcasm.

"Do I have to do all the thinking for you young kids of today? What's the matter did you guys smoke too much of that marijuana in college?" He quizzically looked each of them in the eye, one by one. "So, who buys art?"

"Art dealers, I guess." Pete was the first to tune in.

"Correcto!" beamed El Tío, feeling a sense of success with his

star pupil. "We just have to find one who's a little shady," he added. "One who can get his hands on a few million bucks."

Not uncharacteristically, Joe reacted first. "Let me see if I got this straight. We're looking for an art dealer who's Colombian. He has to be a crook. And he has to have access to millions. Glad we're narrowing it down." He shook his head as he scanned the others for eye contact. "Narrowing it down to zero."

El Tío held up his hands reassuringly. Something was up his sleeve. His smiling eyes hinted that the search was further along than he was willing to say. Maybe the initial reactions were premature. Maybe, El Tío did indeed have it narrowed down, and to a number greater than zero.

Chapter 12

The private phone line of Julian Muller rang in his office suite at the U.S. Embassy in Caracas, Venezuela. His personal secretary stood up from his lap to answer. She smiled at him provocatively as he nodded permission to put the call through to his desk. It rang a number of times as he groped her twice more for good measure before walking back into the private office and shutting the door.

"Muller here. What's up?"

"They goin' to esteal the estuff this week. I think maybe tomorrow in the night."

Muller knew the accented voice. It was one of his best men.

"This week? Tomorrow night? Holy shit, man! I thought they weren't even decided yet. We're not ready for it. Not set up."

Muller was visited by a pang of regret. Maybe he should've taken this more seriously, made it a higher priority. And maybe he should've devoted less time to the Miss Venezuela beauty contestant he had been pursuing in his off hours. Failure to live up to expectations could have serious overtones. His type of work required him to always be a step ahead, to anticipate and to activate. He promised himself it wouldn't happen again. Self-doubt did not sit well with him.

The voice responded, "Then I handle? We jus' do what we can from here, no?"

Muller paused to think. Was that the best he could hope for on such short notice? He knew his man was good. Smart, resourceful, capable of taking independent action.

"Okay. That's the way it's gotta be then. You take care of it. And no screwups. You get this right and I'll see that there's a nice bonus in it for you."

Chapter 13

It was 5 p.m. Pancho, Pete, and Joe waited at the apartment. Adrenalized, Pete and Joe were pacing anxiously. Anticipation added to the stuffiness of the inside air. Joe could feel the turbulence in his gut as he walked to the vented window to suck in some of the fresh air from outside.

If Pancho was nervous, he did a remarkable job of not showing it. His composure validated something. Perhaps he was more up to the task than Pete and Joe. Or, maybe some of those stories about his youth in East L.A. weren't exaggerated. Perhaps Pancho had had some practice for the mission at hand.

"I can hear El Tío's flatbed. He's here," announced Pete. "Right on time."

"I could use a shot of rum," Joe kidded.

"That's all we need. Not even I am thinking about a drink right now," Pete remarked.

Two sets of feet were ascending the stairs. One pair unmistakably belonged to the long legs of El Tío.

"The commandant has arrived, and with his star attraction," El Tío declared, as he presented Anita stepping into the apartment just behind him.

"Anita, what the hell're you doing here?" asked Joe in total surprise, trying not to gawk at her breasts, barely contained in a tight-fitting red top.

"You didn't think I'd let you guys do this without your best 'man,' did you?" she retorted.

"We didn't even know you knew," added Pete.

"Well, one of us did." Pancho finally spoke up. He stood and grabbed center stage in the small living room. "Okay, hear us out. The distraction of that watchman is of critical importance, right?"

This was indisputable.

Standing next to Pancho, El Tío took over the explanation. "I've gotten pretty friendly with the guy. He's even willing to have a shot of rum with me now each time I go to the warehouse. His favorite subject is women. Kind of like you guys. So, what's gonna keep a guy like him, a pretty normal sort of guy, preoccupied? A lusty-looking American woman with big . . . well, you know," he stopped short of overdoing it. After all, she was standing right there with four sets of eyes trying not to fix upon the subject matter.

Pancho reinforced the line of reasoning. "El Tío and I had a long talk about this. Diverting that watchman's attention is key. We have to make sure his mind is on something more appealing. We figure he'll let his guard down a little anyway, because he's used to seeing El Tío. Anita here, playing it up a bit, should be enough to keep him from focusing on what we're up to. The added insurance, it could make the difference."

Joe couldn't argue with the reasoning. But dragging Anita into it would not digest. It kicked up pangs of guilt. "I dunno," was all he could come out with for the moment.

"I was gonna tell you guys about it," Pancho continued. "But I kept holding off, you know, hesitating. I didn't want to get into any more arguments, didn't want to get sidetracked. Besides, personally, I have all the confidence in the world in Anita. But I was afraid. Afraid maybe one of you might underestimate her."

"It's not a question of confidence, Pancho," Joe pointed out, looking over towards Anita. "It's a matter of, why do we want to have her taking the risk, just because we are."

Anita stated her own case. "I'm doing this of my own free will, guys. Believe me, no one pressured me. I'm not gonna be involved after the warehouse part. I don't want a share. Just direct some of the proceeds to the three clinics I work in. That's all I'm asking. For me, it'll be like I was never part of the actual heist."

Then smiling, she added, "Besides, I'd never forgive myself if anything ever happened to you, and I wasn't there to cover your sorry asses. And if that isn't reason enough, I have Jewish blood on my mother's side. A little revenge against the Nazis will be good for our collective souls."

"Very profound, Anita, but the three of us are leaving Venezuela, and the Peace Corps altogether, as soon as this bullshit is over. You'll be sticking around, for how much longer? Another year?" Joe was still concerned for her.

"And I've thought about that. When the clinics get that donation, they'll be able to replace me. So, I've already begun a transfer request. I'll go to another host country to finish out my tour. I'm a nurse. They'll find a spot for me with no trouble, somewhere. Anyway, life won't be the same around here without you crazy kids and all your mischief."

"Then it's agreed, amigos, no?" Pancho knew the question was beyond the point of reconsideration.

Joe looked over at Pete, who just shrugged his shoulders. "Closure," Joe declared, as if it hadn't been reached already.

El Tío took over. "Good. Now let's go over the plan one more time, in case all that rum has finally fried your brains."

But everyone knew the details by heart. Each knew his, and now her, respective role. Anita now would join El Tío with his distraction routine.

The sea of enthusiasm had swelled. Once the heist was decided, there was no putting it off. After all, what if the transshipment to Argentina were to occur earlier than expected? Then they would have missed their chance. And they might wonder about it for the rest of their lives, a tale of what might have been. No, it had to be done sooner rather than later. They needed to get on with it, to get it behind them.

It was November. They had told their North American friends in the area that they were suspending their pro football pool for the rest of the season.

Chapter 14

The tall, muscular blond-haired man was finishing his early dinner at the Bavaria Restaurant. As was his nightly custom, he dined alone. He had not been in the area very long, and he had not gotten close enough to anyone with whom he might share a dinner table. He preferred it this way, at least for now. He would be long gone, he hoped, by Christmas.

Nonetheless, he did stop in the beer hall section from time to time. As long as he could keep his distance, he didn't even mind an occasional conversation with other patrons, sometimes in German with a fellow countryman, or sometimes in his Argentine-accented Spanish with anyone in general.

He was an imposing figure, much taller than the average North American, let alone the average Venezuelan. He was pushing forty and in remarkable physical shape.

He paid the dinner bill and nodded to the maitre d' as he marched towards the front exit. He would make his first of several drive-bys at the warehouse. Customarily, he would view the crates, the ones with the unmistakable lettering "Zurich-Mars," from outside the fence. In between rounds, he might stop at the Bavaria Beer Hall for a cold draught or two.

He and his associates did not relish the fact that the long-awaited cache from Switzerland had to remain at the remote Orinoco River port for such a long period. However, the chance to get it out of Europe through the port of Marseilles had come up rather suddenly, and they had to seize the opportunity.

Another ship would come soon to pick it up, and then take it to more secure surroundings, nearer to the center of their little network.

To date he had not noticed anything to cause suspicion. By day, the warehouse was a bustling place. There was only one entrance in or out. The high barbed-wire fence presented a formidable barrier to any would-be hijackers, even if they somehow knew that the innocent-looking crates contained millions of dollars worth of European art.

In the evening, there was only one watchman. But he was armed and seemed quite alert. He had a two-way radio, which meant he could call for backup from port security personnel. The German had inquired about this evening watchman. Through his sources, he found out that the man had served in the military. This was positive. The watchman would not only have acquired some necessary skills, but he would also be possessed of a certain discipline. This added to the German's peace of mind.

After midnight, the gates were closed. No one was allowed to enter. A different watchman took over. And a guard dog roamed the interior.

Lately, an American trucker was just about the only person going in and out during the evening with any degree of regularity. The German learned that the man had some mining machinery stored inside, and that he went in to tinker with it. Maybe it needed some new parts. The middle-aged American was always alone, and he always drove a sky-blue pickup. The German kept a sharp eye for any changes. Perhaps, if the American were to come in with a larger truck, or if he were accompanied, then it would be time to hover more closely.

As the tall German approached his rented jeep in the parking lot, three well-dressed men, apparently Venezuelan, suddenly scurried up to him. He swore to himself for being careless. Why hadn't he seen them approaching? Maybe they too were pros. Dusk had darkened into night, yet all three were wearing sunglasses.

"Señor?" The heavy-set man looked up at him as they reached the driver-side door simultaneously.

"Hay un problema?" asked the tall foreigner. Is there a problem?

The pot-bellied man who spoke flashed a badge from an open wallet. The German man didn't catch the name, but he did hear *"Policía Técnica Judicial,"* or PTJ, the Venezuelan National Police.

"Cédula, por favor," demanded the PTJ officer holding out his hand. Every person in Venezuela had to carry an official I.D. called a *cédula.* This included foreigners, unless they were only staying a short time, for which a passport served the purpose.

"Passport. I have a passport," responded the tall blonde man, as he slipped it up from a front shirt pocket, and slapped it impatiently into the upturned hand of the intruder.

"Argentina," observed the officer examining the document.

He officiously thumbed through it for several more minutes. Then the officer looked up into the steely eyes towering above him and spoke again, "Just as was reported, *señor,* there has been a mix-up. You'll have to come with us."

"What kind of mix-up? Tell me what is wrong. Precisely, please." The German was making every effort to keep cool and to exhibit uncharacteristic patience.

"Nothing, I hope," answered the officer with calculated vagueness. "We can clear it up in a few hours. Perhaps."

The German knew what a "few hours" could mean in a culture where people didn't take the clock as seriously as he did. But he was no fool. He could see they had the upper hand, at least until he could get in touch with his own contacts. So, he might miss a round or two at the warehouse. Probably not a big deal. What were the chances that the unthinkable would occur on this of all nights?

"We need to search the vehicle," the officer added, holding out his hand for the keys.

The German paused, glaring down condescendingly at the fat man in front of him. By his own estimation, he could simply manhandle all three of them, and then just drive away. But then where would someone as conspicuous as he hide? No. He had to play along. If there were some kind of bureaucratic snafu, his contacts would navigate him through it.

The officer elaborated, "Keys, please." His hand pushed forward more aggressively, but not enough to provoke resistance.

The German reached into his pocket and jingled them a few seconds before pulling them out. He handed them to the pushy fat man, who in turn opened the door and motioned the other two officers to conduct the search.

It was after they pushed back a blanket in the rear of the jeep that they found the Walther pistol. One of them held it up for the lead officer to see.

Shaking his head, the fat man commented, "Then again, this may take more than just a few hours, *Señor.* I am very sorry."

Chapter 15

The five-person team assembled around El Tío's two trucks. Pancho, Pete, and Joe placed their packed bags under a canvas tarp in the back of the blue pickup. They planned on being away for several days. Who knew if they could come back at all? The payload also carried some tools and mechanical parts. El Tío took the wheel. Pete rode shotgun. Anita rode between them.

Pete wore coveralls. They had him choreographed as the mechanic—El Tío was bringing in a specialist to work on the mining machinery that he himself had been struggling to make operational. In reality, the machinery was little more than an obsolete pile of junk he had salvaged at little cost. Originally, he had figured on recovering his investment by selling the parts. Now the investment would have to reap a different kind of dividend.

Pancho and Joe rode in the large flatbed with high side rails. Pancho drove. It was preferable that he be the more visible man when they checked in at the guardhouse gate. Although Joe was black-haired and rather dark-complexioned, Pancho clearly looked more like the native Venezuelan.

El Tío had told the watchman that he and his helpers would be back soon to pick up some cargo he had recently moved into the yard, a shipment that, allegedly, would be bound for La Guaira, the port just north of Caracas. This shipment consisted of dummy crates that had been brought in several days before by El Tío and two of his employees. They were placed less than sixty feet from the crates with the black "Zurich-Mars" lettering. El Tío had cleverly negotiated for space near the mining machinery, reasoning that he wanted to keep his stuff as close together as possible.

The twenty-four dummy crates were almost identical in dimensions to those containing the loot. Working at his garage under cover of night, El Tío and his three accomplices had stuffed the dummy crates with rags and scrap wood. They wanted the dummy crates to be maneuverable enough for one man to handle with a pushcart, but not so light as to be blatantly distinguishable from the crates that would be missing. They lined the inside walls with plastic so no one could effectively peer between the outside boards. The targeted crates appeared to also have such an inside lining.

The later anyone discovered the worthless crates, the better the chance for success. This was a principal argument for doing the heist sooner rather than later. With some luck, no one would realize a switch had occurred until the dummies arrived at their final destination in Argentina, or wherever.

With a homemade stencil, they had meticulously spray-painted the lettering "Zurich-Mars" in the same relative position on the dummy crates that it appeared on the target crates. They then covered the paint job with large black stickers with lettering that read "La Guaira", the port for Caracas. They had ordered well over a hundred of these stickers. They had made sure that they could be easily peeled away by hand. However, they also had made sure they were not of such low quality that they would fall off on their own.

Pancho and Joe carried an additional supply of these stickers in the cab. In the back, on the flatbed, they secured a portable hydraulic lift to the side rail posts. Since they were doing the loading at night, it was understood that they would not have use of the warehouse's forklift. They had practiced using the device at El Tío's livery when they hoisted the dummy crates onto the flatbed for their delivery to the warehouse.

With the pickup leading the flatbed, the two-truck caravan approached the warehouse. El Tío's radio was blaring loudly, evoking a festive atmosphere. After all, it was Friday night and the rest of the city was already ringing in the weekend. Perhaps the power of suggestion would make the guard all the more distractible.

El Tío honked the pickup's horn. The watchman appeared quickly and unlocked the gate welcomingly, recognizing his newfound gringo buddy.

"Hola, capitán," El Tío greeted the man. Hello, captain.

The guard flashed what appeared to be a trusting smile. "Working on a Friday night?" He shook his head, implying he himself would not be, given the choice.

"You know how it is. Gotta take the help when I can get it. Killing two birds with one stone tonight. Maybe I won't have to bother coming by next week. So, get your money's worth from the old rum bottle while you can, since it is Friday night, no?" El Tío temptingly patted the one-liter bottle of Cacique secured between Anita's knees.

The man smiled again. "Perhaps. We'll have to see. The night is still young. Who are your companions?"

"My men back there are taking the cargo we left the other day. Time to get it up to Caracas. I should say, La Guaira, the port. Needs to be there by Monday." El Tío noticed the man checking backlogs on a clipboard hanging in the guardhouse to confirm the delivery that was being referenced.

"Ah, *sí.* That's right. You did mentioned it to me, the one you said you'd pick up one of these nights."

"And tonight's the night. Gotta waste a Friday. Well, not

completely, I hope." El Tío was still working the power of suggestion.

"And who are these friends?" He became especially curious about those in the cab as he nosed closer to the driver-side window and caught a glimpse of Anita.

"The young man here is the mechanic who's gonna get that messed up machine working right. Even if it takes until midnight. He's German. They're the best mechanics, know what I mean?"

"Yes, of course. German. There're lots of Germans in town."

"And this charming young lady, she's my 'wife.' " El Tío said this with such a mischievous laugh that the man got the message that she was anything but, that she was whatever the imagination might conjure up. Anita played the deception, grinning invitingly, like a Times Square street hooker. She held out the rum bottle, the added prop. The power of suggestion was beginning to penetrate the watchman's veneer. They could sense he would soon lower his shield.

"Go ahead in." The watchman's tone was congenial, as he waved the two trucks through.

"My 'wife' and I will be right back here. Hope you'll join us in a little taste of rum to celebrate the weekend. I just want to make sure these young guys get started on the physical work."

The man nodded. His smile implied interest. They'd reached first base, it was time to move into scoring position. The trucks rolled ahead to the far end of the sheltered yard, where the two sets of crates stood like skyscrapers flanking the useless mining machinery.

Pancho parked the large truck closer to the Nazi crates than to the dummy ones, but not noticeably so. Pete got out of the pickup, grabbed some tools from the back, and started puttering with the mining equipment.

El Tío then drove Anita and himself back to the gatehouse.

He carefully inched forward for the last few yards, calculating the optimal parking position. The idea was to obstruct the sight lines between the guardhouse area and the crate area in the distance. Every detail, nothing left to chance.

By the time El Tío and Anita reconvened with the watchman, they found him in a more relaxed mood. The music on his own radio was turned up, and was pumping out Venezuela's most popular English-lyric song of the time, "Sugar, Sugar" by the Archies.

Within minutes they were seated on boxes and making small talk between pours from the rum bottle. Anita flirted as if she were on loan from one of the local brothels, all the while moving and gesturing as provocatively. It seemed to be working. The watchman kept gawking in her direction and away from the important activity going on in the rear. The watchman's rifle and two-way radio were behind him, about an arm's length away.

It had been prearranged that if the guard had the urge to check on the crew in the rear, El Tío would shout out a warning to Pete in English. It would not be unusual for El Tío to be communicating in English with his "German" mechanic. The boss would simply be inquiring as to how his workers were doing. And Pete would be sure to answer, in English.

Pancho and Joe hustled like athletes trying to score before the final gun. Each time they loaded a crate containing the art onto the flatbed with the hydraulic lift, they replaced it with a dummy crate from the nearby stack. Pete feigned working on the mechanical equipment. But most of his time was spent coordinating the operation, attending to the details. It was Pete who slapped on the new "La Guaira" stickers to the Nazi crates, covering their "Zurich-Mars" lettering as each one was loaded. And it was he who peeled off the stickers from the dummy crates as each one took the place of the crate being heisted, exposing the counterfeit lettering "Zurich-Mars" they had stenciled on several nights before. By the fourth or fifth switch, the determined amateurs had reached assembly-line efficiency.

When Pete got ahead with the stickers, he helped with the hoisting and moving. It was hard physical work, and at a pace that would put a longshoreman to shame. They were pulled along by their own adrenalin, hardly noticing the drenching sweat.

Back near the guardhouse, El Tío continued to fake each sip of rum as he raised his paper cup to his lips. Whenever the watchman turned his back, or fixated on Anita, he would pour some onto the ground behind him. As the leader of the pack, he could not afford to compromise his level of alertness. There was a long night ahead.

Anita, on the other hand, hoped to be safely back at her apartment soon. Nonetheless, she too tried to sneak a few drops onto the ground. She thought if things got tense, she'd have to be prepared for whatever improvisation might be called for. However, the watchman did not turn his back on her nearly as often.

Despite their own efforts to preserve sobriety, El Tío and Anita did all they could do to get the watchman to lose his. They couldn't pour him enough, replenishing almost every sip he took from his paper cup.

Suddenly, El Tío and Anita heard the sound of approaching footsteps by the gatehouse. "Everything all right in there?" questioned an official-looking man in uniform.

"Port security," El Tío whispered to Anita in English as he hid the bottle behind him.

The watchman stood at near attention and answered, *"Sí."*

"With the loud music, and all that laughing, I thought there was a party going on."

Anita crossed her arms over her chest and sat as stoically as a nun administering a test.

"No, the party is later," El Tío butted in in his heavily accented Spanish. "My 'wife' and I are just waiting for my workers to finish up back there. We're just keeping *el capitán* here company."

"Workers? What're they doing back there at this hour?"

Conveniently, the watchman beat El Tío to a response. "He has a German mechanic back there working on some machinery. Two other guys are loading a shipment to take to La Guaira. Tonight." The watchman handled the quiz. He demonstrated he was indeed on top of the situation. But did it reassure the uniformed intruder?

"They know they have to be out of here before midnight, right?" the port security guard added.

El Tío and Anita nodded along with the watchman.

"Maybe I'll stop back later." The port security officer turned and walked off. His parting statement raised up red flag number one in El Tío's mind.

Red flag number two came right on the heels. The watchman was looking to regroup. As he stood tall and stretched, he asked El Tío to put away the bottle. "Maybe I'll take a little walk," he announced.

Grabbing the rifle and the two-way radio, he started heading towards the rear of the warehouse yard. El Tío wasted no time. As gracefully as he could, he stood and walked alongside the watchman. "I'd better check on my boys," he commented, disguising the apprehension. He had to think, and fast. He shouted out in English, "Here we come guys, pretend you're taking a break." He figured they could not be far from finishing the job.

"We're ahead of schedule," Pete responded in English.

Pancho and Joe were sitting on the back of the flatbed when El Tío and the watchman arrived. They looked spent. Sweat poured profusely from their foreheads. Pete was pretending to be studying a blueprint while having a cigarette. Wearing the coveralls, he was sweating even more. He wouldn't have been much wetter had he taken a dip in the Orinoco. Why hadn't the refreshing nighttime breezes kicked up? El Tío wondered. Or had they, only to be irrelevant in the tense air encircling his crew.

El Tío did not have to count the crates on the flatbed. Noticing there were only four of the dummies left, he knew his energetic young team had loaded twenty containing the looted art. Impressive, he thought. A brief nostalgic vision of the physical phenom he himself had been as a young Marine some thirty years before proudly flashed to mind.

If worse came to worst, and the watchman remained with them until they finished, they would simply load on the four remaining dummy crates and forego the last four with the booty. Yeah, and it would be just my luck that the *Mona Lisa* is in one of those left behind, El Tío quipped silently to himself.

At that instant, out of the corner of his eye, El Tío caught a glimpse of the remaining "La Guaira" stickers on the ground near where Pete was studying the blueprint. The watchman had not noticed. Not yet. The watchman spent his first minute or two noting the payload on the flatbed, and checking out the hydraulic lift the men had brought in with them.

El Tío's quick thinking paid off again. "Pete, the stickers are on the ground, in plain view," he calmly stated, once again in English. "Move over by the watchman and offer him a cigarette. Make sure you get him turned in the opposite direction."

At that instant, Pancho and Joe also took the cue. Pancho hopped off the truck and motioned the watchman over to the hydraulic. He asked him in Spanish if he'd ever seen one before.

"Of course," the man answered. "I've seen all types of equipment for lifting. Lord knows I've worked around here long enough. Did you guys bring this one in?"

"*Sí,* we brought it in on the truck. Had to. We knew the forklift wouldn't be available at night." It was hoped that Pancho, or Joe, would not have to talk at all. Although they both spoke Spanish very well, without typical gringo accents, neither sounded like a native Venezuelan. With El Tío, Anita, and Pete being obvious foreigners, they had hoped that at least Pancho and Joe could appear as un-noteworthy as possible, even presumed to be natives. But necessity had now eroded that concept.

"Where're you from?" the man asked Pancho, somewhat surprised to glean an accent in a man who looked so native. "You're not from here, are you?"

"Yes, I am. Born in Venezuela. From Maracaibo. But I lived for many years in Mexico with my family. My father was a laborer for one of the oil companies." It sounded like a story Pancho had on file for occasions where it behooved him to be perceived as a native Venezuelan.

Joe held his tongue. He did not have to say anything. If he did, he would have had to claim to be the son of one of the many Italian immigrants in the area.

The watchman glared at Pancho with a quizzical look. "Maracaibo? You don't sound *Maracucho* to me. I have lot of friends from there. You can't be a *Maracucho.*"

Pancho didn't rattle. "I agree. It was that Mexican influence. Spent my whole adolescence there. Had to blend in. Easier to score with the Mexican *muchachas,* you know?"

The watchman turned to Joe. Was he hoping that at least one out of five spoke like a true native?

Just as it appeared he would say something to Joe, Pete held a cigarette in front of the man's face. The watchman accepted it with a smile of appreciation. Pete positioned himself with his back to the outside perimeter as he provided a lit match for the man. El Tío had more than enough time to toss the pack of stickers behind a box and out of view. Then he puttered around for a few moments to camouflage what he had just done.

"Well, when're you guys getting back to work?" chided El Tío, this time in Spanish. "*El capitán* here has to finish his rounds and I . . . I need to get back and check on my 'wife.' She gets lonely with no men around." He winked mischievously to the watchman.

The cue had its desired effect. The watchman concurred that he should continue on his walk around the inside perimeter of the barbed-wire fence. The power of suggestion was working overtime. He mentioned how he too wished to say a proper good-bye to El Tío's "wife," waiting by the guardhouse. By the sheepish smile, it was clear he wanted to indulge her sultry flirtations, and to fantasize over her one more time before they all left him to his monotonous solitude.

When the watchman passed out of view, Pancho, Pete, and Joe quickly re-mobilized. Maintaining an awareness of where the watchman was, and of where he was headed, El Tío made a beeline back to where Anita had been waiting.

"Well?" she asked, anxiously.

"We're okay. He didn't catch on to anything. The boys did good."

"Thank God," she exhaled. Jokingly, she added, "I swear, under normal circumstances, if this guy were to rape me one more time with his eyes, I'd bust that bottle over his head."

El Tío laughed. "But, Anita, I'd think you'd be used to that by now. Having a hard time myself. You know, staying focused." It was true. It was also the only kind of flattery he knew.

Shortly after the watchman arrived back at the gatehouse area, the engine of the large flatbed roared to life. This meant all the crates were on board, and that they were ready to move out. Pancho circled the truck around the inside perimeter, and within seconds pulled up to the gatehouse. The watchman took out the necessary logs and paperwork to sign them out. El Tío signed for his end of the transaction. The watchman signaled for Pancho to drive on out.

But just as the idling truck began to inch forward, the uniformed port security guard reappeared to block its advance. El Tío had hoped that his "maybe-I'll-stop-by-later" annoyance, would amount to nothing more than a polite way for him to have said good-bye. No such luck.

"That was quick. You loaded all that in such a short time?" The official seemed to be taking an interest in a matter for which he was not directly responsible.

Then the thought hit El Tío. What if the man was on someone's private payroll? Could it be that he was being paid to watch over certain cargos, to keep a special eye on certain wares? Such an arrangement would not be unheard of. And what if it were the cache from Zurich? Would he be familiar with the size, the shape? The number of crates?

El Tío decided to respond directly to the question. "Always in a hurry to get done and get the weekend started. Can't enjoy myself, you know, 'til I know these guys are on their way."

The man stepped to the side and directed his flashlight on the load of crates. After moving his forearm in a circular motion, he fixed the beam on one of the "La Guaira" stickers. El Tío noticed that Pete had done a perfect job of slapping them on. Damn good thing. No one realized a quality control inspection would occur so soon.

"La Guaira," the officer repeated under his breath. He turned off his flashlight. Then he circled around to the gatehouse and picked up the papers signing out the cargo. He conducted himself in a way that left little doubt that he represented a higher authority than the watchman who had been so successfully deceived. But the transaction papers would only indicate that everything was properly logged in and out. No problem there.

"The Americano brought these crates in the other day." The watchman once again had made an inadvertent commentary that could only prove helpful.

"Correcto," El Tío confirmed. "And just got word today to get the whole shipment to the port of La Guaira by Monday morning. It's a long haul, you know."

The port security officer still would not tip his hand. They could not tell if he was falling for their story, or if he was becoming even more suspicious.

"Wait here. Don't let them leave," he ordered the watchman.

Carrying the clipboard with the papers, he began marching towards where the large truck had been. He stopped short once the dummy crates with the lettering "Zurich-Mars" came into view.

The Americans held their collective breaths. The dummy crates were not perfectly identical to those they had heisted. But it would have required a very discerning eye to notice, especially with crates of all types and sizes represented in the vast yard.

Fighting back complacency over a job well done, El Tío forced himself to think one step ahead. What if the security guard asked to open one of the crates on the flatbed. Could they physically overpower the two armed men before any shots were fired? El Tío maneuvered over to the driver-side window.

"We may have to overtake them," El Tío posed to Pancho in whispered English. "Stay cool, but strike fast. As soon as I make the first move."

Pancho relayed the message to Joe in the passenger seat.

"No fucking way," cautioned Joe. "How far would we get? Unless we outright kill 'em. Or beat them silly. Not acceptable, man."

Pancho didn't argue. He knew Joe was right. The Nazis were

meant to be the only victims of this escapade, and no one else.

Pancho glanced alternately at El Tío and at Joe. "Then, we need a decision, and fast."

"Try bribery first," Joe blurted out. "If he has a special interest in the crates, maybe it's because somebody else paid him off first. Let's up the ante."

"Not bad. Could be the solution," Pancho added, looking over at El Tío for a reaction.

El Tío processed the options. "Okay, here's the plan . . . when the guard comes back, if he asks me to open a crate, I'll bitch and moan how we're in a hurry. I'll mention how our customer's waiting by a phone for our call to tell him we've picked up the stuff. I'll give him the rum and offer him the cash in my wallet, about a thousand *bolivares.* Probably what he earns in a month. I'll make him feel we're just buying time, that we can't delay on account of any hassles."

Pancho relayed the idea to Joe who was slightly out of earshot of El Tío's lowered voice.

"It's the best play," Joe acknowledged, looking somewhat relieved. "The corrupt little bastard, he'll probably collect twice. Afterwards, he'll claim how vigilant and diligent he was, but that how could anyone have ever figured on the dummy crates."

Yeah, but who was it that he was collecting from in the first place? El Tío kept wondering. Maybe the answer would become evident all too soon.

El Tío saw the security guard turn and begin his slow march back to where the crew was waiting. The river breezes began to kick up. Finally. Where were they earlier? Now, all they brought was the chill of apprehension. The man was in no hurry. He seemed to be reveling in the authority he had over them. Upon approach, he scanned the crates on the payload one more time.

"Everything in order, amigo?" El Tío tried to reintroduce an air of informality. He exuded more calm than any of the younger men could have.

The official put the clipboard down and approached the driver-side window, hands on hips, the back of his right hand practically leaning on the handle of his holstered pistol. "Okay," he said to Pancho.

Okay, what? Pancho did not want to speak. He waited instead.

The uniformed man looked up at him impatiently. "Well, are you going, or what?"

He waved them through. Pancho and Joe looked at each other with relief. The port security guard was not a very accomplished entrepreneur after all.

The large truck accelerated off into the distance. As El Tío and Anita watched it disappear out onto the main road, they each breathed a long but inaudible sigh of relief.

"Well, let me go see how my mechanic is doing." This time El Tío did not leave Anita alone. She followed him to the pickup and they drove inside to fetch Pete.

On the way back out of the gate, El Tío addressed his watchman friend, "That screwed up machine still isn't working. Needs a part. So, I'll be back in a few days."

"Bring your 'wife.' I didn't get to say a more proper good-bye."

"I'll do that," El Tío smiled. "If she doesn't move back home with mama."

No one in Puerto Ordaz ever laid eyes on El Tío again.

Chapter 16

El Tío's small fleet of trucks was not long for the roads. The Venezuelan government had informed him that he was in serious arrears on his tax obligations. They had been threatening to close him down until it was settled. Then, with the decision to go ahead with the heist, El Tío had his lawyer in Caracas alter the terms of negotiation.

He promised to sell his business and use the proceeds to pay what he owed in taxes. He had found a buyer, a company in Caracas. And he was due to arrive there to close the deal.

Right after leaving the warehouse, the hijack team returned to El Tío's livery. There they transferred the stolen crates from the flatbed onto a similar truck that he had rented for a one-way trip. Then they loaded twenty-four additional dummy crates, also with "La Guaira" stickers, onto the flatbed used for the heist.

One of El Tío's regular drivers was coming to pick up the truck with the phony crates at midnight. His instructions were to drive it to Caracas, to the company of the prospective buyer. It would kill two birds with one stone. The buyer would receive a sign of good faith—the delivery of one truck, and the fake shipment to the Caracas area would provide a helpful deception.

Puerto Ordaz to Caracas was about a ten-hour drive. The truck would have to pass through a number of National Guard checkpoints, called *alcabalas.* If the *guardia* at any of the checkpoints logged the plate number, time, and cargo type, then any investigation in their wake would reveal the shipment was indeed headed for the port of La Guaira just north of Caracas. El Tío had instructed the driver to drop off the crates at the port before surrendering the truck to the buyers in Caracas. The crates were noticeably light. The driver was unaware they only contained scraps and filler. But he would be more appreciative than suspicious.

The four men boarded the rented truck for the long trip across Venezuela to the Colombian border. The trip would take over twenty hours. El Tío would do most of the driving, with Pete doing most of the relieving. Therefore, Pete sprawled out in the back with the crates in an attempt to get some needed sleep.

Pancho and Joe rode in the cab with El Tío. They would cross the vast central plains, the renowned Llanos of Venezuelan folklore. Then they would arrive at the foothills of the Andes in the southwestern portion of the country. They would weave along the narrow roads clinging to mountain slopes until they arrived at their destination on the Venezuelan side of the border with Colombia, the city of San Cristóbal.

At dawn on Saturday they peeled off the "La Guaira" stickers on the stolen crates and replaced them with stickers of the same color that said "Frontera," the "border." They wanted to avoid suspicion from any of the numerous National Guard checkpoints they would have to pass. La Guaira was to the north. The border was to the west, the direction in which they were headed.

After a number of rest stops for coffee, food, etc., they arrived in San Cristóbal at about 2 a.m. on Sunday. They chose a modest hotel with a parking lot large enough for a truck. They rented a room with three beds and a private bath. Each man took his turn staying in the cab of the truck.

By early afternoon on Sunday, they all had had some much

needed rest, and each had had the opportunity to shower and change into fresh clothes. With the rest, the cleanliness, and the combed hair, they had undergone a major makeover. For the moment, they looked more like businessmen than tropical truckers.

The venture was about to reach its climax. The question that had puzzled them—how to liquidate the goods—was now going to receive its answer. Cashing in such a cumbersome booty had presented no small challenge. They had brainstormed and strategized for days, obsessing over the single most important criterion, the minimization of risk.

Therefore they had decided against driving the cargo across the border into Colombia. It meant settling for less money. It also meant that the Colombian buyers would be the ones crossing into, and out of, Venezuela. They would shoulder that risk. The important thing was that they were bringing satchels with two and a half million U.S. dollars, in cash.

The buyers, or brokers, whatever they were, stood to make a substantial profit. But the four Americans did not much care about that. Where the art ended up was no cause for concern. Even the black market was preferable to the South American Nazi underground. They just wanted the cash and a hassle-free getaway.

On Sunday evening, the customary clusters of people were hanging out in the main plaza, strolling, socializing, courting, or whatever. Pancho stayed behind, on guard duty with the truck, while El Tío, Pete, and Joe positioned themselves on a cement bench in the plaza, looking purposely conspicuous.

They expected to be approached by the art dealer, or his representative, as early as this evening, but no later than Tuesday evening. This was prearranged. It would be obvious that they were the North Americans that the buyers were there to meet.

The art dealer idea took on a cloak of feasibility when El Tío claimed to have established some back channels. According to him, he had come upon the Colombian buyers through a network of art dealers in Caracas. Without revealing specifics as to what he had for sale, he was given names. From there, he found an interested party, one who could generate the required cash.

His name was Oscar. Or so they were told. According to El Tío, this Oscar had been aware that art looted by the Nazis had been making its way into the underground markets of Europe and North America. And as soon as it made its way onto the South American scene, Oscar wanted to be in on the early action.

With the number of ex-Nazis who had immigrated to South America after the War, Oscar reportedly had been anticipating the inevitable arrival of paintings, artifacts, sculptures, and heirlooms that had been scooped up from Holocaust victims and from museums in territory overrun by the German war machine. According to El Tío, Oscar figured that such works would appreciate in value over time, especially as the rightful heirs died off, lost hope of recovery, or were distanced further from their former possessions.

Pancho, Pete, and Joe fully expected that this Oscar would possess a connoisseur's knowledge of the authenticity of the works and that he would come with a trained eye. Logically, they were expecting him to show up personally to review the cache. And since he stood to turn a substantial profit, he should have nothing to gain by turning them in.

At about 7:30 p.m. a young man walked by the bench and asked if anyone had a cigarette. Pete produced the pack from his shirt pocket.

"You don't have a Piel Roja?" asked the man, indicating he preferred the popular Colombian brand. This was the signal they had established.

"No," responded Pete. "We can't get them in our part of Venezuela. We're from the eastern end of the country." The Colombian detected the gringo accent in Pete's Spanish. This should not have been necessary if Oscar was indeed nearby. Presumably, Oscar should've at least known what El Tío looked like.

"You must be 'El Tío'?" the man inquired. Big Don Buchanan had not used his real name in setting up the deal.

"In Person," laughed the older American. "Is Oscar with you?"

"Oscar will be here. We want to meet tomorrow. We want to see the stuff. If it's authentic, you get the pesos."

"You mean the dollars," El Tío was quick to clarify.

"*Sí,* we mean the dollars," the man acknowledged.

"We?" inquired Joe at this juncture. "Who's we?"

"Oh, pardon me." Colombians from the Andes region always seemed so formal and polite. "I should have mentioned that there are four of us. My brother and I are here with our father, Oscar. And he has his very trusted assistant. And there are four of you?"

"Correcto," responded Joe. "Our fourth man is with the truck. In a secure area, of course."

Joe waited for eye contact. Then he continued, "Here's what we propose. We drive the truck to the yard of the rental company. It's a busy place, especially on weekdays. So it won't be unusual for anyone to be examining and transferring cargo there. We open the crates. If you find everything in order, which you will, you give over the agreed amount. We transfer the truck rental agreement to you so you can take the stuff to Colombia, or wherever. We're ready first thing in the morning."

"We're ready, too. We will not need the rental, however. We have our own truck. We will simply transfer the material. But we can still meet at the company yard. Where is it?"

"I'll meet you here tomorrow and show you there." They did not want to take the chance that the buyers might case out the place and prepare some kind of ambush with planted weapons or the like.

Joe added with reciprocal formality and politeness, "And we will search each other and the respective trucks for weapons? So we know we are doing the transaction in good faith, of course."

"Of course."

It looked like it would happen as El Tío had said.

Joe met the contact at 8 a.m. on Monday morning and asked if he could ride with them. The Colombian agreed. Their truck came by within minutes. Joe gave directions to the driver, a rugged-looking man who only nodded, then he jumped on the back along with the contact. He noted there were three men in the cab, but he had only gotten a good look at the stone-faced driver.

They rode the short distance to the yard. Joe hopped off and directed them to pull up alongside the loaded rental truck where his three colleagues were already waiting.

The young man who was riding in the middle indeed looked like he could have been the brother of the first man, the contact. The older man who rode shotgun was assumed to be "Oscar." But he looked too rough hewn to be the artsy type. Certainly, he didn't match up with stereotypes Joe had imagined. And the large, stone-faced man with long black hair, the driver, he had to be Oscar's so-called "very trusted assistant." He looked very formidable, like a young bull. If he was not some sort of bodyguard, he sure looked the part.

"Good morning, everyone. Good day to get rich, eh?" El Tío broke the ice, but not loudly enough for third parties to overhear. As expected, there was a good deal of activity going on around them. This was good.

Oscar spoke up for the buyers, "Good morning. Hope you all

had a pleasant trip. So, why don't we open one crate at a time. And then, if intact, we will reseal it, and move it to our truck."

"Sounds efficient," agreed Joe. "Let's do our weapons check. If you don't mind."

"No. Of course we don't mind."

They looked inside the respective cabs. Then they patted down each other. Joe had occasion to exchange searches with the "trusted assistant," or whatever he was. It felt like he was patting down a statue carved out of marble. When the man patted down Joe, Joe felt a chill run up his spine. What would it be like to be punched in the face with one of those meat hooks?

"Okay?" Oscar concluded.

"Okay," approved El Tío, as ranking member of the hijack team.

They set the process in motion, in assembly-line fashion, opening, resealing, and transferring the crates. Unbeknownst to even the Americans, there was an inventory list in a plastic pouch inside each one. How about those Nazis? Joe thought. So meticulous. They'd even made inventory lists for what they'd looted. And this made it much easier for Oscar to know what to look for.

The inspection part therefore went very quickly, much more so than anticipated. Oscar barely examined any of the individual works. Good thing. The paintings were well secured by individualized wooden casings retrofitted to prevent any damage. One had to peel back a canvas cover and peer between the cross-boards of the casings to make any attempt at identification. The vases and the sculptures were similarly packaged. The inside walls of the crates were lined with plastic for added protection. Repackaging every piece would have been terribly tedious.

Nonetheless, it seemed odd that the buyers did not scrutinize the merchandise more painstakingly. Oscar did not comport himself in the manner they had envisioned. Shouldn't a real art connoisseur at least have a magnifying glass? But then again, who really cared?

When the twelfth crate was loaded, El Tío interrupted the process and asked for half the payment in his own inimitable, nonthreatening way. Oscar wasn't sure whether or not he was kidding. Nevertheless, he motioned to his brawny assistant.

The young bull, who had yet to speak a word, fetched a small satchel from a compartment beneath their truck. It dawned on Joe that no one had noticed this compartment earlier, and no one had therefore looked inside it for weapons.

"There's half," declared Oscar. His expression indicated that he was not put out by having to show this good faith gesture.

El Tío accepted the bag from the young bull, and went into the cab to count it. Joe sat inside with him and watched. One million dollars! In cash. In his hands. El Tío had led an eventful life. Guadalcanal. Iwo Jima. But this was a first.

But one million dollars wasn't half. The deal was for two and a half million dollars. El Tío and Joe looked at each other, a little concerned.

"What do you think?" Joe asked. He could see El Tío's brain was abuzz with thought.

"Better not to haggle it out now. Maybe it's nothing. Maybe that brute of an assistant can't divide by two."

Joe still smelled smoke.

By noon, Oscar had performed his cursory inspection of the final twelve crates. Everything was loaded onto his truck and ready to go. El Tío stood poised to receive the rest of the payment. The "assistant" pulled out another satchel and handed it to Oscar.

"Señor," Oscar began. "Since we spoke I found that this material would be harder to distribute than I first thought. I was not able to get financing for the full two and a half million. There is

another million dollars in this bag." He handed it to El Tío, who was looking back at him with piercing eyes.

The Americans had discussed contingencies. They had reviewed several scenarios to predetermine how they might handle each. Two million dollars was indeed above the bottom line amount they would accept, just to be done with it. On the other hand, they knew that this type of ploy, a bluff made by a negotiator with nothing to lose, was not uncommon.

So they also had nothing to lose by countering with a prepared script of their own. Although Oscar did not examine the individual works as meticulously as they had anticipated, Joe did notice how the man could hardly contain his gleeful surprise each time he perused one of the inventory lists. Oscar had to realize how much the stuff was really worth. And even if he wasn't an authentic art connoisseur, he had to know enough to determine that the works weren't counterfeits.

"This is not right, my friend," Joe began. "A deal is a deal. We had many expenses." Then he tried a bluff of his own. "When we first found out about the cache, we saw some inventory lists. We made inquiries, we checked up on its true worth. We were told, by reliable sources, it was worth well over six million dollars. And that was just in Caracas. These same sources told us it might be worth double that in Buenos Aires or São Paulo."

Impressed, the other three Americans gazed at Joe with admiring approval. El Tío's smile seemed to say, "Not bad."

Oscar, on the other hand, looked as though he suspected such claims to be exaggerations. However, it was evident that these Americans were not so naive. They all seemed to realize that it was a veritable giveaway at only two million.

But Oscar persisted, "Surely you don't want to kill the deal now, at this point."

As they began to tango, Joe couldn't help fixing the corner of his eye on the scary-looking "assistant" standing only several feet away from Oscar like a bull ready to make a run at an untrained matador. His mouth never twitched into the slightest semblance of a facial expression. He never spoke. But he listened and watched, as if he could sense an ant crawling across the dirt parking lot.

Joe's Spanish wasn't as good as Pancho's. But they had agreed the latter was likely to lose his temper if a situation developed. And they wished to avoid waving a red cape in the faces of potential fighting bulls.

"Señor Oscar," Joe continued, "you were recommended to us as a man of your word. We preferred to suffer the additional expense, and the lesser payment, to avoid the risk of selling it in Caracas, or at the port of La Guaira. But it is not too late. We can simply reload the crates and head in that direction."

Joe wondered what would happen if the Colombians tried to pull away. Should they risk a physical confrontation? After all, they did already have two million dollars. He calculated that El Tío could easily handle Oscar. The two sons didn't look very imposing, physically. But then who'd be the lucky one to have to take on "El Toro"?

But Joe figured Oscar also had to worry. If the Americans accepted the lesser deal and went away angry, who would know whether they might alert authorities? Or worse, whether they might reveal the new custodians to the Nazis who'd been separated from their valuable loot. Oscar had to know his profit would be substantial, even if he forked over the last half million. It would still be a sweetheart deal.

Oscar faked a pained sigh. "This is going to break me, my friends. My family and I will barely be able to eat until I sell some of this stuff. I hope we can buy enough gas to drive this truck back to Bogotá." He went through this litany of exaggerations as he motioned to the man-bull who was reaching into the back lining of his leather jacket.

For a brief moment Joe tried to recall if the man had been wearing the jacket when he'd frisked him during the weapons check. No, he had not been. For a second, Joe fully expected to be staring down the barrel of a pistol. He sensed his American colleagues beginning to stir.

Feet started to shuffle, but then they all noticed it was indeed a money pouch, bulging at the seams, and not a weapon, that was coming into view. Without further deliberation, Joe walked forward spontaneously.

The stone-faced man did not extend his arm forward. Joe stopped short when he noticed that the man's free hand was curled into a fist the size of Ecuador. Now what? he wondered to himself.

"Let him have it," Oscar ordered.

Just as Joe pictured himself falling backward under a flying tackle and a barrage of brick-hard punches, the pouch bounced against his chest. He barely got his forearms up in time to catch it.

It was done! They got the two and a half million. The Colombians and the Americans waved farewell. They went their separate ways, each group and each individual to pursue the life course this transaction would affect, whether they knew it or not.

The Americans turned in their rental truck. They walked as fast as they could back to the hotel. They gathered their belongings and took a cab to the airport. All of them had tickets to Caracas. Now they just needed to get seats.

Their luck continued to hold. There were two seats on an Avensa flight at 3 p.m., and at least two on the Aeropostal flight at 5 p.m. Since El Tío was anxious to get to Caracas to sign the papers for the sale of his company, it was agreed he'd go on the first flight, with Pete. Pancho and Joe would take the later flight.

The money was easy to divide up. Once it had been settled that they would receive two and a half million dollars, it was decided that El Tío would get one million. After all, it was his mission from the start. He did the lion's share of the planning and preparing. It was he who'd located Oscar and the Colombians. El Tío also had to cover the operation's up-front expenses. He simply kept the first satchel with one million dollars for himself.

There was one and a half million dollars left over to set up permanent financing for the Peace Corps project, and to make an annual donation to the three clinics where Anita worked. And the Nazi underground was that much poorer. Their success smelled sweet. The poetic justice had a pleasant resonance.

At the airport, when it was time for Pete and El Tío to board the 3 p.m. flight, the reality of what they had pulled off finally hit. It was time for their adrenalin supply to replenish.

"Pete, we'll see you in Caracas," Pancho began. "El Tío Don, don't know when we'll see you again. Be careful." Pancho gave El Tío an *abrazo,* a hug.

Joe stepped over to do the same. "Tío, hope it won't be long before we meet again. I'll never forget you." That was an understatement.

"By the way, where will you be going, Tío?" Pancho asked.

"I'm not really sure yet," he answered with his sly smile. "All I know is it won't be Venezuela . . . or Colombia . . . or anywhere near where my ex-wife is living."

It was the last time Pancho would ever see him, or hear from him.

Chapter 17

Inefficient subhumans. How many times had he cursed them over the past three days? Everything had been going along without incident for Heinrich Klaus. Then those self-important Federal Police agents with the stupid sunglasses had to come along and hassle him over some minor immigration problem.

It had cost him the entire weekend. Two of the agents had accompanied him to Caracas early Saturday morning, after staying with him all Friday night. They took him to Immigration Hall as soon as it opened on Monday morning.

The Immigration officials were puzzled. They couldn't find anything wrong with his Argentine documents. The Federal Police agents shrugged their shoulders, apologized for the inconvenience, and told him he was free to go.

They didn't even offer him a ride to the airport, the bastards. They refused to return the Walther pistol they had confiscated. And they conveniently lost the keys to his rented jeep.

Good thing he had his "people" to contact in Caracas. A replacement pistol was the first order of business. The ride to Maiquetia airport, and a ticket back to Puerto Ordaz was also no problem. There was no substitute for efficiency. His people were the embodiment of competence. Same day service.

The flight arrived on time, just before 6 p.m. on Monday. Pleasant surprise. Probably the only time all week that would happen, he guessed. He flagged a taxi and headed straight for the Orinoco River port.

He asked the driver to wait near the warehouse as he proceeded on foot to where he could view the valued freight. There it was, just as it had been before the weekend sideshow. Four tightly packed rows, each with six crates. The unmistakable lettering "Zurich-Mars" struggled to remain visible in the dim lighting. And the mess nearby, the mining machinery uncrated and strewn along the ground, continued its ugly presence. When was that buffoon of an American going to give up and get it out of everyone's way?

Chapter 18

The finish line was in view. No time for tripping and falling. Can't blow it now with amateurishness. The dangerous part, presumably, was over. But could they still be discovered? Unlikely, after they set up the account in the Cayman Islands. Pete, Pancho, and Joe had figured it was as good a place as any to use up vacation days that were still on the books. And that's where they had flown after landing in Caracas.

As for the financial mechanics, Pete had done the research. His father worked for a New York City bank, and his mother served on boards of several philanthropic organizations. Of course, he had posed the question on the grounds that they had come up with a wealthy benefactor.

This was to be the official tale. Their Peace Corps project, called *Oportunidades Sin Límite,* Opportunities Unlimited, would have a permanent funding stream thanks to an anonymous donor with more money than he could spend in his lifetime. The interest and dividends from the account's investments would be enough to fund the annual operating budget and to make an annual donation to the clinics where Anita worked. The financing would exist into perpetuity. The concept still carried a melodic resonance. After a few days of paperwork, interspersed with some beach time, the three entrepreneurs returned to Venezuela and made their way to Puerto Ordaz for the final chapter of their Peace Corps experience.

They met with the Board of Directors of *Oportunidades Sin*

Límite. The members were particularly gratified to know they could continue the project by hiring host country nationals to replace the departing Peace Corps volunteers. *Permanencia* and *perpetuidad,* these concepts fulfilled their dreams as well. The final Board meeting was festive. It turned into a *despedida,* a farewell party, right after final business was conducted. After several *Cuba Libres,* heartfelt good-byes were expressed by everyone.

The curtain closed on this final act. Or so they hoped.

Chapter 19

Heinrich Klaus had already swung by the warehouse one time. His rounds had gotten back to routine. New keys were made for the jeep. His replacement pistol was kept on his person, in an ankle holster. And, most importantly, the crates were still in place.

It was actually getting monotonous, he reflected, while sipping a Polar beer at the Bavaria Beer Hall. Maybe he wouldn't bother making another run by the warehouse tonight. It was Sunday. Maybe he'd have another Polar. Or two. It was about the only thing in Venezuela that met with his approval. They probably had a German brewmeister.

His eyes wandered. He missed the accompaniment of a woman. Back in Buenos Aires, he was in high demand. Tall, athletic, cultured. And never married. Tonight he could always go down the road to one of the *puterías,* to one of the whorehouses, he figured. But these people, the European blood had been too diluted. No telling whom he might be mixing with. No, it would be better to hold off. Simple matter of discipline.

But the porcelain-skinned woman standing by the booths where the young Americans were celebrating exuded a certain elegance. Of course, his hormones were also in a heightened state, and he had no trouble envisioning the ample bustline beneath the loose-fitting yellow blouse. He broke into a smile, perhaps his first of the day. Sometimes he resisted letting his guard down. Feelings could be dangerous. Empathy, especially for the wrong kind of person, could lead a man astray.

She didn't appear to be coupled off with anyone. She seemed a bit older than the American guys around her. Certainly, she conducted herself in a more refined way. The guys seemed to be kidding her about something to do with playing the role of a slut. But he could barely hear, and his English was a work in progress. Then he saw her pull a skimpy rose-colored top from a bag and hold it in front of her to a chorus of laughs. Minutes later, the three young men appeared to be playing a stupid hand game to see who would take it as a souvenir. How childish these young Americans could be when they had a few beers.

A number of locals seemed to be stopping by to shake hands with the three young American men. The more he observed, the more he concluded that they were being toasted for something or other. Maybe they had achieved something in the community. That wouldn't be difficult around here. Anything would be an improvement in this backwater.

Then it became obvious. There was a finality to the *abrazos,* to the hugging he observed. That's it. They must be leaving town. Lucky bastards. Soon it'll be my turn. As soon as that freighter chugs up the coast and into the Orinoco to pick up those crates.

Ah, the fucking crates. Just sitting there, next to that mess of machinery, the so-called mining equipment. That American trucker must be persistent. He shook his head as he revisited the picture of the strewn-out rubble. But the vision stuck. The beer must've heightened his senses, or at least blocked out competing thoughts. That machinery had not been touched all week. Each part was in the same position from the weekend before. Why would the American leave it out like that, and then not come and work on it?

Suspicious? Probably not. But checking on neighbors was part of his deal. And like serfs living next to a castle, the mining equipment was neighbor to the great works of European art.

Klaus peered at his watch. It was approaching midnight. Too late to get into the warehouse. Tomorrow evening would be better. The watchman who seemed to know the comings and goings of the tall American trucker would be back on duty. He'd be the best person to ask.

He went back to thoughts of a less taxing nature. Like the light-skinned American woman with the intelligent demeanor coupled with the proper endowments. Every so often he put himself in a different picture, a world of normalcy, unencumbered by the "calling," the one true cause that had been his life to this point. Would it be his life forevermore? He preferred not to dwell on such things. Normalcy, like misplaced empathy, could lead a man astray. As far as the American woman was concerned, maybe some other time. Maybe if the freighter to pick up the loot were delayed. And maybe when she wasn't surrounded by those "kids." Or, maybe he would just forget her.

Then it dawned on him. She reminded him of someone. The wholesomeness. The quiet dignity. The gracefulness around men, the air of self-control. This must be a woman of culture and taste. Surely, with the amber hair, strong bones, and what appeared to be eyes of blue, a person with much Arian blood. Abruptly, he found himself wiping the wetness from his eyes as the memory of his mother, killed in the flower of her womanhood, paid a visit to his beer-induced reflections.

They felt a welcome release. Here they were at home, back in the Bavaria Beer Hall. Comfort, safety, security. Too bad it would be the final time ever. The nostalgia was already starting to kick in. This had been their HQ. The jump-off point to their social, and even to their work lives. How many times had the alcohol and the conversation led to some new idea, or to some new venture? Including this last one.

But that was fast becoming a memory. Like an out-of-body experience. Joe could hardly believe he had participated in something so inconceivable only a few short months before. It was like he'd been in a movie, as if he had played a fictional character in some unlikely adventure caper. And to his relief, it felt like the screenplay was over, with no prospects of continuation or of ramification.

"You looked great even as an alter-ego the other night," Joe kidded Anita when they were alone for a moment. "Which way do you prefer to be remembered?"

"I must have been nuts. Then again, young man, maybe you should know, most women have a secret side, a certain mysteriousness."

"With your kind of class, ma'am, you can have all the mysteriousness you choose."

"Thanks, José. You're going to make me cry. Especially if you call me ma'am."

"You going to be okay here without us?" Joe looked into her glassy eyes. "Anything suspicious happen since we took off with the stuff?"

"Not that I could see. Not so far. And it looks like I won't be around here much longer. Transfer's going through. Looks like I'll be going to Guatemala. Just waiting for the official date."

"Guatemala? Gee, that's great, Anita. I hear it's a beautiful country. Send me your address. I'd like to come visit."

"Sure. It's a good place to kill off my alter ego. I'll probably be wearing one of those ponchos all the time as a coverall."

"You'll fit in just fine. Just like you did here. I'll feel better when you're out of here. So will you, I assume?"

"I guess. Especially with you crazy assholes gone."

"Nice talk. Be ladylike."

"Sure, with you guys gone, my bad side isn't likely to resurface. Can't say I minded the gawking, though. Once in a while it can be reassuring."

"Anita, don't shortchange yourself. You don't need to be prancing around like the star of the local cathouse to be noticed. I doubt if you ever escape the notice of discerning men. The man of your dreams is probably taking note as we speak." Joe scanned the room for emphasis. But neither of them noticed the brawny German sitting at the far end of the bar, lost in thought.

"Hey, José. Where the hell's your buddy Carlos?" It was Pancho, starting to feel the Polars he was pumping down. "What'd'ya think? We put him to shame, now he won't show his face. He should be over here kissing our butts."

"Keep it down, Pancho. We're not the only ones who understand English around here. And who the hell knows about Carlos." Joe waited for Anita to step out of earshot, then continued, "If he got lucky with that *señorita* he was chasing, then he's probably in the sack. You know him. We're low priority when he's getting laid."

"Yeah, yeah. I think we just out-machoed the smooth-talking sonofabitch, and. . . ."

"And he doesn't want to listen to you carrying on about the legacy of Pancho Villa," Joe interrupted.

"Fuck 'em if he can't handle the truth."

It set Joe to wondering all the more as to why Carlos hadn't shown up. The time was washing away quickly through each mug of beer. Anita had gotten word to Carlos about the send-off, and he had sent back word that he'd attend. With departure scheduled for the following morning, Joe was beginning to feel stood up.

"Maybe, he wasn't as good a friend as we . . . as you thought." Pancho seemed to be hiding the fact that he, too, was hurt by the apparent no-show.

Joe wondered if Carlos wasn't as confident in their triumph as they had become. Then he imagined Carlos reacting to the ostensible success of the heist. And it troubled him to practically hear Carlos' sobering words. Something to the effect that it wasn't over yet, that the authorities, if not the Nazis themselves, would soon be sniffing their trail.

Was Carlos fearful of continued association with his American friends? Was he wanting to avoid being seen with them? Shit. That had to be it. Not the señorita. If he was getting any by now, he could be getting it later just as easily.

After last call, Pancho, Pete, Joe, Anita and her roommates, along with several local die-hards, paraded out and headed home.

When the curtain closed, Carlos still hadn't come by for his cameo.

CHAPTER 20

Heinrich Klaus waited impatiently at the gatehouse for the evening watchman to show up for the 6 p.m. shift. Sure, the crates were in place, just as they'd been for the last several weeks, but that mining machinery kept replaying in his mind. Why had it been disassembled and then left untouched? Asking about the American trucker was a precaution worth taking. Maybe he could exert some influence. Maybe he could get the apparatus moved out from under the shadow of the valuable bounty.

When the watchman arrived, Klaus wasted no time with formalities. "Excuse me, *Señor,*" he began in Spanish. "I am *Señor* Klaus. I represent the owners of freight that is stored here, awaiting shipment." He showed him an invoice and a business card with the name of the company in Argentina that served as a "front." "Here are my documents." He held up his passport.

"Let me get settled in here first." The watchman picked up on the foreigner's impatience and it annoyed him. He placed a bag he was carrying inside the gatehouse, then fidgeted for a timesheet to sign himself in. He was in no particular hurry.

Klaus glared at him with a blank expression that masked his disgust. He loathed the idea that this underling would make him wait. He rejected the notion that friendly banter could personalize the interaction and maybe leverage cooperation. Heinrich Klaus would rather just demand the cooperation.

Finally, the watchman looked over at him. "Okay. What can I do for you?"

"The American, the one who was coming in here every night . . . the one working on the machinery back there? He hasn't been around? The parts have been unattended. Do you know if he plans on coming back?"

"Hmm. Now that you mention it, he did say he'd be back. Said something about new parts, I think. Why do you ask?"

"I may need to hire him. To do some hauling," he lied, resenting any need for explanation.

The watchman reached for his logs. "It was a week ago Friday he was here. Hard to forget. He came with a sexy American woman with a red top." He added to the description by gesturing with cupped hands up by his chest and flashing a sly smile. "And there was a mechanic. German, he said. He tried to get the machine working, but couldn't. First time I ever saw a German mechanic fail to fix something. Anyway, the American said they'd have to come back. But he hasn't yet. At least not on my shift."

"If the German couldn't fix it, it must be junk."

"Huh?"

"Never mind. Did he say when, when he'd be back?" As he asked, Klaus reminded himself that time specificity was very loose in this culture.

"No. Come to think of it, he had his large truck with him that night. And two workers. They loaded some cargo for Caracas, or La Guaira, I think it was." He picked up the clipboard with the logs and thumbed back a week. "Yes, that's right. They picked up twenty-four crates. I remember the stickers. The lettering said La Guaira. Maybe the American went with the big truck to make the delivery. Maybe that's why he hasn't. . . ."

"Twenty-four crates!" The coincidence hit Klaus like a dagger to the gut. Swallowing hard, he regained some semblance of restraint. "I need to go in and check on my stuff."

"Your papers are in order. So, go ahead." The watchman waved him through.

The German wasted no time. Within seconds he was in the jeep speeding along the inside perimeter of the yard until he came to a skidding halt within yards of the large crates with the "Zurich-Mars" lettering.

Grabbing a crowbar from behind the seat, he stepped forward rapidly and wrestled the nearest crate down onto its side. Too easy, he immediately noticed. The weight should've been more of a challenge, even for someone as strong as he.

Manipulating the crowbar with the dexterity of a craftsman, he pried the crate open. Sweeping his huge hands firmly inside, he began pulling out the mixture of rags, paper, and wood scraps.

His blood was at a boil. He could feel it almost percolating in his veins. He pulled down another crate. Too light. Then another. Same. He was almost too angry to proceed. But he forced himself. He opened all twenty-four in less than a half hour. It did not take long to identify the filler once each crate was unsealed.

His rage flowed, unrequited. Marching over to the mining equipment, he began to trash it, hurling pieces of machinery in every direction while cursing alternately in German and in Spanish. The sound of the approaching motor signaled the arrival of a pickup truck. It looked like the same truck he'd observed the American driving. Was it the American trucker, happening into his awaiting clutches? Klaus scurried forward ready to yank the man out of the driver seat like a crash-test dummy when he noticed it was the watchman who was riding shotgun. And as the focus snaked through the rage, he could see the driver was not the American trucker.

"*Señor,* what do you think you're doing?" the startled watchman began as he got out.

With a bug-eyed expression, the driver also exited. He was more stunned than the watchman. In a weak voice, he attempted an explanation, "I've just arrived to pick up that machinery. The American sold it to us last week. Part of the sale of his company. Like this pickup truck. I don't understand. Why are you throwing it around?"

But the German was not in the mood for explanations. Before the watchman could exert any control, Klaus glared at him and immediately took the offensive. "Look over there, you incompetent bastard. Do you see anything in those crates but garbage? Your American friend! He robbed you. I should say, he robbed *me,* right under *your* nose. I don't want to hear about that pile of rubble you call mining machinery. It's worthless. But it got him in here, didn't it?"

He kicked one of the open crates and stormed towards the jeep. With one fluid motion, he opened the door, slid in, started the engine, and keeled out. The watchman, still paralyzed with embarrassment, made no attempt to follow the streaking vehicle. The accelerating motor sounded like an extension of the big man's roar.

As Klaus proceeded through the gate, he slowed to look for any of the port security officers. When the cargo had first arrived in port, he alerted each of them one by one, promising a generous bonus when the crates were safely loaded onto the ship bound for Argentina. Within seconds, a security officer appeared. Unbeknownst to Klaus, it happened to be the same guard who interposed himself the night the crates were switched.

"Hey, you," the German called him over to the jeep. "Nice security you have here. That little bonus of yours just washed down the Orinoco."

"What? Your merchandise? It's there. It's still there. I've

counted the crates myself, each day. There must be some mistake."

"Mistake! You and your useless watchman in there . . . you are the mistakes."

The guard seemed to search his memory for what could've gone wrong. But he didn't get to respond.

Klaus continued, "That asshole you call a watchman probably was socializing with the robber himself. Fast friends, eh."

The uniformed officer seemed to be getting the German's drift. Like the confluence of the Orinoco and Caroni Rivers, Klaus' accusation and the guard's recollection converged into the same mental picture.

"The American?" he finally mumbled.

"Brilliant conclusion, Detective."

"Why that lazy drunk," the officer scapegoated. "He couldn't take his eyes off that *gringa* whose *tetones* were bulging through her tight red top. I'll get his ass fired. He was too preoccupied to open one of the crates, even though I asked him to."

"And, of course, you couldn't open one yourself. I'm going to get *your* ass fired. Or worse!"

Heinrich Klaus disgustedly pulled away from the port and headed back towards town. His mind was racing. He had never before failed in a mission. Despite the apparent setback, this one was still not over. He would search the far corners of the globe before admitting failure.

But where would he begin? The bankers in Caracas came to mind. Were they in on it? They better have had theft insurance, especially if they'd hoped to spend Christmas with their families.

And how did that goddamned American even know what was in those crates? And where could he have gone to fence the merchandise? He's only had it little more than a week. Checking with art dealers in Caracas right away, that made clear sense.

And that American woman that distracted the watchman.

Who was she? The description the watchman and the port officer gave replayed in his mind. American with a red-colored top and big tits. Suddenly, it hit him. The figure of the American woman he had fixated upon the previous night at the beer hall flickered through the adrenalin and into his mind. The skimpy red top she held up to the chorus of cheer!

Coincidence? Maybe. But it was a ray of hope too promising to ignore. He had just discovered the "crime," yet he might already have a suspect. He wasn't losing his touch. This would appease his "people." For now.

He would find this American woman again, and very quickly. No question.

Chapter 21

"You guys are gonna freeze your asses off," Pancho commented as he watched the VIASA jetliner touch down on the runway. Maiquetia Airport was the international gateway to Caracas and to the rest of Venezuela. It was Tuesday morning, and the departure process was winding to a close.

Pancho, Pete, and Joe had left Puerto Ordaz early Monday morning on a domestic flight. They then spent the rest of the day at the Peace Corps office processing their discharges. On Monday evening, they did their farewell tour of the Caracas night scene, a final opportunity to eyeball the potpourri of women of every shape, size, and color, dressed like models, and strolling by the clubs and cafés along Sabana Grande. And then Tuesday, it was fly-home day.

"Not for long," Pete responded. "Christmas with the folks in New York, then I'm out of there."

"Where to?" Joe asked.

"D.C., I hope. Gonna apply for a government job of some kind. You gonna stay in New England, José?"

"Maybe. If I get into grad school at U. Mass., I will. Hear they're doing some progressive things at their School of Education. I can hustle a Master's without hardly ever attending classes."

"Sounds like you," Pancho kidded.

"Yeah, look who's talking," Joe countered. "Where're you gonna work your next hustle? With your cronies in East L.A.?"

"Hell, no, I'm through with that scene. I'm gonna try grad school, too. San Diego State maybe. A brain like mine would be a shame to waste."

"Yeah, like you haven't been wasting it on delusions for the past two years," Joe chuckled.

"You guys will be begging to come out for a visit within a month. You'll see. After two years of sunshine, you won't even be able to get it up with that cold air blowing up your assholes."

"Maybe Pancho's right, Pedro. Maybe we should head out to California after the holidays. And wait out the winter."

"And do what?"

"I dunno. Same thing we always do. Drink. Look for *señoritas.*"

"Sure. Come on out," Pancho urged. "In California you can even use your Spanish. Then I'll come east in the summer."

"Yeah, lots to do in the summer," Pete agreed. "I'll show you New York. Maybe Washington. Up Joe's way there's . . ."

Joe shrugged his shoulders. "Trees, lakes, mountains."

"There's Tanglewood," Pete reminded him.

"There's what? Never heard of it," Joe answered.

"You never heard of it?" Pete was surprised. "It's right in your backyard. Boston Symphony Orchestra's summer home. Outdoor concerts. Damn. I should've known you were a cultural buffoon."

"*Outdoor* concerts? That's probably the only reason you heard of it, Pedro. You can drink while you listen to the music. I'll bet you don't know the difference between Beethoven's Fifth and a fifth of Irish whiskey."

"Doesn't make any difference to me," Pancho chimed in. "As long as we can party."

The announcement of the flight to New York's Kennedy International Airport came over the loudspeaker. In Spanish. Then again in English. Joe and Pete were leaving on the same flight, with Joe connecting on to Albany, New York, the nearest airport to his parents' home in Western Massachusetts. Pancho's flight to L.A. would depart an hour later.

"Guess we better head over," Joe suggested.

Pancho walked with them. "So, be seeing you guys in a couple of months?"

"Could be," Pete answered. "We can down a *cerveza* or two and reminisce. Embellish our stories a few times over."

"Yeah, especially the last one," Pancho agreed. "What do you think? Won't it sound better with real Nazi SS guards holding back their attack dogs? Picture it." He looked half serious, like he was ready to submit a screenplay to Hollywood.

"Yeah, truck ramming the barricades, guns a-blazing," Pete laughed.

"What's the purpose of embellishing it?" Joe asked soberly. "We're only gonna be talking about it to each other. Right?"

A wet blanket fell upon Pancho's and Pete's imaginations. Joe's reminder sounded more like a warning.

"Right," agreed Pancho.

"I should hope so," Pete emphasized.

"And let's hope El Tío doesn't get carried away," Joe added. "You know how he likes to sling the shit when he gets going."

"El Tío, wonder where the hell he is," Pete posed.

Joe chuckled. "He's probably trying to figure a way to double his take. Probably into another scheme by now, I'd bet. . . . Wish I could figure out why Carlos never came around. We were pretty tight."

"Fuck 'em, I told you. Don't even think about it," advised Pancho.

"Maybe you're right, Pancho. I guess my biggest worry is Anita. I'll be happy when I hear she's safely out of Venezuela."

"Yeah, me, too," Pancho nodded. "Guatemala, right?"

"It looked pretty sure, she told me. She said she'd send along her new address. Should be soon."

It wasn't.

Chapter 22

Heinrich Klaus awoke before sunrise on Tuesday. Disgust and anger had prevented a restful sleep. After discovering the heist, he had spent much of the evening at the local CANTV, the Venezuelan telephone offices. Those without their own offices or their own home phones had to rely on these public telephones, especially for long distance calls.

By late Monday evening, he had informed his "people" in Caracas, as well as those in Buenos Aires, about the heist. Members of his network were not known for patience or passivity. They set their recovery efforts in motion immediately. Revenge measures would follow shortly in their wake.

He was instructed by "Rudy," his superior in Argentina, to stay in Puerto Ordaz. He was to uncover any leads lurking in local shadows. Others in the Nazi underground would deal with the bankers in Caracas—a good theft insurance policy would be their only hope.

Klaus was pleasantly surprised that Rudy didn't sound more vindictive towards him. Sure Rudy was angry, and sure Klaus' thoroughness was called into question. But by and large, Klaus sensed they were showing uncharacteristic tolerance. Perhaps because he'd been so valuable over the years, a favored operative. It reaffirmed his exalted status with elder class, the SS alumnae.

Of course, it didn't hurt being the son of Jurgen Klausmeyer, the infamous SS Colonel who'd been sent to Paraguay just prior to the end of the War to pave the way for many of his SS cronies to escape to South America. It was a privileged assignment, one that was precipitated by the death of his beloved wife in February 1945. She had been a prominent member of Dresden's cultural elite until the controversial Allied bombing of that city made Jurgen a widower.

Even a hardened SS Colonel with a string of mistresses felt grief at the loss of a wife with such desirable qualities. The departure to South America helped him to forget. And it helped young Heinrich also to forget. No son of his would waste time on sorrow and tears. The budding brotherhood of ex-Nazis hiding undercover in South America would be Heinrich's new family as well.

In Germany, Heinrich had been a gung-ho member of the Hitler Youth. Leaving with his father for Paraguay, he missed out on the opportunity to "defend to the death" his beloved Fatherland against the mongrels invading from the East. It was not until his later teens that he grew and thrived. Excelling in school and on the athletic fields, he was a favorite of his father's generation. His promise as a special agent put him at the front of the line for all phases of special training. Martial arts, demolitions, commando operations, and his primary specialty, human disappearance.

Paraguay was a small country. But it did have a government sympathetic to the cause. Nonetheless, it was too confining. A man of Heinrich's talents, not to mention his tastes, required a more cosmopolitan base. He moved to Buenos Aires and fronted as a respectable businessman, shortening his surname to Klaus, and often going by the first name Enrique, the Spanish version of Heinrich. But he relished his special assignments, and he prided himself in doing them well. At least until now.

But it wasn't he who had slipped up. He wasn't responsible for the snafu that necessitated the side trip to Caracas at the same time the American trucker was switching crates. No, but he hoped it would fall to him to find out who was responsible. It would make for complete vindication, and his record would remain unblemished.

For now, finding the American woman was the order of the day. Locating her proved to be as easy as he had expected. After all, he had just seen her at the Cervecería Bavaria Sunday night. Inquiring with the manager as soon as it opened, Klaus discovered she was indeed a regular. She did not come in as often as her female Venezuelan friends, nor as often as her male North American friends, the manager explained. But all of the American Peace Corps volunteers received phone calls and messages from their main office in Caracas at the Bavaria.

The manager explained that a messenger would be sent to their apartment if none of them were around when a call came. The Americans would then come by to wait for the prearranged call.

"I guess that really does make them regulars," Klaus acknowledged, projecting some uncharacteristic warmth and friendliness. Perhaps the heist had forced him off his pedestal, at least for the moment. "Thanks. She's an attractive woman. I saw her the other night and would like to meet her, if you know what I mean."

The manager smiled. "This would be the place. Her name is Anita."

Klaus returned to the CANTV phone offices. No time to waste. He called the bar. Disguising his voice, he stated he had an important message for the American woman named Anita. He would call again between 7 p.m. and 9 p.m. that evening, he lied. A two-hour interval would give ample time to strike up a conversation. And then to enjoy her company. Until "Rudy" would give the order.

★ ★ ★ ★ ★

Anita saw the message in her door when she returned from work shortly after 5 p.m. It must be regarding the transfer to Guatemala, she guessed. It uplifted her spirits after feeling down over the departure of Pancho, Pete, and Joe.

She had seldom gone for drinks on weekday evenings. But tonight would be an exception. The important call provided a rationale to go along with the urge. Ever uneasy about going to bars alone, Anita got her roommates, Carmen and Marta, to agree to accompany her. If it was the bittersweet news regarding Anita's transfer, they wanted to be there.

The three women arrived before 7 p.m. and had their choice of booths. It was early and the place hadn't begun to fill up. Anita sat across from her two friends. When they ordered the first round of drinks, Anita told the waiter that she was there awaiting an important phone call. He assured her that he'd inform the rest of the staff of her presence.

The booth was in earshot of the telephone. Anita could also see it from where she was seated, and found herself looking up each time it rang to see if they would signal her over. But it was early. The message had said between 7 p.m. and 9 p.m. As things went, that usually meant closer to the later boundary, if not beyond.

The frequent glances, however, caused her to notice the large handsome man with blond hair half sitting and half standing over a bar stool. Not bad, she remarked to herself. Why haven't I seen him around before?

When she noticed that he noticed her stares, he seemed to force a smile. She hadn't meant to convey interest; she never wanted to come across as too forward. But what could she do? She couldn't very well explain that it was the phone that kept drawing her attention. At least originally. It didn't hurt that this well-chiseled statue of a man seemed to be standing guard over the phone, over her pathway to the future.

After her second beer, Anita was feeling very relaxed, optimistic about her transfer, and now a bit flattered that the handsome man was looking at her quite interestedly.

"What's the matter, Anita? You seem distracted," Marta asked.

"Oh, just anxious, I guess. Wish the call would come. I'd like to get the news, one way or the other." She looked up again, fixing a longer look upon the tall man who was smiling in her direction.

Curious, Marta turned to see what was so interesting about the phone sitting behind the bar. "Ah, I see," she chided. "Do you think he's American?"

"Who?" answered Anita, quickly realizing it was too late for denial. Smiling sheepishly, she conceded, "I would guess European. German maybe."

Anita wondered if she could've dressed more appealingly. Not the tight-red-top-style, of course. She was through with that act. Maybe she could've given a little more thought to preparation, but it was only the phone call that had been on her mind. The loose-fitting dress wasn't very revealing, but it was comfortable and ladylike. She was back to being herself, modest, unassuming.

"Why don't you wave him over to join us?" Marta egged her on.

"No-o. I can't do that. If he's interested . . ."

Before she could finish, Marta was nodding and waving the man over to join them. Carmen laughed. Anita's face turned red.

"Marta, what're you doing? He's gonna get the wrong . . ."

The tall man confidently stood up and started his approach. His long strides were graceful. The beer in the half-full mug he held hardly rippled. The smile had become warmer, more reassuring. It had now broadened upward into his piercing blue eyes.

"Ladies," he greeted. "May I have the privilege of buying a round of drinks for three such charming young *señoritas?*" He fixed his gaze on Anita, leaving no doubt that it was she that he'd really come over to meet.

Anita felt flattered. Carmen and Marta nodded at her encouragingly. They approved. His Spanish seemed natural, but the accent indicated another country. Chile? Argentina, maybe. His Nordic looks, however, were an indication of other origins. Perhaps he was an engineer who came to South America from Germany or Austria. This was not uncommon in this newly industrialized zone.

Impatient that Anita didn't jump to the cue, Marta took it upon herself to respond to the offer. "We'd be delighted. Please, join us if you like."

The vacant space in the booth was next to Anita. She slid towards the wall to give the tall man some room. His knees almost touched the underside of the table as he got comfortable.

He called the waiter over and each of them ordered another drink. When Anita spoke, he noted her accent and asked where she was from.

"Norteamericana," she answered. North American.

"Canada or the United States?" he asked politely.

"The United States. I work here as a nurse. And you?"

"I am from Argentina. I work for an import-export company in Buenos Aires. Here on business."

"You don't look Argentine. At least not like those I've met."

"Well, I was born in Germany. My family left before the war. Thank God."

"A wise decision by your family."

"Yes, of course. Those were bad times. I was spared. Many of my schoolmates ended up with the Hitler youth. That wouldn't have been for me. No way. I am too easygoing. A lover, not a fighter."

"That's nice to hear. But you look big enough to be quite a fighter."

"Oh, no. Not for me. I use my energy for sports. Soccer, rugby, skiing, things like that. Do you mind if I practice my English?" he asked in Spanish.

Anita looked at Carmen and Marta for permission. They nodded. It was clear that it was a way of achieving the privacy he wanted.

Two separate conversations ensued. Carmen and Marta were soon up and about socializing with other acquaintances, while Anita and her new friend Heinrich lost themselves in their English dialogue with one another.

Time seemed to stand still. It had been quite some time since Anita met a candidate for "Mr. Right." He was easy to talk to. His English was impressive. And he seemed to hang on every word, sincerely interested in knowing about *her.*

He was perhaps eight to ten years older than she. But that was fine. She was a bit tired of the early twenties subculture she'd been limited to for so long. This was a different dimension. More sophistication, perhaps. Her shrinking social circle forced her to look beyond for new ventures. Maybe fate had preordained this chance meeting, simply holding it in reserve until the others left. Uncharacteristically, Heinrich even mentioned how he lost his mother as a young teen. Perhaps he picked up on Anita's sympathetic tendencies, and he wanted to endear himself that much more. True to form, Anita's do-gooder nature came into play. This vulnerability seemed to blend well with his ostensible strength and confidence. It heightened his appeal, and it lowered her guard.

They had common interests. Concerts, theater, movies, even

sports, such as skiing. Anita had been to Germany as an undergraduate, and was intrigued by Heinrich's wealth of knowledge about its history and culture. A touch of resentment filtered through when he mentioned how much of Dresden's legendary beauty had been destroyed by Allied bombs. Anita practically apologized for her countrymen.

They must've discussed everything. She wondered if she'd saved some topics for next time. And she truly hoped there would be a next time. But then she remembered the impending transfer. Why did she have to meet such an interesting man just before her own departure? Was it too late? Could she abort the transfer, like changing the TV channel back to the previous one? She tried blotting it out of her mind for now.

It was now well after 10 p.m. And no phone call. Maybe there was no news after all. Maybe the transfer to Guatemala was still on hold. All of a sudden, the delay was the good news. Ironic. She had come into the beer hall anxious for closure. Now she was more interested in an opening.

Carmen and Marta came back to the table and announced it was time for them to leave. It was late and they had to teach the next day. Anita knew the choice was hers. If things were going well, Anita knew that her two friends would understand that she wanted to stay. She was American, and therefore was not subjected to the same rules. If she didn't have a chaperon on the first date, her reputation would not be scarred forever.

"I'd be happy to drive you home," Heinrich offered.

Anita paused. She gazed back and forth between him and her two friends, searching for the right decision. What if she put him off and he took it as lack of interest? And how much time did she have left? Could she afford to waste time playing games? Being from Argentina, he would know the difference between a tango that was real and one that was contrived.

Heinrich took her hand. "Anita, I assure you that I am a

perfect gentleman . . . and you will be in good hands."

Smitten, she fell for the nudge. She nodded. Carmen and Marta said good night and left.

Anita never made it to Guatemala.

Book III

Chapter 23

San Diego
April 1998

Joe arrived before Pete. He was jittery. Whatever it was that Pete had to tell him couldn't be good. He had never seen Pete so shook up.

Joe took a private table in the popular Italian restaurant in the historic Gaslamp Quarter. His wait wasn't very long. Pete arrived within minutes. He looked no less troubled than a few hours before at the funeral home.

"Good choice," Pete acknowledged, gesturing to the surroundings. Perhaps under more ordinary circumstances, the Romanesque decor and the aroma of sauces and spices would have eased them into a more relaxed frame of mind.

"Shall I order some wine?" Joe asked.

"Sure. We'll need it. Go ahead. You choose."

"Why not? One of my few skills." Joe called the waitress over and pointed to a Tuscan Sangiovese he had been wanting to try.

They sat in silence as they perused the menu. The deliberations were interrupted by the prompt delivery of the wine. As the waitress uncorked the bottle, they mumbled to each other about the entree choices they were considering. The waitress poured a splash into Joe's glass for sampling. He swirled and sniffed for a second, then took a sip. He nodded and she poured both glasses.

She was ready to take their orders, so they hastened their

decisions. They each seemed disposed to getting the minor stuff out of the way.

"To Pancho," Joe toasted, holding up his wineglass.

"To poor Pancho," Pete repeated somberly. When he put down the glass, he fidgeted with the silverware and napkin. It was time to unlock the gate. Joe braced himself.

"José, it seems surreal," he began. "I got an anonymous call at my office the morning after you announced your candidacy . . . you know, after I sent you the congratulatory message by E-mail. It was a man's voice, strong and articulate. Very serious and right to the point."

"About?" Joe barely whispered.

"He told me the news about Pancho. About being killed in the accident. Then he laughed. Real sinister-like." Pete took a sip of wine, then breathed deeply. "He said it was made to look like a car accident."

"You mean it wasn't? It wasn't an accident?" At that instant Joe recalled what Marialena had said about Pancho never neglecting his seat belt. About how they'd found him thrown from the car. Was this little puzzle related to what Pete was now revealing?

"That's when he told me it was connected to our 'not-so-well-kept secret,' his words, from our Venezuela days."

Joe felt like he'd been flipped upside down. His face nearly turned the color of the wine in the glass he twirled nervously between his fingers. He could feel the moist outpouring of sweat on his brow and forehead. And a jolt of dread oozed up and down his spine like mercury in a thermometer.

Finally, Joe's vocal chords untensed, and the sound of his voice filtered through. "The heist! The fucking heist? That was over twenty-five years ago. How could that bite us in the ass now?"

"He laughed, José. The caller laughed, mockingly. He was

poking fun at our thinking no one else knew about it. Big joke on us, he said. Or something to that effect."

"So, who . . . ? What . . . ?"

"Then . . . that's when he made the connection to your candidacy, José. He said your candidacy for the U.S. Senate was a threat to some people, important people willing to pay money, big money. And he was the one to whom they paid it . . . Pancho's death was the first warning. The first warning to you, Joe."

Suddenly Joe's bewilderment transformed to anger. "What? You mean to say Pancho's life came to an end because some assholes feel I'm some kind of threat? What kind of crap is that? And what threat? And who the hell are they?"

"Sh-sh. Stay calm, José. I can just imagine what you're feeling right now. And I'm not even the one they're trying to stop."

"But, Pedro, they killed Pancho, didn't they?"

Pete understood the implication. By the look on his face, it was clear that he recognized his own predicament. And his own dependency on Joe's course of action. "The man gave me a message to deliver."

"And what is it he expects?" Joe ranted. "For us to keep it to ourselves? For me to get out of the race? All this without an explanation. Are we supposed to forgive him, too, for killing Pancho? Just a political casualty, I suppose."

"Joe, the explanation is part of the deal. They want to meet with you."

"You mean this is negotiable?" Joe responded sarcastically. "My God, Pedro, you had it right. This is surreal."

Pete finished the remaining wine in his glass and gave himself a fresh pour. When Joe nodded, Pete topped off Joe's glass as well. "Are you ready to hear the rest, ready for your instructions?"

"Instructions!" Joe reacted, once again dueling with the

outrage he felt. "They killed Pancho, and now they're gonna instruct me? Screw them!"

Pete pressed on soberly. His own health was somewhere within the equation. "He said . . . he said that it would be in everyone's 'best interests,' again his words, for you to meet with him so he could set you straight. He said, if you went alone, nothing would happen to you."

"Go where?" Joe wanted the explanation now. But Pete couldn't provide it. So, if going somewhere to get it was the only alternative, then he would need to take his chances. He had to know what the hell this was about.

"They must like doing their work outside the country," Pete noted. "He wants you to drive up to Montreal after you get back. Go there a week from Friday. Go to Place Jacques Cartier after 6 p.m. Grab a bench right there in the plaza. Someone will come for you, to invite you to dinner."

"Considerate of him. It's only about an hour and a half drive from Burlington," Joe commented.

The pause lasted several minutes. Joe tilted back his head and peered up at the ceiling. The fake Roman columns joined the ceiling at a point directly above. He closed his eyes and massaged the back of his own neck with his fingers. He pressed harder and harder, hoping beyond hope that he would awaken from this dreamlike predicament and find himself back in his sunroom overlooking Lake Champlain. But it was not to be. He knew Pete was awaiting some kind of response.

And it was Pete who broke the silence. "Are you gonna go?"

"It's critical we find out all we can. Living the rest of our lives with this . . . this uncertainty is a risk in itself. I don't know, Pedro. Guess I need to think hard on this. But right now, in all honesty, it doesn't seem avoidable, does it?"

"Wish I could go with you, Joe," Pete expressed what he hoped was obvious.

"I know you do. But looks like your mystery man is the one playing the tune, at least at this stage of the music. Funny, isn't it? After all these years. I barely remember that we even did that crazy heist. Feels more like having been in a movie. And having stepped back into real life after it was over, like it never really was a part of our reality."

"Yeah, I know what you mean, Joe. But with this fucking guy knowing all about it, it's the same as having it in some cinematic archive."

"I never told a soul about it, even though it would've been a great story. It was for fear of this very thing, that it'd somehow come back and haunt us."

"Ditto with me. Never even told my wife, or ex-wife, I should say. I didn't even get a chance to tell you, José, we've just separated."

"No shit? Sorry to hear that. Like you really need this nonsense on top of that."

"Really. But like I've always said, that's what alcohol is for." He took another gulp of wine for emphasis.

Joe couldn't help suspect that any marital breakup for Pete might be more attributable to alcohol than assuaged by it. "Looks like we're going to need each other for a few weeks, amigo," Joe concluded.

"Yeah. I don't think we can run to the authorities. What're we supposed to tell them? We robbed six million dollars worth of art. Be great for relations with Venezuela."

"And I'm sure the Peace Corps would use us on their next recruiting drive—'the hardest robbery you'll ever love committing,' or something to that effect," Joe said.

"Maybe 'the scummiest people you'll ever love robbing.' "

"That's right. Assuming they really were Nazis. We took El Tío's word for it, remember?"

"Yeah, I thought about that afterwards. Hope we at least got that part right."

"Pedro, you don't think this caller was . . . ?"

"Nah, if he was part of the Nazi underground, and knew about it all this time . . . hell, they would've surfaced before now. It was a lot of money, don't forget. They must've been bullshit."

"I can hardly remember who did know about that heist," Joe speculated. "I'm positive that Pancho never told anybody. I did some probing in my conversation with his daughter, Marialena. On the flight out here. She didn't give a hint that she'd heard anything remotely related to it."

"Outside of the participants, only Carlos Santiago knew," Pete reminded him.

"So when we left Venezuela, the only ones who knew were you, me, Pancho, Carlos, El Tío, and Anita," Joe summarized. "Unless someone overheard us and took note. Seems if it'd become known at the time, we or the Peace Corps would've heard from Venezuelan authorities. Wouldn't you think?"

"That makes it all the more mysterious," Pete added. "Have you ever heard from Carlos? I've gotten correspondence from El Tío over the years, but he's never included a return address. We've always corresponded through people he knew who were visiting the U.S. He was always living somewhere overseas. And he apparently moved around quite a bit. Probably hiding from his ex-wife."

"Or from whomever else he scammed. Yeah, I remember you telling me that about him. I received a few Christmas cards from him years ago. Pretty much on the same basis. But getting cards to him was too confusing, so our correspondence just ended. As for Carlos, he never resurfaced. I never heard from him again after he failed to show for our farewell party. And Anita . . . well, you know that story."

"Sure do. She never corresponded with anybody. We know

she was gone from Venezuela when you tried reaching her shortly after you left. And she never sent any of us a forwarding address."

"She was supposed to go to Guatemala to finish her Peace Corps service. But I never tried to reach her there. Always figured she'd send me her new address when she got around to it. When she didn't, I felt offended. I was a little pissed she'd forgotten me, forgotten us, so soon. So, I let it go. You never tried finding her, Pedro?"

"No. Like you, I just waited to hear from her. Figured she was tighter with you, and if you didn't get any word, then. . . . Maybe when I get back to Washington, I can check with the Peace Corps to see if they have an address."

"If they don't, why not ask if she ever, in fact, served in Guatemala, or wherever, in early 1973."

"Good idea," Pete agreed.

"And what about Pancho's family? We can't tell them anything. Makes me sick. I'm flying back with Marialena. Sitting with her for over six hours. That'll keep the old emotions in turmoil. Shit, knowing what I know, and having to keep it from her. What her dad did, for noble purposes. And what it ended up costing him. And costing her." Joe was shaking his head in continued disbelief. He stared at the wall long enough for his eyes to dry.

"That's a tough one, José. Our mystery man didn't supply us with instructions on any of the human aspects."

"He sounds like a man without many human aspects, Pedro."

Chapter 24

As anticipated, Joe had to fight off his uneasiness. For the first hour or two, his conversation with Marialena was forced and superficial. Knowing what he now knew, he wished he were flying solo. Soon after they were aloft and had been served breakfast, they were offered a movie choice. Thank God, Joe thought. A chance to hibernate for a while. He gladly paid the five dollars, even though the selection held little appeal. It didn't surprise him when he was soon lost in thought.

He needed to get his feelings under control. A veritable cocktail of emotions was being sipped into his brain. Anger, regret, frustration, even helplessness. Helplessness was the dangerous one. It was the one most likely to zap him in his tracks, before he could emerge from the starting blocks.

No, he wouldn't succumb to a feeling of helplessness. Not before giving it his best shot. He needed to get clear, to think rationally. Strategies, plans of action, contingencies.

He was not a strand of wheat wavering in the wind. He reminded himself that he was a candidate for one of the most prestigious offices in the land, the U.S. Senate. An emerging public figure. But then again, it was this fact that was aggravating the dilemma. How could he resolve such a personal matter in a private way?

This trip to Montreal, would it allow the light to shine out from under the bushel? Or, would it just deepen the quagmire? Would he be playing into the hands of some sinister puppeteer?

And what about the physical risk of this Montreal meeting? Come alone and you won't be harmed. He was supposed to trust the people who murdered Pancho? Pancho was alone out there on the highway when they got him. How hard were accidents to arrange? Especially if these guys were pros. And he had every reason to suspect they were. It wouldn't be your run of the mill street punk who would safeguard a six-million-dollar secret for over twenty-five years, only to pull it out of a hat when it could best serve a purpose.

Grappling with this Montreal question was like exercise for the brain. It required the focus of a game of chess. Gradually, his capacity for reason was being restored. The storm clouds of emotion began to lift.

The meeting with this tormenter was only a week away. The idea of hearing him out was like a magnet to his sense of curiosity. But then what? If, as Pete had been told, it was about his Senate candidacy, he would be threatened, or blackmailed, to abort it. And that was the least bad thing that could happen.

What about hiring protection? Could they hover in the shadows, undetected? Would he get into a vehicle if so instructed by the contact meeting him at Place Jacques Cartier? Hell, no. But he'd better have a prepared reason to refuse, something that would tilt the balance back in favor of his living to see Vermont again.

But the meeting in a restaurant, as proposed, that might be okay. He would be safe in a bustling Montreal restaurant brimming with Friday night's bon vivants.

He considered how he should get to Montreal. Should he drive or take public transportation, a bus or the train from Essex Junction. And if he were to drive, surely he would not want to drive back alone at night on the lonely rural highways between Montreal and Burlington.

Could he get someone who wouldn't be noticed to tail him

as insurance? He thought of Terrell Jackson, his friend the retired FBI agent who taught criminal justice courses at the University. "T.J." had also signed on as a campaign adviser, a member of Joe's inner circle. Someone with his skills and background would make anyone feel much safer.

But there was the problem of conspicuousness. Unfortunately, there was little chance that Terrell Jackson would simply go unnoticed, even if the blackmailers, or whatever they were, had no idea that he was anything to Joe. Even though T.J. was around fifty, he still had the look of the athlete he once was. In his twenties, he was a wide receiver with the Washington Redskins. He stood six-feet four-inches tall and was still lean of build.

Although as an African American he would not stand out as much in Montreal as he did in Vermont, he was still more likely than not to be noticed by any security types sure to be eyeballing Joe's movements. It was disappointing not to be able to call on such a valuable resource. But, at least, he might go to T.J. for advice. That alone would be a help. He knew he could count on his trust.

Maybe private detectives were an option. Could be expensive. But what if this Montreal escapade aroused media suspicion? That had to be avoided, sure as shit. So how could he arrange inconspicuous protection that was also confidential? And that could handle the job, of course? So much to think about. Thank God he had a few days.

When they landed in Pittsburgh to catch their Hartford connection, Joe and Marialena resumed the small talk. With time to kill, he offered to buy her a beer.

Seated on bar stools just off a busy concourse, she remarked, "José, this ordeal seems to have emptied your tank a bit. You seem more dispirited than me, even. And Dad and I were very close."

He stared at the beer, watching the bubbles fizz upward

towards the head. He wasn't sure how he'd respond.

"Am I right about that?" she persisted.

"No, it's not that, Marialena. I'm sure your sadness is deeper. Maybe with me there's a selfish element. Your father was a contemporary. This kind of thing is a wake-up call to us old geezers. You know, a reminder of mortality, of how quickly it can just end."

"Well, it can end quickly for anybody, us youngsters included. Time needs to be put to good use. Look at you. You may be entering into your most notable years."

"I can't help thinking about all the good years your father had left. Knowing his thirst for challenge, certainly there were going to be eventful happenings in his future."

"I guess we'll just have to appreciate him for all that he did accomplish in his life. It was a lot. He even died giving of himself—while on the way back from the orphanage where he volunteered his consulting time. He'll always be an inspiration to me," she declared.

Joe thought how her declaration alone might've made one's life worth living. He wished he had someone that close, someone for whom he could have been such an inspiration.

They began making their way to the departure gate for their Hartford-bound flight. Strolling along the concourse, they peeked into a few shops and people watched. Then Joe heard the announcement that jogged his memory, rearranging all the pieces of the puzzle he was working on. It was the boarding call for a flight to Boston's Logan International Airport.

Boston. With the announcement of his candidacy at the beginning of the week, and with the unplanned trip to San Diego, he had forgotten to RSVP to his cousin's wedding in Boston. Taking place tomorrow. No problem, though. He knew that with a last-minute phone call, they'd be happy to hear he was coming and would set him a plate.

And why not? He would be in Massachusetts minutes after they drove north from Bradley Airport. It'd been a while since Joe had seen the relatives on his mother's side, including cousin Sal. Funny how a good idea could come out of nowhere when you most needed it, he thought.

"Marialena, could I ask a favor? Do you think you and your housemates could put me up for the night? I think while I'm so close to Boston, I'd like to attend a relative's wedding. I had almost forgotten about it. If not, I'll just grab a motel room on the way down the pike after I drop you off."

"Don't be silly," she answered. "We'd be honored to have a future member of the U.S. Senate as a house guest."

CHAPTER 25

"The living-room couch folds out. Will that be okay for you, José?"

It was a little after 8:30 p.m. They'd just gotten back to Marialena's apartment in Northampton, Massachusetts, after a full day flying over the purple mountain majesties and fruited planes.

"More than okay," Joe reassured her. "The floor would've been fine. We ex–Peace Corps guys are easy to please."

"I'd offer you a nice Venezuelan hammock," she kidded. "But the one my father gave me is still at my mom's in San Diego."

"Logical. I'm sure it gets more use there than here in this climate."

"Well, I think I'll freshen up. Maybe go out for a while. Care to join me? Northampton's a fun town, and it's too early to turn in."

It was only about 5:30 p.m. west coast time, Joe thought. So he wasn't ready to call it a night, either. "Sounds good to me. You can show me around. I could use a bite to eat. Can I treat?"

"I'm not that hungry. But I'll show you to a restaurant of your choice. We have quite a selection."

She really hadn't eaten much all day, he noted. He could see how she maintained her world-class figure.

"It's a deal. While you're freshening up I'll call my aunt to tell her I'll be at her granddaughter's wedding."

As expected, Aunt Carmella was glad to hear from Joe. She was his deceased mother's youngest sibling, the only one still living. Joe's mother's family settled in Boston when they immigrated from Italy, and Joe had visited them often as a youth, especially during the summer when he could include a Red Sox game or two.

For family, there was no such thing as late notice. Aunt Carmella always looked forward to seeing her out-of-town relatives. She had heard Joe was a busy man, involved in some kind of politics. Nonetheless, Joe did apologize for the short notice, citing the San Diego trip as the complicating factor. She promised to put him at a table with his first cousins.

Marialena got ready quickly. She changed into a brightly colored spring dress that highlighted her long black hair and smooth olive-colored skin. But what wouldn't look great on her, Joe concluded.

"My God, you sure look lovely, young lady. Aren't your friends going to wonder what you're doing hanging out with your grandfather?"

"My friends know I like older men. Are you ready? We can go on foot if you like."

"A walk would be great."

It was a pleasant April evening, warm and dry. Spring was surely in the air, an optimistic time for New Englanders. The harsh winter had faded, soon to be a distant memory. The downtown sidewalks were flowing, people strolling between restaurants, clubs, cafés, and theaters.

They put their names in for a table at a restaurant that served "eclectic fare." They sipped margaritas at the bar while waiting for their names to be called.

"It's funny, I forgot to ask if you're even old enough to drink. I have trouble thinking of you as a kid," Joe remarked.

"Don't worry. I turned twenty-one over a month ago. Want to see my driver's license?" she kidded.

"No, I believe you. Just that I can't run for Senate and do

things like contributing to the delinquency of a minor.

"So, Marialena, seriously, don't you have a man in your life? Here it is a weekend night and you're spending it with a friend of your father. I would've figured someone like you to be in great demand."

She laughed. "I wasn't kidding when I told you I liked older men."

"Older? Older than twenty-one is twenty-two on up," he reminded her.

"I've dated a few guys since I've been here. But most of the men my age don't interest me. The supply of older men, late twenties on up, is a bit smaller. Many of them are married or in relationships. Besides, I'm in no hurry to settle down. Got a lot of living to do first. Maybe I'll join the Peace Corps after I graduate," she teased.

"I'll write you a character reference." He chuckled to himself—a character reference from a guy who'd stolen six million dollars while he was on the Peace Corps clock!

"By the way," she changed the subject. "Could you use some help with your campaign? You've certainly won my support. And I'm sure it'd be a great experience. Will you have a campaign committee in Brattleboro, maybe?" Brattleboro, Vermont, was less than an hour from Northampton.

Campaign? Oh, yeah, what about that? The idea seemed to be back beyond the backseat, somewhere in the trunk, maybe. A locked trunk. "Sure, there'll be a steering committee in Brattleboro. You sure you'd have the time?"

"I'd make the time. This summer, maybe?"

"I'd be honored. I'll get back to you as things get organized. You still owe me a visit. I'll introduce you to the campaign staff when you come up to Burlington."

"Sounds good. That may be soon," she predicted.

"Marialena, you're welcome anytime. It doesn't have to be

campaign related. Hope you know that. Any time you'd simply like to talk, about your father, or whatever." It would be gratifying, he thought, to be supportive. At least it might counterbalance the unspoken awareness of why Pancho was killed.

After the late-night dinner, they exited into the balmy night air. She paused and took in a deep breath. It seemed to ratchet up her energy level.

"I feel like dancing," she announced. "That'd be fun, don't you think? Cathartic, that's what it'd be. Cathartic. I just learned the word."

"Cathartic? Cathartic for you, maybe. For me, it would probably be orthopedic—I'd probably throw my back out."

"Just for a while. It'll do us both some good."

It was the last thing he would've suggested. But for some reason, he couldn't say no. "All right. You talked me into it. I'll grab a quick espresso in that coffee shop, and then you can lead your 'Uncle José' around by the nose."

They were back to her place shortly after midnight. She had been right. The dancing had been therapeutic.

But they had not gone unnoticed.

Chapter 26

Joe woke up later than expected. Then he took his time conversing with Marialena and her housemates over coffee and bagels. Her housemates seemed impressed having a senatorial candidate at their breakfast table, and the inevitable questions came up: his chances, his main issues, his reasons.

When he finally hit the Massachusetts Turnpike, he realized it would be too late to make the wedding ceremony. So he headed directly to the reception hall in Boston's North End.

It was a neighborhood that brought back memories of his childhood and his youth. An Italian ethnic neighborhood that made him feel bicultural, almost. He remembered how this had been a helpful frame of reference when he made the adjustment to the Latin culture in Venezuela as a Peace Corps volunteer.

The beautiful spring day had drawn many people to the narrow streets. Shopping, running errands, socializing. He savored the bittersweet nostalgia.

Skipping the wedding service, he was one of the first to arrive at the reception hall. He went directly to the bar and readied himself to greet long-lost relatives and cousins. These occasions were few and far between. As a kid, he had been close to his first cousins, those in his own generation. The families used to get together regularly. But now everyone was spread all over the Boston suburbs, bringing up their own kids.

The cousin Joe had been closest to was his Aunt Carmella's oldest son, Salvatore Gionella. They were the same age. They had gone to Fenway Park together as kids. Cousin Sal also included cousin "Joey" in the neighborhood mischief he and his cronies perpetrated almost as an avocation.

But for Sal, the mischief later took on more sophisticated dimensions. Or, so everyone just assumed. No one seemed to know, with any degree of specificity, how Sal managed to put food on his family's table. Or supported their three cars. Or maintained the vacation home in Fort Lauderdale.

Joe's parents' generation had aspired to have the next generation surpass the accomplishments of its own. Better jobs, more money. This tended to mean more education. And most of those in Joe's generation followed that recipe, scraping and sacrificing to get through college. But not cousin Sal. He didn't need to.

Sal now lived in a large house in an upscale suburb. But he was as much a fixture in the North End as cappuccino. To those in the family, it was no secret that Sal had "special friends," and that these friends could exert undue influence in certain circles.

Soon there was a steady trickle of familiar faces arriving by the bar. Despite thinning hairlines and expanding waistlines, Joe had no trouble with the recognition game. Conversations were fast and eager. It could've been truly enjoyable, were it not for this Montreal meeting that kept gnawing on his brain.

And that was why Joe kept looking towards the entrance. The relative he most wanted to see was keeping him waiting. Even the bride and groom had made their grand entrance by this time.

Surely, while in the North End, Sal would've needed to circulate around the neighborhood before coming inside. Sali "Giones," a.k.a. "Jones," the shortened version of the surname Gionella, always paid his respects.

Finally, the gleam of sunlight in the entryway was eclipsed by the wide, round figure shuffling forward waving to all in view. The wide, toothy smile was unmistakable. Cousin Sal's short, stubby legs propelled the barrel-sized body inward until he shook the first set of hands, slapped the first row of backs, and hugged and kissed the first cluster of ladies. Almost a caricature, Joe decided, himself smiling from ear to ear.

Joe waved to get Sal's attention. It only took a minute or two. Sal was the type who would notice everyone "in the joint" right after making his entrance.

"Hey, Joey, how the hell ah ya," Sal bellowed out in his thick Boston accent. The short legs churned like pistons, as the corpulent cousin Sal came to within arm's length.

"Sali. Great to see ya." As they shook, Joe wondered if the fingers of his professorial hands were being fused together by Sal's grip.

"Joey, Ma said you called 'n was gonna be here. How many years it been? Gee, you look great. What you doin' to stay in shape? Look at this guy, doesn't look a day over thirty."

Joe appreciated the flattery, and he smiled profusely as Sal's accent added color to recollections of times past.

"It's been too long, Sali. Glad to see you're still out of jail," he chided.

Joe didn't reciprocate with any insincere commentary about how Sal looked. Sal's once thick black hair was now fully gray. His waistline required additional airspace. And the thickening skin looked like it could stop a bullet—maybe some day it would take on the challenge. But Sal still looked like a man to be reckoned with. His forearms were straining the sleeves of his suit jacket, and his fists were almost the size of bricks.

"Jail, whatta you talkin' about? Everybody loves Sali Jones around here. Always doin' favors. So, you're a politician now. Why didn't you tell me you wanted to be a crook. I coulda got ya started thirty years ago."

In Sal's world, "politician" and "crook" could very well have been synonymous terms.

"No, I'm gonna be an honest one, Sali. Thank God you and I have different last names," Joe joked.

"Joey, seriously, I know the best thing I could do to help is to not let anybody know we even know each other. But really . . . if there's anything I could ever do, behind the scenes maybe, . . . *Whatever.* You jus' let me know. Understand? You know there's nothin' I wouldn't do for family. And don't worry, you wouldn't owe me nothin' after. Not a thing. Not ever."

It was a familiar refrain. Sal always offered to help Joe out with "whatever," every time they got together. It was part of the ritual. Joe never took him up. He never needed to. Not until now. Now, he might finally find out what was in the "whatever" package. Yes, he had counted on running into Sal, and yes, he welcomed hearing it once again, the perpetual standing offer.

"Well, Sali, now that you mention it. Maybe there's something you can do, 'behind the scenes,' as you say. You ever been to Montreal?"

Sal perked up. Joe pulled him out of earshot of everyone else, and proceeded to explain his apprehensions about the Montreal meeting. Sal demonstrated acute comprehension of such matters; he didn't need to ask any questions. Backside protection needed, inconspicuous and undetectable—understood. Can't go to authorities for reasons Joe couldn't reveal—understood. No publicity or public attention—understood. No gratuitous violence or rough stuff—understood.

Sal was almost overcome with excitement. He acted flattered. Maybe it was the opportunity to do well by a relative who was about to make it big in the "legit" world.

"Piece a cake, Joey. Consider it done. I got friends in Montreal. And I'll go up there myself, to make sure everything goes perfect. Jus' send me some of that Vermont maple syrup after."

"I thought you said I wouldn't owe you anything," Joe kidded back.

Chapter 27

His own home felt like a refuge. But he knew it was only a mirage. Friday was but a few days away, and the wheels were grinding forward. Joe was going to go to Montreal.

He punched in the number to Judy Bennett's office. Time to check in with his campaign coordinator.

"What's going on?" he began.

"Well, it's about time," she remarked. "Tore yourself away from the California sunshine, finally, eh?"

"Yeah, real pleasure trip. A friend of mine died, remember? I'm pretty fried, Judy. Hope you don't have anything lined up for this week."

"Not really. But you shouldn't be wasting valuable time. I can think of a hundred different initiatives. . . ."

"Not in the mood for initiatives. Next week . . . maybe.

"Okay," she sighed, hating to relinquish all control. "But I have you lined up for Sunday 11 a.m. on statewide TV."

"Sunday?" He paused to think it through. The Montreal ordeal would be finished, one way or the other. If he were going to drop his candidacy, he could simply announce it Sunday on the program. "Sunday's good. I'll be back from Montreal by then."

"Montreal? Since when did *they* vote in Vermont elections?"

"Just need to be alone for a few days, Judy. Nobody knows me up there. Anything else?"

"That reporter from the *Rutland Free Press* would like to do an in-depth interview. You know, biographical stuff. I can blow her off for another week."

"What reporter? That sexy Vicki something-or-other that was at my announcement?"

"Rivier. Vicki Rivier is her name."

"Married? Single? Available?"

"Cut the shit, Joe. This is a small state, and we don't need any scandals. Or even gossip, thank you. Take cold showers for the next six months, will ya? Or do whatever it is men do to get by."

"And what would that be?" he chided, now enjoying the fact that he'd gotten her worried.

"Just wash your hands before working the crowds."

"And I'll wash them afterwards, too. So, I'll see you Sunday . . . I hope."

Chapter 28

The phone rang at the Washington office of Senate Majority Leader Blake Ross. The caller spoke, "This is Julian Muller. Senator Ross is expecting my call."

Ross kept him waiting for a fashionable three or four minutes. After all, the Senate Majority Leader was one of the three most powerful figures in the U.S. Government. A man of Muller's ilk had direct access only when it served the senator's purposes.

"Mr. Muller, this is Senator Ross." He liked keeping it formal.

"Hey, how you doing?" Muller preferred taunting the formality.

"What is it, Mr. Muller?"

"Well, here I am in Montreal. Hotel St. Bonaventure. Nice town. Just had a massage from a sexy young thing with a French accent. . . ."

"To the point, Mr. Muller. I'm a busy man."

"Joe . . . I'm sorry, *Mister* LaCarta, is meeting me here this evening. He just left his home. Alone. He's somewhere along Interstate 89 as we speak."

"Just as long as it's never *Senator* LaCarta," Ross caught Muller's sarcasm. "I have enough problems. That asshole will get all the middle-of-the-roaders working together."

And if that happened, it would be a pretty good guess that there'd soon be a new Majority Leader. Ross was a Conservative Republican in his public persona. But he was a right-wing reactionary in his heart. And he had an inner circle of other senators and congressmen, with whom he shared what was in his heart.

"Asshole? Senator, where's your sense of decorum?"

Ross sighed. "I trust you will achieve the desired outcome, Mr. Muller. That you will succeed in making him realize that he's better off where he is, doing what he's doing, rather than becoming a U.S. Senator—if he were to win, that is."

"Oh, he'd win. Why, I'll never know, but he would indeed win."

"Then that's all the more reason to be persuasive, isn't it?"

"I have every confidence, Blake . . . I mean, Senator. I should have him pissing in his pants right at the dinner table. I don't think he'll make a scene like his buddy down in Mexico. The jerk got carried away, then had a fucking heart attack right on the spot. We had no choice, had to make it look like an accident. . . ."

"I told you I didn't want to hear details," Ross shouted into the phone, unaware of the fiendish grin on Muller's face.

Muller was shaking the wall of deniability that insulated the Senator Ross–types from the Julian Muller–types, and he was getting a kick out of it. Men like Ross, men who just pushed buttons while others did the heavy lifting, deserved to share the risk once in a while.

"Pardon me, Senator. Don't know what I could've been thinking. Forget I ever mentioned his buddy."

"I'm forgetting this call ever took place. Now, is that all?"

"Unless something unforeseen. . . ."

"That's all, Mr. Muller. Call only if you have to. I will be reading about his withdrawal in next week's papers." Ross hung up.

Muller enjoyed putting the senator on edge. And he figured the rest of the good senators and respectable congressmen in Ross' hard-liners group would share the uneasiness. If they viewed him as a loose cannon rather than the professional he truly was, then so be it. It was Muller's way of undermining their phony sense of security.

Having Ross and his cohorts as clients was for convenience purposes. What they were paying him was hardly worth his while. The big bucks were coming from the likes of drug cartels and corrupt police at home and abroad. These were the ones who stood to lose if the relaxing of drug laws ever took hold. They were well aware of how the old bootleggers had to find new rackets when Prohibition was repealed in the 1930s.

It had been Muller who approached Ross to sign on as a client. Muller was an opportunist and knew how to recognize mutual self-interest. Conveniently, he already knew Senator Ross from back when they really were on a first-name basis.

Ross was a young senator on the Intelligence Committee back when Muller was a principal operative in the overthrow of President Salvador Allende of Chile. Allende had been duly elected by the people of Chile. But he was a Socialist, and therefore was perceived as a threat to U.S. influence in Latin America. He had to go. The overthrow resulted in a military dictatorship, more friendly to U.S. interests, and more advantageous to Julian Muller's career.

Not that he wasn't already a rising star. After a stint in Army Intelligence in the Vietnam of the mid-sixties, he was assigned to the U.S. Embassy in Caracas, Venezuela, in 1969. There, he was in charge of monitoring guerilla activity and kept tabs on the activities of the Communist party. He had recruited and assigned a number of native and Latino operatives who reported directly to him. It was important that a country like Venezuela, with all its petroleum and mineral wealth, not succumb to the folly of left-wing domination.

His organizational prowess in Venezuela led to his being in demand for the more critical circumstances in Chile, once the

Socialist Allende had been elected. Muller's effectiveness in the successful overthrow brought him positive recognition in Intelligence circles. Soon it was not financially desirable to remain on the CIA payroll. The lure of becoming an independent contractor, the prospect of selling his services to the highest bidder, delivered both fame and fortune. And his client list grew to include almost everyone conceivable by the 1990s.

Now, he had his own fortune to protect. But he was still not the kind of man to entrust such measures to underlings. Besides, what challenge, what fun, was that? For him, excitement and stimulation were their own rewards. Let others hide in a cocoon of deniability. He could hide, too, but because of his inconspicuousness to the mainstream world. And he reveled in this ghostly existence.

After his phone conversation with Senator Ross, he jumped rope in his hotel room for twenty minutes. Then, after his daily three hundred sit-ups and one hundred push-ups, he remained on the floor stretching out the muscles on his lean fifty-five-year-old body. He showered, then plunked himself down onto the king-size bed to prepare mentally for the evening objective.

He remembered Joe LaCarta from their Venezuela days. They hadn't ever met. But Muller knew all about Joe. He shook his head on the pillow as he reflected. What could possess a man like LaCarta to continue to frustrate himself trying to make things better. Peace Corps. Policy wonk. It was laughable, Muller thought. What a futile life path. Why was reality so hard to grasp? Maybe the lesson LaCarta was about to learn would be like a favor. Maybe, LaCarta should pay him, too, he chuckled, for the wisdom he was about to impart.

Chapter 29

Old Town Montreal brought back memories. There was Paula before she reconciled with her husband. And then there was the brilliant psychiatrist, Dr. Roberta Guerette. How much nicer it would've been to walk among these old colonial buildings on this delicious spring evening if the agenda were recreational rather than confrontational.

He arrived at the Place Jacques Cartier and, as instructed, took a seat on an available bench. People of all ages meandered along the sidewalks and zigzagged through the plaza. Vehicles inched along the narrow roadways, some getting stuck behind horse carriages carrying tourists, honeymooners, and the like.

Joe had parked the rented car several blocks away. He had chosen to rent for the flexibility it afforded. He could simply leave the car behind if necessary. After parking, he walked to the front of Notre Dame Cathedral, where he stood for fifteen minutes. It was the prearranged stake-out point for cousin Sal and his crew. From there they picked up Joe's tail, presumably, and would follow him until he was safely back home in Burlington.

So he hoped. If Sal and company had indeed picked up his tail and followed, they were certainly discreet, because he hadn't noticed any sign of their presence. Damn Sal, he worried to himself, he better not just be all talk.

Joe's senses were sharpened to the people around him. Every face, every clatter of footsteps, caused him to wonder. Who would be the messenger? Who would lead him onward into the tunnel?

A street vendor approached. Joe shook his head. He didn't have anyone for whom to purchase roses. Then another handing out brochures, some promotion or other. Joe waved him away. But the young man didn't accept the refusal. He shoved the brochure into Joe's resisting hand until Joe took the cue and grasped it.

Joe immediately noticed the handwriting, blue ink on the cover: "See you in the Chateau Laurent. Ask for Mr. Jones' Table."

Mr. Jones? As in Salvatore Gionella, a.k.a. Sali Jones? What the . . . ? Maybe it was only coincidence. It would have to be a desperate situation for Sal to want to make contact. Chateau Laurent, where was that? Joe looked up and scanned the area surrounding Place Jacques Cartier. Finally, he noticed the messenger gesturing and saying something in French that could've meant "around that corner." When Joe stood to head in that direction, the young man nodded and walked away.

Joe slowed his walk. He needed time to think. What if it was Sal? What if there was some kind of warning that Sal needed to communicate? Or, did Sal maybe take some ill-advised initiative? Joe wondered. Maybe cousin Sal and his crew didn't exactly operate with the precision of the Corleone family. But then again, Joe reminded himself, he hadn't really had the luxury of checking references.

The maitre d' greeted Joe at the entrance of the Chateau Laurent. The restaurant was indeed located just around the corner. It had a narrow storefront, but the floor space extended inward beyond eye view. Every visible table was already taken, and a few people had gathered near the entryway, apparently getting posted onto the waiting list.

"Oh, yes, Mr. LaCarta, Mr. Jones is expecting you. Right this way."

Joe followed the maitre d' down the tight walkway separating two long rows of tables in the deep, narrow layout. They squirmed by a scurrying waitress or two before the back wall came into focus and Joe noticed the one man sitting tall and making eye contact. It wasn't cousin Sal, and he was much too "waspy" to be part of Sal's crew. There was a place setting across from him. The maitre d' gestured to the vacant chair.

The man stood and extended his hand. "Mr. LaCarta, I'm Mr. Jones."

The haze lifted. This was the meeting Joe had come for. It had nothing to do with Sal. Why couldn't this asshole have chosen an alias other than Jones? Smith, maybe. Or something more creative, like Eichmann.

"Call me Joe. Dispense with the formalities. Let's get on with it." Joe sat.

The imposing gentleman had a face that said mid-fifties, but the posture and musculature of a man in his prime. "Fine. We dispense with the formalities. Call me, Jules. We're on a first-name basis, just like old friends."

Joe slapped the palm of his hand on the leather-bound menu. "Look, don't make light with me, scumbag. For what you did to Pancho Morales, you should burn in Hell, starting tomorrow, as far as I'm concerned."

Julian Muller appeared amused. Perhaps he hadn't expected such a feisty prey. "Temper, temper, my friend. You'll need to keep a cool head. Trust me on that. I'm far more experienced than you in these matters. It's quite normal that you hate my guts. And I don't really care . . . unless you get elected, of course," he chuckled. "But that's the agenda for this evening's chat. But, please . . . relax. Order some food. It's some of the best in the city. And I know you have a taste for good red wine.

A bottle you could never afford is on its way."

Joe took the advice. He was here on a mission of discovery. There was nothing to gain by telling the man what any idiot would already know—that an adversarial relationship had been established for once and for all time. Joe opened the large leather-bound menu. It looked more like a reference book.

"Joe, before you get into that, I need for you to head into the men's room. Just a precaution. This is a private meeting, you understand. Just making sure you're not wired. Go ahead. My assistant is waiting for you in there. Don't worry, nothing's going to happen to you. At least not tonight."

Feeling the need to relieve himself anyway, Joe complied. He pushed open the men's room door and sure enough, the "assistant" was waiting. It felt like déjà vu. "Assistant?" That was the term Oscar the Colombian art dealer had used in referring to his bull-like assistant many years ago when they'd fenced the Nazi loot.

And now, was this the same character? He fixed his gaze on Joe as if they indeed had met before. The brawny figure was the spitting image, only a generation older, of that young bull. The stone face had not changed. The thick hair had simply turned gray. The shoulders and torso surely had been chiseled from the same chunk of granite.

And true to the vision, the "assistant" barely made a sound. Maybe, he called Joe by name, but it sounded more like a quiet grunt. He patted Joe down thoroughly. Even the firm hands felt like the ones that had frisked him that day in the truck yard. When the bull reached between the legs, Joe cringed. Wouldn't it be cute if someone walked in on us now, he thought.

Stone Face nodded to Joe that he was clean. Then he exited. Joe made a quick stop at the urinal before returning to Jules' table.

"Just like I promised. Routine drill," Jules stated, as Joe re-seated himself.

The wine had arrived and been left to decant. When the waiter noticed Joe's return, he came and poured him a glass. Jules raised his in toast.

"To our agreement."

Joe refused the gesture.

Jules shrugged and took a sip anyway. "Now that's what I call a gift from the gods. Perfect. Helps one to live forever."

Joe sat silent, perusing the menu. He figured that the food order was the gateway to the explanation, and he wanted to move the process along.

When the waiter returned they both were ready with their choices. The waiter took the orders and left them alone.

Julian Muller began, "Your friend wasn't supposed to die. Sure, they were gonna work him over a little, to make sure he got the message, and to make sure he delivered you the message. But, he lost his cool, he tried to fight back, all excited-like. Well, he was no match. His heart must've given out. He croaked on the spot. There was no choice then, but to make it into an accident."

"That's why he wasn't wearing a seat belt," Joe added.

"Hmm. Guess those guys must be slipping. Better have a talk. Good observation, my friend."

"Why did you involve him at all? I was the target."

"True enough. But no sense for us to take unnecessary risks. You're high-profile, well known in some circles, especially that pea-size state you live in. And Morales . . . we knew we could get to him outside the country. We found out about his Mexico routine, wasting his time with those street urchins at the orphanage."

"Pancho did more for the world in those few occasional trips to the orphanage, than parasites like you do in a lifetime. And that's even if you don't discount the harm you do."

"All right, all right. We're not getting into any philosophical discussions about each one's place in the world. Suffice it to say, we have a problem. And this problem can go away very easily."

"If I withdraw from the Senate race."

"Bingo."

"And if I don't? You send your goons after me."

"Well, they're not really *my* goons. They'd come after you, anyway. And your friend Pete in Washington. And maybe your families, like that hot-looking daughter of the deceased. Boy, I wouldn't mind crawling all over that for a night."

Joe tightened his hand on the wineglass ready to empty its contents in the man's face. But rationality descended like a straightjacket and gave him enough pause to probe rather than to provoke.

Muller smiled, almost tauntingly. "Don't waste the wine, Joe. Like I say, it's the best you'll have for a while."

The man must have seen Joe's hand twitch. Once again he was right. But not because the wine would be wasted—Joe's palate was desensitized, lost among other priorities, but because Joe needed to make the best use possible of this face-to-face audience.

Joe took a sip. "Okay, they're not *your* goons. But you can call them off. Is that what you're saying? If that's so, what do they have against all of us?"

"Come on, Joe. Make this easy. What do you, Morales, and Pete Donovan have in common?"

"I don't know. We were in the Peace Corps together. Maybe there was an angry brother or two, whose sisters we chased after."

"Very funny. Any of those brothers in the Nazi underground?"

Joe felt like he was smacked upside the head. Pete had forewarned him that the heist was not the ironclad secret they'd come to believe it was. But Joe still harbored hopes of diffusing the suspicion. But was it more than mere suspicion?

"Tell me something," Jules continued. "Did you really think amateurs like yourselves could've hoodwinked the Nazis so easily? Did you really think the stuff was unattended? They had one of their best operatives hovering around that loot. And if he had gotten to you characters you would've been food for the Orinoco river creatures. Lucky for you, I did know about it, so we could cover your sorry young asses. My men impersonated Venezuelan Federal Police the night of your coming-out party and diverted Mr. Gestapo off to Caracas."

"You must have us mixed up with someone else."

"When're you gonna stop wasting my time, Joe?" Jules sighed. "Guess if I were in your shoes, I'd keep trying, too. Keep planting doubt, keep obfuscating. But I was in Venezuela. We watched it all unfold. And, by the way, did my man in the men's room look familiar to you?"

The man was right again. It was a waste of time. "So what're you telling me? The Nazis now know? And they're ready to exact revenge? Unless you call them off? We don't have the money, you know. We gave it to a good purpose."

"Very admirable," he said sarcastically. "Glad we paved the way for you to do something to benefit the poor and the downtrodden . . . as if that were a concern."

"Well, what *was* your concern? And who the hell *were* you."

"That's all secondary. Suffice it to say, the nature of my role included the prevention of any international incidents. As for my operatives, well, they were a bit luckier. They saw a chance to make some profits. They were contract people, not on any government payroll at the time. Anyway, years later, the ex-Nazis and I, sometimes we had occasion to cross paths."

"Yeah, I can imagine. Let me guess. The governments favorable to them were the same ones favorable to your kind?"

"Right on, Professor. At the time, it would've been better for me had you guys not done the heist. But, once we detoured Mr. Gestapo from jamming a longshoreman's hook up your butts, we figured, 'what the hell?' Maybe my contract guys could make a few bucks off the deal, and they'd stay happy. Little did I know the secret would come in handy so many years later for yours truly."

"So if I don't renounce my candidacy, you tell the world I robbed a bunch of Nazis years ago to fund a Peace Corps program that might not have survived otherwise. This is supposed to cost me votes in Vermont? Are you sure Pancho's heart attack wasn't induced by laughter?"

"Nice try, again. I think you have a more accurate picture of what the consequences would be. Use your imagination." Jules' taunting smile disappeared into his stern gaze.

Jules savored a sip of wine, then continued, "Okay, let me give you a little chronology. It was the guys who worked for me who found your crooked art dealer in Colombia. There was a commission to be made, that's why they did it. And that's why the Colombians tried to get a discount at the last minute. Or so I was told."

Joe remembered how the buyers had tried to sneak away for two million dollars instead of the agreed upon two and a half.

"Anyway," he continued, "the so-called art dealers didn't know art from donkey turd. But they did know the value of the shipment—thanks to the information supplied from our end."

"They weren't art dealers?" Joe recalled his suspicions over how half-assed they had been in their scrutiny.

"Quite to the contrary, my friend. Oscar was a front for a fledgling drug cartel that needed capital to crank up its international operation. You know, getting cocaine onto U.S. streets so it could poison our kids. The fruit of your good works."

"Bullshit. Even if what you say is true, they would've gotten it here, anyway."

"What I say *is* true. And your assistance was indeed appreciated. Shall I go on? I'm enjoying this."

Joe could see that the man was reveling in the disillusionment being radiated by the blood churning in Joe's veins.

Joe gulped some wine. "I can hardly wait," he said.

"The Colombians paid you two and a half million. Then they ransomed the whole stash back to the Nazis for five million, which they didn't mind paying because, from what I was told, they collected four million on theft insurance through the Caracas bank that oversaw the shipment."

"You've gotta be shitting me. So the fucking Nazis got the stuff back? They lost only a million dollars."

"At first, more. Don't forget, my contract operatives were taking their bite, ten percent here, ten percent there. You know, setting up and brokering the deals. But the Nazis were stubborn about taking losses. So, they held on to the stuff a while longer. They let the trail get a little colder, let a few more victims die of old age so the stuff wouldn't be recognized or reclaimed. The works kept appreciating in value. They unloaded some of it in New York City, I hear. They made out, big-time."

"So, if everyone benefited, as you say, why are the Nazis out for revenge now? And besides, aren't they all a little old?"

"Pride, my friend, pride. You let people fuck with you, especially a group of do-gooder amateurs, and soon you won't command any respect. And no they're not too old. The old SS and Gestapo guys from World War II may be. But they never gave up on dreams of a Fourth Reich. They organized their offspring. Their grandchildren, even. They're still kicking around, believe me."

"What makes you so privy to all this information? And how do you know all these scumbag organizations?"

"It's what I do. And I'm quite good at it."

"And your so-called operatives, who were *they?*"

"You don't need to know that. Doesn't matter, anyway. They went off on their own after all these deals. They took their profits and multiplied them. They established and controlled the main drug-trafficking route through Venezuela. Got to hand it to them. No one even knew the stuff was coming through all those years. They owned the river routes right across Venezuela, along the Orinoco, up through the innumerable tributaries of the Orinoco's Delta Amacuro, and right out to the Atlantic.

"As for me, I left Venezuela soon after you did. They needed me down in Chile."

"The Allende overthrow?"

"We're getting off the subject."

"And you're not gonna divulge your clients?"

"What for? They're obviously quite powerful, and willing to go to extreme measures. Or they wouldn't have hired me."

"So your Nazi friends are awaiting some kind of go-ahead if I don't abort?"

"The man who was tailing you in Venezuela was named Heinrich Klaus, son of former SS henchman Jurgen Klausmeyer."

"Big name change," Joe interrupted. "Must've fooled everybody."

"He wanted to get the best of both worlds. A different legal name, but one that would still intimidate pain-in-the-ass informants. Klaus is now over sixty. At the time, he'd have fed you assholes to the anacondas around the Orinoco. Now, he's a commandant in the Nazi underground. He gives the orders."

Joe paused to digest what he was being told. Certainly, he wasn't having much luck digesting the food. "When do I give my answer? And how do I get in touch?"

"I'll get my answer the same time everyone else does. When you renounce your candidacy. Until you do, I'll take it to mean that you're proceeding. At peril to yourself. And to whomever.

As for getting in touch, there's no longer any need."

Joe stared around the room. He'd hardly touched the gourmet fish concoction he had ordered. Everyone else in the restaurant seemed to be relaxed and enjoying themselves. Couples, groups. Some looked like honeymooners, at least they seemed in the throes of romance. Maybe they were cheating spouses. Who knew? A few street vendors trickled in, selling flowers, usually roses. An occasional photographer offered to memorialize the occasion for couples exhibiting any degree of infatuation. Flashes from the cameras sparkled in the dimly lit ambience from time to time.

"Cheer up, Joe," Jules added, as he called for the check. "You can go on and live happily ever after. You just can't do it as a U.S. Senator. Hell, the public wouldn't want a founding member of a Colombian drug cartel, anyway. And that Orinoco trafficking route through Venezuela, it practically has your name on it. And you want to scale back drug enforcement? That's pretty inconsiderate of you. Every time they clamp down in Mexico, the Orinoco route benefits. Don't you see that? Hey, maybe I will get them to name it after you. What a great idea."

"Fuck you." Joe couldn't hold back any longer.

"Yeah, sure. Fuck me," he laughed. "I think you know better."

Julian Muller paid the waiter, leaving what appeared to be a generous tip. The stone-faced, bull-like figure appeared out of nowhere, slowly walking from the rear of the restaurant towards the main exit. He stopped halfway and looked back at the man Joe knew only as "Jules." When Jules nodded, the man continued through the main door. Would he be waiting outside? To accompany his boss? Or, to put an exclamation point on the warning to Joe?

"Don't worry." Jules noted the troubled look on Joe's observing face. "He's just going to get the limo. Unless I need him, of course. We have no further business this evening. Just remember all you've learned tonight. Chalk it up to wisdom. Maybe you'll get rid of that naive idealism. Finally."

"Gee, thanks. You mean now I can be like you? Yeah, this session has been a real character builder."

Jules was about to stand when he seemed to think of something to add. "You remember that watchman?"

"Huh?"

"The watchman who fucked up, the night you heisted the crates. He rests in peace in his Orinoco River grave. Died way too soon, don't you think? And the banker in Caracas who was in charge of the shipment. Disappeared. But luckily for his family, he reappeared, several years later. Minus his tongue and vocal chords. They didn't like how poorly the secret of the shipment had been kept. But they did go easy on him, thanks to his having had the good sense to take out theft insurance.

"Anyway, thought you might like to know how some of the innocent bystanders fared in all this. Seems like your initiatives had a spillover effect. Gee, I hope the poor and the downtrodden all benefited enough to compensate, to make up for the 'benefits' you brought about on behalf of so many others."

This time the man stood up to leave. "Remember you are now playing by Jules' Rules." He waved good-bye, and fast-stepped out the door.

Joe sat and absorbed all he'd been told, the final warning still ringing in his ears. "Jules' Rules." It was like having his own biography rewritten, like events being reinterpreted by a historian with deeper insights. And this revision was now the prevailing one, like the victor's version after a war is won. And it sure seemed like this war was won. And not by the good guys.

Joe wondered if it were possible to feel any worse. He finished the wine in his glass, more to stall than to taste. He exited the restaurant and headed for the cathedral once again. He strolled in front for fifteen minutes, then returned to the rental car. He wanted to go home.

Heading south on I-89, his mind reached back and cross referenced Jules' entire tale. It was all too believable. He could find no contradictions. Only more questions. Like what happened to El Tío. And more frighteningly, like what happened to Anita.

Chapter 30

The front door buzzer was being rung aggressively. It woke Joe up. He had been revisited by the dream, the one that leached into otherwise peaceful sleep at various times over the years. It was the element left hanging from his past, an element that he seldom dwelled upon when he was awake. There had always been the faceless pursuer zeroing in, getting closer and closer to discovering his secret. But now, for the first time, the pursuer's face was on the dream screen, and in vivid focus.

He peered at the clock radio where the red numerals indicated he had overslept. It was 11:15 a.m. He remembered tossing and turning until the wee hours. He must've lapsed into a deep sleep somewhere around daybreak.

"Be right there," he shouted out.

He felt the blood flow get jumpstarted as he shuffled to the street entrance of his house. Opening the door, he saw a young female of high school age. At least, it wasn't an assassin or leg breaker. Not yet, anyway.

"Yes, what can I do for you?"

She held out a large manila envelope. His imagination conjured up the possibility of a letter bomb. But that was before he noticed the name in the left-hand corner. He recognized the name of the photo shop.

"I was told to deliver these to a Mr. LaCarta," she said.

"Oh, thank you. Wait here." He was about to go for his wallet.

"No, it's all set. Everything's paid for."

"Well, how about something for you?" He felt obligated to give a tip for such door-to-door service.

She laughed. "I'd feel guilty taking anything. The man who sent them tipped me in advance. More than I make in a week." She turned and started towards a rust bucket of an old car.

"Who? Who's it from?"

"There's a note inside." She kept walking.

Joe walked towards the kitchen and started the coffeemaker before unsealing the envelope. He immediately recognized the color blow-up photos of his host from the previous evening in Montreal. The indelible image in his mind of the infamous Jules could now be forever reinforced by hard copy.

He unfolded the accompanying note. It read:

Joey,

Thought you'd want to hang on to the memories of your private dinner in Montreal. Have a good summer. Call anytime.

Love,
Cousin Sali

Joe was smiling from ear to ear. What a pleasant surprise. Sal and his crew *were* there, and they really *were* pros. He recalled how there had been flashes going off every so often. Someone must've sneaked a picture of Jules when he least expected it, like when he was riveting his stare on Joe's tortured face. Maybe he'd send cousin Sal that jug of maple syrup after all.

He poured a coffee and picked up the phone to call Pete. Before he'd punched in the full number, he hesitated. Shit, what if my house is bugged. Can't let Jules know what we're thinking. He hung it back up, and took the coffee to the bedroom where he quickly got dressed.

★ ★ ★ ★ ★

"Pedro, good morning. Or is it afternoon by now? Look, I'm calling from someone else's phone at the university. It dawned on me we could be bugged."

"Yeah, makes sense. We'd be smart to figure on it. How'd it go? You sound healthy."

"I am. Physically. Emotionally is another matter. Listen, I e-mailed you the number where I'm at. Get to another phone and call me, okay?"

Pete called back within fifteen minutes. "José, let's hear it, man. All the details."

Joe proceeded with a blow-by-blow description of how it all went down. He described Jules, the "assistant," the restaurant, everything. Most importantly, he retold the whole sordid chain of events centering around, and proceeding from, the legendary heist.

"Unbelievable. Unbelievable. Unbelievable." It seemed like Pete was stuck on the one word.

"Pedro, what do you think? CIA? This Jules character must've been CIA back in our Venezuela days."

"Makes the most sense. And the other operatives were probably Latinos. People who could blend in."

"Yeah, this Jules guy didn't strike me as a blender."

"Remember, the seventies were still the Cold War years. The Cuban Revolution was only a dozen or so years before. And there was guerilla activity in Venezuela."

"And Uncle Sam would've wanted to keep Venezuela safe for democracy, with all that oil, and all those minerals down where we were. So somebody must've just gotten wind of our plans . . . and the CIA took an interest. I dunno."

"Could've happened that way, José."

"You think El Tío blabbed once too often. Or was he CIA himself?"

"Don't kill yourself trying to figure it all out, José. This Jules revealed a lot, but I doubt if it was a hundred percent."

"Oh, I already know it was less than a hundred percent. He was evasive about who he represented. Except . . . except he harped on how relaxed drug enforcement would actually hurt some of the traffickers, like the ones with the Orinoco River route."

"You think the cartels hired him?"

"Could be. But why wouldn't they do their own dirty work? Why does he have to unleash the Nazis? After all these years."

"So what're you gonna do, José? Listen, don't bag it on my account whatever you do. I'll hire protection if I have to."

"It's a consideration, Pedro. My decision will have ramifications for not only you and me. Who knows how far they'd go. Marialena, maybe? They got Pancho, and he didn't even know I was running. At least, not yet."

"Take a day or two," Pete advised.

"I'm scheduled for a TV interview tomorrow. I'll take at least till then."

Joe paused to think, then added, "Pedro, I'm gonna send you Jules' photograph. He doesn't know we have it."

"Photograph? We?"

"Never mind for now, Pedro. You know how resourceful I always was," Joe kidded. "With your contacts in the Immigration Service, maybe with the Passport Office, see what you can find out."

"I'll do my best from this end, in Washington."

"Speaking of your end, did you check with the Peace Corps Office about Anita? Did she serve in Guatemala?"

"Yes, I checked. No, she didn't serve in Guatemala. Her Peace Corps service ended in Venezuela shortly after ours did. They didn't have an address for her. And I couldn't find anything here for an Ann Jeffries."

"Marvelous. That's real encouraging."

Chapter 31

If it weren't for the strands of gray throughout the close-cropped full head of hair, Terrell "T.J." Jackson might still pass for the professional athlete he once was. At six-feet four-inches tall, he bragged that his current weight was within five pounds of what it had been when he played wide receiver for the Washington Redskins half his lifetime ago.

Nagging injuries had cut his career short. Then he went to work as an FBI agent for twenty years before taking the teaching "gig," as he referred to it, in Criminal Justice at the University of Vermont. He lived alone in his lakefront condo through much of the year. He spent free time with his wife at their home in Alexandria, Virginia. Their kids were grown, so the long-distance marriage was manageable, enabling Mrs. Jackson to retain her teaching duties at Georgetown Law and escape the steamy D.C. summers in July and August.

"Well, look who's back from the west coast," T.J. greeted him at the door. "Come on in. When did you get back? Have a beer?"

"Been back all week. Been laying low. Yes, I'll have one of those Magic Hats."

"Why you been hiding?" T.J. went into the fridge and pulled out two bottles of his favorite micro brew. "Have a seat. Was just getting set to catch the Orioles game on TV, since they're playing in Boston."

"I make it a point not to waste time watching the Red Sox until August. If they're still in the race, then I'll watch. They've busted my balls too many times over the years," Joe explained.

"Judy Bennett told me you wanted to see me. But I thought that was tomorrow, at the TV station."

"Yeah, that's right. But what I have to see you about can't wait. Need your advice. Before tomorrow."

"Oh?" T.J. looked over at Joe, no doubt noticing his troubled expression.

"I thought about coming to you sooner. But . . . but some things needed to play out first. Anyway, let me begin at the beginning."

It was the first time he'd ever told the tale of the heist to anyone since they had done it. But he knew he could trust T.J. And besides, having an ex–FBI agent as such a close friend was on the positive side of the ledger. It was a card he'd have been foolish not to play.

"That's all pretty amazing, Joe. And I've heard a lot of shit in my time. . . . So, you guys robbed a bunch of South American Nazis. I never would've guessed that about you."

"Well, I never would've guessed that about me, either. All that beer and rum must've fried my brain cells."

"There's a certain beauty to it. Robbing Nazis to help the poorest of the poor. I can see where you'd be tempted. In fact, it's damn admirable, I'd say."

"But according to this Jules character, sounds like the Nazis were none the worse for it. They got the stuff back, and collected on the insurance besides."

"The important thing now, Joe, is what're we gonna do about it."

"I'm glad you said 'we,' T.J. That's reassuring. But I don't really want to drag you into harm's way. I just figured your advice, your take on it all, would be invaluable."

"I've been in harm's way before, my man. Listen, you got a guest room at your place, right? How about I move in for a few days. A little added reassurance for you. I'm still licensed to carry a piece."

"Are you sure? Shit, T.J., you got a wife, and grandkids."

"Stop trying to make me feel old. Maybe I could use a little excitement. Besides, these guys, whoever they are, the ones who want you out, *really* piss me off. The fact that they're fucking with an election, *really* pisses me off." The gritted expression on his face could evoke pity for anyone caught in the crosshairs of his wrath.

It was an offer only a fool would refuse. "When're you moving in?"

"Tonight. Dinner's on you."

Joe downed the remainder of the ale. "It's a deal. I'd better get going. Got to see about getting an alarm installed."

T.J. arrived at the house and noticed that Joe was already fumbling around the microwave, reheating some cartons of food. "What? Chinese take-out. Figured the least you could do was pasta with some good homemade marinara sauce."

"Hell, I don't have enough focus right now to boil the water," Joe replied. "Besides, we've got to eat and run. Can't talk here until I'm sure the place ain't bugged."

"I was gonna mention that."

They ate and ran. First to Ben and Jerry's where T.J. treated for dessert. Then to one of their preferred downtown watering holes on Church St. Being it was Saturday night, they were fortunate to get a free table.

"I've been mulling this over all day, since you left," T.J. began. "Tell me. Who might've found out about the heist, outside of those involved?"

"Only one guy that I know for sure. His name was Carlos Santiago. Hung out with us socially. A real party guy, and skirt chaser. He wasn't Venezuelan. He was from Mexico City.

Worked outside of town, mostly. Agriculture, animal husbandry, shit like that. He was affiliated with the University system. Why, you don't think . . . ?"

"CIA. Why not? Someone could hold a job and be on the CIA payroll. Or be on the CIA payroll in a job that was only a cover."

"Come to think of it, none of us ever actually saw Carlos at work. We never knew where he was off to. Shit, now you got me thinking. I thought the bastard was a legitimate friend. But you know, after we stole the shit, none of us ever saw him again. He just disappeared. Never even came to our *despedida,* you know our send-off party."

"How'd he find out? Did you tell him? And when?"

"Beforehand. I told him. I wanted his take on it. I even wanted him to be in on it—if we decided to go for it. I respected his opinions. In spite of his roguish social habits, he was pretty astute when it came to serious matters. The dude knew how to handle himself."

"Sounds like he'd be just the type. Just the type the CIA would want on its payroll."

"I don't know. What about the agreement where Peace Corps and CIA are supposed to be mutually exclusive? They wouldn't have had him hovering so close to us."

"Maybe they didn't do it on purpose. Maybe it just happened that way. You said you were friends socially. Surely, he wasn't there spying on you guys."

"No. If he were CIA, he'd be there to keep tabs on guerilla activity. Maybe the Communists. Hell, I even got to meet a few of the Communist organizers in the area."

"There you go. You and this what's his name, Carlos, simply traveled in the same circles, and you hand him the information on the Nazi loot. . . ."

"And he tells whoever it is he reports to at the embassy in

Caracas. Probably this Jules character."

"You would've made a good G-man, Professor LaCarta."

"Still, I think our imagination's getting the better of us."

"It's not about imagining. It's theorizing, reconstructing, analyzing," T.J. corrected. "Where can we find this Carlos?"

"Who the hell knows? Who knows if he's even alive? If I were to guess, I'd bet he went back to Mexico. He spoke of it as if it were Nirvana. His signature song was "Mexico Lindo," a real nostalgia piece. And Mexico's a big place. And I'd guess Carlos Santiago's a pretty common name."

"It'd be a start. What's his second last name?"

It was a good point. Spanish names included the mother's maiden name as a second last name. How could Joe forget? Carlos' second last name was Huerta, the same as one of Pancho Villa's adversaries. It had been a source of banter between Carlos and Pancho Morales.

"Carlos Santiago Huerta was his full name," Joe answered.

"Maybe that buddy of yours who works for Immigration can run a check. Have him contact our embassy in Mexico City. Meanwhile, I may have a source or two up my sleeve."

"While you're at it, you might want to check on a photo I have back at the house. It's of this Jules I met with in Montreal."

"Photo? How the hell did you pull that off?"

Joe wasn't ready to create a nexus between this ex–FBI agent friend and his lovable cousin, profession unknown, from Boston.

"Oh, I'd rather not get into that part. Let's just say that resourcefulness is one of my strong suits, the one that I was hoping would get me elected."

Despite staring at him skeptically, T.J. didn't pursue an explanation.

"So, where does that leave us?" Joe asked. "Suppose we are able to put some pieces together. Doesn't make the present situation any less dangerous. These guys don't strike me as patient. They're not gonna be waiting around for my answer. And I sure as shit don't want them delivering any more messages, like the one they delivered through Pancho."

"So what're you telling me, Joe? You gonna give in? You gonna just walk away and quit?"

"Well, my life hasn't exactly been misery, T.J. I could just go back to being Joe LaCarta again. Teach, write, maybe even get laid once in a while."

T.J.'s expression was somewhere between disappointment and disgust. "Don't these bastards piss you off enough to just want to . . . to just want to tell 'em to kiss your ass?"

"Easy for you to say, T.J. One of my old friends got croaked and I can't even tell his daughter why."

"Oh? Easy for me to say, eh? Don't give me that jive. You think I've never been threatened, or my family? Told to back down or back off? Look at the color of my skin, man. Check where I grew up. And where I've been. Shit, man. Threats were a way of life. You ever hear of Dr. King?" T.J. took an agitated sip off his beer.

"Look, don't get riled. Your point's well taken. But my political ambitions, or issues, are hardly at that level of societal importance."

"Oh, really? Are they really that different? Look, Joe, you're a legitimate candidate in what should be a fair election in a free society. And these dirtbags, whoever they are, are fucking with that. And to the point where they already murdered somebody. You want it that your friend died for nothing?"

Joe tapped his wineglass, then took a nervous sip. The pause in the conversation continued as Joe scanned the crowded room. T.J. looked up from his beer and fixed his gaze on Joe's wandering eyes. Joe was aware that the former athlete was waiting to hear if the pep talk had spurred any combativeness.

"I need more time," Joe finally said. "I need more time, but we also need to keep them at bay."

"You said they didn't strike you as the patient type. And they're obviously not."

"Tomorrow, on that TV show, I'll announce that I am *suspending* my candidacy. Then, I drop out of public view, and they'll think the campaign is over, done. Later, if I resume, for whatever reason, I explain that 'suspended' simply meant 'deferred.' What do you think?"

"I think you politicians all have a way with words." T.J. smiled. "But it could work. Could buy some time. And it could hold them off. At least until they interpret your meaning."

Chapter 32

He wanted her to know before he made it public. He owed her that much. He knew she'd be disappointed, probably more so than anyone, that he was about to "suspend" his candidacy.

"What the hell does that mean?" Judy Bennett asked.

"It means I want everyone to think it's over for now. But my choice of words means I can explain it later as 'having been on hold.' "

Joe didn't give her details. He explained there were personal reasons involved, reasons centering around potential blackmail. He needed to buy time. And he needed to count on her supporting this ambiguous position.

"Fucking beautiful," she added. "Finally, I get a crack at the top spot in a big-time campaign. And what do I do? I latch onto a guy with a past."

It must have been frustrating for her, he realized. Until now, Judy had run some local races, and had been a gopher in a few national and statewide runs. But it wasn't until she and Joe hooked up that she got elevated to the major leagues. If they were successful, her next stop could be a Presidential race.

"At least it's not a sex scandal, Judy. That means press interest may be minimized. They have been spoiled—the President has given them all the bimbo stuff they could ever want."

"How do I know it's not? Hell, Joe, you were lusting after that reporter from the Rutland newspaper, weren't you?"

"Judy, I'm divorced. Remember. Even if it were about sex,

I'm a free man, right?" By now the conversation was only half serious.

"They're calling you. It's time to go on. Good fucking luck." Judy only used vulgarities when she was clearly in a state of frustration.

Joe took his seat in the semicircle with four members of the local and statewide press. The live Sunday morning show began with the host introducing the panel and tossing the first question.

Not surprisingly, it was about candidate LaCarta's call for more creative strategies on the illegal drugs question. Soon after, the panel segued to some of Joe's other pet themes. Campaign finance reform, bipartisan cooperation, volunteerism, energy independence, cutting the national debt.

With less than five minutes of airtime left in the program, candidate LaCarta dropped the news. Viewers across Vermont were told his campaign was being suspended. Most would think that "suspended" meant "ended." That's what Joe hoped. But inevitably, there would be those who wanted to know why. And, of course, there'd be a few who wanted to know what "suspended" really meant.

Joe raced out of the studio as soon as time expired. The unprepared panel of reporters stayed seated to share their bewilderment with one another. Judy Bennett went home, dejectedly.

Chapter 33

"How bad did it look on TV," Joe asked T.J., who had stayed behind at Joe's house to get a viewer's perspective.

"Not great. But not really so bad, either. Hell, there's nothing to evaluate it against. How often are campaigns 'suspended' two weeks out of the gate?"

"Everybody's gonna think I'm some sort of flake. I better get used to it. All the more reason to lay low."

"Speaking of laying low, phone's been ringing off the hook. I let the machine take 'em all. There was one that might interest you, though. Senator Parker."

"She called? She must be in town. I should return that one."

Senator Elizabeth Parker Shannon was a moderate Republican who held the other Vermont Senate seat, the one not up for election. She was one of a growing number of senators growing frustrated with inertia and partisanship. She had told Joe that she was amazed at the number of diversions and digressions that had little consequence beyond media entertainment.

Joe had been personal friends with Senator Parker and her husband, Attorney Patrick Shannon, for about eight years. Elizabeth Parker possessed a charismatic personality and had become quite popular in Vermont. Her more hard-core colleagues in the Senate, however, felt an uneasiness towards her—she was seen as too conciliatory. Indeed, her name was even on bills co-sponsored by Democrats.

As a Republican, she could not endorse candidate LaCarta,

the Independent. However, her expected endorsement of Lester Bryant, a conservative Republican vying for the same seat, had become conspicuous in its absence. Joe LaCarta was more her cup of tea. They knew they could work quite well together, and that their collective efforts would promote constructive bipartisanship. And with a little luck, they could relegate hard-core do-nothings like Majority Leader Blake Ross to back-bench status.

It was not surprising that Senator Parker would expect some elaboration or amplification on this "suspension" move. Joe called her at the number she'd left on his machine. She was in the area, and invited Joe to come by her home in Essex Junction.

With T.J. driving, they arrived a half hour later. Both Elizabeth and Patrick were at the door to greet them.

"You remember my friend, Terrell Jackson," Joe began.

"Of course. We met at several University functions. How have you been?" She smiled gracefully.

Patrick shook his hand. "Don't want to make you feel old, Mr. Jackson, but I was quite a fan of yours in my high school days. I grew up in the D.C. area and followed the Redskins religiously."

"No, doesn't make me feel old. Makes me feel good. Someone remembers—I had a short career, you know. Tell me, how is it you stay up here, and Senator Parker, the native Vermonter now works in Washington," T.J. kidded.

"That's why she can get elected and I could never," he laughed as they moved into the living room to sit. "Joe here looked like one of the few who'd overcome the outsider status. And how long have you been here, Joe, twenty years?"

"What do you mean?" Joe said, smiling. "I am a native. Born in Rutland. Of course, I lived there all of about eight months before my family moved back to western Massachusetts."

"In that case, you have maple syrup in your veins," Senator Parker added. A porcelain tea kettle rested on a tray on the coffee table in the center of the room. She took it and poured four cups and invited them to help themselves to the *biscotti* piled on a nearby serving dish.

Then she moved beyond the amenities. "So, Joe, what gives? Here I am enjoying a relaxing weekend at home. I turn on the TV to hear candidate LaCarta once again talk about his creative ideas and his practical approaches, and very articulately, I might add. And then at the end, just as I'm contemplating your soon-to-be arrival on Capitol Hill, I hear a bomb go off. And my ears are still ringing."

"I'm sorry, Betty. I should've alerted you that I was going to do this," Joe lied. "But it came up all of a sudden. It's very personal, and I can't get into the details."

Her expression had suspicion written all over it. With the President's celebrated dalliances, sex scandals were the first thing that came to everyone's mind. Maybe she imagined Professor LaCarta having a tryst with one of his students.

"Don't worry, Betty. It's nothing to do with a young babe. Nothing like that. Nothing of interest to the media."

"You hope. They'll pry and speculate, of course."

"I'm gonna lay low."

"If you don't talk, they'll just speculate all the more."

"I appreciate your concern, Betty. But I just gotta do this for now."

"For now? You mean this is a temporary state of affairs?"

"I chose my words carefully, Betty. But, please, I'd appreciate it if you don't even hint of that possibility to anyone. There're reasons why it must look like I'm out, period."

"Well, this should make some of those regressive old farts on the Hill pretty happy," she sighed.

"Will they be that obvious in their glee?"

"They'll try to disguise it. You know about Blake Ross and his little circle of obstructionists. Now they'll be hopeful that lamebrain Bryant will get elected."

"Gee, that's not a very nice way to speak about a fellow Republican."

"Yeah, well . . . it's just that the idea of another do-nothing bootlicker. . . . There'll be glaciers in the Amazon before Bryant and I collaborate successfully on anything."

"C'mon now, Betty. You mustn't lose your can-do attitude. Regardless of what happens."

"Don't worry. I won't. I stay just pissed off enough to keep at it. But Ross seems to be preventing any legislative action on anything. He keeps licking his chops at every new revelation in the President's sex scandal. Of course, he'd be the first to sweep it away if it were a political ally instead of a Democrat."

Joe chuckled. "Why is it that Democrats always screw around with women who need book deals? That's why they get caught."

She smiled, too, getting beyond her frustration. "And Republicans have their affairs with the country club set, is that it? They already have money."

They spent another half hour with small talk. Then Joe and T.J. nodded to each other.

"We should get going, let you two enjoy the remainder of the weekend," Joe said, as he and T.J. stood up and stretched their middle-aged spines. Senator Parker and Patrick accompanied them to the door.

"Betty, I want to tell you it's meant a lot to me to have your moral support. This state is lucky to have someone like you representing us. It'll be a source of permanent regret if I never get to join you on Capitol Hill. So . . . let's see what develops."

"Just do me one favor. If I get stuck having to host a visit for Ross when he comes here this summer to stump for Bryant, sneak up behind him and pour a cold Long Trail Ale over his perfectly coiffured head."

"It's a deal. But only if I don't get back in the race."

CHAPTER 34

Washington, D.C.

The Monday morning call was put through to Senate Majority Leader Blake Ross.

"What're you calling me for? I can read. He's out. History."

"Is that how you interpret it, Blake? I mean, Senator." Julian "Jules' Rules" Muller was in his usual feisty form. "Have you looked up the definition of 'suspended' lately?"

"Don't talk to me about mincing words."

"The bastard is buying time. 'Suspended,' 'deferred.' Sounds to me he can jump back in at any time."

"Hey, if he's on the sidelines, they won't vote for him."

"Then I better make sure he stays on the sidelines. Let's see, what can I do next?" Muller teased.

"Mr. Muller, I believe we're finished here. I am quite confident that Joseph LaCarta will live happily ever after, teaching Political Science at the University of Vermont." Ross hung up the phone.

Rutland, Vermont

The Following Day

As instructed, Vicki Rivier drove down to Rutland to meet with her managing editor, Jack Epstein. He had told her it could not wait.

Upon arriving at the main office of the *Rutland Free Press,* she checked her desk. Not much clutter. In this age of computers and faxes, she could spend most of the time working from her home in Middlebury, halfway between Rutland and her primary beat in Burlington. It was convenient, as well as time efficient, especially now that she had been assigned to profile Senate candidate Joseph LaCarta.

She proceeded into Epstein's private office. "Hi, Jack. What's up?"

"Here, look at these. Looks like we discovered LaCarta's 'personal reasons.' "

Vicki thumbed through the pack of color photographs. Each one showed Joe LaCarta with a dark haired beauty less than half his age. In several, they were dancing together. In several others, they were conversing over what appeared to be margaritas. In another, they were dining together. The last two photos showed LaCarta accompanying the young lady through the front door of a home, once apparently exiting, once apparently entering.

"Who sent them?" She was trying to hide her disappointment. She had come to be intrigued by the popular candidate. Sure, she maintained her objectivity, but she couldn't help liking what he'd been saying. Also, she found him appealing in other ways, and was well aware that he was divorced. But she never figured him to be the type to exploit his celebrity on women young enough to be his students. No, she had figured him to be of more substance than that, a man who didn't need that kind of trophy. She found herself bracing against a tide of disillusionment.

"Don't know," Epstein responded, handing her the accompanying note. "Postmarked from Burlington. Yesterday."

The note read:

Good riddance to another adolescent,

From,
A Disgusted Citizen

"Do we know if she's his bimbo?"

"Looks that way. But, no, we don't know. That's why I called you down here. Drop everything else and find out. You can bet we're not the only paper who got copies of these prints. So, we've got to be ready to go to press tomorrow. Because the others sure as hell will."

"What if there's some sort of explanation?" she asked quietly. "What if it's just some typical scandal-mongering? You know how things have gotten."

"Any answers you get make it into print tomorrow morning, Vicki. If there're no answers, then I have no choice but to print the questions. We can't afford to get beaten on this. Time's a-wasting. Good luck. And happy hunting."

Chapter 35

Washington, D.C.

"I'd better call Judy Bennett, just in case she's left holding the bag on something. I'd feel guilty," Joe explained to Pete Donovan.

It had been a spur of the moment thing. But he and T.J. had determined that a trip to the nation's capital, with its myriad government agencies, might render some research benefits. Since Joe wanted to be incommunicado, it would kill two birds with one stone. Same for T.J., who used it as a chance to stay with his wife in Alexandria, Virginia. Joe was staying with Pete. They planned to get an early start the following morning.

"Joe, where the hell are you?" Judy Bennett's agitation practically shook the receiver on Joe's end.

"D.C. Making some inquiries. Why? What's the big deal?"

"The big deal is that there's someone else making inquiries. Vicki Rivier from the Rutland newspaper. You know the one that turns you on. Gee, I'm surprised you even give her a second look, she's probably over forty."

"I'm afraid I'm not following, Judy. What does she want? She still after that biographical piece?"

"I think the puff piece is on hold, Joe. She's been trying to get some answers all afternoon about some photos. Photos of you with some voluptuous babe less than half your age, dining and dancing somewhere out of town. And, quite frankly, I think I'm entitled to the same answers myself."

It didn't take a computer model to piece it all together. Joe's mind processed everything quickly enough. Evidently, his situation was keeping more than one amateur photographer busy. Or maybe not so amateur. Certainly, he hadn't noticed anyone watching Marialena and himself that night in Northampton, Massachusetts.

Joe took a deep breath. "The young woman in question? I assume she had long dark hair, very Latin-looking?"

"Yes, Joe. Just like in your fantasies. Is she it, Joe? Is she your 'personal reasons'? Are the photos the blackmail you were worried about?"

"Fuck, no, Judy. This is bullshit. Harmless as hell. That's Marialena, the daughter of my friend who died. San Diego, two weeks ago, remember? We traveled together. I stayed at her place in Northampton one night on the return trip—I had to head to Boston for a wedding the next day."

"What were you doing dancing? Thought you were supposed to be mourning?"

"I don't know. It was her idea. It was supposed to be therapeutic, I guess. And you know something? It was.

"Look, Judy," Joe added. "She's more like a niece. I can't help it if she's a knockout."

"Weren't you worried about being seen? Massachusetts isn't exactly in another solar system."

"Didn't even cross my mind. If it weren't totally harmless, then it might've entered my mind. And again, let's not lose sight of the fact that I'm no longer married. I am a free agent."

"I'm well aware of that." Judy sometimes gave off hints that if she weren't married herself, she might have tampered with Joe's free agentry.

"So I better call this Vicki Rivier right now."

"I would say. And you better hurry. Her deadline for the

morning paper is fast approaching." Judy gave him the phone number.

"Ms. Rivier, this is Joe LaCarta. I understand you've been trying to reach me all day." He maintained decorum despite the outrage over the dirty-tricks tactic. He had reminded himself beforehand that it wasn't the reporter's fault, that she was merely doing her job. And he knew how critical it was to be personable with reporters who had yet to draw conclusions.

"Mr. LaCarta, thanks for calling. I'd almost given up trying to get a statement from you. In fact, I'm minutes away from e-mailing the story down to the Rutland office. I work out of my house," she explained.

"I kind of gathered that. I noticed it was a Middlebury phone number. Look, this is one colossal mistake."

He went on to explain the whole San Diego trip in detail. He told her who Marialena was, and why he spent the night in Massachusetts.

"And the young lady?" she asked. "She'll corroborate your story?"

"Can't we leave her out of it?"

"I'm afraid she's not being left out of it, Mr. LaCarta. We have every reason to suspect we're not the only news organization to receive those prints. Wouldn't it be to both your advantage to have your side of the story in at least one publication?"

Another troubling prospect. The story would run unchecked in how many other newspapers the following morning? What a mess. And this was just a sampling of Jules' Rules, as his arrogant Montreal host had boasted.

"I guess you're right, Ms. Rivier. And thank you for your sense of fairness. Hold the presses. Let me call the young lady.

To explain, and to clear it with her. Hope she's home."

"José, what a pleasant surprise. So nice to hear from you."

"Marialena, thank God you're home. First of all, how're you doing?"

"I'm doing okay. Really. Still think about Pa, and not being around when he died, but, bottom line is I'm fine."

"Marialena, I hate to bother you with this, but I don't have much time."

Joe explained it as an aberration, maybe some nut with an ax to grind. He didn't get into the Jules' Rules factor; he wasn't ready for that yet. He'd let the guilt of what happened to her father continue to be pent up inside, at least for a while longer.

"Gee, these reporters must have bimbo on the brain," she remarked. "Sure, Joe, I'd be happy to call and straighten it out. It's a simple matter of telling the truth."

"Exactly. Simply tell it like it was, and the two stories will corroborate. Listen, I'd better leave you to make the call. In the meantime, Marialena, you be careful. I don't know who it was around Northampton that shot the photos. But I think you should check in with the local police after the stories hit the papers. Have them check by your house from time to time."

Joe was explaining "photogate" to Pete when the call came.

"Mr. LaCarta, I spoke with Marialena," Vicki Rivier said.

"She gave you her name?"

"Unabashedly. But I won't use it. I think the decent thing to do is to keep her unnamed. The story's about you. She faxed me a copy of her father's obituary; her account is the same as yours. Your explanation will make it into our morning edition. I barely made the deadline."

"Thank God. There'll be at least one accurate report out there tomorrow morning."

"She's quite a self-assured young lady. She didn't mind adding. . . ."

"Adding? Adding what?"

"Well, she said she did like older men and that if you weren't quite so old, and if you weren't her father's friend. . . ."

"Please stop right there."

"So, why are you in Washington, may I ask? That's ironic, isn't it? You bag your candidacy, but you go directly to the Capitol anyway?"

"Just getting away from it all for a while. Staying with an old friend for a few days. Male friend."

"Mr. LaCarta, I shouldn't compromise my objectivity, but I tend to believe yours and Marialena's explanation of the photos. What is undeniable, however, is the fact that those photos being circulated is a story unto itself. Do you have any theories?"

He had had enough for one day. But he couldn't blow his cool at this point. The last thing he needed was to have the press triggering some sort of response from Jules and the Nazi dogs he held on a leash.

"I haven't a clue, Ms. Rivier. Surely, every candidate must have someone who hates his guts, someone just waiting to find something they can use. At least it wasn't an assassination attempt."

"We'll talk again soon, Mr. LaCarta."

Chapter 36

"Nice of you to show up," Joe taunted T.J., the last one to arrive for the breakfast meeting. It was shaping up as a beautiful May morning. Springtime in its glory almost erased the tensions.

"Mind if I spend some time with my wife?" he shot back.

"Didn't think it mattered to guys your age."

"Anytime you want to try and keep up, my friend, let me know," T.J. held out his hand to Pete. They'd never formally met.

"You broke my heart more than a few times, T.J. I was a Giants fan those years when you were burning them with touchdown catches," Pete began.

"Well, it wasn't for very long. I was out of the NFL before I was twenty-seven. But I gotta admit, doing it to your Giants gave me special satisfaction. They'd led me to believe they were gonna draft me in the first round. But they passed. Then the 'Skins took me in the second. Cost me some of that big-time bonus money. Seems like a century ago."

"If they'd paid then like now, you wouldn't have had to find a second career," Pete noted, referring to T.J.'s twenty-year stint with the FBI.

"Ain't that the truth? But then again, I wouldn't be here now having all this fun."

"Speaking of fun. . . ." Joe went on to update T.J. about the photos and about the newspaper coverage.

"So they were tailing you even before the Montreal meeting,"

T.J. concluded. "Obviously, this isn't a low-budget operation. Funny, I thought they'd come at you with that drug cartel shit first. I thought that'd be the logical forewarning."

"I don't know," Joe said. "The drug cartel might have trouble fielding a credible spokesperson. Too easy to refute. At least with the young babe story, they had photos to spread around."

"Still, I wouldn't discount it. Could be next in their repertoire. Why would they risk harming somebody if they could just ruin your reputation instead?" T.J. reasoned.

"Because they already did," Joe reminded him. "They already did harm somebody. Pancho. Maybe they've already conceded that the phony scandals wouldn't be enough, that I could handle a few jabs. The threat of harm, that's the trump card, the knockout punch."

"Not bad. You reasoned all that out by yourself?" T.J. remarked.

"You think a guy has to have FBI training to have an analytical mind? So, where you off to today, T.J.?"

"Gonna check in with an old friend at the Bureau. I'm trying to remember if he owes me any favors. Hell, I may need my old job back the way I'm taking time off from the University to come here."

"I'll vouch for you," Joe said. "Who knows, maybe you'll get a book deal—'retired FBI agent saves Senator LaCarta from the villains in his past.' "

After breakfast, T.J. parted for the Hoover Building, FBI headquarters. Joe accompanied Pete to his office at the Immigration and Naturalization Service, the INS.

Immediately on arrival, Joe called Judy Bennett. "How bad?"

"Could be worse," Judy answered. "Lucky you caught Vicki Rivier before deadline. Her story gives your account in full, and mentions that it had been corroborated by the unnamed young woman. In fact, the article concludes that someone may be setting you up. She used a couple of the photos, but the captions reflected your explanations. Pretty favorable all in all. And, they put it on the front page above the fold."

"Not bad. And what about the others, the other papers?"

"Believe it or not, only one of the two Burlington area papers covered it at all. The *Herald* told me that they needed specificity in the sourcing of the photos. Not so with the *Patriot,* however. They're so conservative that they'd probably be outraged if the woman were your own age and were to be your fiancée as well. They're supporting Bryant, anyway. They'd love to put you away once and for all. They used the photo of you dancing. Big surprise, eh?"

"Fortunately, it's the lesser paper in the Burlington area. Most of their readers wouldn't vote for me anyway."

"They must've passed on the story in Brattleboro. Or, they didn't get the photos. The Bennington paper printed it, but portrayed it as a rumor. They used the photo of you having dinner together. Same with the Montpelier paper."

"And what about our friends in the Hub?" He was referring to possible coverage in the regional sections of the Boston papers.

"As far as I can tell, only the *Tribune* carried it. Back pages. But three small photos. Dinner, dancing, and one on the front porch of what must be her apartment house."

"Figures. I had a bad feeling about their editors, anyway. They're not too big on me or on reforming drug policies. Their idea is that the military should surround our borders and coastlines.

"Judy, fax me the Vicki Rivier article. And the *Patriot* and the *Tribune* articles for now. No hurry on the others."

The faxes arrived in priority order. Joe read the three he'd requested as they slithered through the machine. He didn't wait for the rest. Pete could hold them for later.

Joe started heading for the hallway. "I'll catch you later this afternoon, Pedro. Happy hunting."

"Where're you going?" Pete called after him.

"Capitol Hill."

Chapter 37

"Terrell Jackson here to see Dr. Drake," T.J. announced himself at the reception desk outside his friend's private office at FBI headquarters.

Dr. Lucas Drake was not only a friend, but had been T.J.'s boss at the time of his retirement. Before that, Drake had been somewhat of a mentor. About the same age as T.J., Drake nonetheless preceded him at the Bureau during those years that T.J. had made a living on the gridiron. Drake had been one of the earlier African-American agents recruited by the Bureau, and in turn helped recruit the young Terrell Jackson after his NFL playing days were over. They became fast friends as Drake took the ex-jock under his wing.

Drake didn't keep T.J. waiting. He burst out of the back office with a wide smile and extended his hand. "Welcome home, my man. You here for your old job back? Got an opening for an undercover guy. On a senior citizens scam."

"Hell, no. I'm holding out for a naked pole dancer scam," T.J. kidded back as he followed Drake into the privacy of his office, after a long handshake.

"So how's that teaching job? Bored yet?"

"No way, Doc. It's great not having to track down slime for a living. I told 'em to hold a position for you."

Drake not only had a law degree, but he'd also achieved a Ph.D. in forensic science.

"Not me, man. Too damn cold up there. I'll do a summer

course, maybe. So, what're you doing here? Isn't school still in session? Or, are you missin' the old lady?"

"Yes and yes. But I'm *here* because I need some help."

"Yeah, figured it wasn't a social call, since you came to the office instead of the house."

"I've been co-opted to do some private investigatory work. And I thought you might welcome your former star agent with open arms."

"Let's hear it, T.J. You probably already have a sense of what I can help with and what I can't. But I suppose you're figuring I'll stretch those boundaries in your favor, given that you were such a star agent, as you so humbly recall."

Smiling briefly from ear to ear, T.J. began, "I'm trying to prevent a crime. A little information might serve that purpose. I'm trying to locate some people. Maybe you could run a check with some subordinates, maybe fire up the computers. If we can get to the bottom of it, might save you guys some work later."

"Oh? And it's not something we should know about *now?*"

"Doc, to be honest, I'm out on a limb on this one. If I could trust everyone the way I trust you, maybe I could present a broader picture. But until I can find out what we're dealing with, I think I'm going at the proper pace. If we can find these few people, it should illuminate the roadway somewhat."

"Who's the 'we' you keep referring to? Anything to do with that guy you told me you were supporting for Senate? You know, the one who's incorporating some of my ideas on drug policy reform?"

Drake had a good memory. Indeed, T.J. had picked Dr. Drake's brain back when Joe was first researching, and first brainstorming ideas, on the drug issue. It had proved quite valuable.

"Can't say, Doc. But you're as sharp as ever."

"Tampering with elections, T.J., would be a serious matter."

Drake paused, but T.J. didn't lead him any further. "All right, let's have the names."

"There's a Carlos Santiago Huerta. Mid-fifties. Mexican, we think. Probably still lives there. There's a Heinrich Klaus, early-to mid-sixties. German born. Probably lives in South America somewhere. Unless he's fictional, he may have ties to the Nazi underground."

"What Nazi underground?" Drake interrupted. "Haven't heard from them in years."

"I wonder why," T.J. answered sarcastically. "CIA probably recruited them all during the Cold War."

"Only those two?"

"No, there's one more. But we only have an alias, 'Jules Jones.' Here's a picture, present-day edition. This guy's American, could be living anywhere. Might've been CIA at one time."

"Got any easy ones?" Drake chided. "Anyone living along the Potomac, for example?"

"If they were easy, I would've brought in the local computer hack."

"See what I can do, T.J. But you know the drill. Can't tell you what I can't tell you."

"Yeah, I understand. And I'm confident that you'll make a fair interpretation of the word 'can't.' "

"You've been hanging with too many politicians. So, when are you gonna make a social call. The wives would like to see each other, I'm sure."

"Count on it, Doc. Love to have you see Lake Champlain this summer."

Chapter 38

"I'm afraid you just missed her," the receptionist in Senator Elizabeth Parker's senatorial office informed Joe. She gazed at him like she should know him from somewhere, as if she were deciding whether it was in a positive or negative context.

Seeing this, Joe added, "I'm a friend from Vermont. Until two days ago, I was running for the other Senate seat."

"Oh, yes, of course. I heard the senator mention your name this morning. You missed her by a couple of minutes. You might even be able to catch her in the hallway if you hurry." She pointed Joe in the right direction.

Joe walked briskly down the corridor in the opposite direction from whence he'd come. At the far end he noticed a woman who could be Senator Parker having a conversation with a well-dressed man. Seeing that the conversation was about to end, he quickened his pace. As she pulled away, Joe recognized her for certain.

"Betty," he called out. When he called her name a second time she turned and focused.

"Well, if it isn't. What brings *you* here? Chaperoning a high school bus trip?" Was she disgusted or just poking fun?

Joe caught his breath as he caught up. "So you've read the morning papers, I take it?"

"Get them every morning. By fax or on-line. You didn't answer my question."

"I'm sure you have a lot of questions. That's why I'm here. I felt I owed you an explanation, especially since I told you Sunday there was no bimbo factor."

"You came down here for that? You could've called."

"No. No, I was already in Washington. Flew down yesterday afternoon. Didn't find out about those photos until late last night. That's why only one paper has my account."

"Yeah, I noticed. Vicki Rivier's report. She's very fair. Very thorough. The best reporter in the state for my money. Your explanation seemed pretty plausible."

"Then you believe me?"

"Yes. I figure if it were true, you're smart enough to have been more careful," she laughed. "But who provided the photos? Didn't realize you had enemies that serious."

"Probably some crank."

"Anything to do with why you've suspended your campaign?"

"Hell, Betty, you sound like one of the reporters. Give me some space."

"Come on, walk with me, Joe. I'm on my way to see his highness, Blake Ross. Shouldn't take long. He'll politely tell me why they can't move some of my bills, and I'll be out of there. Maybe we can grab some lunch."

They strolled along the corridor, then took an elevator to the top floor where they entered the suite of the Majority Leader from South Carolina. It was elegantly appointed. Joe didn't know much about furniture, but he guessed it to have an antebellum South motif. He wondered if Ross sported a Confederate flag in his back office.

A number of staff aides kept busy in a side room open to the reception area. Some appeared to have a phone receiver attached to their heads. Others opened mail, while a few well-dressed young twenty-somethings pounded away on computer keyboards.

The largest wall in the reception area was covered with

photographs. "Behold the 'wall of fame,' " Senator Parker said softly as they waited for Ross. "Wall of *shame,*" she then whispered out of the side of her mouth.

Blake Ross emerged from his private sanctuary and greeted Senator Parker with an affable smile. She introduced Joe.

"Oh, yes. I've seen you on TV a number of times. Read some of your stuff. Very interesting. You're running for the other Senate seat in Vermont?" Ross asked innocently.

"The pleasure is mine, Senator. I've always admired your leadership and dedication." The mutual insincerity could've filled the Capitol Rotunda.

"Joe is not a candidate at the moment," Senator Parker added, as if she believed Ross hadn't already known and been privately gloating.

"I'm sorry to hear that," Ross said.

"Personal reasons," Joe added, shrugging his shoulders.

"Yes, I can understand. It's a large commitment. Politics can really undermine your private life. Sorry we won't have you around here. Although, I'm sure there's little you and I would agree on, based on what I know."

Joe was pleasantly surprised by this glimpse of honesty. "Oh, you'd never know. As an Independent, I reject a lot of so-called liberal positions, too."

Ross and Parker started to head for the back office. Ross shook Joe's hand again and said, "Hope we meet again in the future."

"Likewise," Joe agreed, determined that his own idea of "future" would be far more optimistic than Senator Ross'.

Joe walked over to the aforementioned wall of fame. Showing an appearance of interest couldn't hurt. The recent photos were the usual standard fare. Ross with several recent presidents, Ross with a visiting world leader or two, Ross being honored by one conservative group or other. Pretty boring stuff, Joe thought.

Joe decided that Ross' early years might be more interesting. How did someone who did so little become so powerful? Joe slid towards the corner where some older photos seemed to be clustered, and began to scan for faces from the past. President Nixon. Henry Kissinger, maybe.

Sure enough, some of the heavy hitters from that era were indeed included. But there were so many faces that were not big newsmakers. As that fact occurred to him, one face grabbed his attention like a head-on collision.

Mouth agape, he pulled the folded photocopy he'd made from one of cousin Sal's color blowups from his pocket. A match? Was it a match? A match made across twenty-odd years? The man in the wall photo had the exact same facial features, the same smirking expression. Even the same athletic build. The man in Montreal was in such great shape that he couldn't have looked much different as a young man.

And there he was. In a photo with a young Senator Ross and several others. The caption read *Senate Intelligence Committee, 1976.* Joe focused on the face until his eyes tired. Shuffling his feet, he continued to scan some others until once again he saw the face. Still no name. But he and Senator Ross were standing with someone Joe surely did recognize. And the caption was confirming: *Delegation to Santiago, Chile, 1976* The man in the center was none other than General Augusto Pinochet, President and supreme ruler of Chile after the overthrow of Salvador Allende in 1973.

Joe and his co-investigators had already pretty much figured that the author of Jules' Rules had been a CIA man at one time. But to have had contacts at such high levels. Senators, heads of state?

The circuitry in Joe's brain was as engaged as the computers in the adjoining room when Senator Parker emerged from the brief conference, rolling her eyeballs for Joe to notice. "Entertaining?" she asked, referring to the photo display.

"More than you could imagine." He didn't elaborate.

They exited to the hallway together. Should he have asked a staff member about the man's identity? Maybe. But maybe not. Would it have triggered suspicion? Would such an inquiry get back to Jules himself?

"You seem distracted, Joe. What happened? Did you see a ghost in one of those photos?" she chided, not knowing how close to the bull's-eye she was with her observation.

"Yeah, the ghost of candidacy past. Listen, Betty, you don't think Ross would actively try to prevent my candidacy, do you?"

"I can't see Ross a*ctively* doing anything. Why? What're you driving at? Sounded like he didn't even know you were out until I mentioned it. Granted, he was threatened by the prospect of having you in the Senate. He is supporting Bryant with all the clout he can give. Your being out, and Bryant now with a strong chance of getting in, he sees it as another opportunity to fortify his power base."

"And that sticks in your craw more than it does mine?"

"Yes, it does. I didn't spend my life trying to get here, only to be put on hold every session. Joe, if there's anything I can do to help get you back in, let me know. Whatever. It has to be behind the scenes, though."

Joe smiled. "Whatever," "Behind the scenes." Where had he heard that before?

After lunch Joe began a leisurely stroll back to Pete's office. It had become a delicious spring day, as warm as a summer day back in Vermont. Whenever a light breeze kicked up, pedestrians were treated to the sweet smell of flowers in bloom. Joe was in no hurry. The walk and the fresh air were cleansing some of the cobwebs in his head.

Could the connection between Ross and this Jules lead

somewhere? Certainly, it could lead to a name, a true identity for the puppeteer seemingly holding the strings. Joe came upon an inviting patch of grass between some buildings, where several others were absorbing sunrays before returning to work.

Stopping his stride, he plunked himself down on the edge, just off the sidewalk. The momentary relaxation was a welcome respite. The street activity provided a distraction, but he kept returning to the mental exercise of trying to connect the dots.

That's when he noticed the young man in jogging attire standing by the curb near a street sign. The shorts and tee shirt were dry. Maybe, he was awaiting a running companion. Or maybe he had stopped to mull around after Joe had sat. It was worth trying to find out for sure.

Joe stood and resumed his walk, varying his pace and discreetly peering over his shoulder every so often. After several subtle look-backs, he caught sight of the jogger maintaining a comfortable distance. Why was that so surprising? he thought to himself. It can't be the first time he'd been tailed. After all, they'd shot the photos of Marialena and himself.

But the idea that they now knew he was in Washington was troubling. They would figure this was a fact-finding mission. They would notice that he trekked up to Capitol Hill, that he was hovering around Pete at INS. And God forbid, they might have noted T.J.'s little excursion to the Hoover Building.

He gritted his teeth trying to ward off the feeling of being overmatched. There was little doubt. He and his fellow detectives would have to rally against a tightening time clock.

Chapter 39

"My compliments," T.J. said to Joe, gesturing to the strand of smoke ascending skyward from the large cigar Joe had given him.

"Nice touch, José. Where'd you get them?" Pete asked.

"Some shop I walked by. Needed to stop a time or two to figure out if that jogger dude was still following. They're Arturo Fuente's Doble Chateau."

"Hope none of the passers-by bitch about the cloud of smoke," Pete said.

"Fuck 'em," Joe answered. "Honest Abe over there freed the slaves." They were seated on a bench in the shadow of the Lincoln Memorial. It was a prearranged meeting.

"Nice talk," Pete kidded. "With that attitude, the antismoking Nazis won't be voting for you."

"So happens I'm only worried about real Nazis."

"Okay, what've we got," T.J. began, seemingly taking the chairman role. "We all know about the jogger and Joe's coming across the photos in Blake Ross' office.

"My man at the Bureau came up with some good shit," T.J. continued. "A man fitting the description of your buddy Carlos Santiago Huerta is living in Mexico City. As for Mr. Gestapo, he gave me a Heinrich Klaus, living outside of Santiago, Chile. Early-to mid-sixties.

"As for the man in your color photo, my friend Dr. Drake said, quote, 'there is no available information on him.' "

"Which means?" Joe asked.

"Which could mean anything," T.J. answered. "Could mean there's nothing at all. Could mean there's nothing that can be given out. Now, if you're sure about this match with the photo you saw in Ross' office, the guy maybe is, or was, a government operative of some kind. Possibly known to the FBI. And very possibly, there's an overriding reason why Drake couldn't tell me anything."

Joe sighed, and turned towards Pete, who was nodding.

"No luck, either, on the photo," Pete reported. "Scanned it into the computers, maybe to see if there was a link to a U.S. passport photo. No luck. But some such information is blocked."

"Which means?" Joe asked again.

"Similar to what T.J. just explained," Pete said. "Might not exist. If it does, might not be accessible."

"Shit, who the hell is this guy, the phantom of the opera?" Joe felt a little frustrated. He figured Jules had to be American. And if the FBI and INS were buffering his true identity, this was not a good sign.

"It's not all bad, José," Pete added. "My other information confirms what T.J. picked up at the FBI. Not only that, I called a phone number for Señor Carlos Santiago Huerta in Mexico City."

"What?" Joe perked up.

Pete held up his hand. "But he wasn't there. I spoke with a young female who said she was his daughter. Carlos spends most of his time in Acapulco where he owns a hotel. Guess what it's called. The Mexico Lindo."

"The title of his theme song. It's gotta be him," Joe answered. "Owns a hotel in Acapulco? Where'd he come upon that kind of cash?"

"That I didn't find out. Figured I'd leave the decision to you, if you wanted to call him in Acapulco. As for our Gestapo friend,

Heinrich Klaus indeed lives outside of Santiago, Chile, in a ski resort town called Portillo. It's a popular place for ski bums from North America and Europe to go during our summers. Their winter season is the opposite of ours. And, our friend Klaus has a listed occupation as ski instructor."

"Must be a front. Besides, he's pretty old," Joe noted.

"Maybe he keeps fit," T.J. interjected, patting his flat stomach. "Besides, he's probably not the muscle anymore, assuming they're still in business. They've probably brainwashed a fresh batch of new young nutcases to handle the dirty work. Probably, he just gives the orders."

"I don't know about the giving orders part," Pete continued. "But the ski instructor part looks legit. Are you ready for this?"

Pete waited for Joe and T.J. to rivet their attention. "Heinrich Klaus, using his own name, teaches skiing in the United States during *our* winter months. The guy must be allergic to summer. And you'll never guess where."

"Don't tell me Vermont!" Joe was on the edge of the bench.

"Killington."

Joe stood up to pace, almost fumbling the lit cigar from his hand. "Fucking Killington. He's two hours away from where I live."

"Here's the address." Pete handed him a slip of paper. "And we don't show him as having left yet. He must still be hanging around up there."

"Spring skiing," Joe offered in the way of explanation. "Not out of the question for Killington to still have some skiing in May."

Joe sat back down, shaking his head. There was a pause as he relit the cigar that had gone out. Looking at T.J., he asked, "Do you think his young nutcases are nearby?"

T.J. shrugged his shoulders.

Pete had additional news. "You guys want to hear about El Tío?"

"You found El Tío Don?" Joe perked up. "Donald Buchanan is still living? That's good news. I hope. Hell, he must be what, mid-seventies?"

"At least," Pete answered. "He's living in San Jose, Costa Rica. I got an address and a phone number. I guess he finally settled in one place."

"He was the mastermind of the heist," Joe said to T.J. to refresh his memory on names. "El Tío made all the arrangements. It was he who came up with the art dealers who turned out to be narco traffickers. Pedro, do you think El Tío might've had links to those characters, that he might've had another side deal going?"

"Who knows? Wouldn't put anything past him. Then again he seemed anti-drug. He always busted our balls for having smoked pot in college."

"Do you think he moved around so much to stay one step ahead of *them?* And not his ex-wife's lawyers like he'd claimed?" Joe was thinking out loud. Suspicions now invaded his every thought.

T.J. broke a momentary silence. "Gentlemen, we need a plan."

Chapter 40

T.J. watched as the car pulled into the driveway. The young man in the jogging shorts got out, walked to the mailbox, and proceeded through the side entrance into the house. T.J. drove forward and slowly passed to see if there was a name on the mailbox. Arturo Kaiser.

He'd already written down the Maryland plate number from the car. T.J. had picked up the man earlier when Joe had done a dry run, a walk to the Capitol, for its own sake. When the man in the shorts finally went "off duty," T.J. followed him to his parked car, then stayed behind him through rush-hour traffic all the way to College Park, a case of putting a professional tail on the man tailing Joe.

T.J. was no longer accustomed to such long days in a car seat. But it could prove fruitful. A name and a license number. Finally, they knew the identity of one person definitely on the opposing team. T.J. figured he could run it by Dr. Drake if need be. Drake, after all, had complained that the previous requests hadn't included anyone living close to the Potomac.

As he approached the University of Maryland campus, T.J. decided it was time to get out of the car to stretch. Maybe he would grab a coffee, and take a walk on campus.

He parked his wife's car and started in the direction of the stadium. A sedan slowed as it passed him on the left going in the same direction. The well-dressed man on the passenger side seemed to fix a prolonged stare. Now what? T.J. thought to himself. His guard went up. He was unarmed, but he did have his wife's cell phone. He watched the dark vehicle proceed well beyond him before it turned to the left.

He ducked into a building to find a men's room. When he exited he scanned the road in front just in case. No sign of the dark sedan.

He stopped walking once the stadium came into view. It rekindled memories of his college days, when his University of Virginia football team played Maryland in an away game his junior year. It was a two-touchdown performance that launched him into the national limelight. The good old days when he didn't have to stretch after sitting in a car for a few hours.

On the return walk, he heard a slowing car to his back once again. This time over his right shoulder. Shit, they're back. This time he stepped quickly behind a light pole all the while focusing his eyes sharply on the vehicle to recognize all that he could. Sure enough, it was the same sedan.

The white male driver was also well-dressed and didn't look much different in the face and hair from the passenger. When the driver noted T.J.'s evasive maneuver, it became apparent that the wily ex-agent had become aware of their surveillance. The car sped off too fast for T.J. to get a plate number. But he could've sworn they were neither Maryland, nor Virginia, nor D.C. plates. The fact was they could well have been federal government plates.

Was he being followed by a government vehicle? What kind of shit was this? Here he was tailing the man who'd been tailing Joe. And now someone was tailing him. What had he gotten himself into?

On his way back home to Alexandria, T.J. drove to Pete's apartment in Arlington. He called Joe on the cell phone, and Joe came down to join him for a front-seat conference. It was still unconfirmed whether or not Pete's apartment might be bugged.

"Pete get off okay?" T.J. asked Joe.

"Yeah, left from Dulles. Should be getting there soon. I'm a little worried, his going alone like that."

"Well, this is a dangerous proposition all around. I was tailed myself. Apparently, they picked me up when I was following jogger-boy."

"What? How was that . . . ?"

"Kind of strange, to tell you the truth. They looked more like Feds than like thugs."

"Oh, that's real comforting. Who's on who's side here? What the hell can be going on? You sure about your buddy, Dr. Drake?"

"Hey, man, knock that shit off right now. I got three brothers, and this guy's closer to me than any one of them. I'd trust him with my life. I *have* trusted him with my life."

"Sorry, just touching the bases. I'll be on paranoia medication soon. Tell me about the jogger."

"Got his name and plate number. I'll check him out. Don't know if that'll lead us to who he's working for. Unless I slap him around a little. But gotta be careful they don't retaliate. Any other news?"

"Yeah. Good. And not so good."

"Start with the not so good. I'd like to head home on a high note," T.J. said.

"I may've fucked up, T.J. My curiosity was reaming out my insides. So I called Senator Ross' office. Said I was a student at American U., a constituent from South Carolina, and that I had taken a tour of his office. Said I was doing a project on Chile and that I had seen the photo of Ross with General Pinochet. But that I was curious about the third man in the picture."

"Oh, man."

"I know. But it sounded like a good idea at the time. And I

figured if it worked, it would make for a major shortcut."

"Small possibility against a high risk," T.J. said.

"I know that now. The receptionist said she didn't know, but that she'd check, and call me back. Not wanting to give a number, I told her I'd be the one to call back later. So I did. And got a bullshit answer. She said that the senator didn't remember the name, but that the guy was a member of the Chilean delegation that had met with him."

"Yeah, I'd put that in the category of a bullshit answer."

"Yeah, especially since the same guy was in another photo a few feet away, the one labelled *Senate Intelligence Committee, 1976.*"

"Hopefully nothing'll come of it. What's the good news?"

"The good news emanates from the bad. As I mentioned, I'm getting borderline paranoid. After making the calls to Ross' office, I started to figure he would take down the pictures. Especially if they checked with American U. The name I gave was a complete alias, just made it up. A Billy Joe something or other.

"So I rolled the dice again," Joe continued. "We're gonna find out how much Senator Betty Parker dislikes his highness Blake Ross, and how sincere she is about supporting yours truly. She'd extended the offer of behind the scenes help, so I called to take her up on it."

"The suspense is killing me," T.J. chided.

"I described the two photos, told her what the captions were, and asked if she could check, or have someone check if they were taken down on account of my having inquired about them."

"And she didn't ask why?"

"Of course she did. I told her the guy in the photos might've been behind the photos of me and Marialena. She wanted more, but she gave in when I assured her that it would be better for her to not know anything more."

"So she's gonna check? If Ross takes those photos down, indications will be pretty damn strong that he's in on this."

"No shit. And as powerful as he is in the government, it may not just be a question of being in on it, he could be behind it, the real puppeteer."

"What about the narco traffickers and the Nazi operatives, then?" T.J. was contemplating out loud.

"Maybe Jules' tale was nothing but myth. Then again, maybe they're all connected," Joe speculated. "Anyway, Betty Parker said she'd go a step further than just checking on the photos. She told me that if they were still up, she'd figure a way to photograph the photos. Maybe take a picture of the whole wall if that was the best she could do. She would need to figure an excuse. Contrive some sort of photo op. I dunno."

"Sounds like it's been a good month for clandestine photography." T.J. started the car engine.

CHAPTER 41

The call came in to Senator Ross' office just after 9 p.m. He'd been expecting it.

"It's me, Senator," Julian Muller said. "You sent a message for me to call you."

"I did indeed. This office received a call today from an American University graduate student inquiring as to the identity of the third man in a photo of myself and Gus Pinochet. Don't know if you ever noticed, but that third man is you."

"Gee, I must've been hot stuff in those days," Muller teased, knowing full well that his position on the shady side of the mountain was higher up now even than it was back then.

"My secretary checked with me. I had her check the name out with American University."

"Let me guess," Muller interrupted. "He's one of the busboys."

"Do you know who was in my office the other morning?"

"I dunno. General Pinochet? He wanted a duplicate, maybe?"

Ross was trying not to let Muller get under his skin. "Your dinner date from Montreal. Joe LaCarta."

"I'm jealous. What the hell was he doing in your office? . . . Though we did know he was in the building."

"He was with that pain-in-the-ass lady senator from the pain-in-the-ass moderate wing of my beloved party, the incumbent senator from Vermont."

"Elizabeth Parker Shannon, or Elizabeth Shannon Parker, or whatever her name or names are? Who can keep track nowadays?"

Ross could do without the levity. "It may've just been coincidence. He dropped in on Senator Parker, and waited for her in my reception area while I gave her the brush-off on some harebrained health care legislation. If he recognized you, it was dumb luck. Why don't you get flabby like most other fifty-five-year-olds? And why did you have to meet LaCarta in person?"

"Because I've got to have my fun, Senator. Some people like to sit on their ass. I like to kick some ass. I'll retire when I'm eighty. I'll buy a whorehouse in South America and bang twenty-year-olds till the ticker gives out."

"Mr. Muller, LaCarta's made a connection between us. I can't afford to be linked to you and all your baggage. The photos are coming down tomorrow. And. . . ."

"Oh, Senator. You mean I'll no longer be on the wall of honor?"

"And I think our association on this matter is finished. He's out of the race. And you've been paid."

In spite of his taunting demeanor, Muller did not relish losing Ross and his congressional cronies as clients. Of those paying for his services, they were the ones who provided a cloak of respectability. It was a counterweight to the drug traffickers and the complicit law enforcement officials they owned. It was a respectability that opened doors and cushioned blows. It helped keep Muller's little shadow world safe and secure.

"I don't share your optimism, Senator. I don't believe he's out nor that we've seen the last of him. I don't like the way he's poking around. And that little bimbo scandal we tried to plant didn't stick. Hell, one newspaper made him sound like a victim. I should have tried the drug association. That might've worked better."

"Mr. Muller, dispense with the little irritations. I don't know whom you may be working for, nor do I know what they may've asked you to do. As for our association, please consider it . . . well . . . 'suspended,' that's the word I'm looking for."

"Very original, Blakey. I'll be calling again. To say 'I told you so.' "

"Only if I call you first, Julie." Ross hung up.

Chapter 42

San Jose, Costa Rica

Costa Rica had long since been on Pete's list of places he wanted to visit. When he discovered that Don "El Tío" Buchanan lived in San Jose, the capital, he called the phone number anonymously to establish that the septuagenarian was at home. The journey was a responsibility Pete would take on for the team.

As the taxi rumbled along the roadway from the airport, the verdant mountains all around made him wish the trip were recreational. Instead, it might unearth skeletons that he had never known existed.

Sure, the prospect of seeing "El Tío" kindled some enthusiasm. But at the same time, apprehensiveness was welling up inside. Could the very insights he came seeking drag them down from discouragement to outright despair?

The taxi driver took pride in pointing out the fashionable houses in the neighborhood. One belonged to a justice of the Costa Rican Supreme Court, another nearby belonged to an ex-President. Pete surmised that El Tío was not only living among the elite, but he had finally surrounded himself with those who, at least ostensibly, dealt from the top of the deck.

The cab arrived at a cul-de-sac. The address Pete had corresponded to a large modern home whose worth would be into the million-dollar-plus ranges back in the Washington, D.C. suburbs. Pete paid the driver and asked him to wait until someone answered the doorbell.

She was a woman of about forty, most likely local. Pete addressed her in his still fluent Spanish. "I'm looking for *Señor* Don, Don Buchanan. I am an old friend. My name is Pete . . . Pedro, Donovan."

She smiled politely. *"Un momento, por favor."* She shut the door behind her. Evidently, she had been schooled by El Tío on taking precautions. Pete heard the taxi's motor rev and glanced over as it pulled away. The wait endured for several minutes, minutes that seemed simultaneous with the day's lapse into dusk.

Pete felt the eyeball in the peephole just before the door swung open and the unmistakable grin disengaged his anxiety. The facial expression was the same. The hair was whiter and thinner. The six-foot-four frame was partially hunched over to the left side where he leaned on an aluminum cane.

"Pedro, it is you. It's really you. I thought my wife was pulling my leg." He extended his right hand to Pete. "Come on in. What the hell brings you here? Gee, after all these years. How'd you find me?"

"Hell, Tío, don't you think it was about time. I work for the government, Immigration and Naturalization, so I had ways to track you down. Always knew you were moving around. Hiding from your ex-wife, tax collectors, whomever." The "whomever" concept triggered a slight shudder along Pete's spine.

"I've been here a while. Got tired of moving around." They moved into a living room area. El Tío motioned for Pete to put his bag against the wall and take a seat.

El Tío finally introduced the woman who'd first answered the door. Her name was Rosita. He asked her to bring two beers as he plunked himself into a leather easy chair. She walked off to the kitchen with an obedient smile on her face.

"She was a real find," El Tío explained in English. "They

don't make'em like that back home. Takes good care of me, especially since the little stroke last year."

"You okay?" Pete was concerned.

"Small potatoes, can still do the important things," he said through a burst of mischievous laughter. "She's forty, I'm seventy-eight. What do you think? Isn't Costa Rica great? I try to keep up. Maybe I need some of those pills, what do they call 'em, Niagara, or something like that?"

"Viagra. With a 'V.' " Pete chuckled along with El Tío. "Well, at least you have a wife. I'm separated, looks like we're headed for divorce," Pete explained. "My two kids are off to college, maybe they won't feel it as much."

"Sorry to hear that, Pedro. You're looking none the worse for it. A little lighter on top," El Tío patted his own forehead. "Not too much in the gut, considering the way you used to like the old *cerveza.* Tell me, how's them sidekicks of yours? You keep in touch? I think I saw José on CNN once or twice. Recognized him right away. Hair's not as long, and it's grayer. But overall, he looked pretty good. Got quite a kick out of seeing him."

"Yeah, he's doing well. He was running for the Senate, the U.S. Senate, from Vermont. But had to bow out."

"Oh? That's too bad. That he dropped out, that is."

Pete looked for signs that El Tío might know more than he was letting on.

"News isn't so good about Pancho. He died last month. Car accident in Mexico."

"Gee, I'm real sorry to hear that. He was still a young man. I guess compared to me almost everyone's a young man. I always had a lot of admiration for that kid. He had a lot of balls."

Pete paused. He didn't add that Pancho's balls might've sparked the heart attack that put out his flame.

"Nobody's heard anything from Anita," Pete added. "You haven't, have you, Tío?"

"No. Not me. Why? You ask as if you're worried something may've happened to her."

"Well, she was in line for a transfer to Guatemala. But I checked with Peace Corps in Washington. It never happened."

Again there was a pause as Pete scanned for clues on El Tío's face or in his mannerisms.

El Tío broke the silence. "My life since we hit the jackpot has been pretty peaceful. No complications. Not ever. I never told anyone. My ex-wife never found out about the million bucks. Rosita doesn't even know how I made my money, how I afford all this." He waved his hand to indicate the spacious, tastefully furnished home.

Rosita reentered the room and signaled that she had prepared some food. El Tío waved Pete into the dining room where three places were set. The conversation in English about old times flipped over to a conversation in Spanish about the present-day lives of Mr. and Mrs. Donald Buchanan.

Pete politely asked Rosita about her life. She had been widowed at a young age and now had two grown daughters. She not only did not need to work, but she and El Tío had the means to hire domestic help as they pleased.

They had been married for about five years, and led a comfortable but simple life. El Tío told Pete he had a satellite dish and they spent much time watching TV. Rosita's daughters lived in San Jose and visited often. El Tío's son and daughter from his first marriage also visited, but each only about once a year.

When the meal concluded, Rosita busied herself with clearing the table. El Tío suggested that Pete and he transfer to the back breezeway, where they reverted back to their native English. El Tío asked Rosita to bring them some brandy.

Two half-filled snifters arrived within minutes. "This is the good stuff from Spain," El Tío boasted.

"Nice aroma," Pete commented. For once, Pete was being careful not to get ahead of himself with the alcohol. He would need the skills of a diplomat to ferret out whatever secrets El Tío might've kept locked away. If the old man had once operated on a need-to-know basis, then it fell to Pete to convey there was a new need-to-know dynamic.

"So, Pedro, you never mentioned. You here on business? You're welcome to stay with us. As you can see, we have plenty of room. Have you graduated beyond Peace Corps accommodations?" he teased.

"Thank you, Tío, that's nice of you. And, yes, I am here on business. But it's personal business, I'm afraid. Maybe serious personal business."

El Tío perked up. He must've sensed the urgency in Pete's voice. Pete continued, "None of us ever told anyone about the heist down on the Orinoco. Not even our wives. We figured everything went our way, and that blabbing could only fuck things up. Pretty soon each of us all but forgot about it—we never kept any of the money, as you know. Then . . ."

Pete took a sip of brandy and decided not to mince words. "Then, Pancho dies just as Joe announces a run for the Senate. I get an anonymous call to tell Joe to go to a meeting in Montreal. Joe goes, meets with a scary guy who explains he knows all about the heist. In fact, unless he was making it all up, he knew more about the heist, and what went on behind the scenes, than Joe or any of us ever did. And . . . and he reveals that Pancho's death was no car accident, that he died receiving a message, the message that Joe should stay out of the Senate race."

El Tío looked as if he'd just heard a ghost story. His voice finally worked its way through the ashen face and tense lips. "But who . . . who? . . . Please, Pedro, tell me you're joking. I'm too old for this. You sure you guys didn't go back to smoking that weed again?"

"I wish. I wish someone would just spray cold water on me and I'd awaken from a bad dream. But, it's all real. The scary guy in Montreal claims the Nazis are under his thumb. He's just got to give them the word, and they'll finally get their revenge. That's what'll happen if Joe doesn't abandon the candidacy."

"I thought you said he did?"

"Yes. That's right, he did. But we still would like to know more. Can't go the rest of our lives without answers." Pete kept hoping that the tone would make truth serum fester somewhere inside El Tío's secret memory vault.

"He abandoned the race out of fear?" El Tío said. "Don't know if that's any guarantee. Once he's gone and forgotten, he'll be low-profile again. Easier to do away with. And since they forced him out, they'd have the incentive to silence him permanently. And cover all traces of their handiwork."

Pete let the analysis sink in. It was a perspective they hadn't discussed. But it made sense. And that being the case, what did it mean to other nobodies, like himself? It did have some positive resonance, however. The fact that El Tío proffered this concern seemed to confirm that he himself was not a party to this conspiracy. Indeed, the troubled look indicated that he harbored his own fear of it.

"Did you come here to warn me, Pedro?"

"Yeah. You could say that. Apparently, the Nazis weren't the only ones lurking in the shadows. Obviously." Pete raised his antennae another notch and took another sip of brandy. Did El Tío have anything to get off his chest, and would he unload it?

"Are you saying there were third parties?"

"Perhaps." Pete economized on his words. Purposefully. "Carlos knew."

"Carlos. Oh, yeah, the ladies' man."

"You know, Tío, none of us ever laid eyes on him again. He

never came to our send-off. Never corresponded. Nothing."

El Tío sat pensively, like he was grappling with something, a something he either wanted to bury deeper, or to release into the air. The kind of secret an old man either takes to the grave or gets off his chest at the final hour.

El Tío breathed in the fumes from his snifter and sipped. Forging across a threshold of uncertainty, he began, "Pedro, did you ever wonder why I moved around so much after I left Venezuela?"

"I guess so your ex-wife wouldn't come after your money." By now, Pete was concluding that perhaps there was a more authentic reason.

"Not hardly. No, the real reason was a bit more serious. Remember those art dealers? Just after we sold the stuff to them, I found out their real aims. They were drug dealers. The profits were going to expand their operation. The international marketing of Colombian cocaine was getting another jumpstart.

"I knew these were some dangerous hombres," El Tío continued. "And they knew who I was and how much of their money I had. So I needed to make sure they never knew where they could find me, especially since I wasn't gonna return to the U.S."

"To avoid paying alimony? That's why you stayed abroad?"

"Yeah, my urge to not give in to my ex was almost stronger than my will to be safe. Stupid, eh?"

"How did you find out about them? About the charade?"

"Carlos."

"Carlos! So he *was* involved? That's why he avoided us?"

"Listen, Pedro, I still don't know much about the guy. All I know is he filled in the gaps. Once he found out about the heist idea, he came to *me.* Said he'd tried to talk you guys out of it, but after giving it some thought, he felt it could work. He wanted in on the action if he could come up with a buyer.

Made me swear not to tell any of you guys, not even Joe. How it was that Carlos had contacts across the border in Colombia, I never knew. Nor did I ever figure out.

"I took care of him from my end. Gave him a hundred grand. I really didn't get to keep the full million. I met him in Aruba after I left Caracas. That's why he wasn't at your send-off. Don't know whether he would've attended anyway. But Aruba is where he came for his cut. That's when he admitted they weren't art dealers. I was a little pissed, annoyed that he hadn't told me the truth from the beginning. But the sonofabitch was afraid I'd back out if I knew. Anyway, he at least gave me the heads up afterwards, told me to watch my backside, that they were unpredictable."

"But you were never threatened all those years."

"True. But those drug cartels made so much money that my little stash paled into insignificance. Why would they bother?"

"You know, Tío, the mystery man in Montreal told Joe that the buyers actually ransomed the art back to the Nazis. The fucking Nazis were collecting on an insurance claim after the theft. The bastards used the insurance payment to cover much of the ransom. So they end up with the stuff, anyway. And presumably, they sold it and made millions. With that kind of cash, who knows what they could've bought. Or whom they could've bought."

"Unbelievable. We probably did them a favor. Makes you wonder. Makes you wonder if there were other brokers besides Carlos out there getting a cut."

"Or if Carlos got in on all the commissions that were made."

"Goddamn. That would've been something." There was a glint of admiration in El Tío's eyes. The incurable wheeler-dealer.

"Tell me, Tío. Had you known . . . had you known these were drug dealers and not art dealers, would you still have gone ahead with it? Would you have told us?"

He thought about it for a minute or two. "Knowing how I was in those days, I'd have to say yes, I would've still gone ahead with it, despite the added risk. But, no, I wouldn't have told you guys."

"I'd have to agree with that assessment. I appreciate the honesty." Pete downed the rest of his brandy. "Speaking for the three of us, and probably for Anita, too, I'd have to say we would've dropped out, not done it. At that point it would've contaminated the beauty of it—the idea that it was all win-win, no downside."

Chapter 43

Sleep wouldn't come easy to El Tío. A sense of security that had been building for over twenty-five years had just suffered serious erosion, like a mudslide in the rainforest. Could he, too, become a pawn in this chess game, where candidate Joe LaCarta was being checkmated by unseen power brokers? The tranquility he had envisioned for his final years was fast becoming a mirage.

Why should the drug cartels care? They had made millions. And the Nazis? According to what Joe had been told, they made out better than had the heist not happened. Maybe the desire for revenge was still virulent.

And what was so threatening about Joe LaCarta taking his place in the U.S. Senate? Maybe El Tío needn't worry as long as Joe kept his candidacy in a state of suspension. Maybe he should offer Joe money to stay out. No, Joe wasn't likely to be motivated by money, or power. His reasons for wanting to be a senator most likely went beyond anything El Tío had ever felt. And besides, such an offer would only bring suspicion down upon El Tío as to complicity. He didn't want to be viewed that way, especially now that he'd cleansed his soul in making the confession to Pete.

But if he stayed out, El Tío reasoned, Joe could be more easily eliminated as a nobody than as a somebody. And there'd still be compelling reasons to silence Joe permanently, to prevent any backtracking on his part. Would an "accident" similar to

Pancho's be written into the script for Joe?

If Joe jumped back in, on the other hand, then harm would more likely befall one of the other heisters. Pete? Himself? Pancho had already taken his turn. And maybe . . . maybe, so had Anita.

Because he was wide awake, El Tío was the first to hear the rapid barrage of rings from the front doorbell, a steady fifteen-second crescendo. He felt his heart begin to race. Quickly recognizing panic was a threat in and of itself, he willed himself to de-escalate the urge. Coolly, he swung out of bed, gripped the nearby cane, and stooped to retrieve the loaded 9mm Smith and Wesson he kept in the nightstand. A glance at the digital clock radio told him it was 2:41 a.m.

When his eyes adjusted to the darkness, he saw that Rosita had awakened and was sitting up in the bed, hands shaking. He motioned for her to stay quiet and to remain behind as he exited from the ground-floor bedroom towards the open living area. Plodding forward with the cane in his left hand and pistol at the ready in his right, El Tío arrived to the edge of the hallway.

The living room lights had been turned on. Peering ahead, he could see through the foyer at the far end that the front door was wide open. But the centerpiece was in full view, spray-painted in black on the marble floor of the living room. The symbol that once had terrorized millions, the swastika. And below it, facing El Tío's approach was the footnote "Zurich-Mars." The eerie touch made for a grim reminder.

El Tío heard footsteps descending the stairs, but quickly recognized Pete, who had been staying in the guest bedroom on the second floor. Pete stopped midway down when he saw the artwork. Seeing El Tío proceed towards the open door, Pete scurried down the rest of the way and cautioned, "Tío, wait. Don't go out there."

As he said this, Pete picked up a marble statuette from an

end table and came shoulder to shoulder with the old man.

"I have to check, and shut the door," El Tío reasoned.

"What if they're still in here?" Pete whispered.

The crash of breaking glass in the master bedroom coincided with Rosita's gut-wrenching scream. Recognizing his superior quickness, Pete grabbed the gun from El Tío and rushed to her. Rosita was hunkered down in a far corner of the spacious room, alone. A large rock rested on the floor surrounded by diamond-like particles from the busted window.

When the figure of her husband appeared in the doorway, Rosita jumped up and ran to his arms. Abandoning all caution, Pete broke from the bedroom, and ran down the hallway across the living room to the front door. Gun at the ready and crouched, he slithered through, keeping his back against the outside wall of the house.

Blending with the shadows, he focused all around, but saw nothing. He listened for movements. Still nothing. They hadn't established if there was still an intruder on the inside. But it was clear the rock had to have been thrown from the outside.

After several minutes, Pete returned to the living room where Rosita was just hanging up the phone with El Tío standing guard with a second pistol.

"Nothing," Pete said, anticipating the question on each of their faces.

"Just called the police," El Tío explained. Seeing Pete's gaze upon the small pistol he was holding, El Tío added, "Had an extra one in the study. We checked everywhere inside. They're gone."

Pete shut the front door behind him and locked it.

"How'd they get in?" Pete wondered out loud.

"Probably a window," El Tío speculated. "But if it was, they shut it behind them."

"I think it was meant to scare us only. . . . This time."

"Next time it'll be different," El Tío said. "We're ordering an alarm system tomorrow. And I'm hiring a guard. And getting a guard dog. Screw those assholes."

"Tío, I'm sorry about this. I can't help but think I dragged them here, brought you to their attention. I feel like shit."

"I'm not so sure, Pedro. If you found me, they also could have. They found Pancho, didn't they? And you. They found you to give Joe the message. I figure we're all in their little address book. And besides, maybe I had it coming—a case of the chickens coming home to roost. That heist was my brainstorm. I lived all those years off the proceeds. And I kept you guys in the dark about Carlos, and later about the drug dealers."

"They're running out of patience, looks like. Joe made a statement that his candidacy was 'suspended.' I don't think they're equating the term 'suspended' with 'ended.' I can feel the vultures hovering."

"Sounds like something's gotta give. Listen, Pedro, tell Joe not to roll over on my account. We'll be all right here." As El Tío said this, he pulled back a curtain. Two police cars were pulling up in front.

"In fact, if he resumes the campaign, I'd like to send along a generous contribution."

"He'd be flattered to hear that, Tío. But I can tell you he wouldn't take it. He won't take out-of-state money, even though it's arriving in boatloads for his opponents. Campaign finance reform is a big issue for him."

El Tío shook his head. "He's still idealistic, eh? After all these years."

Chapter 44

Vermont

With the sand sinking through the hourglass as it was, taking time for a newspaper interview should've been low priority. In fact, Joe had to admit, it should've been off the charts. Except for the one factor. He really wanted to get to know her.

But why was she still persisting? What interest did Vicki Rivier have in a noncandidate? The most likely answer was that she wanted to pursue the connection between whoever delivered the photographs and Joe's suspended candidacy. But Joe held out hope that she had another reason, the same one which spurred him on.

Joe had just arrived back in Burlington earlier that day. After a quick stop at his house, to see if it was still intact, he headed south on Route 7 to meet Vicki at her home/office in Middlebury.

T.J. remained in Washington. It wasn't simply to spend more time with his wife; there were some loose ends he wanted to try and tie together, his portion of the detective work. Joe returned to Vermont because he had plans of his own for tomorrow, plans that T.J. had advised against. T.J. wanted Joe to wait until they could go together.

The rolling green meadows with the Green Mountains—some still whitecapped—on the horizon to the left, and ice-blue Lake Champlain and the Adirondacks on the right provided a panorama for happier thoughts. Joe shelved all apprehensions about the following day. Instead, he preferred dwelling on the visit at hand. As he viewed the black-and-white cows grazing in the hilly pastures, he promised himself that the interview should be on his own terms, relaxed and informal.

Middlebury, a college town, was about an hour from Burlington. Joe had spoken at Middlebury College several times and knew his way around. The only reason he arrived late to the address Vicki Rivier had given him was because he'd left late from Burlington.

"Hi. I thought you were going to blow me off." She peered at her watch as she greeted Joe at the front door. But more importantly, she looked him in the eye with a warm, genuine smile as they shook hands.

"My apologies, Ms. Rivier. I'm not the type to be fashionably late. Just that I flew back from D.C. today, and you know how . . ."

"You don't have to explain, Mr. LaCarta. Come on in. Have a seat. Make yourself comfortable. We want this to be as painless as possible. Could I get you some coffee or tea?"

Coffee, tea, or me? Joe couldn't help recall the memoirs written by some flight attendants many years before. He took a seat in an old wooden chair in the den area that served as her home office. "Nice set-up," he commented, gesturing at the array of office equipment.

"It's great. So convenient. It's the computer age. Faxes, E-mail. And since I'm in Burlington as much as I'm in Rutland, can't beat living halfway between. So what'll it be?"

"Oh, if the tea is decaf. . . ."

"You got it. Be right back."

He watched as she shuffled off to the kitchen. She moved gracefully, footsteps light upon the hardwood floor. The lean body looked firm under the revealing sweater and the snug jeans. She seemed totally at ease; informality was not going to be difficult to transact.

Joe caught glimpses of her through the kitchen doorway as she prepared the serving tray. She worked quietly and efficiently. Her serious facial expressions were as intriguing as her smile. They conveyed a depth of character that went with her wholesome look.

She did not possess striking beauty by any means. Her face was different, like it belonged to one European country or other, but not pinpointing which one. Her hair was several shades of red, strawberry to chestnut. Joe considered himself a man of narrow tastes. And Vicki Rivier had the kind of allure that fit within that corridor.

As she returned smiling, Joe couldn't help wondering if she had once been a dancer or gymnast. She poured his cup from a porcelain teapot. There were scones laid out on a dish.

"Have a little snack, if you're hungry. The scones are delicious."

Delicious? To him she, too, looked delicious. "You're too hospitable. Do you do this for all your interviewees? Or is it a ploy to get their guard down?" Joe smiled. The last thing he wanted was to appear adversarial.

"I do it for me. Almost every day as a picker-upper. Often I don't have dinner until very late. Especially when I'm running up against a tight deadline."

"Well, that shouldn't be the case tonight. Nothing I'll have to say will be tomorrow's news. That's for sure."

"That always depends." She grabbed a pen and notepad. "Maybe something incredibly interesting might come out about yourself."

"Yeah, well things that are 'incredibly interesting,' and can't wait for a few days, are usually incredibly bad."

"Why don't you start with a little background? Who is Joseph LaCarta?"

"Gee, right off the bat? Hell, if I try to talk and eat the scone at the same time, I'll get crumbs all over your floor."

She pretended to scribble on the notepad. "So let me get this straight. The man who would be senator from Vermont, is a sloppy eater. Do not invite to dinners with heads of State."

Her sense of humor was a pleasant surprise. He'd had his fill with tight-ass reporters in the past, the kind that took themselves too seriously. Unfortunately, it was a trait he too often found in professional women whom he would've otherwise considered appealing.

"Let's see, where do I begin? I had a happy childhood. My parents were immigrants from Italy. Working class. Stressed education. So, I did well in school to avoid being kicked in the ass. Or should I say 'posterior'? Had a lot of friends. Played sports, but never as well as I wanted to. Worked my way through college, avoided flunking out and being drafted. Then I went into the Peace Corps in Venezuela for two years."

"Oh, that must've been interesting," she stopped him. "The Peace Corps. What did you do in the Peace Corps?"

He smiled as the temptation crossed his mind—I robbed Nazis of art they had pillaged and used the proceeds to perpetuate programs for the disadvantaged. The smile went away when the more sobering version invaded his thoughts—of course, naive me, I didn't realize it would help drug cartels get established, make the Nazis richer, and get some innocent people killed.

"Mr. LaCarta, tell me about the Peace Corps experience."

Joe returned from the daydream. "Oh. Mostly community development work, in a city down on the Orinoco River called Puerto Ordaz. A lot of rural people had migrated into the city in search of a better life. But as is typical, there were never enough good jobs."

"I've been to Venezuela myself," she said. "Caracas, the

coastal areas. I once did a story on the oil wells of Lake Maracaibo for a business magazine. Latin America is a special interest of mine."

"Really? We have that in common. *Hablas español?*"

"Sí, bastante."

"How about that? What d'ya say we run off to Mexico?"

She blushed. The advance was made too soon. But since it was said in jest, Joe could retreat gracefully. "Anyway," he continued. "After I returned from Venezuela, I did a combination of grad school and work, mostly in education and community services. After the Masters, I got serious about public policy and got a Ph.D. It's been academia and writing ever since."

"And TV, and the lecture circuit," she added for Joe.

"Yeah, that stuff, too. Then I let them talk me into politics. And we know how long that lasted."

"Which brings me to the question of 'why.' Of why it hasn't lasted."

"Just not in the cards, I guess. Guess I'm just an ordinary guy who wants to live in peace. You just heard my background. Quintessential ordinary. I'm not a war hero, ex-actor, ex-jock, any of those things."

"I think those types are amply represented in Congress, Mr. LaCarta. From what I've observed, your ideas are anything but ordinary. Especially since common sense is no longer considered ordinary. Mr. LaCarta . . ."

"Call me Joe, please."

"Don't we need to preserve a certain degree of decorum?"

"As I sit in your den taking afternoon tea? You want to know about Joe LaCarta? Then know I like to be on a first-name basis with people . . . with people I . . . I respect." He groped for a cautious word. Especially since she didn't jump at the idea of running off to Mexico.

"Thanks for the flattery. Don't know if I've really earned it. But, as you wish. Consider us on a first-name basis, Joe."

"Great. So, sounds like we're finished here. I'm about ready to head into town for some dinner. I'd like it very much if you'd join me, you probably could choose the best place. I'd even offer to treat, but I know you couldn't accept such a gratuity."

"Whoa, I don't have enough yet to fill a photo caption. You didn't come all the way down here just to run off for a bite to eat, I hope."

She hoped right. He didn't come all the way down just to run off for a bite to eat, unless, she were going to run off for a bite to eat with him. He now realized that if he were going to get to know her better, the real interview would represent first base. "I smell coffee in the kitchen. If you insist on continuing the inquisition, you're gonna have to pump me with some caffeine."

"My pleasure." She went to the kitchen and returned quickly with a mug teeming with the fresh brew. Milk, sugar, and honey were already on the tray.

"So without further delay," she began. "Those photos of you with the student from U. Mass., I felt you and she explained it quite adequately, quite believably. And even if it were so that you were having a fling—I can see where she might be irresistible, by the way—I figure it wouldn't be enough to bring down your candidacy. After all, you are divorced and unattached. Such age differentials aren't unheard of, the male being the old one, of course."

Joe chuckled. "I didn't mention that I was divorced and unattached."

She blushed slightly. "These are things a reporter picks up when covering a candidate."

"And did you also pick up on what I might consider irresistible?"

"We're digressing. The point I'm leading to is the connection between those photos and your suspending the candidacy. And by the way, I've thought about the choice of that word. 'Suspend' does not mean 'end.' So come on, Joe, there're a lot of curious people out there. What gives?"

"The photos were just some prank. Maybe some former student who hates my guts. Candidates go through crap like that."

"Candidates don't suspend candidacies two weeks after they announce, though, do they?"

The only reason he was putting up with this was that he even found her testiness appealing. "Look, Vicki, don't think of it as my quitting so soon, think of it as my having announced too soon. Before I'd really assessed how it would disrupt my life. I still have my core beliefs and will continue to press common sense ideas and needed reforms."

"But you won't be doing it as a member of the U.S. Senate. You'll still be on the sidelines, several steps removed from where you could make a real impact. Won't that stick in your craw?"

"Gee, Vicki, sounds like I would've had *your* vote."

"Joe, why are you *not* convincing me that there's no story here? Put yourself in my shoes. Wouldn't you suspect that the so-called personal reasons might contain a public interest?"

Joe thought how he'd like to put himself in something other than her shoes. "No, not really."

"So you're not going to give me any insights as to who's behind the photos and why they're against you. You're not going to tell me if you're fearful of some further threats. And you have no idea why they don't want you to become a senator?"

She was good. And he was impressed. But, he could not give in. "Vicki, are you sure you're a journalist, and not a novelist?" He let out a phony laugh, then continued, "There's no big story here. But, I promise you, if one emerges, I'll give you an exclusive. You have my word."

Joe watched as her determined demeanor slowly became disarmed. He'd hoped this promise would hold her off for now, that she'd accept it as a fair compromise. She sighed and leaned back in her office chair.

"So, what about dinner? Are you going to join me?"

The pensive look on her face soaked up the silence. She stood and pulled several take-out menus from a pile of papers. "I think . . . I think it would be unadvisable for me to be seen in town with you. Who knows? Your friends from *Candid Camera* might be lurking in our wake. So, how about ordering in? I can clear the table of all that mess, and we'll both have company."

He liked her style. He may've sounded too eager when he said, "Sounds great."

They chose Mexican, the consolation prize after she'd ignored the suggestion to run off there with him. She called the eatery. He helped clear the table.

"Do you like wine with the meal?" she asked as she stood by a small triangular wine rack on top of a bookcase.

"An investigative reporter asking an Italian if he takes wine with a meal?" he chuckled. "I would've thought you'd already know the answer to that."

The smile returned to her face. She pulled a Chianti from the wiry wine rack and slid a corkscrew across the table in his direction. "You want to do the honors?"

"My only dining room skill. And should I light those candles?" He pointed to the two on the table, then wondered if this was too suggestive, especially when she didn't respond. He let it go.

They were ready for the food when it arrived. She wouldn't let Joe treat. She sprang for her half. They unpacked the bags and cartons, and transferred everything onto awaiting plates. Joe poured the wine and they took seats across from one another.

Joe lifted his glass, but she held back and said, "Maybe this place could use a little atmosphere." She stood and reached for a wall switch. She dimmed the lights, then, nodding towards the two candles fixtured on the table, she handed Joe some matches.

With both candles lit, she raised her glass. *"Salud,"* she toasted, using her Spanish.

"Salud," Joe reciprocated. *"Y gracias por la hospitalidad."* And thanks for the hospitality.

"Well now that we got the tedious stuff out of the way, about me and my suspended Senate run, let's hear a little bit about the gracious hostess."

"Oh, there's not much to tell," she said coyly. "Pretty uneventful life."

"Why not let me be the judge of that." His focused brown eyes conveyed genuine interest.

"I'm from Burlington originally. Went to UVM. Then I taught high school English for years. Freelanced a little in the summers, magazines mostly. Then I needed a change, so I took the job with the Rutland paper and moved here to Middlebury."

"Just like that?"

"Well, there was another aspect. I wanted to put some distance between myself and an abusive husband."

"Who would abuse you?"

"Oh, it wasn't physical so much. He was a drunk. He's okay now. But we grew apart. He leaves me alone. I run into him occasionally on Church St. We're friendly."

"And no children, and no one since?"

"No children. And no one at present."

She proceeded to explain how she liked her job. She enjoyed travel, and was active in recreational pursuits such as skiing. Joe asked her if she'd ever been a dancer or gymnast. Flattered, she related how she had once been involved with an amateur dance company. She volunteered her age. Joe would've pegged her to be barely forty, but she was forty-five. Her forthrightness added to her allure.

"You don't miss living in the big city, Burlington?"

"Nah, it's growing too fast. Doesn't even look the same as when I was a kid. Too much traffic. Nice place to visit, though.

"My life is pretty simple. I love my independence, especially after being involved with a husband who had so much baggage."

Joe smiled at her reassuringly. "I'm sure there are a lot of guys out there without baggage who would be interested in a charming woman such as yourself."

The implication might've been too obvious. Joe was including himself in that category before it occurred to him that, if what he was carrying wasn't baggage, what was it? Nonetheless, he could see she appreciated the compliment as she blushed once again.

"What have I done to deserve these nice comments? That's very nice of you. A middle-aged woman like myself will take all the flattery she can get. But I'm fine. I'd be very cautious about getting involved with anyone. It's got to be the right situation. And I'm confident I'd recognize the right situation if it came along."

Which, of course, made Joe wonder if he'd brought along the right situation. Maybe if the Montreal mystery man and his Nazi thugs took their program elsewhere. Nevertheless, this was the time to ask her about dating, about seeing him socially. But before he could form the words, caution overtook him. She was still wearing the journalist's hat, she hadn't declared a moratorium on the interview. What if his forwardness got incorporated into her story on him? He held back on crossing the line.

She broke the uneasy pause with a serious question on Joe's foreign policy views. Joe didn't want to get back onto business, but he'd temporarily lost his handle on the natural flow of conversation.

"Nobody's interested in foreign policy much. It's not what wins in senatorial races. But, it's a big concern of mine. Things are better than they were. Seemed we once did too much for oppressive military governments, helped them against their own people. You know, El Salvador, Guatemala, Chile." The mention of Chile once again conjured up the picture of General Pinochet flanked by Senator Blake Ross and the scary Jules character. Bet those guys could tell a tale or two about that era of U.S. foreign policy, he thought to himself.

"Yes, I do know. I, for one, am pretty interested in it, especially in those countries you named. Maybe we can do a story strictly on your foreign policy views sometime."

"You mean, if I were a candidate for anything."

"I mean when you become a Senate candidate again." She winked.

Joe was beginning to think she had a stronger hunch about what he was going to do than he himself did. Her intuitions towards him were at the same time both endearing and spooky.

He downed the last drop of wine in his glass. They had both finished eating. Vicki reached for the bottle, but it was empty.

"Would you like more wine?" she asked.

He would, but was reluctant to have her uncork another full bottle. "I guess so, but don't waste a whole bottle just to refill my glass."

"It wasn't only you that I had in mind." She got up and grabbed another red. It was a Chilean. "Your mention of Chile must've been suggestive." She held the label out in front of his eyes before uncorking it. "What the hell," she continued, as she replenished the glasses. "I'm all caught up on tomorrow's stories. And you sure as hell didn't give me anything to hold the presses over."

"No one's happier than I about that," he said, touching her glass with his before they each took a swallow.

Spontaneity was the pathway to exciting. The more they conversed, the more apparent it became that her sense of humor ran parallel to his own. She emphasized the laughable aspects when relating past experiences, a trademark he shared.

Time seemed to stand still. But the reality was that it had flown by. The second bottle of wine expired shortly after 11 p.m.

"I don't do this very often," she wanted to point out. "Having been married to an alcoholic, I'm a little guarded about . . . well it's been a while since I've had such an interesting evening."

"Vicki, it's certainly been the nicest evening I've had in a while. Interesting too. But I want to emphasize the 'nice' part. In fact, I hate to see it end. I mean, maybe I could have some coffee before driving back to Burlington."

"Of course. But are you sure you're okay to drive? I have a guest bedroom that you're welcome to."

She said this without the slightest awkwardness. The nonchalant, but considerate invitation resonated like the pleasing finale of a symphony.

He savored the uplifting pause as he mulled it over. It would save him considerable driving time. He would not have to drive an hour north tonight, then an extra hour south tomorrow, on his way to Killington. Killington? At this moment, he did not want to stir up any of those jitters.

"Are you sure it's okay, Vicki? I hate to put you out."

"Of course, it's okay, Joe. It's my house, isn't it? I'm in charge, and *mi casa es tu casa.*" My house is your house—he'd heard it said many times in Latin America. Her lips seemed to honey-coat the words as she voiced them.

Joe went out to get the overnight bag he always carried in his car. Upon re-entering the house, she showed him to the guest room. It was cozy, but looked like it hadn't had much use.

"Let me know if you need anything," she said softly before turning to exit the room.

Just before she reached the door, Joe called out to her, "Vicki?" He walked toward her as she turned.

"Yes?" She looked up into his eyes.

He gently placed his hands on each of her shoulders. Then he bent forward to join his lips with hers. They were warm and relaxed. The kiss lasted several seconds before he pulled her closer. With undisguised passion, he kissed her again. Her excitement also seemed to intensify for several minutes, until finally she worked her forearms between their chests to loosen the hug.

Gazing affectionately into his eyes, she spoke softly, "Joe, I had a wonderful evening. I haven't felt this way in some time. But, we'd better call it a night."

She turned to walk away, then added, "I'd hate to disqualify myself from the big story exclusive you promised."

He thought how he would prefer a private little story between the two of them instead. But he had a nice feeling as she disappeared from the room. The temporary glow would afford some pleasant thoughts, for a change, when his head hit the pillow.

Chapter 45

He awoke before she did. The watch he'd set on the nearby dresser read 8:05 a.m. The heavy sleep seemed to counteract the effects of the wine. Rallying onto his feet, he found his way into the bathroom. As quietly and as unobtrusively as he could, he began to shower.

Pangs of nervousness over the upcoming trek to Killington began their resurgence. His mind strategized over how he might stake out the address Pete had found for the notorious Heinrich Klaus.

But the building angst was interrupted by the knock on the bathroom door. "Yes?" he responded, poking only his head out from the shower curtain he held up in one hand.

She opened the door slowly and peered in demurely. She held out a thick folded towel in one hand. "You'll need a clean towel. The ones on the rack have been there a while."

Joe smiled widely to acknowledge his accommodating hostess wearing a white terrycloth bathrobe that was belted at the waist. "Good morning. Hope you don't mind my grabbing the shower first. Thought I'd get on the road. Don't want to overstay my welcome."

Instead of laying the towel down, she entered. She began advancing forward towards the end of the tub, Joe still following her with his eyes. The knot on the robe seemed to loosen as she pranced forward.

Suddenly, it occurred to him that she had not come in for

morning small talk. Her claim from the night before, that she would recognize the "right situation," breezed quickly into his recall.

She stopped when she reached the end of the tub, arm's length distance from Joe. She placed the towel on the nearby vanity. Then her eyes fixed on his. He hoped he was reading the signals right.

He let the curtain fall from his hand, and reached up to open it further. He was fully exposed. She stood before him unflinchingly. He reached down where one side of her robe overlapped the other and gently undid the loosely tied waist belt. Not a hint of resistance.

There was nothing but bare skin underneath. She freed herself from the sleeves as he rolled the robe off her shoulders onto the floor. Lifting each of her long legs over the side of the tub, she stepped into the warm shower with him.

An hour later, cuddled together in her bed, Vicki broke the silence. "I've got to go into Rutland, to speak with my editor."

Joe didn't flinch as he wondered what this had to do with what had just taken place.

She explained, "I'm hereby disqualifying myself from the Joe LaCarta story."

Joe stared at her admiringly. "Personal feelings versus professional ethics? . . . Damn. There goes my favorite reporter."

She kissed his lips and said, "I hope you can view it as . . . as a gain in some other ways."

"Count on it." Then breaking into a smile, he added, "That editor of yours better assign somebody good to take your place."

"There! You just all but admitted there is a big story to be had."

Suddenly, Joe was visited by the ugly reality of possible jeopardy to those close to him. As he tightened his arms around her shoulders, he answered, "Not if I can help it."

Chapter 46

As he drove up the mountain on the access road to Killington, the pleasantries of the previous hours dimmed away into a compartment of his memory. His mental gears were forced to shift, especially now that he chose to fly solo, against T.J.'s better judgment. But he weighed the element of danger against the element of time, and prioritized the latter.

If Heinrich Klaus' ostensible occupation was ski instructor, then his reasons for hanging around Killington would soon melt away along with the snow. Joe could readily see that activity was winding down. Few cars at the lodging areas. Restaurants closed for the season. The mountains were green except for slopes where snowmaking equipment accommodated the diehards. With more sunny days such as this on the way, it would soon be a futile exercise.

Joe hoped he wouldn't find that Klaus' chalet was already in mothballs until next season. As he drove onto the street with the cluster of A-frames, he noted how it looked like an uninhabited village. Reading the numbers, he zeroed in on the unit matching the address Pete had written down.

Driving by slowly, he wanted to assess whether anyone was home. Peering out the driver-side window, he picked up two telltale signs. A newspaper was sticking out of a receptacle by the front door, and the garage door was up with no vehicle on the premises. The unit was still in use. Possibly no one was home, but probably they'd be right back.

The next step would be to park at a distance. He wanted to get a better look on foot. Things were so quiet that even one car engine would be noticeable for its intrusion on the peacefulness. He could see that only a few units reflected signs of habitation. A car parked here and there. A light on.

Joe parked on the street, around a corner and out of view of Heinrich Klaus' front door. Would he look suspicious walking through the neighborhood? What would he say if asked what brought him there? A real estate agent, looking for properties to list? For properties to rent in the off-season? That might be a credible ruse, he concluded.

Walking leisurely, he came to the front of chez Klaus. No sign of life, but there was no telling if someone was inside. Intuitively, he closed in for a better look. Noticing two white strips near the doorbell, he inched forward to read the names. Sure enough, the top strip read "Heinrich Klaus." Joe's heartbeat raced to full throttle.

He stepped back and resumed his walk, wanting to achieve a comfortable distance while keeping the unit in view. It was decision time. Should he ring the buzzer and get on with it? Or should he wait and come back with T.J.? There was an urgency in the serenity. He came to the conclusion that it would soon be lights out for the entire cluster of chalets.

His indecision was short-lived. The stillness was broken by the approach of a charcoal-colored Audi with a woman barely visible at the wheel. The car pulled into the vacant garage of Klaus' unit. The woman exited the car, but did not continue through the side entrance. Instead, she quickly swung around to the front of the house to grab the newspaper from its receptacle.

She wore a hat and had on a pair of sunglasses. Joe snuck a long look at her, but she paid no attention to him strolling about a hundred feet away in front of what he hoped was a vacant unit. As she fidgeted for the key, she turned towards the door, back towards Joe, an added opportunity to size her up without being noticed.

She appeared to be later middle-aged. Medium height with streaks of silver in hair once blonde. She had a hardy bounce to her stride. The active, outdoors type, typically found in a ski area, Joe thought. He noted she was wearing an aquamarine down vest that was open in the front. Being that it was much more than was needed for the warming temperature, he guessed that she had gone out much earlier in the morning. He watched as she entered the chalet and the front door closed behind her. His curiosity piqued. There was not enough patience in his entire being to hold back the flood of anxiety he was feeling. He had to ring that doorbell.

In his mind, Joe went over the ruse idea. He would claim to be a real estate agent looking for potential properties to list for the next ski season. He would say it was a routine canvassing. If Klaus was at home, he would at least size him up. If he was not at home, he would ask about his whereabouts, maybe in the context of a discussion about the property. Maybe he could find out how much longer they would be around.

He rang the buzzer. As he stood waiting for what seemed like several minutes, he wondered what the button he'd just pushed would ignite in terms of his fate and that of those others for whom he was beginning to feel responsible.

Nevertheless, he rang it again. How could she not hear it? He knew she was in there. Maybe she stopped in the powder room, he thought. If that were the case, then most likely she was alone.

Finally, he heard someone approach. But then, another protracted pause. Was she sizing him up through the peephole? If so, why was it taking so long for her to decide? He wasn't seedy-looking. And it wasn't exactly a crime-ridden neighborhood. Why the screening process?

Finally, the door swung open. The woman he had seen enter

minutes before greeted him with a look on her face which, at the same time, exuded both puzzlement and surprise. "José?"

He was in a state of amazement. She knew his name! The name he was called back in Venezuela. He studied her face. It took another moment before it clicked in. He did know her! He could not believe his eyes. "Anita?"

Joe froze, waiting for the shock to fade. He thought he had seen the last of this old friend from his Peace Corps days. He had come to fear that Anita might've paid the ultimate price for what they had done on that fateful night, that she might've been the one not to escape the clutches of this notorious Heinrich Klaus. Now, the question was, what on earth could be her connection to him? Regaining his wits, Joe flashed another look over at the white strips by the doorbell. Before, when he'd seen Heinrich Klaus' name, he hadn't bothered to catch the name on the lower strip, "Anne Marie Klaus."

"I don't believe it!" they each uttered the words simultaneously.

She approached to give him a hug. After a slight hesitation, he threw his arms around her as well.

"José, I don't believe you're here. I was actually thinking of calling you. I read your name in the paper, knew it had to be you when I saw your picture. But I felt funny because of the circumstances." It clicked. She was referring to the Marialena episode. "But you found me. How'd you know I was here?" She did not suspect for an instant that it was the other name on the doorbell that had caused their paths to cross.

Convenient, Joe thought. Stunned as he was, he needed time to figure how forthright he could be with her. "It was a real long shot, Anita. I thought it was another dead end when I saw the name Anne Marie on the doorbell. I didn't know you went by that name." It was a cautious start.

"Anne Marie is my name. I dropped the 'Marie' in Venezuela.

I liked being called 'Anita,' I guess. 'Ana Maria' or 'Anita Maria' would've been too cumbersome," she laughed.

She had aged well. He knew she was older than he, and therefore had to be at least in her mid-fifties. Her hair was longer, and the amber-blonde had dulled with the encroachment of the gray. Only slightly heavier, she appeared to be conscientious about how she looked. He couldn't help noticing her still ample bosom, the asset they'd exploited for diversionary purposes during the heist.

"Well, come on in, José. We have a lot to talk about. I'd like for you to meet my husband. Unfortunately, you just missed him. He went ahead of me to Boston on some tourist business. I'm closing up things here, and will be joining him for a flight to our other home in Chile. We're year round ski bums," she laughed. "Aging ski bums."

She led him into a large living room beneath the A-frame ceiling. There were smoldering embers in the fireplace.

Joe continued to play dumb. "Chile? The Heinrich Klaus on the doorbell, he's your husband?" That sounded really dumb.

"Yes, of course. I met him in Venezuela. Right after you guys left. We lived in Argentina for a while. Then we moved to Chile, near the capital. We have two children, a boy and a girl. The girl is the oldest. She was born with mental retardation. She's here in Vermont living in a supported home. The boy is more like his father. Very gifted. Graduated from M.I.T. last year and is making big bucks already, with a computer company in the Boston area. He's a ski bum on the side," she added dotingly.

"Your husband is a ski instructor?"

"Yes, and part owner of a tour company. He's been doing it for years. Up here in your winter months. In Portillo, down in Chile, when the southern hemisphere has its winter. He's planning on cutting back, however. Even though he's in phenomenal shape—he's into his sixties. . . . And, quite frankly, I'd like to experience summer again one of these days."

"Anita, I can't begin to tell you how worried we were for you. We never heard from you. Then we found out you never made it to Guatemala. We couldn't help but fear the worst. . . . We being Pedro, and myself."

"And how is Pedro? And Pancho? Are you still in touch?"

"Got real bad news on Pancho, Anita. He died recently. In Mexico. Was ruled an auto accident."

"My God!" Hands on her cheeks, she seemed genuinely startled. No hint of prior knowledge. Of course, if her husband were involved, why would he have needed to tell her such a thing. Then again, Joe still had no clue as to what to conclude about this unlikely marriage.

The barrage of questions she went on to ask about Pancho lent further credence to her surprise. "And Pedro?" she inquired about the third *amigo.*

"Hasn't changed much." He went on to tell her about Pete's job with the Immigration and Naturalization Service and about how his marriage seemed to be at an end.

He brought her up to date about himself, right through the announcement of his candidacy and its subsequent "suspension." Unabashedly, she asked if the alleged affair she'd read about in the papers was true, and if it was the reason he'd left the Senate race. "You can come clean with me, José. I knew how you guys were. Young *señoritas* on the brain. Far be it from me to be judgmental."

"Come on, Anita. I've done some growing up since those days. Besides, which paper did you read? The reporter from Rutland explained the whole thing. The girl was Pancho's daughter! We traveled together to his funeral in San Diego."

"You're kidding? We get the Burlington paper, so I didn't catch that."

"Some photos were sent, anonymously, to several newspapers.

It was part of a planned attempt to embarrass me out of the Senate race. That was mild. These people, whoever they are, will resort to more drastic measures if I jump back in." Senses sharpened, he observed her for any reaction.

"I had no idea you stood for things that might be such a threat?" she inquired, rather innocently.

"Maybe we're entering a new era, post-lobbyist. Buying and selling influence isn't bad enough. Now maybe dirty tricks and intimidation are being introduced into the equation."

It didn't appear she had spent much time pondering such things. He decided to cut to the chase.

"Anita, I have a confession to make. I didn't come here to find *you.* Running into you was as big a surprise as I've ever encountered in my life. Even had my doubts you were still alive. It was your husband, Anita. Heinrich Klaus was the name I was given. It was the name of the man who would avenge the heist, unless I aborted my candidacy."

Her face went blank. "Heinrich? Why? He's completely harmless. You sure you have the right Heinrich Klaus?"

"Anita, whoever these people are, they know about the heist. You said yourself you met Heinrich in Venezuela. Right after we left. I must ask, Anita. Do you know everything about your husband?" He hated to be this hard on her. She seemed to be living a contented life, at least on the surface. Joe did not have the luxury of time, but he did have the luxury of Klaus' momentary absence.

She fell silent with an empty stare in his direction. Either she was concocting a story or was confused about what she had just heard. "Can I get you some coffee, José? What I have to tell you will take a while."

"When I met Heinrich in Venezuela, it was like magic. It'd been a while since I fell for anyone. He was exactly what I'd dreamed about. Strong, smart, worldly. He treated me like a princess. He was very attentive, very considerate. It was a whirlwind romance. I forgot about the transfer to Guatemala. I even quit the Peace Corps early. I moved with him to Buenos Aires."

"It never occurred to you there might be a tie between what we did and a German–South American coming into your life?" Joe interrupted.

"Hell, there were lots of Germans in South America. Some hung out at the Bavaria Beer Hall. And at the Bavaria Restaurant. Surely, they weren't all members of the Gestapo.

"Nevertheless," she continued. "It wasn't that it never entered my mind. I was a little guarded. There was one wrinkle, early on. After being together a few times, he told me he had to beg off, that it had been fun, but he'd be leaving Venezuela soon. Just like that. But he acted strange, like he had some sort of demon to confront. Who knew? But it hurt. I think I'd already fallen in love. And then, just as unexplainably, he returned. I don't know, a day or two later. On the proverbial doorstep. Few words were spoken. He just pulled me into a tight hug. We made love. I still remember stroking his plush blond hair, thinking how boyish he appeared for the moment. Seems like yesterday.

"As for the robbery, and his suspicions . . . what did any of us have to show for it? Nothing. Besides, like many people in the throes of romance, I wanted to believe the best about him. And you know, I think he wanted to believe the best about me.

"He did ask about you guys from time to time. I was never sure why. He heard my friends and me talking about our experiences as a group, so he had natural reasons for discussing you. But, like I say, I was cautious. Never did I speak about that heist. I portrayed you guys as idealists who'd done your jobs in Venezuela, and who'd gone home to get on with your lives. Whether he ever checked up beyond that, I never knew. You guys never kept the money for yourselves. So there was nothing to glean from your lifestyles, I presumed."

"And El Tío was hard to find," Joe added. "He kept moving around, according to Pedro. But still sounds like you harbored suspicions. Yet you married him."

"You're getting ahead of yourself, José. As I said, his way with me was anything but Gestapo-like, for want of a better term."

"You could've tested him. Didn't you tell us one of your grandparents was Jewish?"

"I believe she converted to Christianity before I was born. I just told you guys that so you'd let me come along that night. Had to concoct a revenge factor. I knew you'd be protective about a woman taking such a risk. Are you still such a chauvinist, José?"

"No, I think you cured me that night, once and for all. You were cooler than any of us."

"Anyway, the proverbial shit didn't hit the fan until after we were married in May of '73. We just celebrated our anniversary."

"Congratulations . . . I think?"

"After we were married, he seemed always to be away on business. I thought, with the import-export companies he represented. Then I came to find out who his father was. The old man was still alive at the time. Living in a protected status in Paraguay. He had changed his name from Jurgen Klausmeyer to Jurgen Klaus. Not overly cautious, ay? Anyway, he'd been a member of the SS during the war. When I confronted Enrique, that is Heinrich, he admitted it was true. That's when he also admitted that he himself had been a Hitler youth. But he promised me that had all been in the past, that he had changed.

"He explained how he had been given no choice. In Germany, he had been brainwashed. Then, in Paraguay, he became a product of patriarchal mentoring. Weakness wasn't tolerated.

No mother figure to resuscitate dormant traits like sympathy or empathy. Until he met me, he claimed.

"Needless to say," she continued, "my trust in him started to crumble. I sensitized myself to any clue that he might be leading a double life. But I couldn't point to anything at all that would convince me he was active in any such Nazi organization.

"About a year after we were married, he proposed that we move to Santiago, Chile. He said he wanted to leave the import-export business, and that he'd been offered a job training military officers in Chile, under their new regime. I really hadn't paid much attention to the particulars of that new regime. I only knew that a guy named Allende had been overthrown, that he was some sort of Socialist."

"He was elected by the people of Chile. He was overthrown and killed. A military government took over," Joe summarized.

"Yes, of course. Now I am very familiar with the whole story. Anyway, I agreed to the move. I wasn't settled in Buenos Aires yet, anyway. He promised we'd ski together at Portillo and enjoy the beaches of Vina del Mar. It sounded wonderful.

"After a while, it became rather evident that the military government was not only pretty intolerant, but downright oppressive. Rumors of disappearances and assassinations were rampant. Once again, my suspicions were aroused. He couldn't deny that he was on their side, the side of the oppressors. Oh, he tried to assure me he wasn't directly doing the oppressing. But he trained officers. Taught tactics. Didn't make him much less guilty as far as I was concerned."

"That must've been awful for you, Anita. You still had feelings for him, feelings you couldn't just make go away?"

"You got it. Nonetheless, I threatened to leave him unless he changed jobs. Told him I'd be willing to move anywhere. But to complicate things further, I was pregnant with our daughter. I think the stress and the turmoil of that time led to her being born with a developmental delay. She was diagnosed shortly after birth."

"How did he handle that? The Nazis believed in euthanasia."

"At first, not real well. He blamed me. Said I should've attended to a healthy pregnancy rather than get wound tight over his line of work. But after a few months, he actually began to bond with Adriana, that's her name. It was amazing to see. I was impressed, and amazed, by that sensitive side to him."

"It wasn't an act?"

"Absolutely not," she seemed annoyed with Joe's question. "A mother can tell.

"But," she continued, "he still wouldn't give up his job working for General Pinochet's military government. He tried to tell me it was strictly teaching. And in a classroom only. But I couldn't give him the benefit of the doubt. Common sense prevented it. The only way I could be sure was if he got out altogether.

"We were living well materially. But it went against everything I believed in for us to be doing so at the expense of others. Yes, I demanded absolute reassurance. And I didn't get it.

"Finally, I left. I took Adriana, and we moved in with my sister in Boston. Also killed two birds with one stone. I was able to bring Adriana to some of the most progressive doctors and developmental specialists available. She benefited a great deal from some early intervention programs at that time."

"Heinrich let you leave?"

"He never tried physically to stop me, believe it or not. And he certainly could've prevented my leaving the country, given all his contacts with the military. He did tell me that he still loved me, that he wanted to stay in touch. . . . And that he would definitely visit me and Adriana."

"Did he? Did he come up to Boston?"

"Twice. The second time, he didn't return to Chile. He

resigned the job with the government while he was staying with us in Boston. We moved out from my sister's. I got a job as a nurse, and he stayed home with Adriana. And his changeover was accelerated. It was amazing."

"This story is amazing," Joe added, unable to disguise his skepticism.

"We stayed in the Boston area for three years. We skied on winter weekends. You know, trips to New Hampshire and Vermont. He was already an expert skier.

"Soon he began to take grad courses during the week at several area colleges. He made new friends and new connections.

"Then he began to speak freely about his past, not everything he did, of course, but what he'd stood for. He renounced Nazism, fascism, totalitarianism, you name it, in all its forms. He came to strongly resent how he'd been brainwashed as a youth. He developed a bitterness over being offered only one way of life, one singular life path that had consumed some forty years of his existence. His disdain for his father intensified. He didn't even return for the old man's funeral in Paraguay when he died, during this period."

"It's starting to sound plausible," Joe conceded.

"I had every reason to believe he was sincere. He was sought after as a guest lecturer at several area colleges and universities. After all, his was a captivating story. His reformation was the subject of a feature article in a Sunday magazine. Surely, if it were all an act, the last thing he'd want would be publicity."

"So, why did you return to live in Chile?"

"Despite the political considerations, we actually liked it there. We both had made some good friends. Heinrich was offered a terrific job with a tour company that ran ski trips out of Boston and New York. But it involved being based in Chile most of the year. I prearranged a nursing job before we returned. We left Boston soon after our son was born."

"So the marriage was completely healed?"

"And it has been ever since."

"When you returned to Chile, was there ever any pressure to take up where he left off, with the government, that is?"

"As far as I knew, Heinrich was never actively recruited by any member of the Chilean government. And they had nothing against him, even though he'd spoken out and renounced his past. They didn't consider themselves Nazis. As bad as they might've been, they didn't approach those proportions."

"That's pretty damn tough to do," Joe agreed.

"Although a funny thing did happen," she recalled. "This American guy showed up at Portillo one evening and approached Heinrich at a bar in a ski lodge. I didn't overhear much of the conversation. But Heinrich told me afterwards that he'd been offered a rather large sum of money to do a few 'odd jobs,' as he put it. Heinrich knew who the man was. Apparently they'd crossed paths when Heinrich worked in officer training. The man went away angry that Heinrich turned him down."

"Did you suspect the man was CIA, or something such?"

"Oh, Heinrich outright told me he was something such!"

"And the heist, Anita? Did he ever find out about the heist?"

She took a sip of the coffee and searched for the right words. "Our Boston years represented a cleansing period. He admitted why we met in the first place. Sure, he conceded there'd been an attraction. But he may not have put in the time or effort if he hadn't suspected I knew something. He took the initiative. Came over to my table at the Cervecería Bavaria." She was smiling nostalgically.

Joe tried to imagine their meeting. He shuddered to think of how this all could've gone in a different direction, of how she could've simply disappeared: vulture meal on some jungle roadside, or a rare treat within the Orinoco River food chain.

"His interest in you as a woman must've quelled his suspicions as time went on?"

"Evidently. But like I've said, if I'd made money from the heist, I would've had something to show for it. I didn't even own anything of value. With time, whatever suspicions he may've started with, must've just withered away."

"Thank God he never arranged for you to be identified by the watchman, the one who was on duty that night." As he mentioned this, Joe recalled how the man in Montreal had told him of the watchman's disappearance, never to be heard from again. Whatever had befallen the poor man was left to Joe's imagination.

"I would've avoided that at any cost. I was being very careful throughout all this, José. Just in case. Besides, if I recall correctly, Pancho won that skimpy red top at your farewell party and took it as a memento." She was almost blushing.

Joe was getting the picture. Anita's influence on this hardened ex–Hitler Youth must've been something unique, almost mystical. "So, tell me more about Boston and the 'cleansing period.' "

"When he first brought up the heist, my obvious response was 'what heist?' That's when he proceeded to tell *me* about it. How the loot was the reason he was in Venezuela in the first place. I pretended to be very intrigued, but made no comment.

"About two days later, I came clean. Or at least somewhat. I had thought about it. I figured he may have been testing my truthfulness as well as my possible involvement. I told him I had signed on as a distraction for this trucker that I knew. I told him I couldn't even remember his name. I told him he had been a friend, and that he had told me a tale of woe about how the warehouse wouldn't release his crates until he paid some kind of port tax. The trucker felt he was being overcharged and cheated. He said his only choice was to make the exchange using the dummy crates. So, I helped him out, unaware of what was really being taken . . . until Heinrich told me."

"That's still more than any of us ever told anyone," Joe pointed out. "But I'm impressed. Pretty creative story. Did he believe you?"

"I'm sure he did. He told me he'd long since determined the identity of the trucker. Said he and fellow operatives had tried to hunt him down for quite a while. But they were unsuccessful. They were sure he wasn't staying in any one place. Then they forgot about it. Needless to say, I was relieved to hear that El Tío had long since escaped their clutches.

"Heinrich said that the heist didn't hurt them financially as much as they had first thought. There was an insurance settlement. Then some other shady deal, where they actually got the stuff back, through some back channels. The revenge motive lasted a while longer—they wanted to serve notice that the Nazi underground was something to be reckoned with. But it must've worn off with time."

This was consistent with what Joe had been told in Montreal. The loot was ransomed back to the Nazi group by some opportunistic brokers, even though the Nazis collected a partial insurance payment. "And the involvement of the other three of us never came up again?" Joe asked.

"No. He assumed that those helping the trucker were simply his own employees, he said. However, like I say, if he'd ever checked up on you guys previously, through his own channels, what would he have discovered? Were any of you living the lifestyle of the rich and famous?"

Joe laughed. "Hell, I drove a car that wouldn't start when the temperature got below forty. Then I went into debt to continue my education."

As fantastic as her story was, Joe could not help having faith in her credibility. What other explanation could there be as to why a woman of Anita's character would remain with a man who had had such a villainous past. He could barely fathom the moral dilemma this good woman must have had to confront. Plus, she had two children to think about, one of whom had been born with a developmental handicap.

Now it was time for Joe to unload. He chronicled the events of the past several weeks. He described the meeting in Montreal. He related what Jules had explained about the heist and the brokerage of the several transactions by unnamed opportunists. Anita became agitated when told why Pancho really had died. And she was to the point of anger when told her husband had been implicated by name in Pancho's fateful confrontation.

"Heinrich didn't know Pancho was involved. And he wouldn't care one iota if he were now to find out. Who could be trying to frame him, and why?" she asked bitterly. Then, taking several calming breaths, she suggested, "José, why don't you come with me to meet Heinrich before we leave the U.S.?"

Joe leaned back in his chair and breathed deeply. "Looks like the next stop is Boston."

Chapter 47

The revelations took up most of the afternoon. And now that Joe had agreed to go with Anita to Boston the following day, one day earlier than she had planned, it meant another night in a guest bedroom. The overnight bag he carried in his car was getting a workout.

Joe asked to use Anita's phone to call Vicki. He tried the main office in Rutland, but she had already come and gone. He then reached her at home.

"How're you doing?" he began. A rather unimaginative greeting. But its open-endedness allowed her the opportunity to convey potential regrets over the morning's spontaneity.

"Fine," she answered enthusiastically, as if she hadn't expected to hear his voice again so soon. "Had a nice talk with my editor. Without giving details, I confessed that you and I have developed a personal friendship, that I could no longer be objective covering your suspended campaign."

"And he didn't ask for photos?" Joe kidded. He was relieved that it had gone smoothly for her. Losing her professionalism was a small price to pay for the promise of developing something much more special. "Who's taking over, the resident poison pen?"

"He let me recommend who I thought would be best. I turned over all my notes to her. If they run the bio, it'll be under a joint byline. And I didn't even share my suspicions about the sabotaging of your candidacy. She can dig for that on her own. But now that we're friends, possibly more than just friends, I would hope that . . ."

"Vicki, I get the idea," he reassured her. She was trying to tell him that she'd be a sympathetic confidante.

"Listen, I just met up with an old Peace Corps friend here at Killington . . ."

"Oh? Male or female?" she teased.

"Female, Vicki. A friend I haven't seen in many years. It was totally unplanned. I'm going to Boston with her tomorrow to meet her husband, before they both fly back to their other home in Chile."

"Will I see you on your way back?" she asked invitingly. Did she miss him already? Like he did her. Strange how this was developing. More strange was the timing.

"Actually, I planned on driving straight back to Burlington on I-89. Tell you what. How about meeting me at my place? I have wine and candles, too. I'll call you as soon as I get back there."

"I'll be awaiting your call." Her voice seemed to turn sultry.

"Okay, talk to you then," Joe ended. He was just about to hang up when he seemed to arrive at a decision. It was something that had been in the back of his mind since they parted earlier in the day.

"Vicki?"

"Yes?" She hadn't hung up yet.

"Do you have any vacation time coming?"

"Tons. Why?"

"How quickly can you get away?"

"Things are pretty slow. I'd kept my schedule clear so I could poke around about you and your crippled candidacy. But I'm not on that assignment anymore, remember? Why? You want to whisk me off to some romantic far-off place?"

"I'm booked to go to Acapulco next week. Love to have you along."

"Acapulco! Acapulco, Mexico?"

"That's the one."

"I'll do everything within my means to pull it off." She seemed genuinely excited.

"Latest flame?" Anita asked as he hung up.

"Don't believe there's been one quite like this for a while, Anita." He gave off a glow of optimism that seemed to make Anita appear happy for him.

Chapter 48

Ever since the man in Montreal had introduced the name of Heinrich Klaus as the vengeful Nazi operative ready to be unleashed at any moment, Joe was visited every waking hour by an image that sent chills up his spine. Now, as his car sped southeast along I-89 towards Boston, he contemplated the irony. Instead of meeting up with this so-called henchman in a dark alley or deserted roadway, he was about to be introduced to him by his wife.

Joe wanted to believe Anita. But what if she herself were wrong about him? Klaus wouldn't be the first man on the planet to live a double life. Was the makeover Anita described only an act, a charade designed to hold the family together?

Should he have called cousin Sal? Boston was Sal's backyard. The insurance policy would've been even more effective than in Montreal. But as long as Joe was accompanied by Anita, it'd be unlikely that Heinrich Klaus would reveal his other self, even if it still existed. Besides, how advisable was it for Joe to keep cozying up to cousin Sal?

So, if Klaus wasn't involved, then why did this "Jules" character say he was? Was there really a group of Nazi henchmen at his beck and call? Or, was Jules the author of his own dirty tricks, the true enforcer of Jules' Rules? He gave up Heinrich Klaus by name. Why the deception? To confuse any fact-finding efforts on Joe's part? To turn up the volume of intimidation by exploiting the Nazi mystique? There was the convenient tie-in with the heist. A smart psychological ploy? Possibly. Why not? Amateurs like Joe would've feared the Nazi revenge factor for years afterwards. To resurrect it out of nowhere would deliver a jolt to the sense of security that had taken years to forge.

They made excellent time arriving in Boston. It was the weekend. This time of year much of the traffic headed in other directions, to Cape Cod, to the Berkshires. The Red Sox were also on the road, he noted, half listening to their afternoon broadcast from Yankee Stadium on the car radio.

Anita navigated Joe to the parking garage of the Park Plaza Hotel where Heinrich was staying. Joe helped with the luggage and was impressed by how efficiently she was packed. They must've had this dual residency thing down to a science, he thought.

"I didn't tell him I was coming a day early," she mentioned as they approached the lobby. "I wanted to surprise him. So, he better be surprised."

"That means he'll be surprised that you're being accompanied?"

"Don't worry, he'll see right away I'm too old for you."

The levity didn't diffuse his edginess. "You're not too old for any man with good taste." Her smile indicated appreciation of the compliment.

"Can I help you?" asked the check-in clerk.

"Yes. Mr. Klaus. Heinrich Klaus." She knew they wouldn't give out his room number. "Please tell him his wife has arrived."

There was a pause as the clerk fidgeted with the keyboard and scanned a computer monitor. "I'm sorry, ma'am. There is no one here by that name."

"That's Klaus, with a 'K.' He's got to be here. He called me from here the night before last."

"No, ma'am. Sorry. I've checked again. There was no one by

that name here the night before last, either. Are you sure it was this hotel?"

Anita and Joe looked at each other. She was genuinely puzzled. The apprehensions Joe had harnessed began to run loose once again.

She spoke first. "I don't believe this. If he's not here, where the hell is he?"

Joe shrugged his shoulders. "You want to call back to the chalet? Maybe there's a message."

"Gotta start somewhere, I guess." She didn't have a cell phone so she went to a pay phone. She returned quickly, the same worried look on her face. "Nothing."

"His company? Would they know anything?" Joe suggested.

"Doubt anyone's answering phones on a weekend." She tried anyway. "No answer, just a general recording."

"Anita, think. Did he say he was here when he spoke with you the other night? Or did you just presume it? Could he have been somewhere else? Maybe with plans to come here tonight?"

"He definitely said he was here. He told me to meet him here." She proceeded back to the same check-in clerk. "Sorry to persist. Could you check if a Mr. Klaus has reservations for tomorrow night?"

"Sorry again, ma'am. Nothing."

"Well, we're getting nowhere hanging out here." She was the first to state what they both were thinking.

"Let's bring the luggage back to the car," he suggested. "Then . . . I dunno. Want to check the airlines? See if he left?"

"He wouldn't leave." She didn't appreciate the implication.

They exited into the parking garage. It was typically dingy. But quiet. Joe saw no one. Then suddenly, he felt both arms being grabbed. Stopped dead in his tracks, the two men wrestled him to the concrete floor. Two other men were whisking Anita away into a car that had just pulled around. "What's going on?" she yelled.

"Get in," Joe heard one man say. Anita was given no choice. They threw her luggage in the trunk. When the car was gone, the two goons released Joe and ran off. It was over in under a minute.

He felt a bruise in one bicep. And the opposite shoulder hit the concrete pretty solidly. They hadn't handled him gently. Nevertheless, it could've been much worse physically. But it couldn't get much worse psychologically. There he was, alone, assaulted, and without the one person who could've been the buffer if Heinrich Klaus turned into Mr. Hyde.

Should he contact hotel security? Why waste time—he'd better call city police. He headed back to the lobby. There, just as the pay phones came into view, he noticed a man who looked like one of the attackers talking into one of the telephones. Could Joe be sure? Why would the man still be hanging around? Joe's stride came to a halt well short of the man he thought he'd recognized.

Within seconds, Joe felt a large body brush up against him. Then the unmistakable barrel of a gun was poking into his rib cage. "You can't take a hint, can you, buddy?" came the rough voice.

"What's this all about?" It was all Joe could say.

Just then, the man on the phone hung up and darted over to Joe and the man who was inconspicuously covering him. "Come on," he ordered. "Take him with us. We're getting out of here."

This is it, Joe thought. Why go with these bastards and make it easy? If they're gonna shoot me, let 'em do it right here in a public place. He pulled away and sprinted towards the vast interior of the hotel.

"Wait!" called the man who'd been on the phone. "Joe, come back. There's been a mistake."

Yeah, right, Joe thought, I'm really gonna trust these assholes. Coming upon a stairwell, he started ascending, faster than he had since he was a teenager. After several flights, he burst onto one of the corridors and noticed an open room awaiting maid service. He ducked in and closed the door. Looking through the peephole and listening intently, he concluded they were no longer in pursuit. Taking no further chances, he called security from the phone in the room.

Shortly, two security personnel were knocking at the door. He explained what had happened, and they appeared to believe him. They wrote it all down and called the city police. The coast seemed clear by this time. Joe agreed to drive to the nearest station to describe the abduction of Anita to detectives. The security officers agreed to accompany Joe back to his car.

They were walking through the garage towards his car when a blast of relief came into focus. There, standing by the passenger door, appearing to be waiting for Joe, was Anita. What the . . . ?

"Anita! Are you okay?"

She had a sympathetic smile on her face. "Let's get out of here, José. Big mix-up. I'll explain."

The security guards fixed an annoyed stare at Joe. "Thanks for wasting our time, Mac," one of them said. Shaking his head, he turned to the other guard and they started walking back to the hotel. They'd probably seen their share of lovers' quarrels.

Joe didn't like playing the fool. He wanted to include the security guys in whatever explanation Anita was about to give.

But she shook her head at Joe with an expression of futility. "Don't bother," she advised. "Come on. Heinrich's waiting."

"Heinrich?"

Joe was breathing very nervously as Anita knocked on the door at the nearby Copley Plaza Hotel. He didn't think himself capable of handling any more surprises. When the door swung open, Joe watched the tall lean man break into a wide smile as he embraced his wife.

Heinrich Klaus was even more impressive physically than Joe had envisioned. He looked closer to Joe's age than he did to sixty-plus. His thick head of graying hair was surely blonde at one time. The sculpted facial features were covered with the thick skin of an outdoorsman. As he extended his huge right hand forward for the introduction, Joe couldn't help but think how lucky he was to have eluded this man back in Venezuela. If "Jules" from Montreal and his operatives had run interference, then maybe he should at least be grateful to them for that.

"Heinrich, this is Joe LaCarta, an old friend from my Peace Corps days. Don't know if you recall my mentioning him years ago. I probably referred to him as 'José.' He showed up yesterday, out of the clear blue. He also lives in Vermont, up in Burlington. I wanted him to meet you. And I hit him up for a ride."

Joe noticed that the big man's blue eyes had opened slightly wider at the first mention of his name. He couldn't help but suspect that Heinrich had heard it spoken more recently than the "years ago" that Anita had just alluded to.

"Any old friend of Anne Marie's is a friend of mine," Heinrich smiled. Joe almost had his hand devoured by the man's grip. His English had a slight German accent. "I'm terribly sorry about the mix-up."

Anita had apprised Joe on the way over. The private detectives had been awaiting Anita's arrival to bring her to Heinrich at the hotel where he was really staying. They mistook Joe for someone else. Anita's surprise early arrival had almost cost Joe a trip to a coronary unit.

She was finally able to explain to her "protectors" who Joe really was, after they'd swept her away. Anita's driver phoned ahead to Heinrich, as did the man on the phone in the hotel lobby. The matter got cleared up, but Joe had run off before hearing the explanation. Now, finally in the presence of the notorious Heinrich Klaus, Joe hoped that the explanation game was just beginning.

"The pleasure is mine," Joe responded. "I always wondered who the lucky man to marry Anita would be."

"Lucky is an understatement. Love and marriage in general tends to be life changing. But in my case . . . well . . ."

Unbeknownst to Heinrich, Joe understood the reference.

"Come in and relax. After that little episode, I'm sure you could use it." Heinrich showed them to the sitting area. He cleared a pile of papers off one of the sofas to make room.

"Thanks. I'm only staying a short while," Joe explained. "Need to get back to Vermont tonight. Just wanted to meet you before you and Anita left the country."

"That's nice of you to take the trouble. It was also nice of you to drive Anne Marie, even though it set off the little skirmish earlier. However, I'm afraid both of you coming here was for nothing.

"We are not returning to Chile," Heinrich continued, this time speaking directly at Anita. "Circumstances prevent it. My past has reared its ugly head. We'll be safer here in the U.S."

Here we go again, Joe thought, dropping his chin to his chest. Not another surprise. Nonetheless, he offered to step outside so they could discuss whatever the problem was privately.

Heinrich waved off the offer. "It's not only a private matter." He looked Joe in the eye. "It involves you. And rather directly." This explained why Heinrich appeared to have recognized the name Joe LaCarta when they were introduced.

Joe looked over at Anita for her reaction. She knew something was afoot, or there would not have been the need for private detectives. But he could tell that she too was poised for the explanation. She wanted her husband to cut to the chase. "Heinrich, I told Joe a great deal yesterday. About us. He knows about your past life. You don't have to give any background."

Heinrich looked at Anita. "I didn't want to break it to you until being sure I could pull it off. Didn't want to frighten you. I didn't come to Boston on the usual end-of-season business. I came to line up a permanent change. A changeover that would keep me based in the U.S. year round. Also, I needed to make arrangements to get our condo in Chile sold and our belongings out. The Chilean consul was very helpful."

"Then it's a fait accompli?" Anita appeared to be pondering what this all meant in terms of a future lifestyle.

"Forgive me for not involving you in the decision, Love. But there was only one option once I knew everything could fall into place. Besides, I knew you'd like to be closer to the kids year round, and that you were yearning to experience a true summer." He sounded like a typical family man pointing out the advantages of a job transfer that wasn't optional.

"Well, yes, that's all true. But I didn't expect to cut off our life in Chile so abruptly. What has happened?"

"Do you remember the time, Anne Marie, that I was approached by an American at a ski lodge in Portillo? I told you the man was pressuring me to come work for him, and I turned him down? Remember my telling you how angry he was?"

She nodded. Little did Heinrich know that Joe was also tuned in, thanks to the previous day's history session with Anita.

"Well, he came to see me again last month. He showed up at the Grist Mill one night. It's my regular beer stop, so I'm not hard to find. Anyway, he said how he understood I was long since out of the game, but he would pay me two hundred thousand dollars just to put on a little act. The act being to reincarnate the old Heinrich Klaus and to scare the wits out of one Joe LaCarta, candidate for the U.S. Senate in our very own state of Vermont." Heinrich nodded at Joe when he said his name. "He even offered to supply a couple of his thugs . . . for effect."

"What did he say when you refused?" asked Anita, clearly presuming that Heinrich was no longer capable of such mischief.

"I didn't. I didn't refuse. Not at that meeting."

Both Anita and Joe fixed a steely stare upon him, as they braced for some kind of rationale.

"It was the second time the man had caught up with me since I had buried my former self. This time I wanted to find out why he was hounding me. So I told him I'd consider it, but I wanted to know the reason he wanted it done. This didn't sit well. He operates on a need-to-know basis."

"You know the man's name, don't you?" Could Joe finally be closing in on an identity?

"I should know it, but unfortunately it's long since forgotten," Heinrich continued. "When I first went to work in Chile, in the seventies, he headed up a CIA contingent supporting the military government. Covert stuff designed to prevent the Socialists from ever getting another foothold. Mostly I worked with his subordinates. They seldom referred to him by name. But they told me it was he who had recommended me for work in Chile in the first place. He had first heard of me in Venezuela, even though I only had been there a very short time. After coming to Chile, I met him in person, but only once or twice. He said he knew who my father was, that his own father had worked for the American Office of Strategic Services after the War. He told me his father actually helped some of my father's colleagues to get out of Germany, in exchange for information against the Soviets."

"Small fucking world." Joe was shaking his head.

"When he reappeared in Portillo that time, I recognized him, but could not recall his name. He said that it was irrelevant, that he was better known in Latin America as *El Espanto.* As you know, that means 'The Ghost.' He knew I'd heard of El Espanto. Everyone in our profession had. By then he was a private operative. He had left the CIA to operate more freely, and to make huge sums of money. He was known to be . . . very effective." Klaus was nodding for emphasis.

At this point Joe took the folded copy of Jules' picture from his pocket. "Would this be the man? If that copy isn't clear enough, I have a blown-up color photo I can get from my car."

"No need. This is definitely him, El Espanto." Heinrich enunciated the man's nom de guerre with the kind of awe one shows for an adversary that is formidable, if not unbeatable.

"So what did he give as reasons? For wanting to end Joe's run for the Senate?" Anita now was almost as anxious as Joe to solve the riddle.

"Well, I never knew anything about Joe beforehand," Heinrich nodded in Joe's direction. "El Espanto simply said you were a threat to people he represented, and that your ideas were gathering too much support. They feared your success might influence others, other senators maybe, to break party ranks and effect reforms and changes. Changes that would cost money and influence to his clients. He didn't name names.

"But I'm aware of how these things have worked in smaller countries. People with money, on both sides of the law, people who could afford to hire dirty tricks specialists, could simply do so. To preserve the status quo, to protect their interests. That's how my father and his Nazi cronies lived in their South American sanctuaries. Much of it was paid for out of what they had looted during the War. I would've thought such things couldn't happen in U.S. politics, however."

Joe realized he was a threat to the status quo. But he'd thought it was confined to the usual give and take of the political arena. He hadn't dwelled upon how his ideas could affect wealth and the balance of political power. He could understand where drug cartels and corrupt officials might employ a hired gun like El Espanto. But it seemed like a leap for individuals who otherwise fancied themselves to be pillars of respectability.

Heinrich continued, "He did mention the drug traffickers as an example."

"But I've never concluded I'm for legalizing," Joe pointed out. "I want the matter reexamined, maybe decriminalized, with efforts being more realistic. Smarter use of resources."

"Well, he said they were threatened by any reexamination of the issue. Relaxation of the drug laws would undermine the profits of the people who own the trafficking routes.

"But," Heinrich added, "he implied that this was not the only group he represented. The man is very skilled at working behind the scenes. He said he had several other clients as well. El Espanto seemed to scoff at your idealism in wanting to reform campaign financing."

"So how much did you string him along?" asked Anita. "When did you give him your refusal?" There was some angst in her voice. Heinrich still hadn't described giving an answer.

"I didn't know how to reach him, of course. He called me back two days later. He'd become presumptuous that I would do it. After all, it didn't entail anything dangerous. I was simply going to pretend. I would be avenging the heist in Venezuela."

He stopped to make eye contact with both Joe and Anita. "Yes, he told me how Joe had been with the American trucker that night in Venezuela. And, yes, now I know Anita kept it from me all these years. And, no, I couldn't care less anymore."

There was a collective sigh of relief all around. They paused to look at one another's faces. Heinrich's expression seemed particularly sincere.

Then he added, "And that revenge was supposed to be the ruination of your political career." He nodded towards Joe. "Or else. But he was going to take care of the 'or else' part, if it ever came to that.

"So when I refused, he was pretty pissed off. Said he'd lost all respect for me, that I was a disgrace to the profession. I got a kick out of that distinction.

"Anyway, that's when he threatened to effectively ruin my life in Chile. He still had friends in high places. Life would become a colossal hassle. That would be bad enough. But it wouldn't be a big leap from hassle to jail time on some trumped-up charge, or on some kind of frame-up. Unfortunately, or maybe fortunately, I no longer have the kinds of contacts in Chile that could counteract his influence.

"That's when I came to the conclusion we should stay in the United States. We have good reason to live here year round anyway. But then I got apprehensive about pulling it off. When I sensed they were following me en route to Boston, I had to take some precautions. I let my reservations at the Park Plaza cancel out. I slipped away and checked in here under a different name. I knew Anne Marie was coming tomorrow, today at the earliest, so I hired the private detective agency to be on the lookout. They got overzealous when they saw the two of you together. Isn't that an irony? They suspected you were using Anita as the ticket to reach me. In effect, you would've been working for El Espanto."

"I should've called," Anita said.

Amen to that, Joe thought. There was enough real danger. He could do without being manhandled by private detectives working for the good guys. And he was becoming convinced that Heinrich Klaus had indeed joined the good guys. Why would he be revealing all this if he simply were going to take on the contract offered him by El Espanto?

Joe was mentally drained from the compelling stories of these last two days. He thought of how much more overwhelming it might've been had he not recharged his emotional jets during the pleasant interlude with Vicki Rivier.

Joe related the events of the past weeks to Heinrich, with the death of Pancho being the centerpiece. He emphasized how El Espanto, a.k.a. Jules, had implicated Heinrich by name.

"You see how clever the man is," Heinrich said. "He planted the idea of Nazi vengeance, threw you off track, and got even with me for turning him down."

"Maybe he's not that clever," Joe countered. "Had he not mentioned your name, I wouldn't be here. For whatever it's worth, I wouldn't know what I now know."

Heinrich shrugged his shoulders hopefully. "Joe, I can imagine what you must think of me. In my younger days, I did some awful things. I don't expect any right-thinking person to excuse it. But in the way of explanation, I had known no other set of values. Only those hammered into my psyche by my father and his fellow war criminals. They portrayed the world as a we-they thing. And stupidly, I came to fancy myself a warrior. A soldier whose role it was to preserve and promote the movement, in hopes that someday the younger generation would return to Germany and establish a Fourth Reich. Pretty warped, ay?

"Fortunately, my eyes were opened later. Anne Marie here was the best thing that ever happened to me. And then when my daughter Adriana was born, it became a blessing. One that virtually salvaged my humanity.

"You see, Joe, my youth was nothing more than lockstep submission to constant brainwashing. The network was the only family I knew. No emotional or heartfelt bonds. That changed when I met Anne Marie. God, I shudder to think of what I would've been ordered to do, had we discovered her involvement in the heist before . . ." He gazed into her eyes. ". . .

Before she could work her magic. The thought scared me so much, I tried to break it off with her. But it was too late." He was shaking his head, pensive.

"It was as if she were sent from Above to help me discover that a soul was buried beneath the hardened, dutiful exterior. Later, when Adriana came, and my capacity for love grew even more, the genie was out of the bottle. Who knows, maybe this epiphany would've come earlier, had my mother survived. I'd been discouraged from dwelling on her by my father. But when Anne Marie came into my life, I couldn't stop thinking back to my childhood in Dresden, and to what could've been a normal life."

It was more than convincing. It was almost touching. "Your story is too astounding to be a fabrication," Joe said softly. "I think I believe you."

"Well, if there's anything I can do to convince you fully, let me know. Anne Marie and I are staying in the U.S. And we'll have some time on our hands this summer."

"As a matter of fact, there is something. Something I've thought about, but without knowing where to begin."

Anita and Heinrich were all ears.

"It's something that might be cleansing for all three of us. El Espanto said that the artworks were eventually sold to U.S. buyers, mostly in the New York area?"

"That is correct," Heinrich said.

"What do you say we begin to try and trace them? Maybe get at least some of it back to rightful owners, or their families?"

"That might be a very gratifying use of my newfound free time."

Joe was encouraged by the level of enthusiasm in Heinrich's voice.

"Count me in," Anita agreed. "In fact, I'd better be the out-front person."

"Then it's a deal," Joe said. "Assuming we all remain in good health."

Chapter 49

Alexandria, Virginia

Already dressed for church, T.J. strolled onto the front porch to savor the morning air, as his wife inside applied some finishing touches. His stay at home was winding down.

Peering along the residential street, he immediately noticed what didn't belong. The dark sedan, remarkably similar to the one he'd seen at the University of Maryland campus, was parked about fifty yards away. The two well-dressed white men with short hair standing on the sidewalk had descriptions matching the heads he'd seen through the car windows. They returned his stare. No room for doubt—T.J. was the reason they were posted where they were.

There was no hesitation. Annoyed that anyone would impose upon his home life, T.J. descended the front steps and strode forward aggressively. Caution did not restrain the impulse.

Just before he came upon them, the shorter of the two clean-cut young men spoke up, "Mr. Jackson, we were hoping you'd come over. We preferred not to bother you in front of the Mrs."

"That's big of you. Now, what the hell are you doing here? And who the hell are you supposed to be?"

Both men flashed their IDs quickly, in a manner to indicate they were FBI, but not to divulge their names. The shorter man spoke again, "We're off duty. So our names are unimportant."

"Oh? I think that makes them all the more important."

"Listen, Mr. Jackson. This visit is strictly in the interests of diplomacy. We know you were at headquarters this week. You inquired about a certain gentleman whose picture you had. We thought you'd appreciate knowing that it would be in your better interests to back off. This particular individual has been very valuable to many of us in our work. It's very important that he not be dragged down over anything . . . anything, let's say, trivial."

"Why don't you let me be the judge of what is or isn't trivial."

"Well, putting away scumbags isn't trivial. This man does for some of us what we can't do for ourselves. He can go outside the rules. In fact, he makes his own rules. Doesn't have to worry about going by the book. I would think you would have appreciated having someone like him to call on."

"You mean to do dirty work," T.J. challenged.

"Call it what you like. You never had to bend the rules? Come on. We heard you were a pretty effective agent. A credit to your people after Hoover opened things up."

T.J. gritted his teeth. It wasn't the first time he'd encountered this attitude, this arrogance. It was somewhat disconcerting that this vestige of the sixties and seventies had slithered into the present day.

Glaring at the man, T.J. responded, "For your sake, I'm gonna assume that when you refer to 'my people,' that you're referring to honest law enforcement officials. And as for your wet-behind-the-ears interpretation of history, if your Mr. Hoover had had his way, nothing would ever have gotten 'opened up.' Now you and your mute friend here can get back in that car and drive on out of here before I forget I'm on my way to church. And don't let this gray on my head fool you. I can kick your two sorry asses on my worst day." T.J. wasn't sure he believed this to be true, but he wanted them to be assured he would not be afraid to try.

"Whoa, my man, don't get so riled up. This is a diplomatic

mission. Among brethren."

"I'm not your . . ." T.J. stopped himself. They were right on the one point. Diplomacy was more apt to give insight than would an ass-kicking. "Okay. Give me more. You want me to back off, you gotta give me a reason, a reason that's better than the one I've got for pressing ahead."

"Can't be specific, man. It's just that the guy can work the shadows. Goes where we can't. Deals with people we don't even know exist. Counterespionage, counterterrorism, you name it. Gives us a drug trafficker every now and then."

T.J. got the picture. The man threw some agents a bone every now and then. Probably gave up a competitor or some other unsuspecting dupe he wanted out of the way. He could take shortcuts that saved hours of investigatory toil. He could see why his friend, Dr. Lucas Drake, couldn't shake things loose for him on this one.

"You delivered your message. The visit is over." T.J. turned back towards the house.

"So, what're you going to do?" the man called out, persisting for the answer he wanted to hear.

"What do you mean, 'what am I going to do?' I'm going to go to church with my wife. Gives me inspiration. And you can't underestimate inspiration."

Chapter 50

Burlington, Vermont

"But they spray-painted a swastika across his living room floor," Pete said.

"Since when do you have to be a bona fide Nazi to draw a swastika," Joe countered.

Pete had returned from Costa Rica, and Joe had returned the previous night from Boston. Vicki had joined him at his home shortly afterward. She waited at the table while Joe spoke with Pete from the pay phone in the lakeside eatery. Peaceful Lake Champlain with the Adirondack Mountains rising in the background helped Vicki keep her patience as the buffet brunch table awaited.

"I dunno, José. I never would've doubted Anita back in our Venezuela days. But hell, that story's right out of fantasyland. How can we take it to the bank?"

"Hundred percent guarantees are impossible. On any of this. But think about it. As fantastic as it sounds, there's some logic to it. Sure, this Jules wanted us to get freaked out about the evil Nazis. Other than that, there are some common threads between what El Tío told you, what Klaus told me, and some of the things Jules was willing to reveal."

"Then there are no Nazi operatives? You think the threat is strictly a domestic one?"

"That's what I now think, Pedro. This Jules, or El Espanto, is American. He's gotten to know every shady element that does business in the U.S., and he's set himself out for hire. A back-door link between greed and politics. He takes the risks. Does the dirty work. And his clients provide cover."

"If the threat is strictly domestic, José, maybe it's time to involve the authorities. See what T.J. thinks."

"Yeah. He'll be back tomorrow. Then I'm taking the trip to Acapulco, to see what old friend Carlos has to add."

"José, are you still gonna go? Seems like all the shit that happens is happening outside the country."

"He doesn't know I'm coming. There won't be any planned welcome." Joe didn't have time to tell Pete about Vicki. It seemed frivolous to explain that, even if Carlos turned out to be a dead end, he'd have a few days of relaxation with her in paradise.

"Just be careful, José. I need a place to visit this summer."

"Don't forget. Anita's anxious to see you."

"Might even have El Tío talked into a trip up."

"That would be something. Be a helluva reunion."

When Joe returned to the table, Vicki feigned an annoyed look. "About time. I'm just about coffeed out," she chided.

"Sincerest apologies, my dear. But in a few days, time will stand still as we cavort along Acapulco Bay."

"Well, what do you say we cavort over to the buffet table?"

"Ah, the romance is dead."

After they had eaten their fill, Joe called for the check. Vicki excused herself and started off to the powder room.

"Indulge me one more phone call." Joe stood. "I'll make it quick. Should beat you back to the table." Vicki was still in the dark about the mental gymnastics pinging around her. Joe hadn't even explained why he wasn't making the calls from the comfort of his own home.

Judy Bennett, his on-hold campaign coordinator, was at home

and picked up. "Well, howdy, stranger. Hope you have some good news. I'm getting a little itchy."

"Well, boss, not quite yet. But things may be looking up. Getting a little dose of optimism." Joe wasn't sure why. The Nazis may have evaporated, but El Espanto could be as nearby as the afternoon's shadows.

"You mean I might still have a job? I won't have to go work for some lightweight."

"Can't say much, Judy. But the 'personal reasons' may not be as complex as I thought. May know more when I get back."

"You're taking another freaking trip? And, oh, by the way, what's this about the Rutland paper pulling Vicki Rivier off our beat? Anything I should know about this?"

"I'll call when I get back, Judy. You're getting ahead of yourself. Sit tight."

Joe and Vicki returned to the house. The hefty brunch made them lazy. Before napping, they frolicked through some afternoon delight. Later, he awoke before she did and decided to tackle yesterday's unopened mail.

The large manila envelope was reminiscent of the one Sal had sent after Montreal. More pictures? Joe wondered. As soon as he unsealed it, he noted that the photography groupies were still in business. Two color blow-ups. But a pleasant surprise. He'd almost forgotten about the favor he'd asked of Senator Elizabeth Parker Shannon.

The envelope contained one photo of the so-called wall of fame *without* the two suspicious photos of Blake Ross and El Espanto together with others, such as General Pinochet. The two vacant spaces were conspicuous.

But the other photo was the greater success story. Senator Parker had managed to take a shot BEFORE Ross had removed the pictures from the wall. Now Joe had a documentable link between the Senate Majority Leader and the infamous El Espanto. He read Senator Parker's accompanying note:

Joe,

I don't believe I did this! Quite a challenge—his office is always busy. But, happy to help. I trust your purposes are honorable. Be discreet. Remember, hard as it may be to believe, he and I are in the same party.

Regards,
Betty

P.S. Don't forget to destroy this note.

Chapter 51

Chesapeake Bay

Julian Muller lounged on the bow of his yacht with the slender young blond he had invited as his special guest for the day. Sunset was approaching, and they would soon motor back to his private island marina somewhere in Chesapeake Bay.

The day had served its purpose. His handpicked guests seemed to have enjoyed themselves with the open bar and the "adjunct" crew members. Several guests were crossing the threshold of inebriation. But that was standard fare. The young members of his staff were discreet. Muller himself limited his intake to one or two drinks. His agenda always included more than just the enjoyment. His antennae had to maintain clear reception.

Muller heard his name called. Looking up, the young man named Arturo, wearing his trademark jogging attire, approached with the cell phone.

Muller motioned for his companion to throw a towel over herself. He encouraged the other young women to cavort topless on the deck. But he was more guarded about what he felt belonged to him.

Muller stood to accept the phone. "Thanks, Arturo."

Arturo returned to the cabin. Muller walked a few feet away from his tanning princess so he could speak in private.

The voice on the other end began, "Sorry to bother you, sir.

Our contact just got some information from Vermont. Seems like our trap worked. She said our boy was confident he'd get back into the race. Said something about the personal reasons not being as complicated as he'd thought. Do you think he figured out the Nazi thing was just a scare tactic?"

"Possibly. They've got more brains and balls than I gave 'em credit for, I know that much. Didn't smell right when he went to D.C. with that ex-jock friend of his. It'll cost them. I've had it. Should be fun. Good work on your end. Keep me informed."

Muller walked towards the cabin. One of the revelers, a first-term senator, looked up from the bevy of beauties flirting with him and raised his margarita glass. "Hey captain, where you been hiding?" he asked, speech slurred. "What're'ya antisocial 'r somethin'?"

Muller indulged him. "Got to spend time with my special guest," he nodded towards the bow. "She might feel neglected."

"They're all pretty special far as I can tell." He pretended to reach out towards the backside of a young woman wearing a thong bathing suit. She skipped away coquettishly. "We should do this more often. Hell, ain't got nothin' better t' do." It was as if he were poking fun at his own irrelevance.

Muller was taking note. The man was still a relative lightweight. But lightweights could become heavyweights overnight. And it was important to keep the soil cultivated. Whenever the likes of Blake Ross decided to distance themselves from what he was selling, Muller would have a ready reservoir of new clients willing to open their coffers.

But that was investment for the long haul. Right now he had to deal with the problem at hand. Muller descended the steps into the cabin. Arturo was sitting below with the man old enough to be his father, but a man whose bull-like physique could still inspire fear. And in this matter, it surely had. Once long ago on the Colombia-Venezuela border. Another time in

Montreal. And just before that, near Ensenada, Mexico. Here was a man whose iron fists could still deliver a skull-crunching blow to the face. Arturo sometimes went up on deck to mingle with the guests. But that was not what gave the aging bull his enjoyment.

Muller handed Arturo the cell phone. When he had their attention, he announced, "We're going ahead with the contingency plan. Make the arrangements."

Chapter 52

Alexandria, Virginia

T.J. exited the house, suitcase in hand, as the car pulled into the driveway. He'd said his good-byes to his wife, and would wait for her to join him in Vermont for the summer.

T.J. tossed the luggage onto the backseat, and greeted his friend. "Thanks for coming, Doc. Had a feeling that little visit I had yesterday morning might raise your temperature."

"We had more assholes like that back when I first joined the Bureau," Lucas Drake explained as the car pulled onto the roadway. "Not surprised that the mentality exists still. Doesn't piss me off any less."

"Does it piss you off enough to tell me why the Bureau is protecting the guy in the photo? Or did you just come by to give your star agent a ride to Reagan National Airport?"

"We're not protecting anybody. Men like that protect themselves."

"I meant protecting his identity."

"If we were, don't you think we have our own self-interest?"

"No question. Let me see if I got it right. He works both inside the law and out. But you only know about the inside part because he is valuable to the Bureau, not to mention to a bunch of other Federal agencies. And the Bureau wants to be able to keep going to the well. As for the outside-the-law part, you don't know, and you don't care."

Drake was silent as he maneuvered the car through the

Monday morning traffic. "You're fairly smart for a football jock," he finally said. "Why aren't you smart enough to tell me what's going on? If there's something we should be investigating . . ."

"In due time, Doc. Trust me. Cut me some slack for just a few more days. Then again, if I can neutralize this guy, maybe the Bureau and I won't be at cross-purposes. He can go on helping you, and I can stop him from going after . . . whomever."

"And to neutralize him, you need a name?"

"Can't hurt. How about it, Doc?"

"El Espanto is his nom de guerre."

"His nom de what?"

"He's a legend in Latin American circles. You know, cloak and dagger shit. 'El Espanto' means 'The Ghost.' Started out in the CIA. Venezuela. Made a name for himself in Chile. Then went private. Doesn't live in any one place, but they say he leases property, usually out of the way islands or estates in many different places. Always under a fictitious name, of course. And, usually, not for very long. He's a real soldier of fortune. And he's made a fortune."

"When does he get to enjoy it? Living in the shadows like that."

"You don't understand. A guy like that, that is his enjoyment. With him, it's sport."

"You sound like you know the bastard."

"On the contrary. Never heard of him until you stopped in. When I made it my business, I kept digging. The man is very intriguing. Anyone below my level at the Bureau couldn't have come by what I was able to. Contact with him is strictly on a clearance basis. But it wasn't just for curiosity's sake that I found out all this shit. Since you were the one asking, it triggered my paternalistic tendencies. You know, to protect your sorry ass. Once again, just like in the old days."

"Doc, I'm not afraid for myself."

"Well, you should be. One on one, I know you match up pretty well with almost anybody. Even now that you're living that cushy lifestyle. But this guy makes his own rules. And he can afford to pay the help. I'm telling you, to him it's sport, he plays for the love of the game. He's so into winning, I've heard . . . I heard he already took out a contract on whoever whacks him."

"How do you do that?"

"He doesn't expect to get whacked, of course. But the idea of losing is so alien, that if anyone does succeed, he figures he'll get the last laugh from the grave. The contract calls for some private operatives, already chosen supposedly, to find out who killed him and to avenge his death."

"Sounds like he's taking the El Ghosto, or whatever you called him, a little too seriously," T.J. scoffed. "What about getting arrested for one of his outside-the-law escapades. Anybody ever think of that?"

"He's so far in the tent, the good guys' tent, that he'd have to commit a crime in front of a U.S. Attorney to get busted. Even then, wouldn't surprise me if the Attorney General intervened."

The car pulled in front of the terminal and came to a halt. T.J. stared at his former boss. "That it, Doc? No name?"

"T.J., my man, as pissed as I am about that little intrusion yesterday, I can't do it for you. Now, if I knew this character were interfering, say, with an election, for example, I might reconsider."

As Lucas Drake said this, he reached over to the passenger side and pulled down the sun visor. A small business card fell to the car floor. T.J. retrieved it. And saw the handwritten name "Julian Muller" in blue ink.

"Thanks for the ride, Doc. I owe you."

"Call me."

Chapter 53

Burlington, Vermont

Joe and T.J. puffed cigars as they strolled along the shoreline bike path outside Joe's backyard. The sunset over Lake Champlain provided a soothing backdrop for the debriefing.

Joe fondled the business card T.J. had passed him. Committing the name of Julian Muller to memory, he congratulated the former FBI agent. The help he'd leveraged from Dr. Lucas Drake could prove to be the Holy Grail of their investigation.

"Makes sense that this guy wouldn't need Nazi operatives to do his dirty work," T.J. agreed. "But that story about this Klaus is something out of Hollywood."

"I know. It sounds crazier when I tell it, second hand. But being there, listening to him, knowing the character of his wife. . . ."

"There's no telling who's paying Muller. But I'm sure the 'who' is plural. We'll probably never figure it out. They're probably well buffered," T.J. speculated.

"You think? Certainly would be nice to nail them all."

"We may have to settle for just neutralizing Muller, at least for now. Maybe we should bring in the authorities. Drake already suspects. He knew about me working for your election."

"I just don't want to force a move, T.J. Can't help but think El Espanto already has a plan, a plan he'll execute the minute he knows I brought in the Feds."

"So what're we gonna do? Hunt him down ourselves?"

"I've got an idea to bounce off you. Got some new photos."

"More photos?"

"For now, I think we'll go ahead with the trip to Acapulco. We've gone this far on our own. Might as well get the final piece of the puzzle. Time for Señor Carlos Santiago to tell his story."

"You'd better watch your backside, Joe. I don't like this being out of the country. Seems like Latin America is 'El Ghosto's' personal playground."

Joe smiled at the Americanized version. "El Espanto," he corrected. "Only Pete and you know where we're going. We'll take care that we're not followed. We'll sit by different departure gates until we notice a boarding line for the real flights."

T.J. stopped and looked quizzically at Joe. "Who's the 'we' that you're referring to?"

"I haven't brought you up to speed on that part yet."

Joe restarted the stroll and related how Vicki and he had evolved a professional relationship into an intimate one in only a matter of days.

"Ain't love grand," T.J. shook his head. "Certainly isn't known for its timing. But why the hell are you taking her along. Even if you can trust her, why would you put her in harm's way?"

"I can trust her," Joe reacted. But the idea of endangering her did weigh on his conscience. He had hoped for reassurance from T.J., not for doubt. Hearing it expressed aloud shook loose the guilt Joe had been restraining. He tried rationalizing. "Thought it could be kind of a pleasure trip as well. In case Carlos is just a wild-goose chase."

T.J. looked at Joe and rolled his eyes.

"You think I should leave her behind?"

"Hey, man, I'm not making that call for you. Your decision."

Joe sighed. "I gotta make it with her. Either way, I have to tell her what's going down. I have to come clean on all this shit.

Then . . . then, if I know her, it will be her decision."

Vicki went through a potpourri of facial expressions as she stood on the bike trail listening to Joe's confessions. The Adirondacks were silhouetted in the darkness, as rising moonlight glittered upon the lake surface. They didn't wander far from the backyard now that daylight had departed.

Vicki had arrived shortly after Joe and T.J. had finished their cigar session. Mouth agape, chin dropping, head shaking, she listened intently to the sound of Joe's voice. When Joe completed the account, he kissed her on the cheek, then stepped back to await a reaction.

"LaCarta, all I can say is, this little friendship of ours better develop into the most enriching one of my life. Because I just lost out on one hell of a story."

"If this little friendship weren't on its way to becoming just that, and if you were still wearing the hat of a pain-in-the-ass reporter, I never would've given you all this on a silver platter."

She came up close and hugged Joe. He took her into his arms tightly.

"You really robbed the Nazis of art they looted in the War," she repeated with an admiring look into his eyes. "To give the proceeds to programs to help the poor. Not bad."

"Not bad if . . . if it had turned out the way we'd thought. You know the old saying about the road to hell being paved with good intentions."

He ran his fingers through her hair. It was time to ask. "So, if you want to bag this Mexico trip, I'll understand. And I'll go with a clear conscience."

Vicki stepped towards the lake. There was a prolonged pause as she seemed mesmerized by the moon glow. Then she turned to Joe. "What the hell, haven't had any good adventures lately.

And maybe I can keep you from doing anything reckless. That, and maybe I can help relieve some tension."

Chapter 54

Acapulco, Mexico

It was just as he'd remembered it. The blazing orange sky over the west end of Acapulco Bay at dusk. Joe contemplated it from the fifth-floor balcony of their room at the Tortuga Hotel while Vicki was inside readying herself for the evening plans.

They'd arrived the day before after an uneventful two-leg flight. No trace of followers. Joe had the taxi driver take a roundabout route to the hotel. Still no sign of followers. Not being high season, they were able to get reservations on the spot.

Upon arrival, Joe called the Mexico Lindo Hotel and established through an assistant manager that Señor Carlos Santiago was indeed in town, and that he'd be around all week. That being the case, Joe decelerated the pace.

He and Vicki decided to spend the first twenty-four hours on a recreational detour. They had dinner in a cliffside restaurant overlooking the lighted bay. The first morning they went to Condesa Beach, across the street from the hotel, where they lunched on red snapper under the shade of a *palapa.* In the afternoon they hired a cab to show them some of the sights, including the famous cliff divers and including the location of the Mexico Lindo Hotel.

When Vicki was ready, they exited onto the inner balcony draped with bougainvillea and descended to the ground floor on the glass elevator. Happy Hour music resonated throughout the lobby bar. As they hit the street, the evening festivities were coming to life. Music everywhere. Streams of people of all ages.

They took the next cab in line. "Hotel Mexico Lindo," Joe said to the driver. They had decided that Vicki would accompany him. There'd be a simple innocence to a pair of tourists stumbling on an old friend as they passed through for drinks.

They arrived at about 7:30 p.m. The Mexico Lindo was a quaint hotel located in the older part of the city. It wasn't like the typical sprawling tourist hotels closer to the bay. Nonetheless, it was valuable real estate for one man to own.

The desk clerk told them that *Señor* Carlos Santiago, the owner, was in the bar, that it was he playing the guitar, and that it was his singing voice they were hearing. Joe was surprised he didn't immediately recognize it. The clerk mentioned that it was *Señor* Santiago's custom to entertain the tourists during Happy Hour, from 5 to 8 p.m.

Joe opened the heavy wooden door leading to the bar. It was small and had a Spanish motif. Vicki said it reminded her of the small wine and *tapas* bars off the Plaza Mayor in Madrid. There were about thirty patrons drinking the two-for-one specials as they listened and sang along with the round-bellied guitarist on the makeshift stage.

Except that the black hair had totally grayed, Carlos was a spitting image of the man who'd strummed his guitar at the many parties and river outings they'd had many years before in Venezuela. He hadn't put on weight because he was fat to begin with. The smiling eyes and the flirtatious manner were unmistakable.

Joe and Vicki found two adjoining seats at the bar. The sight lines to the guitarist were slightly obstructed. Joe wore a cheap straw hat he'd bought earlier that day for protection, both from the sun and from instant recognition.

Carlos had been taking song requests. With Happy Hour

winding down, Joe decided to get in on the act. When he requested "Mexico Lindo," Carlos seemed pleasantly surprised. The typical tourist requests were generally relegated to "Cielito Lindo," "Guadalajara," and a few others well known in parts of the U.S.

As he began the song, Carlos seemed to strain a look in Joe's direction. Joe could pass for Latino, even with the touristy hat. Carlos' curiosity remained in check. Until Joe started to sing along, the only patron doing so. As they sang, Joe noticed Carlos trying to focus.

When he completed the rendition, Carlos announced that Happy Hour was concluded for today, and he thanked everyone for coming. He did this both in Spanish and in fluent English. Amidst applause, he stepped down onto the main floor and made his way to where Joe and Vicki were seated.

He wore a congenial smile as he addressed Joe in Spanish. "Have we met, *Señor?* You remind me of someone, but I don't remember who."

Joe placed the hat on the bar and smiled back. "That's because you didn't want to remember your old friends from Venezuela. You didn't even come around to say good-bye."

Carlos squinted his eyes and concentrated. "José?"

"*Correcto.* Finally, we meet again."

Smiling welcomingly, Carlos grabbed Joe's hand and shook it vigorously. Then they hugged in the traditional *abrazo.*

"This is my lady friend, Vicki."

Carlos and Vicki shook hands, as Carlos commented, "You still like the thin ones."

"Watch what you say. She understands Spanish."

Vicki did, of course, but was unsure whether "thin" was meant as a compliment, based on what Joe had told her about Carlos.

"José, what a surprise. I thought I'd never see you again."

"Whose fault was that?" Joe chided.

"Amigo, you wouldn't have understood. In those days . . . well, I had business to attend to. Compelling business obligations. Anyway, that was many years ago. This is now. Tonight you will be my guests for dinner. My chef is one of the best in the city."

Joe and Vicki nodded in harmony. It couldn't have been better scripted. "We accept, Carlos," Joe answered. "Gratefully. We have a lot to catch up on."

"Then follow me." Carlos led them into an adjoining restaurant and picked out what he said was the best table. He held the chair for Vicki, then he and Joe sat. The waiter came without delay, and Carlos sent him to bring a bottle of their best Spanish wine. Amidst some small talk, Carlos recommended some of the house specialties and repeated once again that he was treating.

Through the three-course meal and a second bottle of the fine wine, Carlos and Joe caught each other up on their lives. Summaries without the details. Joe hoped those would come later.

Carlos claimed he'd inherited the money from a rich uncle, enabling him to purchase the hotel. He changed the name and had it renovated. He said he'd been married for over twenty years and that he had three children. The family stayed in Mexico City most of the year. He returned often to visit. It was a short flight, and now with the superhighway, he often drove.

"Has family tempered your womanizing?" Joe asked.

"That and old age," Carlos laughed.

Joe told Carlos about his own career, stopping just short of the point where he took the plunge into big-time politics. Carlos all but offered condolences when Joe explained how he'd been divorced and never had children.

Joe talked about Pete, and how Pete had visited El Tío

recently. He told Carlos how he'd seen Anita. Carlos almost cupped his hands at his chest, then stopped himself due to the presence of Vicki. "Yeah, that Anita." Joe helped cut off the gesture. No one mentioned Heinrich Klaus.

He saved the news about Pancho for last. He described it as the accident it had been claimed to be.

Carlos seemed genuinely remorseful. He went pensive for a moment, then said, "That's truly a shame. Pancho was a man of substance. A real man. Let's toast him."

They held up the wineglasses and they each took a sip.

"He died in Mexico," Joe added.

Again Carlos seemed to dwell. Then, with an air of fatalism, he commented, "Maybe the ghost of Pancho Villa."

"The ghost of somebody," Joe said.

Carlos went on to explain how he had left Venezuela shortly after Joe's departure. He mentioned working off and on in Colombia, as well as in Chile. Joe asked if it was in the same field, agriculture and animal husbandry.

"More or less," came his evasive answer.

Charming as ever, Carlos suggested that Vicki was being left out of the conversation. Joe was impressed with her self-acquired Spanish when she explained what she did for a living, and included some background about her past.

It wasn't until the table was cleared and Carlos ordered sides of brandy to drink with the coffee that Joe set sail into murkier waters.

"Carlos, didn't you ever wonder about the heist? You knew we were going to do it. And since there was no news that we'd ever gotten caught, you must've figured we'd pulled it off."

Carlos squirmed in his chair and threw a glance at Vicki.

"She knows," Joe interjected, as Vicki nodded.

"I wasn't sure you ever went through with it." Carlos took a sip of the brandy without making eye contact.

"Come on, Carlos. It was a long time ago. You can tell me. You can tell me about how it was you who helped El Tío find the Colombians. How El Tío cut you in."

This time it appeared as if it were Carlos who was visited by a ghost. He took a deep breath, and then made real eye contact. "You would have gotten caught were it not for me. There was a mean young German, a Nazi operative, checking on the crates nightly. I got rid of him for a few days. Gave you guys a safe opening. The small *mordida,* the little commission, El Tío gave me was out of gratitude."

"And the Colombians, Carlos? They didn't cut you in on a little bite, on a little *mordida* as well? Or the Nazis, when they got the shipment back?" Joe could see that Carlos was a tad frustrated, as well as impressed.

"First of all, I want you to know that what you see here," he gestured towards the dining area, "is my real life now. I don't want anything to jeopardize this. I am an honest businessman. But, more than half a lifetime ago, I was in a different profession, one I was unable to tell you about."

"And that profession was CIA?"

"I was a contract employee. I reported to someone in your embassy."

"The CIA was forbidden to mix its efforts with the Peace Corps. There was an exclusivity agreement."

"Yes. I was told after the fact. I never planned to become friends with you guys. They gave me a front, as a professor of agriculture. But mostly I was there to keep an eye on the Communists and their organizational efforts. And you and they seemed to be toiling in the same vineyards. Naturally, I bumped into you along the way. And since we had similar interests, and the young *señoritas* were never far away . . ."

Vicki looked at Joe, who smiled sheepishly and said, "What can I say? We were young and foolish."

"When my boss from the U.S. Embassy found out about our camaraderie, he asked me to distance myself. I was about to. Then the idea of stealing the crates surfaced. When I told him about it, he changed his mind. Told me to find out all I could and to keep him informed. He told me to talk you out of it. He was afraid for your safety. And afraid of any embarrassment to U.S. interests.

"But I knew, even if I talked you out of it, El Tío was likely to go ahead. And maybe with Pancho. Even Pedro. I had the contacts in Colombia from a previous assignment. So I made the connections. There were millions of dollars to be transacted. And I covered the play in Venezuela. And I solved the problem of turning the cargo into money. Why shouldn't I get my *mordida?* The CIA didn't care."

"And you knew how to contact the Nazis."

"Yes. I knew how to contact Heinrich Klaus."

"So you learned his name."

"Of course. I saw his passport in Venezuela. And later, we crossed paths in Chile. And yes, I knew he married Anita. But I never saw her, and I preferred it that way. No one would have to discuss their pasts."

"One big happy family," Joe was shaking his head. "Heinrich Klaus, you. And . . . and the legendary El Espanto."

Carlos' jaw was tight with reticence at the mention of this last name. The eyes glared, seeming to say "off limits."

Carlos digressed. "José, I told you in Venezuela that I'd come from a well-off Mexican family. Not so. At one time they were old money. But it had dried up over the years. I had the benefit of education. My father was a university professor like you. He was staunchly anti-Communist. He was known to debate Fidel Castro himself. You knew Fidel had been in exile in Mexico before the Cuban Revolution? My father considered him a dangerous element. Later, the CIA recruited me, based on my pedigree.

"So I used my position and my resourcefulness to make money," he explained. "That's how I was able to buy the hotel and become a legitimate businessman. There was no inheritance."

"It didn't bother you that you helped the Nazi underground to get back merchandise they never had a right to? And that you helped drug cartels build their business?" Joe asked.

"What the Nazis had looted during the War was now in South America. The rightful owners, even if they were alive, had no prayer of getting it back.

"As for drugs, I considered them a diversion. The only victims were by choice. So what if poor Colombians could make a living selling to Americans who had nothing better to do with their money, and wanted to ruin their lives? You stole from the Nazis to give to the poor, right? Same principle."

"Except we didn't take a *mordida,* Carlos. No commission. I don't own a hotel."

"True, my friend. But you live in America. And you haven't done badly. You have security."

"I did until recently." Joe didn't want the discussion to get heated. "I'm only here to get answers, Carlos. I'm in a situation. Politics. I was about to run for the U.S. Senate, but then was threatened. That's when I found out that the heist in Venezuela touched many more lives than I ever imagined."

"So your dropping in here wasn't a coincidence?"

"No. Pedro did some research in Washington. We narrowed you down. The name of the hotel pretty much did it."

Carlos laughed. "I must be slipping. In the old days, I was suspicious of everything.

"But the old days," he sighed, "that was a dangerous way of life. I was so happy to leave it behind. You know, the drug cartels paid me for several years after. Because I knew the territory, I set up a trafficking route through the Orinoco. Bought off officials, paid for protection. In effect, I owned the portage rights. It was a route not as well publicized as the ones through Mexico. But whenever the major routes got squeezed, the Orinoco route raked in more profits. It's probably still that way. But I don't know, I sold out after only a few years."

"So your moneymaking continued?"

"Yes. I not only own this hotel, I own my apartment building in Mexico City. But like I said, I left that life behind. The cartels were becoming huge. And powerful. I always worried that they could crush me like an insect.

"When the CIA offered me a job in Chile, I jumped. Took my profits and went. Also, I figured there was security working for the CIA under a military dictatorship. The cartels would forget I existed. And the Nazi underground . . . well they would no longer resent me. In Chile, we were on the same team."

"And the coach of that team was El Espanto."

Joe could see that once again Carlos didn't appreciate the subject of El Espanto being brought up. Evidently, he thought he'd deflected the topic earlier. This time Joe persisted. He pulled the copy of the photo from Vicki's bag.

"Carlos, do you have reason to still fear this man?" Joe put the photo on the table facing Carlos. "It is El Espanto, isn't it?"

"It's hard to say. That man is much older." Carlos said this in English. He quickly picked up the copy and handed it back to Joe.

"This man is the one threatening me, Carlos. El Espanto. His real name is Julian Muller, correct?"

"I don't know. Even if it is El Espanto, we never referred to him by his real name."

Joe was skeptical. Somehow, he couldn't picture Carlos putting a call through to a U.S. Embassy and asking for "El Espanto."

"Carlos, the car accident I told you about. The one where Pancho was killed. In Mexico. It was no accident. This man was responsible for his death."

Carlos' expression was wide eyed. His face grew pale as he gazed back at Joe, incredulously.

Chapter 55

He knew he had procrastinated—taking that first day in Acapulco to simply relax was a temptation too strong to resist, but Joe finally put the call through to T.J. in Vermont.

"Joe, what took you so long? Thought you'd call yesterday."

The urgency in T.J.'s voice sparked an uneasy feeling. "Wanted to wait until I spoke with Carlos. Why? What's up?"

"Some bad shit may be going down, man. I called that Marialena Morales, like you asked. To check if everything was okay."

"Oh, shit." Joe braced himself.

"Hang on. I hope she's still okay. I spoke with one of her housemates. They said she took off as soon as the semester had ended. They said Marialena had gotten a call from a tour company, who told her that her old man had a time share in Mexico, and asked her if she wanted to use the week or lose it."

"Where in Mexico?"

"The person I spoke with wasn't sure. You know how it is to a lot of people. Mexico is Mexico. Marialena took off. Her mother was supposed to meet her there, wherever it is. They said it was somewhere where there were beaches."

"That really narrows it down," Joe said sarcastically.

"Anyway, it made me jittery. But I still knew it could be a coincidence, that it could be a real vacation."

"Odds are it was. But leaving the country like . . ."

"Joe, we do have a problem," T.J. cut in. "I got the call yesterday. Whoever it was asked for you. I told them you weren't in town. That's when he told me. Said that a certain young lady, with knockout looks, was not likely to return from vacation before you announced 'definitively and unequivocally,' his words, that your candidacy was over and done with. Then he added, 'she might not return at all—accidents happen.' Then the asshole laughed and hung up. I recorded the call but it was brief."

"T.J., we gotta find out where she is."

"I did. I called her housemates again. Got the name of a travel agent that Marialena had used in the past. Pay dirt. Found out she's in Cozumel."

"It's an island. I've been there. I know it. Not too many ways to get out. They're probably watching airstrips and the ferry terminal," Joe said.

"This Marialena may not even know she's in danger. She may not even realize that, in effect, she and her mom are captive."

"I gotta get over to Cozumel."

"Joe, what've you lost your mind? You're no match for these bastards. You forget what Lucas Drake told me about this guy?"

"That's precisely why we can't go through local authorities. No way of knowing who's on his payroll. And if I did that, he'd figure out I'm here. . . . And Vicki, too. Where's Marialena staying?"

"Couldn't find that out. Travel agent only did the airfare."

"Shit. Cozumel is small. It's still possible to find her. And warn her. Then I gotta figure out a way to get them out."

"It's risky business, Joe. I'll come meet you there."

Joe thought about it. It certainly would be reassuring. But selfishly so. T.J. would be one more person in harm's way. And unlike Joe, he had zero chance of blending in with the crowd.

"Thanks for the offer, buddy. Means a lot to know you'd do it. But I need you at that end. Have Judy Bennett make an immediate announcement, an announcement that I'll be making a definitive announcement as soon as I'm back to Burlington."

"Not bad. To the kidnappers it'll sound like they're gonna get their way. Should hold off any 'accident' plans."

"Let's pray. And there's one more thing," Joe added. "Remember those color blow-ups I left in my study, the ones I told you about the other night? From my inside source at the Senate? Time to put them to good use."

"You got it, Joe. We'll give it a shot."

CHAPTER 56

Vicki had an alarmed look. "Joe, what's wrong. That call sounded bad. And you look like—?"

"Yeah, I look like I saw another ghost." He walked back near the bed where she had been curled up with a magazine. "Listen, Vicki, you've gotta get out of here on the next plane home."

"Wait a minute, back up. I'm not going anywhere until you tell me what's happening." She flipped the magazine onto the bed and stood up to put on a long T-shirt.

"Marialena. She's over in Cozumel with her mom. They think they're on vacation, but they're under watch, accidents waiting to happen. There was a call at my home. T.J. just delivered the message."

Joe paced. As he reached the sliding door to the balcony, he opened it to let in a morning breeze. "They got hostages who don't even know they're hostages. And they're forcing my hand once and for all. Guess they were sensing a lean towards resuming the candidacy. I don't know how. Probably all the probing we've done. Just hope they don't realize we're here in Mexico."

"Joe, I heard you say you were going there, to Cozumel. You can't go it alone."

"There're enough people at risk. T.J. offered, but . . ."

"Let *me* go with you," she interrupted.

"Why would I do that? I just turned away a trained FBI guy."

"Joe, I heard you say something about a warning, about getting them out. That doesn't take muscle, necessarily. We need cleverness. Sneakiness, even."

"And you're an investigative reporter, I know. Still, I don't like it."

"Look, Joe, I've been to Cozumel, too. And I know what Marialena looks like from the pictures. I even have one with me in my work folder. Whoever's watching her doesn't know me, and shouldn't even know I'm in Mexico. I'll go there a day ahead of you."

He walked towards her and put his arms around her shoulders. "I'm sorry, Vicki, the idea of you over there . . . by yourself . . ."

"Cut with the macho act, will you." She pulled away from him. "I'm good at finding things out. And at being careful. I bet I can have everything scoped out by the time you arrive."

Joe smiled. Walking back towards her, he put his hands on her shoulders and kissed her on the cheek. "That would only leave the problem of getting us all out."

"We'll come up with a plan," she was nodding her head with resolve.

Chapter 57

Carlos Santiago sat alone in his office staring into the coffee cup. He was awaiting the return call. The receptionist was instructed to hold all others. When it came, Carlos grabbed it after the first ring.

"Santiago, Jules here. You called my service. What's the problem?"

"The problem? I'm beginning to think *you* are my problem," Carlos answered in accented English. He seldom took such a confrontational tone with El Espanto. "I've been trying to shake free from this monkey business for fifteen years. But you're the one ghost from the past I can't make disappear."

"Hey, Santiago, I like the play on words. What, are you taking English lessons? Why's that? You chasing the tourist babes?"

"You hounded me in April to give you a contact you could use up in Ensenada. I never hear from the guy again. Last night I find out the target wasn't somebody you intended to scare, but somebody you intended to eliminate. And then the real shocker, I find out the guy is an old friend. Damn it. You knew Pancho Morales was once a friend of mine."

"Hey, Carlos, you didn't ask. I operate on a need-to-know basis. Now who was it that came by last night and ruined your good night's sleep?"

"You should know," Carlos said. "You made it necessary."

"LaCarta? Joe LaCarta, himself? That stupid bastard. He's at your place."

"No. No, he came over from the Tortuga, especially to look me up. Came in with his lady friend." Carlos winced. Maybe he was slipping. Why did he volunteer this information? Especially when he noted how careless Joe had been the night before when he mentioned where he was staying.

"What was his business with you? What'd you tell him?"

"Very little. He already knew a great deal about the heist."

"Yeah, it was me that told him. I met with him in Montreal."

"I think he knew more than you told him. Unless you gave him Heinrich Klaus' address, and . . . and your real name."

"He knows my name? Well, how about that? This is getting interesting. A real challenge. Let's see, what would a legendary operative do in this situation?"

"Whatever it is count me out."

"Carlos, I'm surprised at you. Where did your spunk go? I remember when you had balls, a real sense of adventure. Hell, now I bet you're screwing no one other than your wife. Don't you remember the nice setup I made for you in Chile? Half those broads disappeared after we let you have at them. Dropped them from planes into the ocean, to join their husbands."

"Stop reminding me of the past."

"We are what we are, and we are what we were, amigo."

"I've grown out of it. Someday we'll all get what's coming. For now, I have my family and my business, and I want to live in peace."

There was a momentary silence. Then Muller came with his pitch, "Okay, Carlos. You can have your family and your business. And I'll leave you in peace. After one last thing. I swear it. You do this one last thing, and it'll be like your old mentor here disappeared from the face of the earth."

"Don't know if I even want to hear it."

"You don't have to touch LaCarta. Kill the woman."

"What!"

"Kill the woman. She's nothing to you. Kill her and make it look like he did it. He'll be tied up in Mexico for months. No Senate. Probably, no more professor job, either." Muller laughed. "You got guys you can hire. I know you've gotten a little soft."

"Are you crazy?"

"Hell, you know I am. But the clever kind of crazy."

There was no disputing that. But Carlos couldn't help recall that the man had once been a loyal American patriot with a sense of honor and duty. He wondered how his driving principles carried him off into the amoral underworld he now inhabited.

"Carlos, if it'll make you feel any better, I'll ante up some cash. I'll even be generous, so you can help LaCarta with his legal fees."

"And if I refuse?"

"Carlos, I'm calling from Cozumel. My crew and I have two hostages here who don't even know they're hostages. If we eliminate LaCarta's girlfriend, chances are these unsuspecting ladies over here can go home unharmed. So look at it as saving two lives, by taking one. It's beautiful. In fact, I like it so much, I'll send my guys over to Acapulco if you wimp out. But that won't sit well. It's inefficient. Plus, you'd still owe me when I come calling next time. I need your answer by this afternoon."

After they hung up, Carlos poured himself another cup of coffee. He recognized it as the fateful crossroads that it was. He had put much effort into shaking loose from his past. Sure, he still had contact with shadowy characters, but it was mostly incidental. He'd grown accustomed to his newfound normalcy and sense of decency.

On the other hand, how nice it would be to make Muller go away, once and for all. Someone was going to die either way, according to Muller. That being the case, shouldn't Carlos benefit? That line of reasoning paid off in Venezuela. The heist was going to happen with or without him. And he turned it into his gain. But the question also revolved around whether Carlos could count on Muller to honor his pledge to stay away permanently.

And if Carlos turned Muller down? Could Muller make trouble for his hotel business? El Espanto had his ways.

No easy way out. Sitting in solitude, Carlos kept evaluating all the variables. In the final analysis, there was only one choice, the choice that was best for him. He must do what he must do, and it was time to get moving.

Chapter 58

It was a restless sleep. He couldn't make his body relax, nor make his mind go into neutral. The sliding glass doors to the outside balcony were shut. They struggled to ward off the pulsating dance music from the beachfront discos below. But the scratching sound on the glass surface was anomalous to the natural nocturnal order of things.

By the time Joe interpreted this, the glass plate was pushed inward, the music volume jumped, and three dark figures burst into the room. The body socks and ski masks were all black. Joe's heartbeat kicked into overdrive as he sat up in the bed. One man slammed his head back into the pillow and held a wooden club by his neck. "Stay put," he ordered in Spanish.

Another figure sped over to the kitchenette area, then to the bathroom. Returning, he reported to the bull-like man standing in the center holding the sharp knife that had cut through the glass.

"No woman. She's not here."

The broad-shouldered man didn't speak. It was as if he didn't want to reveal his voice. Instead, he pulled a pistol from under his belt.

The man holding Joe down, pressed the club deeper into Joe's neck. "Where is she?" he said angrily. "Where's your woman?"

Joe was dumbfounded. Why did they want Vicki? What was

the right answer? "She left for the United States. Today. She's gone."

The man near him slapped Joe's face angrily with the back of his hand. *"Hijo de la chingada,"* he cursed. He looked up at the heavyset man holding the pistol, who nodded towards the door.

The man who had checked the bathroom, bashed his club through the TV screen and looked back at Joe. "We were told to leave you be. But don't press your luck. You follow, and we'll use your head for a baseball."

In an instant Joe heard them scatter out along the inner walkways. Evidently they would exit by traditional means, after what had to be a more harrowing entrance over the contiguous outside balconies. The idea of following wouldn't have tempted Joe, even without the forewarning. Half paralyzed, he remained in the bed, staring at the shattered TV.

His imagination started to play tricks. What was the deal with Vicki? Was there something about her he didn't know? Was she to be trusted? Her foothold into his life had occurred at an unnatural pace. Had she manipulated it that way?

And she was on her way to Cozumel. Was it to warn Marialena, or to join Jules Muller? He'd come to Acapulco to complete the fact finding. Instead, a wrecking ball was now striking at the wall of answers he had been able to construct.

When the adrenalin subsided, Joe buttonholed his emotions and re-established rational thought. How could Vicki be with Muller? That's crazy. Whoever just invaded the room was truly ready to do her harm. Otherwise, why were they carrying clubs, and why, after going through the trouble, didn't they do a number on him? It jived with what he had been fearing all along—that those closest to him were in greater danger than he himself. And this disconcerting fact was being reinforced. Vicki had escaped by only a matter of hours. And at this very moment, she was alone in Cozumel.

Joe finally pulled himself to his feet, and walked to the sliding doors. Instead of ducking through the opening they'd cut through the glass, he undid the lock and slid them open. He took a slow step out onto the balcony. The music was still blaring against the night sky. Looking at his watch, he noted it was 2:50 a.m. He forced a look down towards the street. There appeared to be a commotion of some kind. Several police cars, blue bubbles spinning. Probably routine. Certainly, the intruders had to have gotten away. There was no 911 to call, he smirked to himself.

The fresh air cleared his head. Finally, it hit him. Carlos. Fucking Carlos. He's the only one I told where we were staying. What made me be so careless? He slapped the back of his head. Tomorrow. Tomorrow he would pay Carlos one last visit before heading to the airport.

Chapter 59

"Señor Santiago is gone," the desk clerk informed Joe. "He left yesterday."

"Can I check his suite?" Joe asked politely.

"Go ahead. But you will see no one is there."

"Forget it." Joe gave in. "Did he say where he was going?"

"No. But when he doesn't say, it usually means he's visiting with his family in Mexico City."

Still unsure of how he would have confronted Carlos, Joe left disappointed. He needed to get to the airport. The feeling of unfinished business with old friend Carlos buzzed through his mind like a persistent fly at a summer picnic.

When the flight from Acapulco landed in Mexico City, where he was to make his connection, Joe wasted no time finding a phone. Fumbling through his papers, he dug out the Mexico City number Pete had given him for Carlos' family.

"May I please speak with Carlos?" Joe asked, confident he would know what to say once he got his ear.

"No, I'm sorry, Carlos is not here. He's out of town. This is his daughter. May I take a message?"

It would've been indecent to leave the kind of message Joe had in mind with anyone's daughter.

"No. Do you know where I might call him? I'm an old friend from the United States." Joe figured she would've noted his non-Mexican accent by now.

"No, I am sorry. My father called yesterday and explained he wouldn't be with us this weekend, that some business came up and he had to travel. Didn't say to where. Maybe several places. He spent most of his time chatting with my mother. Maybe she knows, but she's not here. Can I at least tell him who called?"

"Tell him it was José LaCarta. . . . and tell him my lady friend sends her regards."

Battling both frustration and anger, Joe proceeded to the departure gate for his connecting flight. He was too agitated to take a seat. Pacing, he couldn't digest how Carlos could seem so sincere during dinner two nights ago, and then callously partake in the assassination attempt on one of the dinner guests.

Was he, too, some kind of sociopath? He kept playing it out in his mind. When he shuddered at the thought of what it would've been like had Vicki not left, the picture came into focus. They weren't going to harm him; she would've been beaten to death. Who would've been blamed? That had to be it. There he would've been, devastated by her loss, yet confronted with a criminal prosecution. And the perpetrators would've succeeded in ending the candidacy as well as his career, as if he would've cared much at that point.

Jules' Rules, he thought. The bastard wasn't joking when he promised he would do whatever it took.

Joe's and Vicki's plan didn't call for Joe to fly directly to the island of Cozumel. Instead, Joe landed at the airport in Cancun, on the mainland, and hired a taxi to take him south along the Yucatan to Playa del Carmen, the jump-off point for the ferry to Cozumel. The cab let him off at the private airstrip where small planes could be chartered to cross the strait.

Checking with the charter company, he was told it would be no problem arranging a flight on short notice. No problem as long as his credit card hadn't maxed out, he thought to himself. Joe went to a phone and called Vicki. She had called him in

Acapulco after her arrival to tell him she'd gotten a room at the Casa San Miguel, near the main plaza.

"Joe?" She'd been waiting for the call.

He almost became teary eyed upon hearing her voice. But there wasn't sufficient time to dwell upon the trauma that might've been.

"I miss you already," he began.

"That's nice of you to say. I'll be glad when this is over. One more day, maybe, if all goes well."

"It will." Joe was beginning to feel battle-tested. And the angry edge was adding to his confidence. "What've you found out?"

"Almost everyone filters through the main plaza. So I spent hours there yesterday afternoon and evening. No Marialena. Her mother could've passed through, but I don't know what she looks like. But I thought I recognized the man in your picture, Jules, during the afternoon."

"Vicki, you're being extra careful, I hope?"

"Yes, of course. Why? Something else happen?"

"No time for that right now. I had a little visit last night. No harm done. I'll tell you about it later. Just watch your back."

"Anyway. Good news. I went back to the room and started calling the hotels that had time shares. Seemed like there was a Morales in several of them. Then at the Reina del Mar, they had a Mariana Morales. Just figured they may've shortened the spelling."

"No. Mariana's her mother's name. Great work, Vicki."

"I've rented a car and am heading over there right after this call. I'll invent some pretext to approach her."

"Vicki, I should come over now. I know what her mother looks like. It'll double our chances of seeing them today. Time is of essence. Today's Friday. They'll probably try and leave sometime on the weekend, forcing El Espanto's hand."

"No, Joe. Let's stick to the plan. It'd take you a while to get here. Besides, how're you gonna work it so you'll be seen by the ladies, but not by El Espanto?"

"You are good, kid. Take the number of the airstrip here." Joe read it off. "But listen, if I don't hear from you by the time the last ferry leaves, I'm on it."

Chapter 60

Washington, D.C.

The distinguished gentleman approached the reception desk and showed his ID. "I'm Dr. Lucas Drake, FBI. I have an appointment with the senator."

"Dr. Drake? I don't have you written in," she said politely.

"I called a little earlier. I was told he would squeeze me in between appointments. He knows it's urgent."

"Please have a seat. I'll check with him when he comes out."

Drake turned, but chose to pace for a minute or two before plunking himself down. He noted the spaces on the wall of fame, the spaces T.J. had told him about when he'd called. And there was a match with the fax of the photo of the wall T.J. had sent him.

Drake had been suspicious all along. He knew how to read his old friend Terrell "T.J." Jackson. That was why he gave in on Julian Muller's identity. If T.J. felt strongly about something, then it had to be for a good cause.

In his mind, Drake thought about how he might handle the good senator. He was not a fan of the Majority Leader. Drake couldn't get involved in politics, but he was an astute observer of the action or, more accurately, the nonaction on Capitol Hill since Ross and his cronies took control. Like so many other thoughtful citizens, he was fed up with Congress spending time on nonissues, while important matters were left unattended. This was why Joe LaCarta's politics had caught his eye, and he had paid particular attention when T.J. got on LaCarta's bandwagon.

The phone buzzed on the receptionist's desk. She nodded and said, "The senator will see you, sir. Please go ahead in."

Smiling welcomingly, Ross extended his hand. "Dr. Drake. Nice to see you. You look familiar. Have we met?"

They hadn't. Drake figured Ross was simply covering himself in case they had. "I don't believe so, sir," Drake said politely.

"So, what can I do for you?" Ross held his watch up to his face, implying he couldn't give whatever it was much of his precious time. "Always happy to help out the FBI."

Drake recalled how notably untrue that had been years ago when Ross was a young state legislator in the segregated south of the early sixties. "Senator, I wanted you to know we may be investigating possible blackmail and intimidation relative to the Senate race in Vermont." Drake paused to study Ross' eyes. He was quite expert at interpreting reactions. So far Ross was unruffled. "The efforts have been directed at the candidacy of Joseph LaCarta."

"Yes. I've met the man. A real gentleman," Ross said.

"We have reason to believe that a friend of his was murdered just across the border from San Diego, and that man's daughter and ex-wife are in danger as we speak. They're vacationing in Mexico and being shadowed by the perpetrators. We're in the process of working through channels. But apparently, the man we're up against has his own channels."

"This is outrageous. Who would have the audacity? In this day and age. Intimidating senatorial candidates, no less."

"We've gotten involved at the eleventh hour, I'm afraid. LaCarta and those around him were afraid to come forward. They chose to investigate on their own. And they did pretty well. They had been severely underestimated."

"And what . . . what did they find out?"

Drake noticed a slight flinch. "They know who's after them. A Julian Muller. Has all kinds of contacts, foreign and domestic. Inside the law and out. Street bums and . . . and politicians." Drake stared into Ross' eyes for effect.

"Are you implying that LaCarta's political opponents might be involved? That seems far-fetched. And who is this, this Miller?"

"Muller, sir. His name is Julian Muller. Don't know if you recall him from your days on the Senate Intelligence Committee. It's quite possible General Pinochet might remember him for his work in Chile back in the seventies."

"That was ages ago. Why would this Muller give a rat's ass about an election in Vermont?" The vulgarity was uncharacteristic.

"Of his own accord, he would not. On behalf of certain special interests paying him well, he would. And from what we've been told, failure is not in his dictionary. Julian Muller plays to win once the game begins."

"Do you have an idea who these special interests might be?"

"Ideas? Of course. Proof is another matter. Part of what a man like Muller sells is deniability. Connecting the lines might take forever. But that doesn't mean we wouldn't try, that we wouldn't launch a full-scale investigation. And if there are any public officials or politicians involved, well you know how that goes. That's the one area where proof is secondary. The implication itself would do the damage. The press would have a field day. You know how things are in this town."

By now, Drake was sure that the unflappable Senator Ross was beginning to get flapped.

After the pause, Ross responded, "I thank you for telling me this. But I'm not sure why. If there's anything I could do . . ." Ross stood up, evidently thinking that Drake would take the hint and end the meeting.

Instead, Drake remained seated. Crossing his legs and flaunting a relaxed demeanor, he continued, "An investigation is not a primary concern at this time. Right now our priority is safety. We need to get those women home safely, and we have to eliminate the threat to LaCarta, and anyone close to him."

This time it was Ross who took the hint and sat back down.

"Of course," Ross agreed. "Preventing harm is the right thing at this time."

"Precisely, Senator. And if there are others in a position to do the right thing, it could be a major help to all. Who knows? They might even be helping themselves, especially if a prolonged investigation can be prevented." Drake looked piercingly into Ross' frowning face. Then nodding, he stood up to leave.

Ross extended his hand and said, "I think when push comes to shove, people will do the right thing."

"Yes. If it's in their best interests," Drake added, as he turned to leave.

Chapter 61

Cozumel, Mexico

Vicki pulled into the parking area of the Reina del Mar. Suitcase stashed in the trunk, she was prepared for departure. In the early afternoon heat, she had on her swimsuit beneath the light cotton dress. The sneakers she wore were better bets than clogs if running became necessary.

She passed into the main entryway and took a mental snapshot. The lobby emptied into a pool area to the rear of the building. She already knew the beach was in the same direction. Therefore, the pool and beach had to be contiguous. She wanted to look as though she belonged, perhaps being on her way to her room, perhaps waiting for one of the guests.

Sensing that no one had noticed her, she continued towards the rear entrance and exited to view the pool. Why not? she figured. In the afternoon heat, where better place to be than at poolside or on the sandy beach, sipping margaritas, perhaps.

Her first stab proved to be the right one. There, on the outer periphery, near the gate to the beach, lounged the striking figure of Marialena. Next to her, with similar color and facial features, sat a woman, perhaps a generation older. Both were reading. Both looked as secure as babies in the crib.

Vicki changed gears. Their presence could only mean that El Espanto and company couldn't be far away. In fact, they had to be actors on the same stage. Vicki couldn't just stand there. She realized she was attractive enough that most of the males at the pool had noticed her by now. She didn't have a room number, so she couldn't check out a beach towel from the cabana.

Thinking fast, she placed her bag on a chair and sat facing away from the pool. She took off the sneakers and slipped the dress off over her head. Leaving on the dark sunglasses, she waded down the steps into the pool. It was refreshing, and it afforded additional thinking time. The lounge chairs were about fifty-percent occupied. People of both sexes. Adults of various ages. Only a few children.

When he stood up, she saw him, plain and clear. He seemed to be stretching. Was he about to enter the pool? She couldn't help notice his lean muscular body. The legendary El Espanto was in remarkable shape for a man who had to be well into his fifties. Then she saw him sit back down and lift a newspaper. Grateful he wasn't coming into the pool, she guessed he had simply needed to rejuvenate his finely tuned body.

Muller appeared to be alone. But that didn't mean that his charges weren't close by. There were no obvious candidates sitting in other lounge chairs. No one who looked particularly thuggish. Was he doing a solo shift? Maybe the troops had been given some beach time.

When she turned her attention back to the unwitting hostages, Vicki noticed them stirring. Marialena stood up and took off her sunglasses. The older woman followed her towards the pool steps. Vicki was in luck. They were coming in. That was far better than their going anywhere else. Following them without being noticed by the hovering Jules Muller would've been tricky business. Marialena's mother took a seat on the steps to cool off. But Marialena appeared ready to immerse her whole body.

Vicki removed her own shades and placed them by the side of the pool. She swam underwater, then did a few backstrokes. She wanted it to appear that she had entered the water for exercise purposes. When she saw Marialena lunge beneath the surface for a few underwater strokes, Vicki innocently, but deliberately, moved into her path. Marialena surfaced after the soft collision.

"Oh, I'm terribly sorry," Vicki apologized. "How clumsy of me."

"No problem. No harm done," Marialena responded. "I should've watched where I was going."

They smiled and stepped apart. The icebreaker, Vicki thought. But she waited. She wanted Marialena alone, and out of range of any eavesdropping.

Vicki stalled for time. She retrieved the sunglasses and meandered to where she hoped there could be another chance meeting. Marialena swam a few more strokes, then placed her elbows onto one side of the pool. Now. Vicki launched herself forward to where Marialena was resting.

"Where're you from?" Vicki struck up the conversation.

Marialena smiled. Thank goodness, she was taking a friendly track. "San Diego, originally. But I've been studying in Massachusetts. Tough getting used to the winters. Coming here is more like it. How about you?"

"Vermont. Middlebury, a college town. Is that your mother you're with?"

"Yeah, not as much fun as being with a girlfriend. Or maybe a boyfriend. But we're pretty good buddies. We've both had a rough few months."

Vicki's eyes kept darting in all directions. She couldn't be sure whether she'd succeeded in picking a spot where Muller had to strain to see. Nonetheless, he wasn't the only man now looking in their direction. Vicki was not unaccustomed to being checked out, especially by men over thirty-five. But standing next to the striking Marialena, she noted that every post-pubescent at poolside found an excuse to gawk in their direction. Under normal circumstances, this might've given pause for satisfaction. Now, it only made the exercise of distinguishing between predators and fantasizers a challenge.

Marialena continued with the small talk, "I have a friend in Vermont who was into politics. Joe LaCarta. Have you heard of him?"

Vicki made direct eye contact. "Yes, Marialena, I have. And I'm here on his behalf."

Marialena's tanned face almost turned white with surprise. "What? . . . How did you know my name?"

"Marialena, listen to me carefully. We don't have much time. You and your mom are being followed."

Marialena started to turn.

"Don't," Vicki cautioned. "Pretend we're just having small talk. Speak in a low voice. One of the men following you is over in the corner with a newspaper. There may be others."

"What's this all about?"

"Those that are trying to intimidate Joe out of the Senate race are still at it. Remember the photos? I'm Vicki Rivier, the reporter you spoke to by phone. Remember?"

"Yes, I remember. But . . . what're you doing *here?*"

"No time for background. Joe and I've gotten to know each other. To be truthful, we've become lovers. You have to trust me, Marialena. I came instead of Joe, because they would've recognized him. Joe's bringing in a charter plane from the mainland to get us all out of here. It's got to be today."

The young woman kept her composure. She added a smile for effect, but made it a point to pick out the man Vicki had referred to. Vicki noted that El Espanto seemed to be taking things in stride, at least to this point.

"What do you want us to do?" Marialena asked.

"First off, you've got to convince your mom. And make sure she stays as calm as you're being."

"Don't worry she's cool. She's been through a few things."

"Great. Can you guys ride bikes for a few miles?" Vicki asked.

"Sure, we rented bikes the other day. Went across the island."

Vicki described the plan she and Joe had concocted. When Marialena agreed, Vicki asked, "What's your room number?"

"Two forty-four."

"Okay," Vicki added. "You leave the pool first. Talk to your mom, in private. Stay here. I need a few minutes to go slip a note under your door with the phone number at the airstrip. Call Joe. Tell him to bring the plane. When you hear his voice, you'll know everything I'm telling you is on the level."

"This is all so unbelievable." Marialena was shaking her head.

"I'm sorry I didn't tell you sooner, Marialena. Just wasn't sure what to believe. I wanted to wait till I had some answers. Never suspected it would come down to a situation like this." Joe explained how they couldn't expend more time than necessary, how he had envisioned a sit-down conversation with her when the ordeal was over. But it just didn't happen that way. "You better get going. The pilot's ready at this end." They hung up.

Marialena's mother was waiting with the two bikes she'd just rented from the hotel's bike livery. As instructed, they left their luggage in the room, taking only papers and other essentials, and attaching their beach bags to the rear fenders with bungee chords. Ostensibly, they were taking a trek to one of the outlying beach areas.

They began pedaling in the direction of the airport. Marialena was alert to each car that passed. She looked at each driver, but didn't pick out the man who'd been reading the newspaper at poolside. Probably irrelevant, she thought. He'd have a lackey doing the grunt work. Unless, no one was going to bother. After all, they were only on bikes, and bikes weren't capable of flying or floating off the island.

Then Marialena heard a car slowing. She looked to her left. It was Vicki. Vicki was pointing over her right shoulder with her thumb. She pulled ahead and kept going.

With her mom up ahead, Marialena stopped pedaling to peer over her left shoulder. There in the distance, she could barely see the lone bicyclist. It had to be the man she'd seen. He had on the same yellow shirt, and his height in the saddle distinguished him from the locals. Vicki wouldn't have signaled if it were anyone else.

Marialena's first impulse was to tense. Then a ray of optimism shined in. He was alone. He wasn't driving a motorized vehicle. The plan should be that much easier to execute.

Another mile passed. The lone biker to the rear kept his distance. Surely, they would turn a bend and be out of view at some point soon. Timing would be key. Marialena put herself in Vicki's mind and began trying to anticipate the moment.

As they coasted around a bend, Marialena heard herself whisper. "Now, Vicki. Now. Please zip by now."

When she heard the speeding motorist approaching from the rear, Marialena realized her prayer was about to be answered. Vicki pulled to their rear to block Muller's view, were he to be gaining. Motor idling, Vicki opened the right-hand doors. Marialena and her mom grabbed their beach bags, then pushed the bikes into the roadside thicket out of sight. The car sped off to the airport.

"Do you know where to go?" Marialena asked Vicki.

"Yes, I checked it all out beforehand. Every second counts."

Vicki pulled up into long-term parking, turned off the motor, and handed the keys to a valet. "Park it, please. These people have a flight to catch. I'll be back within the hour," she lied. They grabbed their bags and ran into the terminal and in the direction of the charter gate.

As they neared, they could see the single engine prop with Joe standing on the tarmac talking to the pilot through the left side window.

Joe's elation upon seeing the approaching women was short-lived as the barrier he had been fearing emerged in their path. A uniformed emigration official halted their advance. "Identifications, please." Joe hadn't been sure whether official clearance was needed for a domestic flight. It was practically like taking the ferry. But then again, the ferry always went to a point within Mexico. Once airborne, the charter could make it to Belize, or to some other point in Central America or the Caribbean.

The uniformed man studied the passports. At least, Muller hadn't had them stolen. Small consolation, however, if this official were to have been bought off and ready to play gatekeeper.

The few seconds seemed endless. Then the man picked up a phone, sending a chill down Joe's spine. He watched as the three women stared ahead with their own expressions of trepidation. He was on the verge of calling to them to run forward. But that would've been foolhardy. The officer was armed, and the pilot would've had to be out of his mind to attempt a hostile getaway.

Joe saw Vicki turn to see if the menacing El Espanto would be making his way to them. Was the phone communication going to bring in the reinforcements, guns drawn? Escape ended?

When the man hung up the phone, Joe approached to hear the news, for better or worse. The man looked at the three women, then noted Joe advancing. Still with a very serious look, he finally spoke, "Did you know your government has put us on the lookout for you? They're concerned for your safety. There is a fourth person, a *Señor* LaCarta?"

"That's me," Joe chimed in. Thank God. T.J. and Dr. Drake

were able to call in the cavalry. No longer were they floating in limbo.

"You look pretty safe to me," the man smiled. "So far."

"We all are. Thank you for your concern. But time is of the essence," Joe explained, reaching forward to help with the bags.

The officer noted the urgency, and took the cue. "In that case, proceed." He waved them through.

"Señor?" Joe saw the opportunity to expedite matters even further. "Since you've been asked to help, could you clear us to go directly to the airport at Cancun?" Going directly to an international airport instead of landing at the airstrip and renting a taxi, would put them in immediate access to U.S.-bound flights.

"Of course. No problem as long as your pilot is willing."

Joe informed the pilot as the three women boarded. It would cost extra, but money was not a concern at this point. After Joe handed the bags into the small craft, he reached in to take his own bag out.

"Joe, what the hell are you doing?" Vicki asked with an alarmed expression. Marialena and her mother also sat puzzled.

"It's only a four-seater, Vicki. And you're going the extra distance to Cancun."

Vicki asked the pilot if the plane could handle five to Cancun airport.

The man shrugged his shoulders. He wasn't sure how to answer. Joe had his money out. The client called the shots.

"Ladies, we don't have time to waste. We've seen how these guys operate. It's not me they'll harm. It's those around me. It's important you-all get away. The good guys in the FBI are onto El Espanto's little game, but they may need some kind of proof. Let me have the car keys, Vicki. Marialena or Mariana, do you have the hotel room key?"

Mariana handed him the room key. Vicki explained that the

valet had the car keys. She gave Joe the receipt.

"Joe, let me stay with you." Vicki asked.

"Not a chance, Vicki. It was you they came for in Acapulco—the little visit I told you I had. Now get going." Joe nodded to the pilot, lifted the strap of his bag to his shoulder, and hustled towards the gate where the officer had just waved them through.

The officer gave him a puzzled look. Joe stopped to open his bag. He handed the officer a copy of the photo of Muller. "This is the man the FBI alerted you about. If anything happens to me, he will be the one responsible." Joe left the photo and kept going.

Not wasting any time, Joe exchanged the receipt for the car Vicki had left. The valet had a questioning look, but he honored the receipt.

As Joe pulled out of the parking lot, he saw the familiar figure pedaling in front of the terminal. Joe wasn't close enough to see, but he sensed by the mannerisms that Julian Muller was not in one of his playful moods. His prey had gotten unexplainably ahead of him. Now that he was at the airport, he would take the precautions. Joe watched Muller park the bike and enter the terminal. Perhaps, he would make doubly sure the women weren't sitting by one of the departure gates. But it would be futile this time. Joe watched with satisfaction and relief as the chartered puddle jumper lifted its female cargo into the afternoon sky.

It would take Muller a while to pedal back to the hotel. Maybe I should offer him a ride, Joe chuckled to himself. Of course, if El Espanto suspected there were rescue efforts afoot, he'd ditch the bike and rent a car himself. Either way, Joe would be waiting.

Chapter 62

Joe had no trouble getting directions to the Reina del Mar. He parked under a lamppost. Grabbing his bag, he proceeded through the lobby and went directly to room 244 and let himself in.

He closed the curtains and settled in. He made room for himself to relax on one of the beds. A little time for reflection, he figured. And time to prepare for the final confrontation with Julian Muller. His plans were now hazy at best. The fact that the three ladies would soon be in Miami, New York, or somewhere else en route to safety, lifted a huge weight from his shoulders. He felt like he was now playing with the house's money.

He even chuckled at the thought that he was on Muller's tab. Surely, the time-share story was just a lure, a setup. Muller had to be paying for the room. Joe considered ordering room service. Maybe a filet mignon. A few international calls back to the States would rub it in a little more.

His thoughts ricocheted back and forth between satisfaction and anger. He was gratified that the war had taken a turn in his favor. But he couldn't get the idea of Carlos' betrayal out of his mind. And the more he thought about it, the more elusive was the prospect of closure on the shadowy Muller.

The weakening ray of sunshine seeping through the crack in the curtains soon disappeared altogether. As the room descended into total darkness, Joe recalled what T.J. had warned about people like Julian Muller. He didn't become the legendary El Espanto by losing, by being shown up. When push came to shove, would he simply accept defeat? Or would he pursue another form of one-upmanship?

A light sleep took over. The exhaustion of the previous night. The tension of the day's evacuation. His mind and body had been on overload. The opportunity to stretch out must've carried him across the threshold.

But the vision of Muller followed him across that threshold. The face was large against a blue sky. One hand held puppet strings, the other a large automatic pistol. The trademark smirk was on his face, the expression that always seemed to say, I know what's going to happen next, but you don't. Jules' Rules.

Joe was awakened by the knock at the door. He spun to a sitting position and let the adrenalin fuel for a few seconds. He reached over to open the nightstand drawer and pushed the button. Then he slid the drawer shut, except for a slight opening. He then fixed his straw hat in place and walked to the peephole.

El Espanto. And alone again. Dressed as a waiter. It was probably his ruse in case the women had doubled back and answered the door for themselves. Joe wondered if no answer would mean the lock would get picked. Most likely, Muller had his own key by now.

Joe didn't wait to find out. He swung the door open and flipped on the light switch. "New job, Mr. Muller? What happened, a temporary slump in the rent-a-ghost business?"

Even the seasoned Muller was taken slightly by surprise. He hadn't seen Joe wearing a hat before, but there was no hesitation in recognizing his greeter. If he'd hoped to find the women, Muller didn't look all too disappointed to be face to face with Joe LaCarta himself.

"Well, well. Look who's getting around. What's the matter?

Have trouble sleeping over in Acapulco?" Muller imposed himself into the room.

Joe didn't try resisting. Instead, he lured him over by the nightstand and sat on the edge of one of the beds. Muller took a seat opposite him on the other bed.

"Carlos Santiago," Joe said bitterly, searching for the connection, and referring to the lack of sleep in Acapulco.

"Carlos Santiago?" Muller scoffed. "He's a fat wimp. But I got to hand it to you, Joe. You got around. Did some pretty fancy detective work for an amateur. Didn't hurt having that big FBI guy around. I hadn't figured on that when this all started. A small inconvenience from my end. And nice try with Senator Ross. The hypocrite called me. Asked me to back off. Big of him, eh? I'm sure he was compelled by conscience. . . . Where are the women? I rather enjoy getting an eyeful of that Marialena."

"What women? The ones from this room are back in the States. The one with me in Acapulco got beaten to death."

"You seem to have taken it pretty well," Muller taunted. "Cut the crap, Joe, I know she took off before those assassins showed up. I was happy to hear that. Would've been bad for tourism."

"Then it's over between us. Your cover is blown. But I can't prove anything. So what do you say? Stalemate?" Joe wasn't optimistic. He knew better. But he needed a reaction of some kind.

"Sure, Joe. Stalemate. Senator Ross will protect you. Shit, I couldn't pay for one of my cars with what that asshole was paying me. What do you propose I tell my other clients?" Muller was reaching the point in the conversation where he was visibly enjoying himself.

"Other clients. Oh, yeah, I forgot. Drug dealers. Corrupt cops. On both sides of the border. And the guys who run the trafficking routes, like on our beloved Orinoco River. Anybody else I should know about?"

"Not that you should know about," Muller laughed. "Hell, Ross and his blowhard friends, they were just around to run interference. You may be disappointed to know that some of my other clients also travel in circles of respectability."

"Now let me guess. People threatened by campaign finance reform. They can no longer buy and sell candidates or legislation."

"Not bad guesses. But then again, this isn't rocket science, Joe. Surprised it's taken me this long to develop such a broad client base. You had the bad luck of being on the wrong side of too many issues, while at the same time being positioned to build coalitions from the centers of both parties. Bipartisanship is not good. My clients wouldn't be able to buy one side off against the other anymore."

"I presume you don't advertise your services in national publications," Joe probed.

"Hell, no. But I must admit, the Internet has been good for business. But by and large, I'm the proactive type. I approach them. I convince them of how helpful I can be. And of how discreet and anonymous I am. But somehow, I think you've figured this all out by now."

"Like we figured the Nazi tale was bullshit."

"Hey, it was a nice place to start. Figured you'd go to bed thinking about SS Panzer divisions coming up your driveway. How'd you like the photos we sent to the papers? I never planned on that accomplishing much. It was mostly for entertainment value. And to let you know how close we were following you . . . and that sweet young thing."

"So you had to resort to killing, kidnapping . . . ?"

"Pawns in the game, my man. Mere pawns. Can you even imagine the stakes that are on the table for some groups? Foreign governments, multinational corporations."

"And as soon as I'm off the electoral stage. As soon as I go back to being plain old Joe LaCarta again, I'm a pawn, too. Another accident waiting to happen?"

Muller seemed to be prideful of Joe's disillusionment. Joe felt that the man looked upon idealism as a disease that needed to be cured.

"Morales was pretty easy. He had the regular routine of going down to that orphanage to help out a bunch of little bastards. He might've lived if we'd gotten this ex-Nazi to play the intimidator. But the old guy's gone soft. Turned me down. Had we lined up the ex-Nazi, Morales might've been spared. So he could tell how the Nazis you robbed were finally on to you-all. When I had to settle for using my own people, we figured 'what the hell.' Might as well kill two birds with one stone. Kill him and make it look like an accident. Then call it whatever best served our purposes."

"You're a real credit to the human race, Jules. So, if I resume my candidacy, you'll send another message. And if I don't, I assume pawn status. And you'll need to cover your trail, make sure I never write my memoirs. Either way, somebody's gonna go down."

"Joe, hate to disappoint you. But this game is over. You have a much more immediate problem, my friend. You should start wondering if you'll live to see U.S. soil again. And with that, I believe it's time for me to take my leave."

Muller stood. Just before pivoting towards the door, he reached down into the nightstand drawer and pulled out the small tape recorder. He opened the compartment and took out the tape. Putting it into his shirt pocket, he shook his head mockingly. "You did some nice work, Joe. But don't forget, you are still only an amateur." Muller headed for the door.

"What can I say?" Joe lamented. "Guess I'm technologically challenged." Muller wasn't amused. The door slammed shut behind him.

No time to waste. Joe called room service and ordered a Corona beer. He undid the straw hat held on his head by the same masking tape that was holding the second small tape recorder in place. He'd taken the time to do some shopping when Vicki left Acapulco. Indeed, he was a technological neophyte. For this reason, he opted to run two tapes, hoping one would give him audio decipherable enough for evidentiary value.

Joe pulled a blank tape from his bag and inserted it into the tape recorder Muller had graciously left behind in the night-stand drawer. Putting the two recorders together, Joe recorded a copy of the surviving tape. The voices were audible on the original. He just hoped the copy would give added insurance. He placed the original in an envelope and addressed it to T.J.

There was a knock at the door. Peering through the peephole, Joe was relieved that room service hadn't sent Muller back to him. They probably had no idea he'd even been in uniform. Joe let the man in and paid for the beer. Then he asked the man for the favor of mailing the envelope to T.J. as soon as possible. He handed the man five twenty-dollar bills and emphasized that the man had to handle it personally, and secretly. The waiter agreed. As added incentive, Joe had the man make out a self-addressed envelope. Joe promised he'd send him another one hundred U.S. dollars when the first envelope arrived. The man smiled gratefully, ecstatic over his financial good fortune.

When he was alone again, Joe immediately lightened his bag of all nonessentials. It was time to move out, hopefully before Muller had time to formulate a plan. Or arrange the proverbial accident. The thought of calling the police entered Joe's mind. The fact that word had gotten to Mexican officials about their plight was encouraging. But Joe couldn't feel secure. Muller could have some official in his pocket that would turn out to be the actual perpetrator. Better to just make a break and get to the car.

Quietly, Joe let himself out onto the second-floor balcony. The pool area was dark. No sign of humanity. If he could descend over the balcony, he could tiptoe through the shadows and get out to the beach. Then he would circle around to the parking lot and take off in the car.

He tossed the bag down first. He climbed over the wrought-iron bars and lowered himself to a hanging position. His feet groped for the top crossbar of the first-floor balcony below. His toes were almost touching. If he were an inch taller, it would've been easy. Instead, he released his grip and let his weight push off on one foot, spring-boarding into a jump and landing on the poolside patio. A little too old for this type of shit, he thought to himself.

Thigh bones still vibrating, he retrieved his bag. But he forgot about staying in the shadows. Hurriedly, he broke into a run along the edge of the pool and headed towards the exit gate to the beach.

Like out of nowhere, the tall figure wheeled in from the beach side of the gate. Startled, Joe heard the voice of El Espanto.

"Going somewhere, Senator? I kind of figured you wouldn't wait around. I guessed right this time. Just in case, I paid someone in the lobby to come get me if you went out the conventional way."

When Joe noticed the gun he felt like the fool T.J. and Vicki had warned against being. El Espanto indeed possessed the craziness that went with the cleverness.

"You win, Muller. What more do you want? Tell your clients I'm finished. No more politics. Keep your status quo. I just want to go back and live in peace."

"Nice try, Joe. Guess I'd say anything, too, if I were in your shoes . . . and my life was about to end. They'll find you on the beach tomorrow. Naive tourist, shot and robbed."

Joe reacted as soon as he saw Muller begin to raise the weapon from his side. Joe fired his shoulder bag with a two-hand-push pass directly at Muller's head. Almost with the same motion, he took two steps and leapt headlong into the pool.

Submerging, he heard the muffled gunshots. He felt nothing. He noticed no strands of blood reflecting off the underwater lights. Would he have to choose between drowning and being shot? Unable to hold his breath much longer, he would have to surface and hope for another miss. If it dragged on, maybe Muller would take off before potential witnesses would hear the gunshots.

Desperate for air, Joe's head broke the surface. He made a quick glance towards where Muller had been standing, but didn't see him taking aim. Just as he plunged downward into the depths again, Joe thought he'd heard his name called out. Had Muller changed his mind? He wasn't going to surface and ask.

When his breath ran out, Joe came up again. This time he saw the shorter, rounder figure calling his name and emphatically waving for him to get out of the pool and follow. Carlos! What the hell? Were there now two shooters? Back below the surface he went.

But the image of Carlos' sense of urgency brought the picture into focus. It was as if the film needed a short delay before developing. There was a prone body on the ground near Carlos.

Joe surfaced for air a third time and saw Carlos dragging the body towards the beach. "Come on, José. Can't you see Muller's dead? We've got to get the hell out of here."

Joe swam towards Carlos. Muller's lifeless body had streaks of blood oozing from one side of his head. "Carlos? I thought you were with him."

"Get out! Help me drag him. I'll explain later."

Hope sprang eternal, even if it meant trusting Carlos. His killing Muller served as a nice character reference. Joe hoisted himself from the pool and grabbed the corpse under one of the armpits. Carlos and Joe quickly got the body out onto the sandy beach. Carlos had already taken Muller's pistol. Now he took his watch and emptied the pockets.

"Gringo tourist shot and robbed walking the beach at night," Carlos declared.

"That's how he was going to make it look with me," Joe said.

"Come on. I have a jeep out on the street."

Joe went with Carlos to his room in a nearby hotel. Carlos gave him some dry clothes that were short in the leg and loose on the body. But it was an improvement, especially if they were going to try and leave immediately.

Joe called the charter company. They said they'd have to find the pilot and call back. Joe hoped after all this they wouldn't have to risk flying with a pilot who'd already begun his weekend tequila. Nonetheless, both he and Carlos agreed that it would be best to leave before the body was discovered. They would be checking departures more closely afterwards.

"We'll try to make it all the way to Acapulco as soon as we can," Carlos explained.

"Acapulco?" Joe had visions of catching the first U.S.-bound flight available, from an international airport such as Cancun or Mexico City.

"Yes, Acapulco, José. We fly to Acapulco under assumed names." He handed Joe an extra fake I.D. he evidently carried for such occasions. "At my hotel, I can doctor the records. They'll show neither you nor I ever left Acapulco. You came and stayed at the Mexico Lindo when you left the Tortuga. And I never left for Cozumel. When you leave for the States, you'll leave from Acapulco. Emigration records will show you left from Acapulco, just as you originally planned. My staff will corroborate all this."

"So we won't be under suspicion if the authorities don't buy the mugging on the beach theory?" Joe was getting the picture.

"They might buy it. But murders are very uncommon in Cozumel."

The charter company called back. They found a pilot and he would come to get them. Carlos and Joe headed for the airport.

On the way, Joe broke the ice, "So, amigo, are you gonna explain what happened here tonight? You gonna tell me finally whose team you're on?"

"I haven't heard a 'thank you for saving my ass, Carlos' yet," Carlos chided.

"Carlos, thank you for saving my ass. Now how about saving my sanity with a little explanation."

"When we get to the Mexico Lindo. We need to talk in private. Maybe over a shot of good tequila. You gringos are always so impatient. You don't do anything in style."

Chapter 63

Acapulco, Mexico

"I long since had had enough," Carlos explained. "When he wanted me to kill that nice lady friend of yours, for no reason . . ." He shook his head. "You like the tequila? It's my best."

Drinking tequila at midday was something Joe hadn't done in years. But after a good night's rest, and with his impending departure on the late-afternoon flight, he accepted Carlos' invitation to join him in the bar before it opened for business.

"And you absolutely assure me those guys who came to the Tortuga weren't your people?" Joe looked him in the eye.

"On the contrary, they were arrested thanks to me. Muller had wanted me to kill your Vicki. He offered to spare the women in Cozumel in return. He tried to sell it as the lesser of the evils. Big of him."

"Why didn't you warn me off?" Joe challenged.

"First of all, I was angry with myself for leaking that you were here. I had called Muller's answering service to have him call me, so I could curse him out about Pancho, after you'd told me what had happened. That's how he found out you were here. And that's when he told me he was in Cozumel stalking those other two women.

"A month or so ago, he'd asked me the name of someone who could help his guys with a counterterrorist job near Ensenada. He said it was no big deal, some scumbag who might smuggle explosives into the U.S. Then, from you, I find out it was Pancho that got whacked. And it explained why no one has ever heard from the guy I recommended. Muller's crew no doubt silenced him permanently. Probably the work of El Colombiano. You've seen him, half-man, half-bull. My source tells me he was one of the intruders who got arrested leaving your hotel room."

"There was a large man among them. Broad, solid-looking. Didn't speak," Joe recalled.

"That's him. Now, with Muller out of the way, those guys that went to your room may be facing some real jail time. If Muller had lived to fight another day, he would've gotten them out in a matter of days. He had that kind of juice. Another reason the planet is a better place without him."

"I had no idea the commotion on the street was related to those bastards getting arrested. And I was too scared to go down and find out," Joe explained.

"Police cars at that hour of the night are nothing unusual," Carlos said. "Getting them there was no problem. A local police lieutenant, an old friend, owed me a favor. When I made my plan to go after Muller, I knew he'd be shorthanded in Cozumel. And I wanted to keep it that way, and protect you at the same time.

"When I got to the departure gate in Mexico City for the connection to Cozumel, I recognized your Vicki. I kept my distance so she wouldn't see me. I had on a baseball cap and sunglasses."

"And you figured she was there for a similar reason?"

"To be honest, I was confused. But I knew she wasn't in with Muller, because he wouldn't have asked to have her killed. So I guessed it might have something to do with warning whomever Muller was stalking."

"A damned good guess, Carlos. God, you are pretty good."

"Not that good. Like I said, Muller wouldn't have even known you were in Mexico if not for my slip."

"But since you were going over to eliminate Muller, you thought you could keep Vicki out of harm's way as well?" Joe asked.

Carlos continued, "I was beginning to think fate was on my side, that maybe God had lent me a guardian angel to line things up the way I wanted. Seeing your Vicki meant she was safe from the attack in Acapulco, even without the police protection. I knew they would not harm *you,* so I called my lieutenant friend from the airport in Mexico City."

"You changed the strategy from prevention to apprehension?"

"*Correcto.* Prevention would've kept her safe by keeping the attackers away. But they would've been back in Cozumel the next morning. With Vicki gone, we could trap them into breaking and entering. The police had grounds to charge them."

"Why didn't the police come get a statement from me?"

"I asked them to wait, José. Didn't want anything to upset my plan. Besides, if Muller had survived, he would've gone over the head of my lieutenant friend, and there could've been some adverse consequences career-wise. Now, if you would like to make a statement, we'll talk to the lieutenant before you leave."

"Yes, I do," Joe said firmly. "Let's get these assholes out of commission, especially that animal that did in Pancho."

"It will be better for me as well that they remain in jail, even with no El Espanto to pull their strings," Carlos agreed.

"You followed him all day in Cozumel, but didn't get your chance until dark?"

"It took me the first day and night to find him, at the Reina del Mar. The following afternoon I watched him at the pool. He hadn't laid eyes on me in over ten years, and I kept on the cap and sunglasses. Next thing I know he was off on a bicycle. Can you imagine me keeping up with anybody on a bike?" Carlos laughed, pointing to his trademark belly. "I got in my car and thought about getting him out on the road. But soon I was distracted. Passing a vehicle pulled over to the side picking up passengers, I saw Vicki again, at the wheel. Putting two and two together, I figured they'd be off to the airport, that they would be making their escape from El Espanto.

"With his crew in Acapulco, and with the ladies getting away, I started to smell the kill. I even imagined the vultures circling above Muller's bike. No longer would I need to risk hitting him in broad daylight out on the road, where there could be a witness. Now all I needed to do was go to the Reina del Mar and wait."

"Needless to say, you had no idea I was there. Almost to screw it up." Joe shuddered to think he'd almost bought the farm for no reason. What if he had died seconds before Muller met his own fate?

"Well, I wondered why he went out the back way to the beach by himself," Carlos said. "Maybe he was going out to walk off the frustration of losing track of the ladies and the fact that his thugs hadn't returned from Acapulco.

"Then I went out the front of the hotel and circled along the outside perimeter to the beach. Staying in the shadows, I saw him up ahead just outside the beachfront gate. There was enough light from the pool area to reveal that he was holding a gun, like he was on guard duty. I had to advance slowly. If he were to sense someone coming, he would've turned to shoot. And El Espanto used to be a crack shot."

"Thank God, he must've lost a little," Joe said.

"When I saw him dart through the gate, I knew something was up. I started running, as fast as my fat stubby legs could carry me. I even sped up when I heard the shots. When I entered the gate, I saw him ready to take aim again. Immediately, I knew there were no observers, no witnesses. He never saw me. I put my pistol to his right temple. And the notorious career of El Espanto faded into infamy. That's when I saw you come up for air. I knew it was you when I saw the straw hat floating on the water."

"You're right about that guardian angel, Carlos. And fate. Don't know if I'll ever have another day where the stars are so favorably aligned. And I owe you, amigo."

"Enough to forgive my past transgressions?"

"Yeah, the ones in Venezuela. I don't know about the ones after that."

"Only God can forgive those, José. In Chile . . . I still have nightmares thinking about it. People disappearing."

"What drew you to him? To that line of work?"

"At first, the cause seemed noble. Oppose the Communists. Pretty soon everybody was a Communist. As I told you, I was brought up that way. Muller, too. Sometimes when you become accustomed to using extraordinary means to accomplish your ends, the means themselves have a way of seeming right, no matter how evil or immoral. That's what happened to El Espanto. He took it to another extreme—he coupled it with greed. Soon there were no principles at all, only a game.

"As for me," Carlos continued, "after a while, I knew deep down that we were working in concert with the devil. One day, I felt the evil inside, eating away at my very soul, like spiritual leprosy. That's when I got out altogether. And I've been trying to avoid the devil's messenger, El Espanto, ever since."

Joe held up the tequila glass. "Here's to no more messengers."

"Here's to cleansing. And redemption, maybe," Carlos toasted.

"We'd better get going if we're gonna go see your lieutenant friend at the police station. Will he be waiting for us?"

"She," Carlos corrected him with a sly smile. "My lieutenant friend is a woman. She'll be down shortly."

"If you want redemption, amigo, you better hope God isn't female."

Carlos laughed. He slapped Joe on the back.

"One more request, Carlos."

Carlos looked at him quizzically as Joe walked over to the wall and took down the guitar.

Handing it to Carlos, he said, "One last rendition of 'Mexico Lindo.' "

Chapter 64

Burlington, Vermont

Understandably, Joe had developed doubts that this day would ever come. Several times he'd been visited by the vision of himself standing at the podium to renew his candidacy. But mostly, he'd just fight it off. During the Jules' Rules ordeal, he tried not to think that far ahead. Now, having weathered the threat, he wondered if the full-scale campaign would seem anticlimactic.

But he cautioned himself against thinking it would be easy. He wouldn't want to have gone through what he had for nothing. Pancho's senseless death had been avenged, now a victory might give it something resembling a purpose.

Joe arrived a half hour early to the waterfront. The sun was shining—he almost viewed it as symbolic. The press corps was gathered. There were more than the usual representatives. Word had leaked that there was a story behind the "suspension," that those "juicy" personal reasons might now see the light of day.

Warm-weather attire seemed the order of the day. Sport coats had given way to shirtsleeves, woolens to light cottons. Summer was fast approaching. Joe would have to make up for lost time. More importantly, he needed to make sure that there was no loss of zeal.

Joe's personal entourage was upbeat. T.J. was all smiles. His wife had finished the semester and was with him for the Vermont summer. Marialena's semester was also ended, and she finally made it to Burlington for a visit. Anita and Rick, the name Heinrich went by in the U.S., were taking their first look at Vermont politics. Only Judy Bennett seemed to be preoccupied. The irony was not lost on Joe. This should have been her banner day.

The following morning, the press conference of Joseph LaCarta, the Independent candidate for the open U.S. Senate seat in Vermont was covered on the front page, above the fold, in every newspaper in the state. The press was surprised when Candidate LaCarta came clean about the heist in Venezuela, and amazed by the applause that greeted Joe's explanation of the idealistic rationale for the caper. After Joe revealed that it had not been the Nazi underground that had intimidated him into the suspension, but rather that it had been sinister forces of a domestic nature now run out of business, he was able to spare the details on account of the ongoing FBI investigation.

Once again, Joe outlined his goals and vision if elected. But in virtually every newspaper, these were summarized in two or three paragraphs. The larger story was that Vermonters and many others who were paying attention had now gotten a deeper insight into the true character of the man who might be a U.S. Senator.

Epilogue

November

Joseph LaCarta won the three-way race for the U.S. Senate handily, with almost fifty-two percent of the overall vote. The stories about the attempt to sabotage his campaign had finally died down around September. At his victory party on election night, Joe announced that Vicki Rivier and he planned a New Year's Day wedding, and that she would be accompanying him to Washington. He also pledged to work for the elimination of the "marriage disincentive" in the U.S. Tax Code.

Judy Bennett had resigned as Joe's campaign manager just after he re-started his campaign. It was she who had carelessly leaked that Joe would soon end his "suspended" candidacy. She could not forgive herself for what it had signaled to Joe's adversaries and for possibly triggering the events in Mexico. Reluctantly, Joe accepted her resignation, and helped her catch on with a congressional campaign in Massachusetts.

Vicki had had a very busy six months. She and Terrell "T.J." Jackson, were pressed into action as co-campaign managers after the resignation of Judy Bennett. T.J. was named Senator LaCarta's chief of staff and moved back home to Alexandria, Virginia.

Marialena Morales, as expected, established herself quite well over the summer helping out with the campaign. Joe promised her a job on his Washington staff upon graduation.

Pete Donovan offered to sublet his apartment to Joe and

Vicki, after quitting drinking and reconciling with his wife.

A congratulatory note arrived from Senate Majority Leader Blake Ross, who had actively campaigned against Joe on his one trip to Vermont in late June. Apprehensive about what Joe and the FBI suspected about his association with Muller, he begrudgingly set up a senatorial task force to explore ways that senators from both sides of the aisle could work together to tackle some of the more pressing issues. Ross appointed Senator Elizabeth Parker Shannon, (R) Vermont, to head it up. She promised Joe a seat on the task force.

The most stylish congratulatory note arrived in Burlington the night of Joe's victory party with a limousine filled with boxes of Italian pastries, which Joe added to the buffet table. Cousin Sal had the good sense to turn down Joe's invitation to be present in person. Sal's note told Joe to turn Vermonters onto the *cannolis,* and mentioned that he was still waiting for the maple syrup.

Dr. Lucas Drake and several of his trusted agents continued to investigate the Julian Muller affair. They had some definite suspicions about which groups might have hired him. But they were unable to prove any direct links, or to find hard evidence as to how the money flowed.

Julian Muller's death went down as a murder-robbery, one of the few attacks on tourists in Cozumel. It did not seem that there was any clamor on the part of either the Mexican or the U.S. Government to expand the investigation.

Anne Marie "Anita" Klaus and her husband Heinrich "Rick" Klaus settled in Central Vermont and set up a foundation to trace the looted art pieces and to try and return them to the families of rightful owners. Understandably, Anita took on the more visible role. Heinrich worked behind the scenes from old inventory records to which he had been uniquely privy.

Donald "El Tío" Buchanan continued his peaceful retirement

life in Costa Rica. He did contact Joe to make a sizeable contribution to the campaign, but Joe turned down all out-of-state donors. Instead, Joe convinced El Tío to use the money to hire a lawyer of national prominence to sue the estate of Julian Muller in the wrongful death of Francisco "Pancho" Morales. The case was settled out of court for several million dollars when the tape Joe had made in Cozumel was presented as evidence.

Pancho's ex-wife and fiancée used the proceeds to set up a foundation in the San Diego area, in Pancho's name and memory, to provide scholarships for disadvantaged youths. They also made a sizable donation to Father Villa's orphanage in Mexico.

After winning the election, Joe tried to contact the old friend who had saved his life, Carlos Santiago. He got to speak with Carlos' wife for the first time ever. She told him, regretfully, that Carlos had been killed one night on a coastal highway just outside of Acapulco. It was ruled an automobile accident.

10/22/14

ABOUT THE AUTHOR

Jim Ciullo lives in the Berkshires of western Massachusetts and has family in Vermont. In his previous career, he helped develop a system of community services for persons with developmental disabilities. He continues to work as a consultant and as a volunteer in various human service and education projects, but now spends much of his time writing. A previous novel *A Tango in Tuscany* was published in 2002. Jim served as a Peace Corps volunteer in Venezuela and has traveled extensively in Latin America and Europe.